A-Drift on the Road

Cynthia J Dueringer

Ridiculous Life Publishing
Lenexa, Kansas
2020

Preface and Acknowledgements

As a kid living a few blocks off Lake Erie, on occasion, we'd get a Lake Snow. These snows were like gifts from heaven to my childhood. Heavy, wet, and "packy." We couldn't wait to get outside and build snow forts, fall down, shovel paths, fall down, make snow angels, fall down, throw snowballs, fall down, stick our tongues out to catch flakes, and roll snowman sections until we couldn't move them ...and fall down. The silent blanket of air was fresh, quiet, and comforting. There was no snow-blower racket, no plows, just the titter of snow falling everywhere except for a few screams from kids down the street getting snow stuffed down their necks by their friends. We'd get out sleds and go find a hill, anything with a slant would do. Our faces were red and chapped, and our lips split from the cold, but we didn't care. Snow was wonderful. Sometimes when we came in, mom made us hot chocolate that we got to drink out of adult teacups in the pre-coffee mug age of the 1950's. And once or twice in my life, I remember getting marshmallows on top, or a small candy cane hung over the edge into the cocoa. Life was so good.

The wet snows that blew in off the lake would stick to the north side of trees, bushes, and everything else. The snow was so heavy you could hear the giant black oaks straining and cracking under the weight, and occasionally a huge branch would snap off and crash to the ground. For us kids, the snow made everything look like a world in black and white, just like everything we saw on TV.

Eventually we moved away from the big snows, and I missed it something awful. One winter going home to Saint Louis from my grandparents' house in Cleveland, just as we got a little South of Chicago, we got hit with a blinding blizzard. My dad couldn't see beyond the hood of his car. We drove at a crawling pace, and it was quite exciting for a kid to experience. My Dad loved making up crap, and he talked about what we might have to do if we couldn't drive anymore, namely, get out and walk. This concerned me because I knew I didn't bring a ski-suit.

Every kid in our neighborhood in the 50's had a stupid-ugly ski-suit that was a pain to put on. It got soaking wet with snow and took forever to dry when my mom would hang our stuff down the basement or over the tub to drip and dry. In spite of the ugly, it did keep you reasonably warm in the snow until it got soaked. So in that Chicago blizzard, I secretly fretted about not having it until Dad started another story about walking to school in Cleveland winters in the 1930's. Nobody's parents drove them to school, and he didn't recall having school buses. He said they had feet, and they used them. I loved those stories.

That blizzard of Northern Illinois stuck in my mind for years. Although it was broad daylight in that storm, you couldn't see anything out the window other than white. We talked about how lucky we were that it wasn't dark as it would be impossible to drive, and we'd have to park on the side of the road and wait it out. Dad said he wanted to keep moving as he said the snowplows would plow right over us or bury us in snow.

Many eons later in my genealogy work, we made a drive to Esbon, Kansas, which is six miles from the geographical center of United States. My husband's ancestors lived there in the 1870's. We took all our high tech gear with us, my laptop, our cell phones from two different carriers, and our GPS unit so we'd be able to navigate to the tiny town and have plenty of communication. After driving four hours out into the Northern prairie of Kansas and seeing very few signs of human life, we found that all our high tech gear was useless. We couldn't even get a satellite connection for our GPS. We had to locate the lone gas station and buy a map. That drive discovering we had no way to connect to anything electronically, my memories of the heavy lake snows of the Great Lakes, that blizzard in Chicago, and since then the TV news of blizzards around the country causing interstate pile-ups, and my Dad making up crap about the snow; all of it made me think about getting into a big car pile-up out in the *middle of nowhere in a blizzard and what would we all do if we couldn't call for help. So this is my story about that.*

I'd like to thank my husband for not griping about me not doing much housekeeping, cooking, weeding, or much of anything for the three years I spent working on this book. It's nice when someone isn't ragging on you about that stuff. I also want to thank him for bringing home a lot of take-out suppers on days I was buried under my hand-drawn maps, notes, and printouts trying to figure out where my story was going. I'd like to thank my daughter for encouraging me to keep writing when I wanted to quit the day I learned my computer didn't auto-save a week of my writing, and for her suggestion of "perfume of Bicycle Tires" I want to thank my brother Bruce for telling me it was a very interesting storyline, which encouraged me to research the science and get the book done, and thank him for taking a month or so, "grading my paper." And I want to thank my friends who keep asking me if I'm done with my book yet, and even thank those who pretended to be interested in my writing.

I'd like to give special thanks to Mr. Frank Natoli of Lantern Legal, New York, New York, the kind and patient lawyer that took the time to walk me through a little about "fair use," intellectual property law, and helped me navigate a few scary legal issues.

As always, I wrote this in my tone, and my style, the way I'd tell you the story in my own voice.

I hope it is an enjoyable read.

Contact the author, me.

cynthiajdueringer@gmail.com

Cover image courtesy of Haley Stone

Stones Throw Photography

Contact Haley:
photosbyhaley@yahoo.com

Thank you for your artwork, Haley

Say hi to your mom!!

Table of Contents

Chapter 1

Brittany and the Bad Idea

"Are you serious, Brittany?" said Delphia, who was typically very level headed, mostly because she was very smart. Delphia would graduate with honors in a few months and hoped to be Valedictorian of her class. Her best friend, Brittany, wasn't as studious but was outgoing and athletic, finally making the cheerleading squad as a senior. Brittany was also plain and simply boy-crazy, where Delphia preferred studies to the boys that only seemed to want one thing. The two girls, though mix-matched, were friends from childhood.

"Never been more serious, Delph," Brittany said while looking in the mirror and inspecting a few blemishes. "I don't think I can live another week without seeing Bryce. What if ski bunnies are hanging out there throwing themselves at him? He's going to be there for almost another week yet."

"I don't think there's any way you can get away with this crazy plan without getting busted." Delphia reasoned. "If your parents find out, you'll be grounded and they'll shut your phone off until you are forty."

"Oh, Delph, you always look at the negative side. Look, I've already figured it out." Brittany said as she tossed her laptop onto her bed, where Delphia was sitting inspecting her toenail polish. "Check it out."

Delphia picked up the laptop and tapped through the screens Brittany had pulled up. Delphia saw the pages with maps and other miscellaneous information about traveling from St. Louis to Winterpark, Colorado.

"You are crazy, Brittany. This says it's nearly a fourteen-hour drive, one way! That doesn't count your bathroom stops and getting gas," Delphia informed Brittany.

"Oh, you can't believe everything you read on the internet, Delph," Brittany explained as she checked her hair for split ends. "I looked it up, if we leave in the afternoon, we can drive there, and get there by early morning. We eat a little breakfast, then I'll see him, give him his Christmas gift, he'll give me my gift, we leave, and drive back home the next day before my parents know anything."

"We?" Delphia asked. "What do you mean, we? My parents won't even let me go to the mall for the day without a police escort and a swat team."

"Del-phi-aaaa!" Brittany said in exasperation and turned from admiring herself in the mirror to face Delphia. "I'm not going to tell them I'm driving to Colorado. Are you crazy? I'm going to tell them I'm spending the night at your house then we'll be going to the mall for the Christmas sales the next day. We've had sleep-overs dozens of times and my folks don't bother to check up on me. You tell your mom the same thing. Tell her that you are staying at my house then we'll be shopping. We'd be back before they know anything. I just can't sit here and wait for Bryce to get back to town. I have to do something!"

"Look, Britt," Delphia reasoned, "I think you are wasting your time on Bryce. If he wanted to give you a Christmas gift, you'd have gotten it before his family left for their Christmas ski trip, or he'd have stopped by your house."

"Well, I think you are wrong. He just didn't get a chance. I know he wants me to be his steady girlfriend and just wants us to be alone when he asks. I saw him with a little box and I think it's a ring. I just know it's for me. He's going to ask me to wear his ring this Christmas. I mean, why wouldn't he?"

Delphia rolled her eyes and fell on her back on the pillows. "Oh Brittany, he doesn't even text you unless you text him first. And all his responses have been only one word or an emoji."

"Oh, Delphia, you just don't know men like I do. They don't like to text. But see, he does respond to all my texts, except the ones where he's at football practice. He could ignore my texts, but he doesn't. He always smiles when he sees me, and he sat next to me in math. And he doesn't seem to have anyone else for a girlfriend." Brittany argued.

"Brittany, wake up, will you? He sat next to you because we were seated in alphabetical order and that's just the way it came out." Delphia pointed out. "And he smiles at everybody. But yeah, come to think of it, I've never seen him with a girl other than his lab partner in Chem. Maybe he's gay."

"Oh, that's just you," Brittany frowned, "always trying to analyze everything to death. Ok, so don't go with me. I'm going even if I have to go by myself!"

At that moment, the bedroom door opened and Tawnie walked in. She looked at both girls and asked, "You are going? I heard one of you say you are going. Going where?? Can I go?"

Delphia and Brittany hushed Tawnie then looked at each other. The unspoken words were there between Delphia and Brittany, should they say anything to Tawnie?

Tawnie continued her interrogation. "Ok, what's going on? You two holding out on me? I know you two, you are up to something. I can tell by the looks you are giving each other."

Brittany looked to Delphia and Delphia shrugged her shoulders. Brittany decided to level, "Ok, Tawnie, if you say a word of this to anyone, our friendship is over, and then I'll post that you borrowed your mom's vibrator."

"What? I never borrowed my mother's vibrator. I don't even know if she's got one!" Tawnie began to freak out.

"Yeah, that might be true, but who is anyone going to believe, you or me?" Brittany said point-blank. Delphia winced at how mean Brittany sounded.

Tawnie looked hurt at the comment but took it in stride. She looked back at the bedroom door, saw it was still open, and stepped over to close it quietly and turned to the other two girls. "OK, I won't breathe a word. I'm in. What's the plan?"

"Ok," Brittany began to explain her plan, "Bryce's family went to Colorado for Christmas. They went to a ski resort. I am going to drive there so Bryce can give me my Christmas present, and I can give him his."

"That's the plan?" Tawnie said as she sat on the bed next to Delphia. "You have clearly lost your mind, Britt. Your folks won't allow that in a jillion years."

"Well, that's the secret part, I'm not telling them," Brittany said as she opened a bottle of nail polish and stirred it.

"Oh well, DUH, you don't think they'll miss you not being around?" Tawnie mentioned.

"No, Tawnie, see, I have it figured out. It's about a twelve-hour drive from St Louis to Denver..."

Delphia interrupted, "More like fourteen or more."

"Don't listen to her." Brittany said and kept babbling, "I'm figuring twelve hours according to maps online, but we live a little west of the city, and the ski resort is before Denver, so if I drive a teensy bit over the speed limit, I figure I can do it in ten hours. That'll leave me about four hours to find Bryce, exchange gifts, and get something to eat, then head back and be home for my parents' Christmas Eve party. I will tell my folks that I'm spending the night with Delph, then we'll be going shopping the next afternoon and I'll be home for supper. That'll buy me about twenty-eight or so hours, from tomorrow afternoon until the next afternoon, which is Christmas Eve. My folks will be busy getting ready for the Christmas Eve party and won't even think about me. Besides, if they call me, I can answer the phone and they won't know if I'm here, at the mall, or on Mars."

Tawnie sat there in stunned silence, once glancing at Delphia as if to ask if Brittany was crazy to which Delphia knowingly nodded.

"Okay, Miss Brainiac, what happens if you have car trouble?" Tawnie asked.

"I've had my car for nearly four months, it hasn't had a problem yet. Dad always keeps the oil up to date and does all that motor stuff and wiper fluid. Nothing is going to happen. We drove around all summer in it and never had anything go wrong."

Delphia interrupted, "That may be so, but your car is seven years old and has over a hundred thousand miles on it. Who knows what's wearing out? Besides, gas isn't free. Are you paying?"

Brittany simply said, "I was hoping you'd chip in because you get a vacation too."

Delphia frowned at that suggestion and responded, "I don't have much cash. I spent a lot on Christmas gifts and got myself a few things for the holidays. I don't think I can get another advance on my allowance. Mom is always griping about me asking for more money."

"Well, here," Brittany opened a small spiral notebook to a page where'd she'd made some notes and tossed it on the bed between Delphia and Tawnie. "I figure we'll have to grab something from a drive-thru for supper and something for breakfast, but we can take a lunch from home, take some munchies along. So maybe twenty bucks each for meals. I figure four gas fill-ups, at about thirty dollars each. I've got about seventy bucks."

Tawnie asked again, "So, am I invited? I can chip in about $30 for gas. I have some babysitting money."

Brittany thought a second, she really didn't want Tawnie on the trip, too much of a chance of her blabbing the secret, but it was hard to pass up thirty bucks for gas. "Well, I guess you can go, Tawnie. You'll have to tell your folks that you are spending the night and make sure they don't call my folks and check up on it. Can you manage that?"

"I don't think my folks know I'm alive. I don't see a problem. Do we get to ski?"

Brittany looked mildly irritated at that question. "No, Tawnie. No skiing. Skiing is expensive, and in case you haven't noticed, we don't have skis. We won't have time either. We are only going to find Bryce so we can exchange gifts."

"Why can't you just wait until he gets back?" Tawnie asked.

"Tawnie, don't you ever think? There are ski bunnies at resorts that look for cute guys. I don't want Bryce falling for some ski bunny. If I hook up with him, he won't be looking at ski bunnies or anyone else. Especially when he sees what I got him for a gift!"

"What did you get him? Season tickets to the Cardinals?" Tawnie snarked.

"Ha ha...very funny. No, I copied all the selfies I took of myself and put them on one flash drive. I even took a couple selfies in my bikini, with close-ups of my boobs and the T-bar in back! He'll be able to see as much of me as he wants, whenever he wants!"

Delphia and Tawnie looked at each other and rolled their eyes.

"Jeez, Britt," said Delphia, "is that the bikini you bought that your mom forbid you to wear to the pool or beach?"

"Yep, but she never said I couldn't put it on in my bedroom and take selfies!" Brittany told them. "Well, you guys need to get out of here and check with your parents about spending the night. I'll talk to my mom and ask her about spending the night with you. Once we get that done, we are on our way!!" Brittany said, twirling around in her room until she whacked her hip on the dresser.

Delphia had a troubled look about the mission, but Tawnie was totally committed to the secret trip with her two friends. She turned the page on the spiral notebook and started writing what they'd need.

"What are you doing?" Brittany asked.

Tawnie responded, "I'm planning what to take."

"Are you kidding?? We'll only be gone twenty-four hours."

"Well," Tawnie said, "I didn't get to be a Senior Scout by accident. I spent a lot of years planning how to be prepared. So, since we'll be driving mostly at night, it just makes sense to have a few things, "in case". I already wrote down a flashlight with fresh batteries, phone chargers, laptop and charger, blanket..."

"Blanket?" Brittany asked.

Delphia fielded that question. "Yes, a blanket. We should each have a blanket, actually. What if the heater gives out in your car? What if we want to snooze in the back seat? It just makes sense. Your mom wouldn't ask anything if she saw you taking a blanket to my house to spend the night anyway."

"Ok," Brittany gave in as she painted a nail with electric blue polish, "bring a blanket if you want."

Tawnie added to the list. "Water bottles. Too expensive at truck stops. Besides, a change of water can make you sick, better off having water from home. Two or three bottles each, I would think. A couple of pieces of fruit for each, maybe a bag or two of chips. If we get sleepy, munching on a little something will help keep us awake."

Delphia agreed then looked at Brittany, "So what's on your list, Britt?"

"The important stuff. My makeup, eye-liner, lip-gloss, nail polish, curling iron. The cutest holiday sweater from the mall, white leggings, and boots. I spent all my summer job money on boots from the Fillay of Sole boot store. They are white suede and made by some famous Italian designer, Schultz-somebody! So I have a whole outfit that'll knock Bryce's socks off when he sees me. And of course, Cupid's Quivering Arrows perfume. They guarantee it will 'make a romantic point of a woman's desire to any man that catches her scent!'" She recited half the commercial, then she picked up her old beat-up teddy bear and hugged it momentarily, pretending it was Bryce and trying to decide if she should take Teddy along.

"Oh, for crying out loud, Britt....please tell me you don't buy all that commercial crap you read about perfumes," Delphia and Tawnie both said almost at the same time. "Not to mention, I think that stuff smells like a bicycle tire," Delphia added, making a face.

Brittany was confident, "I'm sure you guys know that they aren't allowed to print stuff that's not true. This will work. You'll see. When we go back to school after the break, I'll be an attached woman!" And Brittany hugged the old teddy bear and twirled around in a circle, avoiding the dresser this time.

Tawnie was shaking her head and quietly mentioned to Delphia, "Yeah, and 'Schultz' is a big name in Italian footwear." Then she yanked out the piece of paper she'd been writing on. "Well, I have my list. You make your own."

Brittany caught the little dig from Tawnie and kicked back a dig, "You two are just jealous because you don't have a boyfriend."

Delphia calmly looked at Brittany and said, "You don't either."

"Yeah, well, I'm doing something about it. I'm being pro-active. And Bryce will be mine when we exchange gifts," Brittany babbled to herself in the mirror.

Tawnie raised an eyebrow then looked at Delphia.

"We have to go with her, Tawnie," Delphia sighed. "She'll end up lost or in trouble unless she's got a couple of leveler heads around."

Tawnie agreed. The three sat on the bed and made their plans for Brittany's secret mission to begin their trek to Winterpark.

Chapter 2

The Rolling Landship

Herman and Louise

"We should have left last month, Herman." Louise fretted. "I don't like driving on holiday weekends, especially Christmas. People are crazy and drive like lunatics. And I always worry about the weather."

"Now now, Louise dear," Herman said in his most calming tone. "I've been driving this old RV for twenty years, and she's been good to us taking us to the warmth and sunshine of Arizona every winter. I did all the maintenance myself, she's tough, not like the new ones made out of foam and plastics. She's heavy enough with the diesel engine in back and the generator in front to take on the prairie storms without blowing over, and she's strong enough to push us up the mountains when we get to the Rockies. I'll just take my time. We'll be fine. If we have to stop for a little snow, I can dump the tanks so they won't freeze, and we'll have everything we need for a few hours until they clear the roads."

Louise knew he was right, but was still very uneasy about traveling at this time of year. She'd been sitting in front of the weather channel all morning, making sure they weren't headed into anything ugly.

"We should have left last month, Herman!" she called out again as Herman went out to tend his RV.

Louise called a neighbor to confirm the usual winter house-sitting they did. Taking in the mail, watering the plants, making sure the house stayed warm, and that the electricity was always on. Minnesota winters get very cold, and they didn't want to come home in spring to broken water pipes or cracked toilets.

"So when are you guys heading out?" Genevieve asked. "You are leaving awfully late this year, aren't you?"

"Yes. Herman's niece got married December nineteenth, and she wanted Herman to walk her down the aisle since her dad died a few years ago. Her father, Howard, and my Herman were twins and were extremely close. Howard started to have heart problems and had to move to Arizona full time. It was hard on the twins being apart during the warm months when we'd return to Minnesota. When Howard died a couple of years ago, Herman didn't handle it well. To this day, I can hear Herman talking to his brother when he's out putzing on something, almost like his brother is there, and they are having a great time."

"No kidding?" Genevieve commented. "I can understand that though, if he was so close to his brother."

"Anyway, Herman wanted to be here for his niece's wedding. She's a nice girl and got married kind of late. It was a pretty wedding and Herman cried walking her down the aisle. The tough old cuss. But yeah, I do wish we could have left in October.

"Well, I hope you have fair weather on your journey as we all know how terrible winter can be on the plains and how fast that winter express can roll in with bad weather," Genevieve said.

"Oh, I know it, Gen." Louise said. "And I do worry as we are getting older and I worry about Herman's health. When we get to Arizona, he has doctors that know him and knew his brother. We've made lots of friends in twenty years of going there every winter. So far, so good. But you know Herman. He thinks he's invincible. I stocked up on his heart meds just in case so we should be in good shape no matter what the weather."

"I know you guys will be okay, but I still worry about the lunatic fringe out there. Two old people in an RV are an easy mark for the crazies," Genevieve fretted.

"Herman has that covered. He has a weapon on board," Louise sighed. "We argued about that for a long time and I finally gave in. He was in 'Nam for a stint, and he knows military weapons. I don't want to mess with it, but he says it doesn't hurt to be prepared and said he couldn't live with himself if something happened to me."

"Well, it sounds like you two have it all covered. Just wish you'd wait 'til after the holidays when the holiday nut-jobs are off the road," Genevieve said.

"I know that makes sense," Louise replied, "but we wanted to make sure to be at our winter place for all the Snowbird New Year's parties, so we have to go now. Four long days of driving, and hopefully, we'll be parked and set up for New Year's Eve. We'll probably have Christmas in the RV by ourselves around Colorado. We'll hook up with the kids by phone. There's not much traffic on Christmas day."

"You guys are crazy making this trip at your ages. But I gotta hand it to you for getting out of this stinkin' cold here in Minnesota. It didn't bug me so much when I was young, but as I get older, it really makes my bones ache, especially when we hit the deep freeze and it's 30-below. I stay by my fireplace and space heaters and do a lot of quilting. Dressing up and going out to a party is the last thing on my list!"

"You should fly down and visit us once, Genevieve. I think you'd like it. You don't have to do the RV thing, you can fly in and there are places to rent, all furnished. You can stay a week, a month, or the season. Dressing up for a party is putting on nice shorts! It's very casual."

"Sounds nice, Louise. Maybe one of these days, we'll make the trek."

"Ok, the offer is always on the table. We're headed out this afternoon because Herman likes to drive the interstates at night when there are less crazy people and more truckers. They are much more experienced drivers than most of the four-wheelers. Thanks again for watching the house, you have our numbers and email. Merry Christmas, Gen!"

"Merry Christmas to you too!"

Louise hung up and picked up a box of medical supplies and rechecked everything, double-checking labels and dates, and took them out to the RV. She made four more trips with boxes of necessities. Everything from toothpaste and soap to coffee and tea, they could never really have enough coffee on board. She was stowing everything in the RV so it didn't rattle or slide around when she heard the big RV doors slamming shut under the Coach, and Herman stepped up into the RV. "I'm about ready to roll, dear."

"Ok," Louise replied. "I need one more walk around the house to make sure everything is taken care of, then get my traveling shoes, a sweatshirt, and Twinkles."

"Don't forget to let Twinkles sniff the grass and do her business so we don't have to stop at the end of the street!" Herman teased.

"Don't start!" Louise reprimanded from the kitchen, "It's a long drive to Arizona!" Herman laughed, heading out to shut the garage. After locking everything, he climbed in the RV and sat in the driver's seat and checked all the gauges and noticed he felt out of breath and coughed a bit. Just excited, he thought. Satisfied that all was "go," he fired up the diesel and it rumbled to life. Herman loved starting the RV and feeling the power under it and listening to it nearly growling to get on the road.

A few minutes later, Louise climbed into the RV with her traveling shoes, sweatshirt slung over her shoulder and balancing a large cup of hot coffee. "House is closed up for the winter and locked up tight," she said. Twinkles jumped up the steps, and Herman attached her little dog bed on the huge dash of the RV and Twinkles jumped in ready to go. Louise shut and latched the door, did a walk-through to make sure everything in the RV was locked down, then sat in her co-pilot seat, fiddled with a few maps, the GPS, and a CB radio mike, then parked her coffee cup. Satisfied that everything was in order to go, she smiled at Herman and said, "Ok baby, let's roll!"

Herman pumped the accelerator, and the diesel shot smoke up the stack shaking the earth in the neighborhood as the giant RV inched out of the driveway making a wide sweeping left turn. They were on their way.

Herman aimed his RV toward the interstate so he could relax driving as cornering the behemoth in the neighborhood was dicey if anyone parked near the corners. "Let me know if you need anything on the way out Louise, I can still stop. Once we are on the interstate, there isn't much out there until Sioux City. I hope to make it to Omaha, or if we're lucky, Kansas City by tonight. The next day we'll head out west on I-70 to Denver and hopefully get there for Christmas Eve, I hope to be in Colorado so we can have some snow for Christmas."

"I hope there's no snow anywhere." Louise scowled under her breath as she examined the maps.

"There's an awful lot of traffic getting out of town today." Herman fussed as he stopped the rig in traffic.

"Well Herm, this isn't a typical workday. We usually leave in October when kids are still at school, but today everyone is out of school on Christmas break. People are getting off work early, or are on vacation, so everyone is out doing stuff before Christmas."

"Oh, crap," Herman griped. "I didn't even think about that, or I'd have left earlier in the day. I want to get about eight hours under our belts today before we stop for a rest." Louise didn't say anything, just stared out the window at all the cars racing around.

"I can't wait to get away from the city and just roll on the interstate," Herman commented. "This traffic is awful."

After a lot of stop and go maneuvers, Herman finally steered his load onto the ramp of I-35 South and pounded on the accelerator sending the RV roaring into convulsions as it picked up speed to merge into the stream of vehicles on their individual quests.

"Thank God for interstates!" Herman panted. Louise could see the stop and go traffic had irked him so much his face was red, but he'd be mellowing out now as he and his RV became one rolling down the highway. Louise turned on the CB and nestled back in her captain's chair with the mike and turned the squelch up so she could hear the trucker's talk. Twinkles jumped out of her dash bed and into Louise's lap and curled up in it while Louise pulled a lap quilt over her legs and over the dog too. Everyone was finally in travel mode.

"Breaker:" the CB jumped to life. "A beautiful afternoon before Christmas," some anonymous trucker said, making Louise smile.

Another trucker added, "Merry Christmas, all you truck jockeys."

"Where are you headed, Mr. Corn Flake?" one trucker asked.

"I'm headed to the Gateway to drop my load then to the home-20 to spend Christmas with my wife and kids."

"I'll be headed to the Peachtree State then back to the Windy City," another commented, "hope to get home for Christmas."

Louise and Herman listened to the trucker chatter off into the afternoon. Louise would dose off for a few minutes but would wake up, making sure Herman wasn't dosing off. Herman wasn't dozing though, he was intent on making Kansas City before resting. He was pushing his pusher.

Chapter 3

We Three Geeks of Peoria Are

Barry, Early, and Joe

"Are you shittin' me?!" One of the young guys commented.

"Nope. This is really happening!" The other replied.

"I can't believe we're really going."

The trifecta of geekdom was loading up their van and excited about going to Vegas for a computer gaming convention for the week following Christmas.

Barry was lugging at least a dozen banana boxes, one by one, in a leap-frog method from his trunk to load into the back of the beat-up cargo van. The boxes were good-sized produce department boxes from the local grocery and packed with magazines that were obviously a bit heavy for Barry's skinny arms whose only muscles were in his fingers from keyboarding for hours a day. A tall, pale drink of water with dark circles under his eyes, Barry was a computer nerd. Quiet, but very tech-savvy, pleasant and polite. He got a job easily as a bench technician right out of high school based on a complicated engineering science fair project he entered and won.

His grandfather started him tinkering when Barry was little, and the two would spend hours together at his grandfather's workbench. Barry's grandfather was a basement inventor. He loved building little robotics and things that did useless tasks, like the snow globe shaker that would turn the snow globe once every sixty seconds to keep the fake snow going. Barry loved spending time with his grandfather at the workbench, figuring out how to make things work. His grandfather passed away over two years ago, leaving Barry his lifetime collection of Popular Tinkering magazines. Nearly seventy years of subscriptions and his grandfather had read them all. Barry thought the convention might be the best place to sell the magazine collection to get enough money to build his own computer server system or take a class in animatronics.

Barry's best pal, Early, drove up and parked his car. Early was a short, round, red-headed guy with intense golden eyes. He wasn't very good-looking, but the intensity of his eyes and his natural-red, flat-top haircut always got attention. Early got his nickname because he was always and relentlessly early for everything. He had an itch to be moving about all the time and was the total opposite of Barry's calm, quiet demeanor.

Early was a computer gamer and was hoping to find new games at the convention that he couldn't easily beat. If nothing else, he hoped to hook up with a company that made games and become a game tester. Or even a game tech. He had his sister help him write a resume that was clever and interesting, knowing the competition for the few available jobs was stiff. He had to be something special to get a foot in the door.

"Jeez, Early, what did you do to yourself?" Barry asked as soon as he saw Early get out of his car.

"My sister thought I needed to look more professional, so she talked me into shaving off my goatee and sideburns."

"Never mind the hair, holy cow, what's with the button-down shirt and sweater vest? Are you changing your career choice to accounting? And where are your glasses?" Barry asked some more.

"I got contacts last week. What do you think?" Early said, blinking his eyes at Barry like a heart-sick goat.

"I think I like the glasses better, at least I couldn't see your bloodshot eyes. You know, you aren't applying for a job with a law firm, you are looking for gamer-land. They will be expecting unkept hair, a wrinkled Hawaiian shirt, sneakers, cheeseball stained fingers.....and glasses." Barry said.

"I know. But I had to do this gig so my sister would do my resume." Early explained. "I can't write myself out of a wet paper bag, so this was the deal. I have my glasses in my bags. When we're out of here, I'll put them on. The contacts make my eyes itchy anyway."

As they were stowing their things, Joe came around the back of the van and threw his sleeping bag in. "Ok, you guys, you each owe me twelve bucks for our first gas tank. We said we'd split everything three ways, except our food, so that's the first settlement." Joe said while holding a computer notebook in his hand with numbers on the screen. As Barry and Early dug through their pockets to peel off twelve dollars, Joe entered it into his computer. Early and Barry pretty much maneuvered Joe into driving them to Vegas for the convention. Joe had an old girlfriend there he thought he could hook up with if the convention was boring. Joe was more into math and science and was studying for his degree in the sciences at night. Still, he did like the purity of computing, no mistakes out of a computer unless you entered it wrong.

The three geeks hung out together when they were in high school. They were generally shunned by everyone else for being too weird until semester papers were due, then they were in demand by a couple of athletic guys that needed to make grades to stay on their teams. The geeks were able to help them out, for a price. Namely, protection from the punks and mean girls. There was a group of really mean girls that enjoyed picking fights by singling out a less than athletic guy, then beating the daylights out of him, videotaping it, and posting it on the internet, dubbing in a lot of laughter and adding girlish screams. After the arrangement with the jocks, the geeks were generally left alone, and the jocks had plenty of help studying for science and math finals.

"Where's your stuff, Barry? All you got is boxes of your old man's magazines." Joe commented.

"I got my gym bag in the back seat of my car yet. It's jammed. My mom made sure I had enough clean underwear and socks for a week....and a sweatshirt.....and a coat.....and gloves. She even rolled up a scarf and stuck it in my gym bag. She didn't gripe about me being gone over the holiday so I just let her add what she wanted. She even gave me boots, but I left them in my trunk. I don't think we'll be needing boots in Vegas. She probably even stuffed a couple dollars in there. She's just that way, prepare for anything, she always said. And these aren't my dad's magazines, these are my grandfather's. My dad's only subscription was Playboy. I probably spent as much time with his Playboy magazines as I did with my grandfather's Popular Tinkering magazines."

All three of the guys laughed and were playfully punching Barry's shoulders, teasing, "No wonder you wear glasses!!"

"Man, Barry, at least your mom cares about you," Joe said, stacking another box in the van. "My mom threw me out of the house when I was 18 and told me to get a job. She hated all the computer gear, wires, papers, and disks. She's Jewish so she could care less about the holiday thing and spends her time playing cards with her lady friends. My dad was Protestant though I went to church with him as a kid until he left. I never went to church after that. I thought God was mean to take him away and make me stay with my mom." And Joe slammed a box on top of the pile.

Early was standing next to the van looking at a weather app on his phone. "Looks to be pretty smooth sailing. Cold, maybe a little windy, but nothing in the forecast to slow us down. Hope you got enough duct tape to hold this rattrap together," he joked to Joe.

"The van is in great shape for a used cargo van." Joe defended. I just wish it had a back seat instead of so much cargo space. It just had a tune-up, a new generator, and got a brake job a few months ago. Not much else can go wrong as long as we don't run out of gas. I have two quarts of oil under my seat and got a few tools just in case. I've had the tools there since the last engine trouble when the radiator blew a hose, and yeah, I always have a roll of duct tape."

Barry was back at his car, lugging his gym bag and sleeping bag out of the back seat and locking up his car. Early was in the van re-arranging stuff and stacking the magazine boxes in the cargo space to create a makeshift back seat and stretched out his sleeping bag across the boxes. Joe tossed his sleeping bag in the van, "Use that if you want, down stuffing, it'll make a comfy place there."

Barry schlepped his sleeping bag in the van too and asked if they were ready yet. Joe checked his tire pressure and said he was about ready, then shut the rear van door. Barry slid the side van door shut as Early finished up his makeshift bench seat.

"Hey, this isn't bad," Early commented as he stretched out on his banana box sofa. "I thought we'd just sleep on the floor, but this is much better."

"Hold on," Joe said, "we all won't be sleeping at the same time. I figure we will drive around the clock. I think we can do this in four-hour shifts. One of us can sleep about four hours while I take the first driving shift, and one of you navigates, then we will rotate, and I can sleep while you two drive and navigate, and so on. That way, we don't have to waste time parking someplace and trying to sleep. It's cold out. If we stop the van, we don't really get much heat.

"Makes sense," Early said.

Barry saluted Joe, "Yes, Captain!"

"Are we getting close to hitting the road?" Barry asked again.

"Yep," Joe said. "I've got all the GPS coordinates in my notebook, listed the places we'll stop to get some exercise, and mapped out our travel plan. All I want to do is stop at Walmart on the way out and pick up some supplies."

Early slid the side van door open again and went back to his car to get a flashlight out of his glove compartment. Barry grabbed it from Early and was going to flash it at Early's eyes to be funny, but the flashlight didn't work.

"Yeah, we need supplies alright, like batteries for Early's flashlight."

"You dork," Early told Barry, "it doesn't need batteries. It's a Faraday flashlight, you pull out the little crank and crank it like crazy. It has a small generator that charges when you crank the handle. The light doesn't last very long, but at least you don't have to deal with dead batteries. Watch." Early pulled out a little crank handle and cranked it like crazy, and sure enough, the flashlight beamed a little beam. Early quit cranking the little handle and the light faded quickly.

"Yeah, um, sure Early. That looks like a high-quality emergency tool," Barry said, as he rolled his eyes at the silly flashlight.

"Don't give me that look," Early commented. "Do you realize if there is ever an electromagnetic pulse or sunspot radiation, when all your batteries are dead, this will still work?" To which Barry put his fingers up to his forehead and made the "loser" sign aiming it at Early. "Ehh, go stuff it, Barry!" Early chided as he smacked Barry in the back of his head with his fingers making Barry laugh over their poking fun at each other. Early then climbed in the van and slid the door closed, still laughing.

Barry looked at Joe. "Does this mean I ride shotgun for the first shift?"

"Sure, I guess so," Joe said.

Barry and Joe got in and adjusted themselves, then Joe chunked the gearshift into drive and they slowly rolled away from the curb. They were off on their journey to Vegas. But first, a stop at Walmart to pick up some snacks, water bottles, and a few liters of pop to fill their cooler. They were excited and did a lot of chattering about the convention and what they were expecting; Barry, hoping for a collector to buy his magazines, Early really wanting that game tester job, and Joe hoping to see the old spark of his life.

Chapter 4

Mr. Preston's Club

"Mr. Preston?" Sherry called, running after him down the hall after he stepped off the elevator. "Tiffany is on line one and says she must talk to you before you leave for the holiday!"

"Tell her you missed me. Take a message. I don't have time to deal with her drama," he said as he rushed to his office. But a moment later, Mr. Preston realized what a crappy thing it was to say, so he stopped, took a breath, and turned to Sherry and said, "Tell her I'm booked with pre-holiday meetings and I'll call her after the holidays."

"Yes, sir," Sherry said, obviously feeling disgusted with her boss. She was still scribbling notes on a pad when she asked him, "Are you leaving soon, or are you staying for the office Christmas Party this afternoon? The gag-gift exchange is always so much fun!" She tried to get him to smile, he did have a gorgeous smile, especially after he spent a fortune on those porcelain veneers, but he rarely smiled.

"No. I have a couple of things to finish up in my office first, then I'm gone. I'm not attending the party. It's always so infantile to watch everyone fawn over stupid gifts." He continued walking in a determined pace to his corner office. "I don't know why everyone decides on this stuff every year. Can't we just have an adult cocktail party once, instead of the Santa baloney?"

Sherry responded, even though she knew he'd never change his mind, "Oh sir, it's just some silly fun to take a break from the seriousness of the company. I wish you'd join us, you might enjoy it."

He ignored her comment and entered his exclusive executive office. Sherry followed him with her pad and pencil but stopped and stood just inside the door, not really entering his private domain. He took off his cashmere overcoat and draped it over the chair then settled into his kid leather desk chair. It made a tiny squeak. "Sherry. Make sure maintenance fixes this squeak before I get back from holiday. I can't have my chair sounding like I have a platoon of mice running around in here."

"Yes, sir." Sherry scribbled another note on her pad. "Anything else?"

"Yes." Mr. Preston went to a wall of rubbed ebony cabinets that looked exquisite next to the lush steel-gray carpeting. Women wearing stilettos hated walking in his office on that thick carpet as the heels nearly got tangled in the lavish lushness. Sherry kept a pair of flats under her desk for just that reason. Mr. Preston opened one of the cabinets and took out a box about half the size of a shoebox and handed it to Sherry. "When you get off today, can you take this package to my ex's house and drop it off. It's for Tiffany."

"Um....sir...," said Sherry, looking at the plain white box, "we do a little drinking at the party, and your ex lives quite a way, I don't think I'm comfortable driving there after dark and after a few drinks."

"Then the obvious solution, Miss Carter, is don't drink." Mr. Preston tossed off the comment without even looking at her.

"Yes, sir," Sherry said tersely, starting to do a slow burn.

Mr. Preston looked up after her comment, saw her look of irritation, and re-thought his statement. "Ok, as a gesture of goodwill, you can take it there tomorrow. Just make sure this gets to Tiffany by Christmas Eve. Can you do that? Or is there a problem with that."

"No, sir. I will make sure she gets it." Sherry was irked. She felt bad for Tiffany, Mr. Preston's only daughter that was now about 14. He almost never took his daughter's calls, and when he did, he was so brusque with her that it irked Sherry. Tiffany wanted to spend time with him, but he was always too busy with work. And that wasn't what Sherry saw as the real truth. She saw Mr. Preston simply as a selfish, egotistical, jerk, which probably explained why he was divorced years ago. But Sherry's job paid very well, so she tolerated his acerbic personality. Much of her job was spent smoothing things over with his clients and other office personnel. He was a partner with the firm, so there wasn't really anyone to complain to.

Sherry was thankful the offices were closed for the whole holiday to get a break. However, even when she was on vacation, Mr. Preston would call her with requests that made her head want to explode. He gave her a personal cell phone for the sole purpose of taking notes for him even when she was on her own time. Sherry was older, single, very over-weight, but had a pretty face and excellent executive secretarial skills. She had a very skimpy social life either because she was dedicated to her career, or dedicated to her career because of the skimpy social life. Sherry didn't mind because it wasn't so bad to have someone as handsome as Mr. Preston call you, even if it was just being ordered to be a gofer. Many times Sherry dreamed about having a romance with Mr. Preston until she got back to work and saw how much of a jerk he could be. She remembered when Mr. Preston hired her, he told her he'd tolerate her weight if she dressed well. Yes, Mr. Preston was a total jerk.

Sherry stood there, holding her notepad and the gift box to deliver to his daughter. "Mr. Preston?"

"Yes, Sherry..." he sounded perturbed as he looked up from his notes. "Are you still here?"

"Um," Sherry knew the next question would bring more rudeness, but she needed to ask because she cared about Mr. Preston's relationship with his daughter, "Is this a Christmas gift for Tiffany?"

"Not that it's any of your business, but yes, it's her Christmas gift. Are you planning to ask me what is in the box too?" Mr. Preston asked, never looking up from his papers.

"No, sir." Sherry was trying not to be snippy back, "I just thought since this is a Christmas gift, it'd be nice if it was wrapped in pretty paper and a ribbon. After all, she is a young lady at fourteen." Then Sherry cringed, waiting for his next insult.

"Sherry. I got her a gift. Isn't that enough already?" he snipped. Without looking up from his papers, he flipped his hand at her to shoo her out of his office.

Sherry felt her anger surge at his attitude toward his daughter, the one time during the year he actually acknowledged her existence. Sherry backed out of the doorway and went to her desk.

Mr. Preston thought for a minute and went to the doorway where he saw Sherry standing at her desk, looking at the pitifully plain white box. "Ok, Sherry, you might be right. If it'll make you feel better, and if you have some paper and a ribbon, and only if you would like to, you can wrap it up nice."

Sherry brightened up right away. "Thank you, Mr. Preston. I know it'll make Tiffany happy."

Sherry headed to the storage closet in the office to dig for some wrapping paper when Mr. Preston called to her across half the office, "It's a cell phone, Sherry. Merry Christmas." And he returned to his office. Sherry smiled and felt she accomplished something with Mr. No-Feelings. A cell phone! Tiffany would be very happy indeed.

Mr. Preston finished up a few files, made a couple of client calls to wish them Merry Christmas and left emergency numbers should they need him. Although he had no plans to take any calls anyway.

He could hear more and more talking, laughter, and desk drawers closing coming from the office "cattle corral," as he referred to the center of the office comprised of desks of the aides, paralegals, secretaries, and research assistants. Then he heard some Christmas music and smelled BBQ coming from the breakroom. Mr. Preston simply wanted out of the office of celebrating people.

He locked up his desk and file cabinets, grabbed his briefcase, and as he donned his cashmere overcoat, he looked around, turned off the lights, then locked his office. A few of the staff saw him leaving and shouted. "Merry Christmas, Mr. Preston!" He did manage to turn around and tell everyone to have a happy vacation. Shaking his head in pity at them hanging Christmas lights and enjoying putting up a tree, he was out of the office and onto the elevator.

"Damn people," he muttered to himself. He checked his watch and grew impatient at the slow elevator to the garage. It seemed an eternity before the doors opened so he could rush out to his parking spot like a man on a mission. It was a short walk, but he set his feet into his "I'm important" power-walk mode to his designated parking spot.

There she sat. His sleek, new, built-by-hand European sports car that he custom ordered when he wanted something conspicuously extravagant to broadcast his success. Something that wasn't assembly-line. She was a totally loaded ragtop Spectaculeer X Coupe. Only a few hundred were made in Europe each year, so it was rare to see one. He read that it was the brilliant merger of top German engineering and Japanese electronics, with hydro-electric fuel cells and a gasoline back up. The interior was hand waxed teakwood trim and black ostrich leather. The best of everything. He clicked the key fob to hear the car bark a few beeps to alert him that he was on the approach. Headlights were already on, lighting up the sign over his parking space. "Mr. Tremont A Preston, Partner, Connoiter, Rabinowitz, Abuchon and Preston Law." When he saw his name in lights like that, it always made him smile, showing off his nearly glowing porcelain veneers.

When he opened the driver's door, his car welcomed him with a warm sexy woman's voice, "Welcome, Mr. Preston." He loved that talking car option.

"Lexie, start the car," he commanded.

"The key is out of range, Mr. Preston," Lexie responded while he took off his cashmere overcoat and hung it on a teakwood hanger in the back, then stowed his Italian kid leather, personally embossed, briefcase in the back too. Slipping into his seat, he put the key in and his car spoke again, "Please wear your seatbelt, Mr. Preston." He grumbled at being ordered around but did put on his seatbelt.

He started the car and it purred so quietly he couldn't even hear it. He pumped the accelerator a couple times, vrrroom, vrrooom. "This baby will scoot when I'm on the road!" he said aloud to no one.

"I don't understand a baby scooting on the road," Lexie said.

He ignored Lexie's comment and checked his tablet for his itinerary. He was going to have to hurry to get to McHavigan's Custom Golf Shop before they closed.

"Lexie, let's go to McHavigan's Golf Shop."

"Yes. Let us go." Lexie droned, and his car seemed to come to attention.

He peeled out of his parking spot and even rolled his window down a bit so he could hear the new tires squealing on the winter concrete in the parking garage as he rounded the exit ramps. He loved driving this car!

He got to McHavigan's in record time and pulled into the parking lot, then donning his cashmere overcoat he swept into the shop. The only thing missing in his entrance of extravagance was an entourage.

"Ahhh, Mr. Preston! We've been expecting you!" Murphy McHavigan, the retired golf pro that owned the shop said, "I hope you are going to be happy this time."

Mr. Preston didn't look all that happy though. He'd ordered custom made golf clubs and had to return them twice for the tiniest minor blemishes in the finish, and one club that he felt wasn't weighted properly. He needed these clubs now to attend a celebrity golf tournament in Palm Springs in a few days as he wanted to look affluent and powerful. He spared no expense on the clubs and matching leather tournament bag.

"Well, Murph, I hope the clubs pass inspection this time. I really can't wait any longer. I'm leaving tomorrow for Palm Springs," Mr. Preston remarked, with some frustration.

Murphy was smiling ear to ear as he brought the clubs out to Mr. Preston, each club nestled in its own custom box. Mr. Preston spent a long time taking each club out of its cardboard nest and carefully examining each one. Then he asked to use the practice net to take some swings with them. Murphy led him to the back warehouse where there was a huge practice tee with lots of draped netting, and a practice putting green. Mr. Preston took each club, re-inspected it, then took a few swings.

Finally, he looked at Murphy with his final assessment. "Well Murphy, I do believe you have outdone yourself. These are the finest clubs I've ever seen." Mr. Preston was smiling like crazy, cradling and petting each club like it was a newborn. And to him, they were all newborns.

"Wait, Mr. Preston, one more thing....." Murphy said and trotted off to an office and came out with a box the size of, well, the size of a golf bag. "Here you go, hope this meets your approval."

Mr. Preston pulled the box flaps off and struggled to get the golf bag out with all the packing materials. All Mr. Preston could do was smile. A smart navy blue with camel leather trim, and his name and country club affiliation embroidered on the front. Lots of zippered pockets, slots, and clips had Mr. Preston acting like a little kid, unzipping pockets, pulling packing materials from the pockets, and tinkering with the clips. Then he tried carrying the bag this way and that until he saw the matching golf umbrella with its own umbrella holster built-in on the side. It didn't happen often, but Mr. Preston was nearly speechless. It was clear he was in love with the new bag. "Damn Murphy, you outdid yourself on this one. This is better than I expected," Mr. Preston said without taking his eyes off the bag and looking at it like it was a naked woman, a well-proportioned, young, attractive, naked woman.

"We aim to please, Mr. Preston," Murphy said. "Look down in the bag."

Mr. Preston looked down in the bag and saw some packages there. He took one out, peeled the paper off, and saw it was a custom club cover that matched the bag. Each cover had the club number and the Scottish club name under it embroidered in gold. He fingered the embroidered word, "BRASSIE". "Damn Murph. I could almost cry."

He dug out the other packages and got the full set of covers. Each cover was also embroidered with his monogram in an elegant formal font that included gold stitching highlights on navy kid leather with the camel leather trim. Tucked down deep and wrapped in floral tissue was a cute putter cover that looked to be hand-made in the same colors as the bag with TAP embroidered in it. As he was looking at the little putter sock, Murphy interrupted, "My wife made that for your putter." Then looked sheepish about it.

"Well, Murph, I like it." Then he slipped the small sock over his index finger and wiggled it in the air. "Tell Mrs. Murphy I like it very much!" He picked up the putter and slipped the little sock over the putter, and he chuckled about it. "Custom made too!" Mr. Preston said as he winked at Murphy.

"You know Murph, all I ever had was second-hand golf equipment. My wife ate up my salary with decorating the house, parties, clothes, shoes, travel, and jewelry, and I always stood back and let her have it all just so she wouldn't be so angry about everything. After our divorce, it was massive spousal and child support checks. As soon as she remarried and I didn't have to fork over alimony anymore, I knew I was going to treat myself to something I've always wanted. I've waited almost a year to get all this ordered and made right," Mr. Preston said, smiling and admiring his bag. "It was worth the wait."

"Would you like to put the clubs in?" Murphy asked.

"Hell yes!" Mr. Preston said.

They took the clubs and bag out to the shop where Mr. Preston picked out tubes to gently hold each club so they wouldn't be injured. Murphy gave him an embroidered golf towel with his name and country club's logo, and Mr. Preston used it to wipe fingerprints off each club, before inserting them into their private tube chambers. "Damn! I feel nearly drunk with this bag of clubs tonight, Murph! I feel so energized that I could take on the entire pro tour!" he said as he loaded up the rest of the bag while whistling Jingle Bells.

Murphy interrupted the Christmas tune with a warning, "Don't fly with that bag, Mr. Preston. People that handle baggage have a way to make the fine sets of golf clubs vanish then say the clubs are lost. Not only that, they throw the baggage. It'll be scuffed up before your tournament!"

"Aha.....well, yes, I know Murph. I've been flying for years and have seen some of the baggage handling troubles. But don't worry, I plan on driving to Palm Springs. I'll keep the clubs in the trunk of my new car. They'll be safe there."

"Driving to Palm Springs?" Murphy questioned. "That is a long drive, Mr. Preston."

"I'm taking my time. I have nearly two weeks off. The tournament isn't until two days after Christmas and it's a three-day tourney, then I'll have plenty of time for some R&R in the sunshine before driving back. I have it all planned out."

Murphy handed Mr. Preston a dozen Pinnacle Platinum golf balls and a little bag of golden tees, fake gold, but gold just the same. "Merry Christmas to our favorite customer."

"Hey, Murph....thanks. This is very nice. Now, what's the damage for all this?" Mr. Preston asked as he adjusted the clubs for a perfect club bouquet look.

"Let me tally it up. Please pick out a nice glove for yourself while I do the paperwork," Murphy told him.

While Mr. Preston was trying on golf gloves, Murphy came over with a bill and a sad face. "I'm sorry Mr. Preston, this is a lot of money. We tried to give you a little discount to help." And he handed the bill to Mr. Preston.

"Wowza. Eleven thousand and some change. Damn! I knew it wasn't going to be cheap though, Murph, especially with customizing each club and all the specialty clubs on the ticket, plus the embossing on the leather and the custom embroidery." He gave his credit card to Murphy.

Mr. Preston was humming "God Rest Ye Merry Gentlemen," appropriately enough, while storing the golf balls into the bag and intermittently caressing the clubs while Murphy went to the counter to enter the card information. When Mr. Preston was finally satisfied with his arrangement of the clubs in the bag and snapped open the bag cover and slipped it over the clubs. He breathed a sigh of relief that all was well.

Murphy came back with all kinds of warranty papers and needed a signature on the ticket. They did a lot of paper shuffling, but Mr. Preston was still smiling his bright veneers. When it was done, Murphy stuck out his hand, "Thank you so much, Mr. Preston. Enjoy your clubs."

"Merry Christmas!" Mr. Preston heard himself say to Murphy as he lugged the bag over his shoulder like a pro caddy and left the shop. Mr. Preston actually felt like a Merry Christmas as he settled his custom golf clubs into his trunk. He was whistling "Jingle Bells" as he got in the car.

"Would you like me to play 'Jingle Bells', Mr. Preston?" Lexie asked.

"Lexie, cancel. Let's go home," he said as he buckled up.

"Yes. Let us go home," Lexie agreed.

Chapter 5

Mr. Preston's Helping Hand

Mr. Preston pulled into his condo garage and parked his car. Once again, he checked his tablet for his itinerary, his dinner would arrive in twenty minutes. He was still elated over his new clubs, so he opened the trunk to let his eyeballs soak them in for a few minutes, then he nearly skipped up the steps to the door. Entering his condo, his house assistant was setting his place at the table.

Mr. Preston, though egotistical, wasn't a complete jerk. He hired young James, who was living in a gang-infested area when he came into the law offices four years ago as Jimmeny, a street nick he picked for himself. His parents weren't present very much, and when they were, they usually had substance abuse issues. Jimmeny had already flunked out of high school and was roaming the streets trying to stay away from the gangs. He came to Mr. Preston as a pro-bono theft case that his firm offered from time to time. Jimmeny was just trying to stay alive and keep the heat on in their Section-8 apartment, so he stole things. He was not an arrogant young man though, and Mr. Preston saw that the kid seemed to steal only out of desperation. The skinny kid was too poor for a driver's license, too poor for a phone, wore ratty clothes, had dirty hands and no haircut. No one would hire him. The kid would be stuck in his social class forever until he ended up in prison.

Mr. Preston saw some potential in the kid that he thought was worth saving. He got his case settled and paid the fines himself then told Jimmeny he could work in his law office to pay it back. Jimmeny was eager to be able to pay back the elegant man that bailed him out of trouble. Jimmeny could be polite when he wasn't on the street, so Mr. Preston began slowly teaching him about the good life and how to act and fit in. Eventually, Mr. Preston took him for a haircut, bought him some office clothes, and took the time to instruct him on good grooming skills. He told him that his legal name, James, demanded far more respect than a street nickname. He explained to James that although it shouldn't matter how you dress and act, it really does matter. It will determine how people relate to you. Mr. Preston told him to be on time at the office, well-groomed, well-dressed even to the point of buying an iron and ironing board for James so he could make sure his shirts were nicely pressed. James worked hard at compliance because he really wanted to learn how to be a class act and be respected like Mr. Preston.

At first, Mr. Preston had him waxing his ebony doors, helping Sherry run a few gofer errands, and doing mundane tasks, like cleaning up in the break-room. After a few months seeing this young man really trying, Mr. Preston had him learning to do a little research in the law library. His reading skills were slow, but over the course of a couple of years, he improved while Mr. Preston watched over him.

When Mr. Preston's alimony had finally ended, he bought himself a nice condo, not a huge one, just a very nice one. He asked James if he would become his house assistant and see to it that his home, car, and various other personal things were taken care of and included a decent raise. James enjoyed hanging out with Mr. Preston learning about living at a certain level of sophistication and elegance. It took him out of the poverty and filth he was raised in. After being employed by Mr. Preston for those first few years, James had managed to improve his living conditions with a one-room studio and a little used car. He even had a few bucks left over to send to his mother, even though she most likely used it to buy drugs.

Mr. Preston's investment in James turned out complimentary for both of them. And they seemed to get along quite well.

"Good Evening, Mr. Preston. Have you had a pleasant day?" James said in excellent diction when Mr. Preston came in and took his coat and hung it in the coat closet.

"Good Evening, James. Yes, thank you. Is my shower ready?"

"Yes, sir," James said and led the way to the master suite. James started the shower, helped Mr. Preston take his suit off so it didn't touch the Italian tile floor. After handling Mr. Preston's other clothing to the appropriate hampers, and hanging his suit in the proper place, he placed two large cotton towels into the towel warmer. While Mr. Preston showered, James set out Mr. Preston's shaving gear and face towels on the counter in a particular pre-arranged order according to Mr. Preston's desires. Mr. Preston went through this same showering and shaving routine every morning before work too, twice a day, as he was obsessively fussy about his physical grooming.

James busied himself straightening towels and wiping lint off the mirrors so he did not spend too much time staring at Mr. Preston in the nude. When Mr. Preston finished showering, James handed him the first warm towel that Mr. Preston threw over his head, then James handed him the second towel that Mr. Preston wrapped around his waist then began his saving ritual. James brought Mr. Preston his underthings, and while Mr. Preston put them on, James handled the towels to their designated places then stood by the closet door until Mr. Preston instructed James what he wanted to wear. This evening it was a simple tracksuit.

During a typical workday, Mr. Preston usually chose his own suit, shirt, and tie, but more and more, Mr. Preston let James choose. James enjoyed choosing Mr. Preston's attire and once in a great while, James would deliberately choose something awful just to tease Mr. Preston. Mr. Preston seemed to enjoy the game and would actually dress in the mismatched outfit and ask James how he looked. Then

James would burst out laughing, and Mr. Preston would laugh too.

Tonight Mr. Preston slipped on the tracksuit, then his slippers, and headed to the dining table.

James took a bottle of wine out of the wine cooler, popped the cork, and poured a glass for Mr. Preston. Mr. Preston swirled the wine in the goblet, then took a couple of sips. "Excellent choice, James." James smiled, realizing he was getting the hang of choosing appropriate wines that accompany food.

The doorbell rang at precisely six-thirty. His prepared dinner had arrived. Seared sea scallops, home fries, steamed broccoli, and a salad of spring greens. He nodded to James, who stepped into the kitchen and brought back a small pitcher of hot melted Velveeta. Mr. Preston poured it over his broccoli. He and James had this Velveeta secret. When Mr. Preston was only "Monty" as a kid (short for Tremont), his mom put melted Velveeta on his broccoli so he'd eat it. No matter how successful he became, he still enjoyed the Velveeta on his broccoli, but only at home, and James was never to breathe a word of the silly Velveeta secret.

Mr. Preston finished dinner, then moved to his lounge chair to watch TV. James quietly cleaned up the dishes and finished polishing up the kitchen.

"Anything else, Mr. Preston?" James asked when he was done.

"Did you get all my things packed for my holiday golf trip?"

"Yes, sir. Everything on your list is in the two bags in the closet by the dressing chair."

"Thank you, James."

"Will you be leaving tomorrow?" James asked.

"Yes, pretty early too. I want to get out of town before the crazy people head out for their shopping and Christmas parties."

"Understood," said James. "Your bed is turned down, and the place is locked down. Will you be needing anything else before I leave?

"No, James, that will be all. Have a happy holiday. I will need you back here next Tuesday," Mr. Preston instructed.

"Yes, sir. Tuesday," James said as he got his coat out of the coat closet. "Have a Merry Christmas, Sir, and hope your golf goes well."

"Mmm-hmmm." Mr. Preston was watching the evening financial report. James opened the front door to leave and Mr. Preston called to him. "Oh, one more thing James."

"Sir?"

"There is an envelope for you on the hall table. Merry Christmas."

James' face actually registered surprise. He looked at the table, and leaning on a vase was a small envelope with "James" on it. He opened the envelope and there was a small card from Mr. Preston's personal stationery with his initials engraved in gold on heavy linen stock. James opened the card, and it read, 'Merry Christmas, Thank you for your service. Regards, Tremont A Preston' and a substantial amount of cash in it. James' face lit up, and he hollered, "THANK YOU, Mr. Preston! Merry Christmas!" and he nearly danced out the door quietly singing, "Boom, chukka-lukka, boom, chukka-lukka…!"

Mr. Preston heard the deadlock click. He was alone for the night but smiled to himself with his bright veneers that he made someone's day. He enjoyed surprising James because James never asked for, nor expected anything, from him. It seemed everyone else wanted something.

After the news, Mr. Preston double-checked his bags and moved them to the front door. He turned off the TV and saw that James had set the coffee maker to begin at five o'clock tomorrow morning then checked his tablet itinerary again. Satisfied he had all his bases covered, he turned into his bed, knowing he would be on his way early tomorrow.

He couldn't wait to drive into Palm Springs in his Spectaculeer and show off with his new custom clubs.

Chapter 6

The Black Diamond Awaits

Four Seniors Gamble on a Trip

"Holy cow, Doris," Jackie said as she got out of her car. "You mean Dave is letting you drive this thing to Vegas?"

"Yeah, well, it took a little convincing. Namely, I said I'd stay in town and accompany him to his ex's family Christmas if he wouldn't let me take the Black Diamond," Doris said. "As it turned out, he thought it would be safer for us than my mini-van."

"Is that thing going to ride like a truck with square wheels?" Rita griped as she walked up to the group with her floral rolling suitcase and ever-jingling gold charm bracelet. "It's nothing but an oversized army jeep."

"Oh, Rita, knock it off. It's been civilized," Doris said. "Dave spent a small fortune the past couple years on a luxury suspension option, the custom ultra-plush interior and all the extras, not to mention the diamond-fleck black paint job and gold trim. We'll be just fine. Plus, if we get weird weather, it'll be like a freakin' tank on the road."

"If you want my opinion, it is a tank, no matter how much you dress it up," Rita snipped.

"I'm surprised Dave let you drive it too," Janet said while patting the hood. "I know he was thrilled when he bought it at the military surplus auction for peanuts a couple of summers ago, and it was his pride and joy, not to mention all the dough he spent customizing it."

"Yeah. It's actually designed after the military Hum-Vee, a lightweight, diesel-powered, four-wheel-drive, military tactical vehicle then retrofitted as a dual-purpose utility transport personnel carrier. The company that retrofits them calls it their Dominator-Maximus, Dave calls his the Black Diamond Coach. Diamond for all the money he sunk in it and Coach, like he's the King, and this is his Coach. He was driving it like he was the King of the Earth for a while until some schmuck yelled at him for wasting gas and showing off, and someone else called him a pimp driver. He's mellowed about it since. I guess people ragging on him about the gas mileage and stuff has taken some of the joy out of it. But it's nearly indestructible and good for us gals traveling alone. So, are you girls ready for our annual holiday Vegas trip?" Doris asked as she loaded another suitcase in the back.

"Yep," said Jackie, "The Gambling Go-Go Gals are ready! I have my lucky dice in my pocket and four credit cards."

"Four credit cards?" Janet asked. "You are going to gamble away all of Jerry's life insurance if you aren't careful."

"Nahh," Jackie countered. "That insurance is tied up in investments. I keep the four cards so I can keep my expenses separate. Food and lodging on one, gambling on another, travel on another, and the spare one for emergencies. I just didn't want to travel with a big wad of cash."

"No cash?? Going to Vegas with no cash??" Rita smirked. "That's funny, Jackie. You need cash to grease a few palms. That's how I get special treatment," Rita commented as she bent the side-view mirror around so she could check her lipstick and smooth the top of her overly-bleached blonde hair. Rita could be nice, but as she got older, she was getting to be pretty snippy with her tone. Doris had called Janet earlier in the month and considered axing Rita from the group, but they decided to give it one last shot. As Rita opened the door of the Black Diamond, all she could do was gripe, "How are we supposed to get in it? Am I supposed to lug a step-ladder?"

"No, Rita, do you see the button that says 'step'? Flip that down," Doris instructed. When Rita found the switch and flipped it down, a black step rolled out from under the vehicle and stopped along the bottom edge of the door forming two perfect steps. "How's that suit you, Rita? You think you can manage now?" Doris jabbed with just a bit of sarcasm.

Janet grabbed Doris' arm and squeezed it whispering, "Don't start her going, please." Doris looked at Janet and nodded agreement. While they were comparing notes, they both thought Rita was on the opposite side of the huge Dominator. But Rita came whisking around the vehicle, flipping her hair to the front of her shoulders while looking at herself in the window reflection.

"And who is riding in front?" Rita snipped.

Janet, as the usual fixer, saw a problem arising and volunteered to ride in the back. But Doris stopped that runaway train and told the group that Janet had to ride in front because she was the only one that knew how to operate the GPS and pull up maps and travel information on the computer. Doris knew Janet could do that from the back seat, but she really didn't want Rita up front and have to listen to her bitch about something every two minutes. At least in back, she might nod off and take a nap.

Rita was quite a character and never seemed to get past the '60s. Not her age, but her high school years. She still thought she looked so cute with her long blonde hair and the bangs of a high school cheerleader even though the reality was that her shrunken and wrinkly face was now framed between sides of straw-like hair. She was always smoothing her hair in front of her shoulders alongside her face, only to unknowingly display a mostly bald scalp in the back from too many years of hair treatments, many of which she did by herself. She thought people looked at her because she was attractive when people were really looking at her wondering, what the hell happened to her?

Rita was also relentless about not eating more than a bite or two of anything to remain slim but was actually looking somewhat anorexic, sporting a boney look covered in flesh-toned crepe paper, but she thought being ultra-slim made her look more youthful.

"You know if you'd eat, you could fill out some of that wrinkly skin," Doris kept telling her at lunches. Rita was so underfed that her hair had begun to fall out in a few more small patches, but she still insisted on starving herself and keeping her long hair bleached platinum even though the ends were horribly split and uneven. And no amount of suggestions from the girls about getting her hair trimmed a bit would move her. She was very attractive fifty years ago, but she was beginning to look rather frightening over time. To make it worse, Rita fixed her hair with a little rat job at the top to give her head a poofy look, even though the slightest breeze disrupted the smoothed cover hairs showing off the "rat pile," as the girls referred to it behind her back.

Rita also went in for particularly horrible fake nails. Twice a month she'd get a new nail job with some crazy design on ultra-long, downward-curving nails that looked like they were tools for cutting grapefruit sections. And even this many years from the '60s, Rita still managed to find hip-hugger pants with bell-bottoms. Thankfully the pants she'd chosen for the trip were not obnoxious prints. She usually wore little bolero vests over a scoop-neck sleeveless shirt because she wanted people to see how trim her arms were. Like anyone cared. She resembled a 60's hootenanny hippie-chick, stuck in a time warp.

The girls overlooked it all though and teased her endlessly, but Rita took it all in stride. The one thing the girls couldn't overlook and was most annoying was her gold charm bracelet. She must have had fifty charms on it. Every time she moved, the jingling of the charms drove the other gals nuts until someone would tell her to take it off.

Still, the four of them had hung out for so many years that Rita was just part of the group, and they tolerated her. They barely saw her in Vegas anyway as she went her own way, which was usually man-hunting.

Doris was kind of the group instigator and planner. She always had some event planned for them, theater tickets, concerts, restaurant dinners, and the annual holiday Vegas trip. Doris talked a lot and was loud, but funny, and the only one that had a current husband. She liked crazy clothes with tropical prints, so she wore large, brightly-colored clothes with glittered parrots or rhinestoned flowers with some kind of sparkling tiki-themed design. She was always wearing palazzo pants with generous amounts of gauzy fabric that looked a bit like Priscilla Curtains. Because she was short and a bit chunky and didn't hem anything, the pants fluttered about her feet in the breeze like a litter of starving puppies as she walked. Doris topped it all off with a variety of glittery oversized jackets or oversized shirts. When her hair had turned completely gray, she'd cut it in a very short little-boy cut and would spike it out when she went out so she wouldn't look so grandmotherly. Her husband hated it, but the kids liked it. She even had sunglasses with rhinestone-encrusted frames. When the girls went out, she wore as much sparkle as she could manage. Lots of color, lots of sparkle, lots of loud. That was Doris.

Jackie was the opposite. She was classy. Always tall and slender, she wore linen suits and heels when they went out anywhere. She had a knack for making a scarf stay on her shoulder or around her neck in an elegant designer way. When she tried to fix one for Doris, it ended up looking like a ski muffler. There's a skill to wearing a scarf and having it look right, and Jackie had it. Jackie's hair was long, but never dyed and just a bit of gray. Jackie kept it in a nice bun or a French twist and always looked like she came from Europe's haute couture set. If Jackie wore jewelry, it was a single string of pearls around her neck, a double-strand pearl bracelet, and pearl drop earrings. Always understated and totally chic. Jackie was also the quiet one. Smiling, kind, and upbeat. It was a shame her husband passed on a couple of years ago as they were very happy together. Still, she managed to remain positive through it all. Janet was always envious of the loving relationship Jackie had with her husband. Janet told Jackie many times, she'd be glad to trade husbands. That way, Jackie could have her beloved husband back from the dead, and Janet could be rid of hers. Jackie thought it was a sweet gesture. Doris thought it was crazy.

Janet was the filler of the group. Always very neat and organized from her dry-cleaned and pressed jeans to her brand name golf shirts with the collars turned up and a cashmere sweater folded over her shoulders with the sleeve cuffs tucked together in front, looking like the tennis set at the country club. From Doris' gaudy sparkle to Rita's platinum blonde 60's look, and Jackie's class, Janet was the normal one. She could blend in anywhere and looked like she belonged everywhere. If anyone had a problem or a gripe, they called Janet. Janet always had the time to listen and offer advice, and her advice was solid and on point. Janet helped everyone else when they needed something or anything. A button sewed on? A recipe for cheesecake? Computer crash? Kids in trouble at school? She brought soup when someone had the flu. Janet had a wealth of general knowledge, so she was always the go-to gal when someone needed anything. Janet also was the "smoother" if there was a squabble between any of the girls. She always managed to know how to make peace without hurt feelings. Janet was a reliable friend. They all liked Janet and trusted her and her judgment, and they also knew she was the only one that could keep Rita in check. She had run interference many times when Rita started getting pissy with someone. Janet was the glue for the group.

The gals had been going to Vegas every year since they turned fifty-five. They spent half the year planning the places to stay, shows to see, places to gamble, shopping for outfits and going on diets, and the other half of the year talking about the last trip, reviewing the shows, their gambling skills, the last hotel accommodations, the buffets, and tales of traveling during their coffee klatches, bridge luncheons, backyard barbeques, and phone calls.

This was going to be their seventh trip. Lucky Seven, they called it and were all hyped up over the fact that the seventh trip should be the luckiest of all. The past two years, Doris and Janet drove alone while Rita and Jackie flew, and they met at the airport in Vegas. Doris would never get into one of those aluminum tubes to fly, so Janet stayed back to ride with Doris. But this year, with Doris' husband's huge Dominator-Maximus, the Black Diamond, they were all riding together and looking forward to having a ball along the way.

Rita was already in the Black Diamond fiddling with the junk in her oversized purse. Jackie was getting her train case out of her car and asked Doris if she wanted the case in the back or if she could keep it in the back seat. Doris told her the back seat would be plenty big enough for Jackie's petite train case, and maybe nine more. Jackie opened the back door and it made Rita jump a foot, as Jackie caught a glimpse of Rita looking like she was kissing a pair of binoculars. Rita gave Jackie a cheesy grin and held one finger up to her lips to indicate to Jackie to shush and keep the secret. Jackie rolled her eyes and plunked her train case on the seat and slammed the door.

Rita slid down farther in the seat and put the binoculars up to her lips again.

Jackie went to lock up her car and gave Doris her car keys. Doris took everyone's car keys up to the house to leave with Dave in case he had to move cars. Janet and Jackie watched her walk up to the house. Jackie elbowed Janet, "You know Rita is drinking already."

"Seriously? It's only ten in the morning. She didn't used to get started until after lunch," Janet said.

"Yes, I know. Funny thing is, she doesn't think we all know about it," Jackie commented.

"That's just stupid," Janet said. "She's been boozing for forty years, how could we not know."

"I know, I know, but get this, she now has a flask that looks like a pair of binoculars."

"Aw jeez. Why doesn't she just bring the bottle already?" Janet sighed.

Doris came back from the house. "I guess I'm ready to roll, Girls!" she announced. "Saddle up!"

Janet and Jackie walked around to the shotgun side and passed Doris on their way. Janet made a hand motion to Doris, indicating Rita was sipping already. Doris rolled her eyes.

They piled in the Black Diamond and belted up. Doris fired it up and they rolled out of the driveway and on their way to Vegas and the neighborhood could hear Rita shouting, "Gambling! Here we come!"

Chapter 7

Heaven Knows

Matthew, Not Mark, Not Luke, nor John

"Dear Lord, I hope I am doing the right thing." Matthew prayed out loud as his forty-five-year-old Minibus puttered along loaded down with everything he owned, which wasn't very much.

"I am so sorry, Lord, that I didn't have the patience and faith that I needed to be satisfied," Matthew prayed as he pulled into a Promptitude Gas-Up to gas up the bus. He was dressed in his "civilians" as he chose not to wear his clerical collar while he was traveling.

He'd felt the calling while playing outfield during a little league baseball game when he was about ten. The game was long, the sun was hot, and the outfield was boring. As he was daydreaming about other things he noticed the tiny yellow flowers on the cut weeds at his feet, he saw that even the unwanted weeds were trying to show that they had something worthy about them. He had a sense that he was much like the weeds that struggled to bloom after the grass cuttings as he struggled to be liked among the other kids in school instead of ignored and cut down.

He'd been picked on at school, and other kids didn't ask him to play because he was emotional, shy, and wore glasses. When he saw those tiny flowers on the weeds, he saw himself, the weed at school that it seemed everyone wanted to get rid of. Even at his young age, he somehow understood that he struggled to show that he had something good to offer, just like those weeds in the outfield.

His teachers tried to help, but they only made him feel worse when they'd tell him, "If you want to have friends, you have to go out and make some." He'd tried, but for some reason, the other kids didn't have any use for a kind, sensitive kid. The popular kids were the pretty girls and the athletic boys. He didn't understand why he was always being left out, so he sought help from a higher power.

His parents didn't do church much, but he knew his Grandmother's Bible was on a bookshelf next to an old set of encyclopedias. He loved his grandmother very much and had wonderful memories of her, but she died just before he turned nine, and he still missed her. She always made him the center of attention when he visited and she took the time to talk to him and listen to him. It felt good to him to have someone truly listen. His Grandmother was very faithful and taught him to pray and be faithful, explaining that God always had time for him, and he should pray to thank God for the good things and pray to ask God to help with the bad things.

It was a few days after that spell of boredom in the outfield that he took the Bible up to his room. He opened it to the first page that was ornate with gold lettering and scroll-work down the sides of the page. He fingered the designs leading him to the middle of the page where there was a handwritten inscription that this Bible was given to his grandmother many years before he was born.

As Matthew flipped through the pages, a few little faded, flattened yellow flowers slipped out onto his lap. It was weird because these were the same kind of flowers he'd seen in the outfield. Matthew carefully turned a few more pages of the Bible where a few more crumbs of flowers stuck to a page with a tattered yellowed piece of paper stuck in the binding crack. He loosened it and looked at the writing. "You made my life bloom. -Hank". Hank was his grandfather. His grandfather must have brought a little bouquet of flowers he picked from a field of weeds to his grandmother, and she pressed them between the pages of her Bible.

He noticed there was a pencil-drawn heart around one of the paragraphs on the page, it was as though it was a mystical message from beyond that his grandparents meant for him to find. It was in I Corinthians. Matthew read it quietly to himself. "Love is patient, love is kind, not proud…" After he'd finished reading the whole passage, he understood then that his calling was to love and care for others, even those that didn't seem to care about him. He remembered his grandmother telling him many times to pray and ask God to send someone to him that would love him. So he prayed. And he waited. Prayed some more. Waited some more.

By the time Matthew was in high school, he'd forgotten about praying for love. He had only one pal, another sensitive guy he met at a church group. They used to hang out, discuss Bible passages and religious dogma, talk about girls, and the relentless meanness growing in the world today. They prayed together before exams and for girls to notice them and for things that young men want. But the love of his life still eluded him. Girls talked to Matthew quite a lot, in fact. But they talked to him because he listened to them cry about their boyfriends and broken hearts. He knew how to listen, a skill he learned from his grandmother, so he offered a shoulder to lean on and gave simple advice. Still, the girls never wanted him for a boyfriend, they only wanted his shoulder to cry on, and Matthew let them as it was his only contact with girls. Hugging a girl that was sobbing about a broken heart was better than no contact at all. He never understood why these girls always went back to the boyfriends that continued to do things that hurt them. He couldn't imagine wanting to hurt someone like that.

After some college and dating a few girls, the relationship he wanted so much never happened, and he still had that feeling of being called for a purpose. Eventually, he came to understand that it was God's way of preparing him to minister to a flock. So he studied to become an ordained minister. He had great hopes of comforting his parishioners through trials of life, helping the poor, marrying people in love, instilling faith, and teaching people to comfort themselves in prayer like his grandmother taught him.

So it came to pass that he was given his first flock in a small suburban church. After a year of ministering there, he was learning that many people in his congregation could still be unkind, even after many of his sermons. "Dear Lord," he prayed, "I cannot change these people's outlook on life no matter what I say in my sermons. Please help me find the words that will have them see their blessings instead of complaining about what they don't have."

He was becoming discouraged that much of his time was spent fund-raising and trying to convince his flock that a small offering on Sunday was not enough to pay the expenses on the church's utilities, maintenance, insurance, and a million incidentals such as candles, sacramental wines, communion wafers, and try to have a little extra left to help the poor. He saw that parishioners, in general, were unmotivated to get involved in much of anything, and many seemed to think spending one hour on Sunday was enough to grant them holy access to heaven.

He prayed again, "Many of my congregants are willing to spend hundreds of dollars going to a Sunday football game with tailgating, parking fees, food, and skipping church. On Saturday nights, they go out for dinners with drinks and movies. I hear them sharing with each other what they spent on vacations, holidays, cars, and everything else. Is it asking too much that a tiny portion of that could go to the church? That wouldn't be asking too much, would it, Dear Lord?" And then Matthew would feel guilty, begging God for a few bucks.

When the coffers were almost out of money, he'd pray some more. "Dear God, please take my anger from me when I have to ask for extra donations to repair the furnace, spray for bugs, or fix the broken window. And take the anger from the parishioners that they have to endure me asking again."

He started feeling some resentment toward people dressing so casually when they came into the house of God to worship. Shorts, t-shirts, and a few cases of terminal flip-flops, and a few young men were wearing ball caps through the service. Did they really need to be told that they should dress in a way to show their respect for His holy house? One parishioner even told him point blank, "I wear a suit all week at work, I'm not coming here to listen to your sermon wearing a choking tie. When we are done here, we take the kids out for pancakes, and we're not going there all dressed up to end up sticky."

Matthew didn't know how to respond to that. He was always amazed at the attitude of many of his suburban flock. Was it a tedious job for them to have to spend an hour in church once a week when Matthew felt that it should have brought them a sense of joy and renewal to be together in the church family. Eventually, he decided it was better to forgive their clothing choices like they were going to the beach than to not show up at all. He always felt guilty about being irritated when one more person came in with flip-flops and dirty toenails. Even Jesus got his feet washed, he told himself. He prayed a lot asking God to forgive him for his judging and asked for patience.

Matthew finally had enough, feeling totally demoralized by his parishioners that seemed to think church was a chore and asked his superiors to be moved out of the suburbs. So they moved him to a small inner-city church in a very poor community. Poor is right, it was the slums. Even though some of the older women church members seemed faithful and helpful enough, he noticed that many of the really poor younger city people seemed angry. Angry about everything. He quickly learned not to mention his previous affiliation out in the suburbs as most of the poor had very unkind things to say about the "rich" and how they should share what they have. At first, Matthew felt agreement with this sentiment, but after months of working with them, he saw that many of the street poor felt they deserved a lot of handouts and they didn't want to work for it.

Matthew knew that idle hands are the devil's playground and thought he would be able to help these people to be more hopeful and productive and had great plans to help clean up the neighborhood. But he couldn't motivate enough people to get involved to dig in and get things done. He didn't seem to have the right words. And because the community was so unemployed, he had even less money to work with. He sold some of his personal things to pay the heating bills last winter for some of the families on welfare. His Minibus had been broken into at least once a month, and pretty much everything he had was stolen, even the spare tire off the front.

Once again, he became discouraged when it seemed clear that many of the people only came to church asking for money to get bills paid, asking for free food, or wanting to use the church basement for their club meetings or a warm place to sleep. He never charged for anything, but he still had to pay the utilities to keep the lights, heat, and water on. The church was going into the hole, and he was spending even more time trying to get funding from community sources.

One day, in total exasperation, he shouted at God, "This is not what I signed up for!! These people don't want a reverend to minister to their faith. They only want free stuff!" After his outburst, he apologized to God. He really didn't mind helping people get their gas turned on or a bag of groceries, but after a year went by, he felt like his church was being the chronic neighborhood meal ticket. The same people over and over. Most were quite able-bodied but didn't seem to want to help themselves or help the church. It was making him feel jaded and uncaring. People didn't want his prayers over dying family or officiating marriage vows or his counseling to the weary and afraid, they just expected the church to provide free things. Matthew would get irritated when he handed out so much to hopelessly, intentionally, unemployed people. He'd mutter under his breath, "The Lord helps those that help themselves, you know," as he handed out a box of groceries again. Then followed up by asking God to forgive him again. "Yep, these people are helping themselves," he assured God.

Matthew didn't mind that many of these folks were drug users. He seemed to understand that drug use was a momentary way out of the filth and stagnation of the slums. He didn't mind the language of the streets, even though sometimes it made him wince that they used it in the church. He didn't mind that most of them had police records a mile long, and he was learning not to let the piercings and tattoos frighten him. But he did find himself wondering how they could afford the many gold and diamond studs and rings in those piercings and how they paid for the multitude of tattoos, fake nails, and hair treatments. Everyone had ink and a lot of it. And shoes. He couldn't help but notice the expensive sneakers almost everyone owned. How could they afford two-hundred-dollar sneakers yet not have food for their children?

Even though some of the elderly women and one man volunteered, they couldn't do the grunt work. Matthew spent many late nights mopping red muddy boot prints off the church floor, cleaning windows, dusting and wiping down the altar and pews, scrubbing graffiti off the brick outside the church, mowing the tiny space of grass, filling holes in the parking lot, chasing off the rats that gathered at the dumpster, and everything else. He would begin to feel anger at having to do it all himself when he could have used younger volunteers for some of these jobs. But he kept his faith by chanting, "Idle play is the devil's playground," "Cleanliness is next to Godliness," and "Work is healthy." And of course, he constantly prayed for forgiveness and more faith." Was God teaching him patience? He wasn't sure, but he knew that this experience was only making him think about giving up being a reverend and look into becoming a therapist or something else.

He asked one more time to be moved to a more conservative congregation. And soon he got notice that he would become a pastor for a tiny church in a farming community in Northwest Kansas. Less than one hundred members. When he got the information on his new congregation, he found they seemed to have a lot of volunteers and even managed to save some money in a church savings account. As a bonus, he didn't have to rent a place of his own, he could live in the attached 135-year-old rectory, but the current pastor lived there too. The Reverend Schmidt was old, and his health was declining. He needed help in both his church duties and daily functioning at home. The congregation hoped Matthew would help Reverend Schmidt in both areas. Matthew was excited. He hoped this would be the answer to his prayers to truly help people and looked forward to the challenge.

Matthew came out of the Promptitude Gas-Up with a bag of chips, two bottled waters, a cup of coffee, and a lottery ticket. He was encouraged by the new adventure and was hoping it would be a peaceful, law-abiding town to minister to. And now on this last leg of his journey, he calculated if he drove all night, he could be at the new church and settle in time to help the old pastor administer the Midnight Christmas services.

He started the bus, then dug around in the boxes in the back for his winter coat. A winter coat by Georgia standards. It was colder up here than where he left, but the cold air smelled fresh and clean, just like his new start on life. Matthew put the stick in gear and puttered out of the Promptitude Gas-Up and into the night bound for Kansas.

Chapter 8

Maple Syrup Runs in his Veins

Bentricular Contraction

Ben was good looking enough to get the two waitresses giggling in the kitchen.

"You ask him," Lucy said.

"No way. YOU ask him," Martha taunted.

Both girls continued giggling and looking at Ben through the pass-through from the kitchen.

Ben had been driving for two days and was tired and lonely, but excited about his new temporary job as a ski instructor over the Christmas and New Year's holidays in Colorado. The ski resorts had hired some temps so the ski resort personnel could take some time off to be with their families for the holidays.

Ben didn't have much of a family to leave behind for the holidays. His folks divorced when he was a little kid and he never really saw his dad after that, then his mom passed away from cancer over a decade ago. So his great aunt and uncle took him in when he was in junior high. They owned a maple syrup farm in the remote mountains of Vermont and never had kids of their own, so they had plenty of room and work for a young man. They had the maple syrup farm since the 1940s and ran the business until his uncle died a few years ago at ninety years old. Up until his uncle got the pneumonia that ended his life, he managed his farm and did much of the work himself. He used to tend the maples all winter on cross-country skis, but as he got older, he finally gave in to using an ATV.

Aunt Katarina and Uncle William were tough New Englanders and didn't take crap from anyone, and during Ben's years with them, they taught him to be tough too, working and living the maple syrup life. He helped to tend the trees using Uncle Willie's old cross-country skis, loving the freedom they gave him.

His Aunt and Uncle also taught him how to take care of himself when he was out working and tapping the trees alone in the cold. There were a number of old wive's tales about maple syrup farmers becoming confused while out tending their trees, and getting lost trying to get back home, then froze to death looking for the way, they later called it hypothermia. Ben was never sure if it was true or a way to get his attention. Uncle Willie hammered it into Ben's head over and over. "You can't cheat Mother Nature!" he'd thunder at Ben while holding one finger up in the air as though he was pointing to Mother Nature sitting on a cloud. They taught Ben to recognize the signs of becoming too cold, how to conserve his body heat and how to build a small shelter with either snow or sticks and branches, then hunker down and wait for help.

Ben really loved Vermont in the snow on their farm. He was on skis nearly all winter, either tending to trees using the cross country skis or just having fun downhill skiing with his friends. Most of the kids his age were into snowboarding, but Ben preferred his skis. Because of his years of work among the maples, he was excellent at maneuvering on them. His friends called him Bentricular Contraction because he could twist and turn so fast and efficiently. He loved the nick. He took in the downhill slopes with his friends, but his favorite was cross-country skiing alone, only the sound of the snow under his skis and the wind in the pines. It was then he felt like he was in his element.

When Uncle Willie died, his Aunt, who was a ball of fire before his passing, became depressed and lost her zest for living. She asked Ben if he wanted to take over the farm and make maple syrup for a living, and Ben didn't seem too excited. She realized that this was the end of days for her maple farm, and Ben would go off and do other things. Even though Ben had learned a lot in his fifteen years with his Aunt and Uncle, he would never know everything about the trees that Uncle Willie knew in his seventy years on the farm.

Ben understood the business end of it. If he had to hire help, there'd never be enough money to pay himself a good wage, and he couldn't do it all by himself. Ben only got a small allowance working for Uncle Willie, so when the maple work was done, Ben did things for other people in the area to earn a few bucks. Snow shoveling, there was almost always snow shoveling he could do, he cut firewood too, and as he grew older, he learned how to repair small engines, help repair barn roofs, and do other carpentry work. Ben was handy and was a natural at mechanics, but learning and understanding maple trees, the insects, tree health, and the weather takes many years of watching for the signs. Ben didn't think he knew enough to take over the farm, but then again, he wasn't sure what else he could do to earn a decent living. He was twenty-three, and Aunt Kate wasn't going to live forever, so he'd have to find something soon.

During his many solo cross-country treks, Ben had time to dream. He had many dreams about being a ski instructor at one of the wonderful Vermont ski lodges as it paid well, but it was seasonal work. The competition from other excellent skiers, the class of people that skied, the resort surroundings like a fireplace and a hot toddy at the end of the day was a social life that interested Ben. He considered that he could do ski work in the dead of winter as there wasn't much to do with the maple trees, then come back to the farm when it was time for caring for the trees, tapping, and collecting syrup.

Ben had been looking online for ski jobs, but they were hard to come by as many young avid skiers were eating up those plum jobs until one day he got a tip from one of his friends about some of the Colorado resorts looking for temporary ski guides and instructors over the holidays. Ben jumped on it. Luckily he landed one quickly when he told the prospective employer that he didn't mind working long hours on the holidays. It also paid an extra differential for the holiday hours so Ben would make a tidy nest egg working for those three weeks, and maybe, he thought, they might like him enough to hire him permanently.

The only difficulty was telling Aunt Kate. She was near 90, and he did quite a bit to make her life comfortable considering she took him in when he was a young boy and raised him through his teen years. He hated leaving her alone, especially over the holiday season. But Aunt Kate was mindful of his situation. She understood he was a young man and wanted to see something more in his life than endless acres of maple trees.

"I'm tough, Ben. I'll be just fine. I'm still gettin' around like a wildcat, except when I'm not," Aunt Kate said with an odd twinkle in her eye. "I love you like a son. I think. I never had a son, so I can't compare, but I'm thinkin' this must be what it's like." She was always on the border of making mischief and being weird, and Ben loved that about her. She was funny as hell too.

Ben told her he'd most likely be gone about three weeks and back in time to start working the maple trees as they come out of their winter sleep. Aunt Kate was glad to see him so excited to go do something he loved after all the years of helping her and her husband on the farm.

"This old sappy farm isn't going anywhere, Ben. Sappy. Get it, Ben?" She delighted in the terrible pun. "Those maples aren't going to get up and wander off. They'll be here when you get back, and if you are late, I'll call down to the general store and hire a couple of young men to come up and help. It's always nice to look at healthy young men," she winked.

Aunt Kate realized that the farm was going to have to be sold, she knew she wouldn't be able to keep up the business end by herself. Eventually, she would have to move to town and live in the senior apartments, or maybe she'd be lucky and die on the farm. She considered walking out among her beloved maples on a cold day, and simply sit down, take off her coat and watch the snow. They'd find her come spring. But she knew that'd be awful for Ben.

One thing many old New Englander's don't want, and that's to look like they might be too sentimental, so Aunt Kate punched Ben in the shoulder and said, "Hey. I think you should take Uncle Willie's truck. Your truck is a falling-apart piece of crap and will never make it to Colorado without a tow truck. Nobody's drove old Willie's truck since he died, and it was practically new when he got sick. He just HAD to have that big damn truck. The stupid old man," she laughed. "I don't think there's 30,000 miles on the blue bomb yet. I can't drive it, hell, I need a jack and a rig to get up in it, those big damn tires he put on it, they'll just dry-rot. I don't want to sell it yet because I think Willie would get mad. So you take it on your trip. Just bring it back, so old Willie don't think I sold his damn truck. I swear he was going through his second childhood at 80." And Aunt Kate laughed again while rolling up today's newspaper, then smacked Ben on the head with it.

"Oh man," Ben said. "I can't take Uncle Willie's truck. He was so proud of that thing when he bought it, I'd just feel awful if anything happened to it."

"Wake up and smell the wet concrete, Ben...Willie is dead," she said matter-of-factly. "Take the truck. Nothing I can do with it but sell it when I need some money and I don't need the money now. And I think he'd enjoy seeing you flying down the highway in his blue mistress. He always wanted to travel, but the damn farm kept him from goin' anywhere. Best he did in that truck was when he took you fishin' up near Canada. So take the damn truck. Don't make me say it again." And Aunt Kate grabbed the keys from the nail Willie hammered into the door trim the day he got the truck and anointed his nail as the official Blue Bomb key holder. She tossed the keys across the kitchen right to Ben, still a dead shot at almost 90. She smiled at the accomplishment. "See, still a wildcat!" And she laughed as she walked to the living room. "I'm takin' a nap now Ben, you better go over the Blue Bomb with that mechanical fine-tooth comb ya got between your ears since she's been sittin' for nearly two years. Look out too, because I think Willie was having sex with her when I wasn't lookin'!"

Ben shook his head and smiled at some of the peculiar things that came out of her mouth, but that was Aunt Kate. He went out to the barn and opened a pen door where he'd parked the truck a couple of years ago when Kate figured Willie was too sick to be driving. She worried that he might try to get out and drive it if he saw it, so she and Ben secreted away the truck to the pen, covered it with a couple of old horse blankets, and shut the pen door.

But today, Ben slid a blanket off the truck and coughed with the dust it stirred up. Then whisked off the other blanket like a magician revealing his trick. Other than a bit of a dull finish and film on the windows, the truck looked nearly new. Ben opened the driver's door, it still smelled like a new car. He put the key in, but the battery was dead.

Ben put the truck in neutral and rolled it out to the middle of the barn. He got a bucket of mild soap and water and began wiping down the interior and cleaning the inside of the windows. Ben drooled over this truck when Uncle Willie brought it home and remembered Uncle Willie saying, "Someday, when you are older and work hard, you'll have a truck like this too." Maybe Uncle Willie knew that Ben would end up with it. For a while, anyway.

Ben got up to the machine shed and found the battery charger, and when the battery was charged, he put the key in and the truck fired right up....it sounded like a fuel dragster. Dang!! Ben drove the truck down to town and to the carwash, where he took the time to hand wash the exterior and dry it with a chamois. He saw how the wheels were sparkling chrome, and the electric blue truck nearly hurt his eyes in the sun. It was definitely an attention-getter. He took the truck over to Ed's repair shop and Ed Junior was surprised to see it after such a long absence. Ben explained hiding the truck from Uncle Willie as Ed Junior wiped his hands on a rag. "Yeah, that Kate is a smart one," Ed Junior said. "My dad dated her many moons ago and was jealous when she chose Willie over him. If my dad was still living, as soon as she put Willie in the ground, he'd have been hanging around her house."

Ben looked at Ed Junior for his cold comment. "Ed Junior, can you put this on the diagnostic and see if she's ready to roll?"

"Yeah, not a problem," Ed Junior said as he walked over to the diagnostic machine and started rolling it toward the truck, "I didn't think Kate could drive this thing."

"Well, she can't, Ed Junior," Ben said. "She's letting me use it to take a vacation in. I'm bringing it back in the middle of January."

"Whoa!! You got a good thing going with Kate, Ben."

Ben ignored the rude comment. He never cared much for Ed Junior, but Ed's was the only car repair joint in town unless he went to the next county over where there were a couple of dealerships.

Ben stuffed his hands in his jacket pockets and wandered out of Ed's garage and stopped in at Shirley's Café for coffee and one of her cinnamon rolls that were out of this world. Shirley had gone to school with Ben's mom, and she had a daughter Ben's age that also worked in the café. Ben opened the door making a little bell ring, and he heard Shirley's voice from the kitchen, "I'll be right there, take a seat." Ben barely sat at the counter when Shirley came out, wiping her hands on her apron. "Hey, Ben. How are you? What'll you have?"

"Hi, Shirley. Things are good. Coffee and a cinnamon roll, if you have one."

She plopped a mug on the counter and filled it with coffee, then opened a pastry box and picked out the biggest roll for Ben and handed him the plate. Ben pulled a corner off the roll and put it in his mouth, then followed that with some hot coffee. Momentary heaven.

Shirley and Ben exchanged some pleasantries then Shirley asked him about taking Celeste out. "You know she pines for you still, Ben," Shirley reminded him. Celeste and Ben had a little puppy love in junior high, but that was it. Ben thought she was "dippy" and Celeste never really changed even though Shirley was always trying to hook them up.

"Shirley, Celeste is a nice girl, but nothing clicked for me," Ben said.

"Well, I'll keep asking for her," Shirley said. "She'll wait for you, you know. Get those wild oats going and out of your system, and when you are tired of it all, she'll be waitin' to make you some dinner."

"I'm sure that'd be nice," Ben said, "but she needs to find somebody else, Shirley. It's been almost fifteen years since we liked each other. Besides, I'm heading out of town to Colorado in a couple of days to work at a ski lodge. And I'm not sure if I'm coming back."

Shirley stiffened and looked shocked. "Oh Ben, I never saw this coming. Celeste and I always thought you two would get together."

"Shirley," Ben said, trying to let her down gently, "I don't know what my whole future holds, but I just don't see Celeste fitting in anywhere. You really gotta start telling her it's time to find her own life, and it probably won't include me." He put another piece of the roll in his mouth and savored the cinnamon when Ed Junior came in.

"Truck is in good shape, Ben." Ed Junior said. "You can drive it from coast to coast, and it won't be a problem. It's damn near like a new truck."

Ben settled the bill with Ed Junior and he paid Shirley's bill with a decent tip.

"I gotta get going," Ben said, "I have a lot of packing to do." And with that, Ben was back in the truck and heading to the farm to do just that.

Ben got his life in order and packed up his things then stowed it in the truck "trunk" made by the trunk-like cover over the truck bed. He packed his specialized ski wear he'd accumulated the past few years. He even took Uncle Willie's cross country skis. Grabbing a few camping gear items and his heavy-duty sleeping bag, he figured it'd be cheaper to sleep in the truck with the down sleeping bag than rent a creepy motel room. He even packed some hand-warming packets. Aunt Kate packed him a half dozen peanut butter and jelly sandwiches and gave him a bag of Oreos. She also helped him fix Uncle Willie's big old thermos of hot coffee, and as they were saying their good-byes, she handed Ben a beautiful, thick, hand-stitched quilt.

"Aunt Kate! I can't take this. I saw you working on this for over a year."

"Oh, I know, Ben. I keep myself busy with these projects. But what am I going to do with a heavy quilt like this? You can use it, and you might need it. I've heard horror stories about driving across those flat Midwestern states. You take it. Put it on the seat next to you in the truck. When you get cold, wrap it around yourself and think of it as me giving you a hug." And with that, she stepped up to Ben and gave him the tightest little old lady hug she could.

He put his chin on her head and said, "I'm going to miss you, Aunt Kate. But I'll be back," and he hugged her back and gave her a big smooch on her forehead. "I'll call you every day just before your supper. If you don't answer. I'm gonna call Shirley to come check on you. If I don't call, send the highway patrol after me!" They both laughed an uncomfortable laugh and Ben got in the truck.

Aunt Kate stepped back while Ben turned the key, and the truck came to life. She felt tears working their way out as Ben rolled down his window and waved a small wave and headed down the driveway. Aunt Kate stood there in the snow, and when the tears finally came, she turned and trudged back to the house, wiping tears with her sleeves and feeling much older.

And now, after two days of driving, here Ben was in a diner just before he was about to cross the mighty Mississippi on the last leg of his journey. He was not rushing this trip, he was taking his time enjoying seeing parts of the country he'd never seen. He had driven through Hershey, Pennsylvania just to see the streetlights shaped like Hershey's kisses, drove through the tunnels on the Pennsylvania turnpike, stopped by the Indianapolis 500 and when the sun began to rise this morning he saw it reflecting off the stainless steel Gateway Arch next to the Mississippi. He was stopping for some hot coffee and a little breakfast, as sleeping in his truck at night and driving most of the day was getting a bit monotonous. So at a small diner just before the bustle of St. Louis traffic, he was taking a break and was aware of the giggling young waitresses.

"Coffee?" Martha asked as she slid a laminated one-page menu on the table in front of him, blushing like a junior high kid taking her first gym shower.

"Yes, thank-you, with two creams," Ben said, looking at her and smiling.

Martha whisked herself away to get his coffee, and Ben looked out the window. The window faced west and Ben saw just a tiny glimpse of clouds just barely edging along the horizon. Ben made a mental note on the clouds then studied the menu. He was drawn to look back at the horizon a number of times. The morning light had a certain color about it that concerned him, but there was nothing on the weather report to worry about though, still, something didn't look right.

Martha interrupted his thoughts, "Your coffee. Two creams." Martha put a steaming mug of black coffee on the table in front of Ben, then sat a little pitcher shaped like a cow on the table. "Cream." She informed him and smiled as though she knew the cow creamer was silly. "What'll you have this morning?" She asked as he glanced at the menu, then back at her. "You aren't one of the regulars, so you are just passing through?"

Ben poured the cream out of the cow's mouth into his mug and smiled. "I'm headed to Colorado," he volunteered. "New job as a ski guide at a resort." Martha looked impressed. Ben looked at the cow. "You know, my mom had a little cow pitcher like this when I was a kid. I never wanted to drink milk, so mom would put the milk in the cow and pour it into my cup. Then I'd drink it."

"Sounds like a nice memory," Martha commented, standing there with her pencil and order pad wondering how to flirt with him.

"Oh, it is a great memory. I don't have many good memories of my mom, so it's especially sweet," Ben said, fingering the cow.

"I'm sorry." Martha thought this guy seemed nice to have fond memories of his mom and a cow creamer. "Sounds like it was tough when you were a kid."

"Well, not tough, just sad much of the time. My mom was sick a lot," Ben said, trying not to sound morbid to a cute girl and looked at the menu again.

"That happens to a lot of kids." Martha didn't know what else to say, so she simply stood there waiting for Ben to order glancing back to Lucy in the kitchen who was making frantic hand signals for her to get his name and phone number. Ben looked up from the menu and looked at her name tag.

"Well, Martha, I'll have a two-egg omelet, hash browns, and a toasted English muffin. "He smiled and handed her the menu and noticed her pretty blonde hair pulled back in a loose bun. As Martha took the menu, Ben didn't let go right away, causing her to stop and really look at him. She noticed he was looking to see if she was wearing a ring. She was not. Ben let go of the menu and smiled.

"I'll get this for you right away," she said, "and if you like that creamer, we sell them at the register on your way out."

Ben's mind zoomed back to his childhood and that cow creamer of his mother's and wondered what happened to it. Maybe Aunt Kate had it stored away someplace. He had such warm visions of that cow creamer back when they were a family, and morning breakfasts he'd pour milk from it onto his cereal.

Martha interrupted his thoughts, "Here you go, Sir," as she sat the hot breakfast plate down with a roll of silverware. "Anything else? Ketchup?"

"No, Martha, just the check, and if you wouldn't mind, could you add one of those cow pitchers to my tab?"

"Sure." Martha smiled broadly as she looked at him and spun around to go figure his check.

"Oh, and Martha," he called after her, "my name is Ben and if you are unattached, when I come back through next month, maybe we could get together for some coffee and talk about cow pitchers."

"I think I'd like that very much," Martha said. Lucy must have heard it because Martha saw her fist-pumping in the kitchen.

Ben ate his breakfast, occasionally looking out at the distant clouds and feeling some concern. To Ben, those pastel colors of the clouds and sky were an omen of incoming storms and big weather changes. He'd learned plenty about reading the winter skies all the years he spent with Uncle Willie outside in the maple groves. "You can't play with winter," he'd tell Ben. "It can come fast and freeze you to death before you know it. After you get the chills, you just get sleepy as your blood cools you down, then you are done for." But Ben was doubting his weather knowledge right now because the weather reports were for cold, but clear skies and slightly windy conditions. Nothing to fret about today.

Martha brought his check with a cow pitcher in a box. She wrote her phone number on a post-it stuck to the box and set it on the table. Ben was still looking out the window at the distant cloud line, and Martha noticed. "No bad weather, they said this morning. Should be plenty of sunny driving today all the way," Martha informed him.

"That's what I heard too," Ben said. "But still, I have a gnawing feeling about that cloud line. Well, thanks for the breakfast and the chat. I'd better hit the road." He noticed the post-it on the cow box, picked it up and stuck it to his pointer finger, then pointed at her with it. "Seriously, I will call you," Ben said as he got up from the table, picking up his check and the box.

"I hope so. I'm looking forward to it," Martha told him as she walked Ben to the register. "Have a nice day."

As the register finished its ding, Ben went out to get in the truck, still looking at the eerie clouds in the distance.

Chapter 9

Do You Know the Way to Santa Fe

The Butcher and his Wife,
He Loved Her in the Wurst Way

Augustus Heinrich Buchbinder II sat in his rocker on the porch and thought about it over and over. He'd been through a lot in his nearly ninety years, going all the way back to when he was a young boy in Germany. His parents had enough vision to see what was happening in the German political arena in the 1930s and decided they wanted to send their five children to America to save their lives so they wouldn't have to suffer through what they knew was coming. They'd already witnessed so much in WWI.

Augustus was only a kid then, but tall for his age, and his parents worried that he and his two brothers would be taken to serve under Hitler, their lives would simply be wasted. Eventually, they found a way through their Lutheran church to send the three boys to a Lutheran church in America. At least they wouldn't be taken away and stuffed into Nazi uniforms. Most families in Germany during that time couldn't afford food to feed their families much less send their children away to a safe place, but the Buchbinders were butchers and butchering always provided well. The rich always wanted meats and sausages, and the Nazis demanded it, sometimes took it without paying. Still, the Buchbinders managed to hide enough money in sausage casings to send the boys through a network of sympathizers to get them on ships to America.

After they put Augustus and his two brothers on the ship in Bremen to America, Augustus never saw his parents or sisters again. They wrote a few times and secreted the letters between the churches, but eventually, letters from his parents and sisters stopped coming. Augustus always hoped another letter would come, and he kept writing until his own letters started coming back. Then he heard that his church in Germany had been bombed during the raids in WWII. He had always hoped for word of his sisters or parents, but it never came.

The three Buchbinder boys were taken in by the Lutheran church in East Cleveland, where there were a number of other immigrants that spoke German. The boys learned English there, and as each of them graduated from the 8th grade, they started working all kinds of odd jobs. Augustus' older brothers spent much of their youth as apprentices learning the trade in the family butcher shop with their father and grandfather. So the three boys saved their money and eventually pooled it to rent a butcher shop in a German neighborhood and quickly began to see that the butchering skills of the old country proved useful. Because they knew the secret recipes of the Old World sausages, brats, wursts, and the art of smoking meats, their business did well. They also enjoyed speaking German with some of the patrons of the shop and talking about their "fatherland".

Auggie, as his older brothers called him, was always relegated to the mundane tasks such as cleaning up and deliveries. If you wanted a nice place, there was always cleaning to do in a butcher shop. Auggie got his cleaning tasks out of the way quickly so he could get to his deliveries. He enjoyed going out and seeing his adopted city and meeting the people.

By 1943 the boys bought their own butcher shop and were getting their business feet wet while America was well in the war. Auggie was 17 and wanted to join the American war effort to get rid of the Nazis that destroyed his family. He tried to enlist but was turned away when they saw his age, but when he began to argue with the men at the enlistment office, and they heard his German accent, they had him come back for questioning. Auggie told them that the Nazis most likely killed his sisters and parents and took away their family butcher shop and how he wanted to get involved with the war on the American side. The enlistment officers knew they could use his knowledge of Germany and the German language. They simply bumped his age up a half a year and signed him up.

Auggie didn't sign up for the Army. He had heard the Americans talk about how tough the Marines were, he wanted to be an American Marine. Auggie's father and grandfather were tough, and they raised the boys to be tough too, so when he was accepted into the Marines, he was thrilled and proud to wear the uniform. His two brothers weren't thrilled though and were dismayed when Auggie told them he'd enlisted in the war.

Auggie went through hell and back in the war. Storming beaches, shooting at Japanese soldiers that were kids his own age, then on to infiltrating German camps and killing young men that might have been his old classmates. Those visions never went away, and in afternoon naps and nighttime dreams, Auggie would relive it all over again. Even so, he was proud that Allies won the war, and he was very proud to be a Marine. After the Pearl Harbor bombing, his middle brother joined the war but was killed in the Pacific. His oldest brother stayed at the butcher shop where Auggie returned after the war.

Auggie had briefly met a pretty German girl on one of his missions in Germany, and they wrote after the war. About a year later, he sent for her to be his wife, and she accepted. They married three days after she arrived in Cleveland. Auggie bought a little house near the butcher shop so she wouldn't have to live around the meat.

The two brothers worked the butcher shop for years. They did very well after the war, and for the next five decades until Auggie's oldest brother died after a short illness. Auggie, his wife Wilhelmine, and their only son, Augustus III, maintained the butcher shop until Auggie finally retired at eighty-three. Auggie always remembered the proud day when his only son was baptized Augustus Heinrich Buchbinder III.

Auggie III, or Henry as he preferred to be called, helped in the shop until he went to college where he studied law and eventually relocated out west. And when Henry married and had a son, their baby was baptized as Augustus Heinrich Buchbinder IV. And now, twenty-six years later, Auggie Four, as they called him, married, and finally had a baby boy too.

And now, Auggie II sat on his porch thinking that his great-grandson was going to be christened at the Lutheran church during the Christmas Midnight Mass, and Auggie wanted to be there to see it. The baby was to be christened Augustus Heinrich Buchbinder V. Auggie was pleased that he lived long enough to know seven generations of Buchbinders that included his own grandfather Augustus Friedrich Buchbinder. Auggie was quite proud of his German roots and just as proud of being a butcher like his father and grandfather.

"Villie!" he shouted as he slowly maneuvered himself out of the rocker. "Villie!!"

"Ja? Vat do you vant? Vhy ist you screaming so?" Wilhelmine said as she left her cup of steaming tea.

"Ve must pack, " Auggie announced.

"Pack?" Wilhelmine questioned. "You haff lost your mind. Ve retired from meat-packing sausages over ten years ago."

"Nah, yah oldt voman! I mean pack zome clothes," Auggie shouted, waving his fist in the air.

"Vhy? Who needs this packing of clothes?" Wilhelmine asked, shuffling out of the kitchen.

"I am going to our great-grandson's christening. I'm going to see zis boy become Augustus Heinrich Buchbinder the Fifth!

You don't pack, den you don't come. Simple," Auggie explained as he hobbled down the hall to find his suitcase.

"You are nuts, you crazy oldt man," Wilhelmine scolded as she followed him. "I pack too. To make sure you don't die on the vay!"

Auggie struggled packing his suitcase. He only had one suit that he purchased decades ago and only wore it for weddings and funerals. He remembered a shirt and tie. Belt. Cufflinks. Yes, the cufflinks. He dug a box out of a top drawer and took a much smaller box out of it. He opened it carefully. His grandfather's cufflinks, his pride and joy. They were the only thing his parents gave him to bring to America when he was a kid. They were gold and his parents told him if he needed money to sell them. He only wore them a few times, for important family events, weddings, funerals, graduations, and of course, baptisms. He carefully put the cufflinks back in the box and packed the box in his suitcase. He knew the cufflinks would not be coming back with him, he would leave them with his grandson to carry on and hand to his great-grandson one day. Auggie wiped his eye, it seemed to be watering.

Although Auggie was nearly ninety, his mind was still very sharp. He always insisted it was because of his handmade liverwurst and fresh meats.

He dug out his Atlas and with his magnifying glass, planned his trip. He jotted down leaving Cleveland on the turnpike to Chicago, then south on Route 66 to St Louis then west on I-70. He thought he could make it to St Louis in one day but considered he'd have to take a nap or two along the way.

The second day, he could make it to Colorado. On the third day, Christmas Eve, he figured to take I-25 south to make it to Santa Fe to the church. He had a few hours left in his schedule for naps and meals.

"I am ready to go, Villie!" he shouted. He always shouted when he was excited. He also shouted when he was angry. He shouted when he was trying to make a point. He shouted at the television news. He shouted all the time. Wilhelmina had learned to ignore it during their nearly seventy years of marriage.

"Ve must call the children!" Wilhelmina shouted back. "Ve must tell them ve are coming."

"NO!" Auggie shouted louder than ever, making Wilhelmina stop in her tracks. "No," he said again softer, realizing he was becoming a little anxious about the trip. "No, ve musn't tell dem. It vill make zem vorry. If ve are late, they vorry more. Ve don't vant to make dem vorry on their baptism day."

Wilhelmina had to think about that. On one hand, Auggie was right. On the other, it made Wilhelmina concerned. Just to be safe, Wilhelmina wrote a note about their travel plan and left it on the kitchen counter. Wilhelmina seemed to understand that they were elderly, while Auggie acted like he was still in the marines, rising every day before daylight, saluting his American flag and doing a few exercises, although the past few years, the exercises were minimal.

Auggie had taken the elevator down to the garage level and struggled to lift the suitcase into the trunk. His trunk was gigantic, the space only one of the 1960's highway landships could have. It was his 1963 powder blue Lincoln Towncar. He bought it new in 1963 and paid cash. He was so proud of owning a car, especially this car. Every week he cleaned it from end to end, polishing everything and detailing even the tiniest specks. He kept up with the service work and updates. Nothing escaped his touch. His '63 Lincoln was still in pristine condition like it had been driven off the showroom floor just hours ago. He loved the big car and the smooth ride. He'd been offered money a few times from people that saw him out running errands, but no, this powder blue baby was his, and now he was excited knowing he was taking it on the trip of a lifetime. He also realized this would most likely be his last trip in it.

Auggie was up and down the elevator like a yo-yo carrying one thing at a time. Wilhelmina wanted to have some tea in a thermos and extra teabags. She packed a few bananas for snacking, then a few sandwiches. She stuffed a few bags with crackers, cookies, and even half a loaf of bread. Auggie started to get peeved at loading his car up with so much but knew it might come in handy.

"Vun more box," Wilhelmine told Auggie as he leaned on the doorway catching his breath.

"Anudder box." Auggie was irked. "Big trunk is full. Notting eltz!"

"Dis box ist important," Wilhelmina warned.

"You say they all important. Enough," Auggie argued.

"Dis box has milky magnesia and prunes, so you can poop," Wilhelmina announced like she was the emcee for a game show. Auggie winced.

"You vorry too much about mine poop!" Auggie shouted.

"Ya. Das ist true," Wilhelmina reasoned, "but I know you shouting on pot when you can't make."

Auggie scowled. Once again, he knew she was right and once more stood at the elevator with his box. Two women got on at the next floor, and both stared at his box and smiled. Auggie looked sheepish about its contents and simply stared at the doors wishing they'd hurry up and open.

Auggie had never taken a cross-country trip anywhere. He was always working, so he'd never driven the vast flat expanse of the Midwest Plains. The little that he'd heard about it, he presumed it would be boring, so he loaded up with some Big Band cassettes, so if they had nothing to talk about or argue about, they could listen to something pleasant. He'd had a cassette player installed under the dash in the seventies but rarely used it, today he was glad he'd finally get some use out of it.

One of his neighbors, Dexter, a good friend and card-playing buddy in the senior complex, came into the garage and saw him loading his trunk.

"You going somewhere now? In December?" his neighbor asked.

Auggie explained that they were going to visit their grandson in Santa Fe for the christening of their great-grandson. His neighbor used to travel quite a lot when he was in sales before retirement and warned Auggie about the monotony of the flatlands. Dexter explained there is barely radio coverage in some places. Auggie tossed him a cassette of Glen Miller hits.

"I listen to dat. Gudt music."

Dexter explained that music wasn't the issue, the issue is communication, and that cell phones are useless in many places if they get in trouble.

"If it is so flat and straight, how can ve haff trouble?" Auggie commented. His neighbor tried to explain that a fifty-some-year-old car, no matter how well he had taken care of it can have problems.

The two argued like good friends do for a few minutes, and finally the neighbor convinced Auggie to at least take a portable CB radio he would loan him. "The antenna is magnetic and sticks to the roof, then bring the wire in the rear door like this, then bring the cord around the back of your seat like so. Then keep the radio on the armrest," his neighbor instructed. He showed Auggie how to work the mike and talk into it, explaining channel 19 to find out about road conditions, directions, weather, car trouble or anything else, and how he should have a "handle". Auggie liked the technology of it but wasn't sure it'd be useful. He politely took the CB, thanked Dexter, and shook hands. When Dexter said goodbye and got on the elevator, Auggie plopped the contraption on the floor of the back seat and went back to packing the trunk.

Wilhelmina got off the elevator in the garage and asked Auggie if he needed anything else and that she had stopped by a neighbor to leave a key. Other than going back up to get coats and lock up, she was ready to go.

They both silently rode the elevator back up to their apartment, then got their coats, both silently wondering if they'd get back home. Auggie took one last look at their apartment with a hundred years of family in photographs on the walls, including one of himself in front of his Lincoln on the day he bought it at the dealership. On the mantle were the awards, trinkets, and accomplishments of a lifetime.

In the center of the mantle was a small old faded photo of his parents sternly standing in front of their butcher shop in Germany. He kissed his fingers and touched them to the photo. "Danke, Mama, Papa," and a little tear began to show that he quickly wiped away. He stuffed his arm in his coat and started to yell for Wilhelmina to get her coat on but saw she was already wearing her coat, holding her purse, and standing by the door with her arms folded, impatiently tapping one toe on the floor.

"Ya, voman. I am ready," he said, waving her off.

They adjusted the lock and shut the door behind them.

They were on their way to Santa Fe.

Chapter 10

The Family Affair

To The Grandparents' House We Go

"Aw Mom, seriously? Do we have to go to Grandma and Grandpa's for Christmas? Can't they come here? There's nothing to do at their farm, and last time we were there, I had no internet or Wi-Fi," Christie pouted.

"I'm sorry, Christie," her mother told her, "I know this isn't fun for you, but your grandfather isn't doing all that well. These are your dad's parents, and he wants to spend one more Christmas with them on the farm. You have to understand that Grandpa might not be around next year."

Christie stomped off, saying under her breath, "I hope they aren't around next year."

"I heard that!" her mother scolded, then heard Christie slam her bedroom door.

"What's up now?" Jeff asked when he came in from the garage.

"Our daughter doesn't want to spend the holiday at the farm."

"Well, she's just going to have to deal with it one more time," Jeff said as he wiped his hands on a paper towel. "I don't think Dad will make it 'til spring, and if he goes, Mom will sell the farm to pay for some kind of senior place."

"I know, Jeff," Carol said. "I told Christie pretty much the same thing. She's at "that age" so you can't reason with her. Oh, and did you get Nick's ski suit out of storage in case he wants to go exploring around the barn and outbuildings again? I hope he can still fit into that stuff."

Carol shouted to the ceiling, "Nicolas, find your boots and try them on!" hoping she wouldn't have to go upstairs to pull Nick off his video games to dig for boots.

Christmastime was always a huge deal for their family. Jeff enjoyed going to his parents' farm for Christmases and remembered so many special Christmases at that wonderful time of year. His parents always made holiday magic for Jeff and his sister when they were kids.

Usually, there was snow, and Jeff's dad would hook up the horse to an old sleigh, and they'd go out and look for a cedar tree to cut for Christmas. They'd cut fresh wood for the fireplace and would add a log or two of the fresh-cut cedar that still had some bark on it. While sitting near the hearth warming their feet, they listened to the fire "sing" when the moisture escaped the bark, crackling as it popped off in the heat of the fire. Sometimes Jeff's dad would tell stories of being a little kid on the farm during the end of the Dustbowl times. His mom might tell a rare story of living during the depression and how they had to ration many things.

Jeff grew up on that old-fashioned farm far from the city and without most modern conveniences. They didn't rely on the TV for nightly entertainment because it was iffy with the old antenna on the roof, trying to pick up broadcasts from distant cities. When TV was out, they read, or Jeff's mom and sister sewed while Jeff's dad whittled or went out to the barn to smoke. Jeff felt that living on the farm and having plenty to eat in light of the stories his parents told of having very little, felt fortunate to have so much.

By the time Jeff was 20, and after spending some time in the Army and seeing some of the bigger world, he wanted off the farm. His father gave Jeff his blessing. Although his dad wanted him to stay, he didn't want Jeff to regret his life, so he wished him well.

Jeff went to live in Kansas City for a while, then up to St. Joe. He worked some jobs, took some classes at the junior college, dated some women, but wasn't happy. The cities seemed so loud and cold. There was never peace and quiet. He walked into a church one Sunday morning for their service to try to get his head cleared up about how he might proceed with his life. As he was leaving, he saw a young lady handing out Advent Calendars at a table. Even though he really didn't want a calendar, he thought he'd use it as an excuse to talk to her.

"Hi," she said quietly. "Have an Advent Calendar for Christmas?"

Jeff was smitten. "I'd love one," he said.

She handed him one, and he leafed through the pages not noticing any of it but wondering what he could say to her next. She interrupted his thoughts.

"You are new here?"

"I'm just sort of passing through," he replied, shifting his weight from one foot to the other.

"You look uncomfortable. Can I help?"

"Nah....well, I don't think so anyway. I just have to do some thinking and this is one of the best places to think," he said, looking up at the vaulted ceilings.

She thought for a minute, then said without looking at him, "If you ever need someone to talk to, I am a good listener."

Jeff was feeling a little self-conscious and shy, so blurted out, "Well, I might like to, um, talk if I know what I want to talk about." He could have shot himself for that stupid comment and started to blush.

Carol liked his nervous behavior, "I'll be done here in a few minutes, maybe we could go for a walk. Walking helps you feel better and helps sort out your thoughts."

"I might like that," he said. "My name is Jeff, and I can wait outside until you finish."

"I'm Carol. I was named Christmas Carol, Carol is my middle name."

At first Jeff was going to laugh at her being Christmas Carol, but the look on her face told him right away that she was serious. "Christmas Carol. That's interesting," he fumbled "and different."

"Yes, I was born on Christmas day, so my mother named me for the holiday."

"Pretty cool," Jeff said, not knowing what else to say. "I'll see you outside when you are done."

And so they met, and they walked. And they walked nearly every day after that talking and laughing. Jeff told her about growing up on a farm in Northwestern Kansas, and she told him about her life on a farm in Missouri, but eventually, her folks' farm was bought out by a commercial corn producer, so they had moved to St. Joe a few years earlier. Jeff and Carol had so much in common that it wasn't long before they were walking and holding hands. They fell in love and were married in St. Joe the following year. Jeff eventually got his degree, and they ended up in a mid-Missouri town where Jeff taught junior high.

When their first child came, she came on Christmas Eve. And so Carol named her Christmas Eve, just like her parents named her Christmas Carol. She hoped the baby would go by

Eve, but as it turned out, everyone called her Christie. The next child was born four years later, the day after Christmas. Carol named him Nicolas Christmas. Aside from some teasing at school, he got along fine with his name. When the third child came, Carol thought for sure it would be born on Christmas Eve, but it was a false alarm. The baby came three days after Christmas, so her mom named her Christmas Holly because of the season, and she went by Holly.

Today, they were loading up the minivan, made by Generic Motors, to head out to Jeff's folks' family farm to spend Christmas with them. His sister, Emily, and her husband and two kids would be coming in as well, so it would be a good time to catch up, and the kids could get to know their cousins better. The women would do a lot of cooking of some of the old family recipes and stock up the folks' freezer with some easy thaw and heat meals. The guys would get some of the farm chores done that were backing up and fix a few things for the folks. They would not be sitting around all week staring at the walls.

The kids used to look forward to the trip before Grandpa's stroke left him ailing. He used to take the kids on sleigh rides or wagon rides. They'd climb up in the hayloft and play on the bales. They had hay fights and made bale forts, and Grandpa would pretend to be the hay monster as he climbed up into the loft wearing a burlap feed-bag over his head to find their hiding places sending the kids into screaming laughter.

And then there was grandma's old farm kitchen and something was always in the oven and it smelled terrific to walk into the kitchen swimming with the scent of cinnamon rolls, apple pie, baked ham, and other goodies. And Grandma always made a big deal out of each of the birthdays during the holiday break. But as Grandpa's health declined, so did the fun. The kids had to be a little quieter and had to entertain themselves much of the time. And Grandma spent a lot of time caring for Grandpa, so her cooking was minimal. Even so, Jeff was determined to make this a good Christmas for his family, because it would probably be the last Christmas the whole family was together.

The minivan was packed up with their suitcases, loaded with wrapped gifts, some groceries for the holidays, and plenty of games for the kids. The house was locked up, kids belted in with Holly in a junior car seat between the other two. Jeff looked at the kids in back and asked if they were ready to roll, Holly and Nick shouted "Yes!" but Christie looked out the window, still pouting and mumbled, "I get to spend my birthday out in the middle of nowhere."

"That's enough, Christie!" Carol reprimanded.

And they were off, heading out of the subdivision on their way to Kansas.

Chapter 11

Chuck It All

Chuck climbed up into the cab of the eighteen-wheeler to check his paperwork while the diesel engine warmed when the traffic manager walked up to his cab and handed him a few more papers.

"I sure hate to see you working the holiday the past few years, Chuck," the traffic manager commented.

"It's ok," Chuck commented, "it keeps my mind off my wife's passing."

"I guess so," the traffic manager said as he reviewed the paperwork, "she left us too soon."

"Yep," Chuck continued as he jumped down to the pavement. "You know, even though it's been a couple of years, the holidays always remind me of how she loved Christmas. Being home now is just plain lonely, especially when I think about how she baked cookies and decorated everything for such a glorious holiday. She was like a kid even though she was getting some gray hair. I can't make myself drag out the tree and ornaments yet. At least if I drive now, one of the other drivers can be home with his family, and I can keep myself busy with traffic and the holiday drivers."

"I understand," the traffic manager sympathized as he signed off on the papers.

"I still think about her quite often on the long drives when there's not much traffic. Sometimes I swear she sits shotgun with me." Chuck saw his traffic manager raise his eyebrows in surprise. Chuck winked at him when he saw the question in the traffic manager's eyes, but the traffic manager didn't venture further.

"You never know what you have 'til you lose it," Chuck said.

"Yep, yep, that's the truth," the manager agreed as he handed the clipboard back to Chuck.

The two men walked around the back of the rig and made sure the doors to the trailer were closed and locked down. Chuck was very particular about his rig, so he walked around it and checked everything as though he was a pilot doing a pre-flight check on his aircraft.

The traffic manager admired Chuck, he was a professional long-hauler through and through and one of the most conscientious drivers at the freight company for over thirty years. Everyone looked up to his professional attitude and his fatherly advice to the young men that came in to begin careers in trucking. Sometimes the freight company would saddle Chuck with a newbie driver when they sensed one with an attitude. After riding with Chuck for a few weeks, the newbie learned to have a better attitude. If Chuck couldn't groom the new driver to a better mindset about long-distance hauling, generally, they didn't last with the company.

"Hope to have this load delivered and unloaded so I can be back for New Year's," Chuck said. "I hate driving on New Year's Day when so many hangovers are out there on the road, and those four-wheelers texting on their phones drives me crazy."

"Oh, don't I know it," the traffic manager commiserated. "We've had so many near misses of some four-wheeler idiot texting and weaving off the road then over-compensating to get back on the road sending them fish-tailing. They don't seem to understand that a loaded semi can't stop in twenty feet. That's how old Dan ended up retiring. Lost his load when a four-wheeler cut him off, and he tried to avoid wiping them off the map and his rig jack-knifed. That load took him down over a guard rail. He said it was enough. He didn't want to kill anyone and have to live with that in the back of his mind."

"I know," Chuck said, "I've had texters and talkers doing all kind of stuff nearly losing control of their wheels. They think no one knows they are talking or texting, but up in our cabs, we can see the phone on their leg or on the seat all lit up. When I see a phone lit up like that, I back way off and alert other truckers. Hope I can make it to retiring without a bad one." Chuck gave the traffic manager a knowing look.

The two men shared a good handshake, and Chuck climbed back into his cab and shoved the extra paperwork into his clipboard. "Have a Merry Christmas," Chuck said as he shut the door. He revved his diesel up a few times, shifted gears, and he pulled slowly away from the dock.

"Breaker," Chuck said into his CB mike. "Breaker-one-niner, this is the Cockroach with my eighteen wheels loaded, headed to Mile-High on the eye-seventy, then on to Sack-of-tomatoes." It was CB lingo saying Chuck's nickname was Cockroach and was driving a fully loaded eighteen-wheeler to Denver on I-70, then on to Sacramento.

"Hello Cockroach," came a crackling response on his radio. "Welcome to the leftbound side. Bring it on up. This is Santa Claus in the CornFlake." More CB lingo indicating the responder's nickname is Santa Claus and is driving for Consolation Freightlines headed westbound and wants Chuck to drive up near his truck.

"Hey Cockroach," another voice crackled through, "if you are a roach, would your rig be 'bugged'? I hope you aren't driving for the FB and I." Chuck laughed and responded that it wasn't the first time he'd heard that old "bug" gag. And more jokes entered the airways about bugs, and all the truckers in earshot were having a good time being silly.

Chuck liked hooking up with a couple of other truck drivers on CB's. They would chat about sports, families, trucks, and anything else that popped up that helped make the time go by faster and helped keep him awake. He enjoyed pulling into a truck stop with other truckers and have dinner with them and shoot the shit for a while. And if there was trouble, the other truckers would always stop to help. He'd met a lot of truck drivers in his thirty-plus years hauling, so he never felt really alone on the road.

Chuck picked the CB handle of Cockroach hoping it would sound creepy enough to keep the hookers that patrol truck stops from wanting to solicit business from him. There were plenty of one-nighters he could have had, but Chuck was all about getting the job done, knowing there were plenty of other drivers and travelers that the women could hit on. Even though his wife had passed on three years ago, Chuck loved his wife so much that since the day he met her over thirty years ago, he was simply never interested in sleeping with other women. Chuck used his rest time for just exactly that. Rest.

The I-70 route across Kansas was one Chuck hated as it was so boring, flat, and nearly desolate once he passed Salina, so the CB chatter was very welcome entertainment, and it wasn't long before Chuck had hooked up with Ten-Point, Santa Claus, and Olive Pit. As they pulled onto the entrance ramp of the toll booths, their air-brakes spewing now and then, they nodded to each other, tossing a two-finger wave as they made their toll road checkpoints. Then they were through the tolls and off chattering into the night westbound on I-70.

Chapter 12

Eddie and Travis Going For A Run

Running Dually

Travis came out of the building walking at a good clip. He opened the passenger door of his brother's truck that was parked at the curb and quickly jumped in and told his brother, "GO. Let's get out of here. Now! Step on it."

Eddie looked at his brother with concern but did as he was commanded. He knew he couldn't argue with Travis when he had his mind set on something.

"Make a left here!" Travis shouted at his brother.

Eddie took the corner almost too fast and after the truck straightened out, Eddie finally spoke, "What did you do, Travis?"

"Just shut up and drive," Travis commanded as he drummed his fingers on his leg. "Take us out to the interstate and head west."

Eddie once again did as his brother said, putting his foot into it and careening onto the westbound ramp and entering rush hour traffic where he was forced to slow down and jockey among the rest of the vehicles.

After a few minutes of languishing in traffic and noticing Travis was way past being a little edgy, Eddie spoke up again. "Was there a problem? Did Grandma lend you the money?"

"Yeah. I got some money," Travis said while watching the traffic behind him in the side view mirror.

"How much, Travis? You already owe her a fortune from all your borrowing, so I know she wouldn't lend you what you ask for," Eddie said.

"Shut up," Travis snapped.

"What's up, Travis? Did Grandma lecture you again?" Eddie was getting more concerned.

"Nothing is up," Travis said as he folded his arms and slunk down in the seat.

"That's just bullshit, Travis," Eddie said. "You came out of Grandma's building very fast, and Grandma wasn't standing in the doorway on your way out, lecturing you about getting a job or going to school like she usually does."

"Yeah, well, she was busy," Travis snapped back.

"Grandma has never been too busy for us. She's always trying to help us out. What did you do?" Eddie demanded as pushy as he could make himself sound.

After more of Eddie's interrogation, Travis was getting irritated and finally spilled it out, "I went up to Grandma's apartment, okay? The door was open. I went in, but she wasn't there. I looked around for her, but she must have gone to dinner early or something. I noticed she had cashed her social security check, and the bank envelope was on her desk. So I took some money and left her a note."

"You WHAT? You took her money? You left her a note?" Eddie shouted. "You were helping yourself to her money and you left a note??"

"No Pigskin," Travis said as he touched an envelope he had jammed in his jacket pocket to make sure it was still there. "I told you that I went in and she was gone, and that I 'borrowed' some money and that I'd pay it back."

"Don't call me Pigskin. Did you put your name on the note?"

"Yeah, I think I did."

"So why were you bookin' when you came out of the building then?" Eddie shouted louder than he thought it was going to be.

Travis rolled his eyes, "I saw her getting off the elevator, and it was too late to put the money back, and I didn't want another lecture about getting a job."

"Oh sure, like she won't tell Dad," Eddie was nearly screaming now, "and then we'll have hell to pay!"

"I don't know what all the fuss is about Pigskin," Travis argued back. "We're just taking a little of our inheritance early." Travis took the fat bank envelope out of his jacket and slapped Eddie's arm with it. "She doesn't need it, and she won't say anything to dad. She won't want to get us in trouble."

"Whoa buddy," Eddie yelled when he saw the bank envelope, "that's the withdrawal envelope! Did you take it ALL? What are you thinking! You are such a total asswipe!" Eddie scolded.

Travis said nothing.

Eddie thought for a minute and continued, "Man, that's the difference between you and me. How could you do this to our own grandmother? And I don't view her social security checks as 'our inheritance.' And yep, she'll be calling Dad as soon as she sees your note and her money missing."

"She's never going to die, Pigskin," Travis said while attempting to count the cash. "She's as healthy as a horse. If I don't get some of it now, she'll burn through it all, and there won't be any left to inherit. She won't call Dad."

"Oh my God, Travis. You have totally lost your mind." Eddie was infuriated. "And yeah, she will call Dad if she thinks someone stole from her. She knows Dad is a cop and she's been itching to sue the senior complex for something, so this might be it, and it will lead right back to US. You never were this way, Travis. Why are you turning into such a jerk? Grandma needs that money, it's her monthly social security. She has to pay her rent out of that, her food, her medicines."

"She's got more," Travis snapped. "She'll just go to the bank and cash a check. She probably will think she left it somewhere anyway, or think some of the aides took it."

"How could she possibly think someone else took it, you idiot, if you left a note." Eddie thought about that for a nano-second when it struck him. "Oh wait, you didn't leave a note, did you?" Eddie glared at Travis. "You just took her money."

"Look, Pigskin, I think there's about eight or nine-hundred dollars here, I'll give you a hundred if you shut the hell up about it. It's a loan, I tell you. I'll pay her back." Travis acted like that made it okay.

"You haven't paid me back the ten bucks you borrowed from my piggy bank in junior high. You won't pay grandma back. You already owe her probably thousands from all your borrowing. You don't have a job, how can you pay her back without a job?"

Well, if you need to know, that's why I needed this money. I needed some traveling money. I need to get to Colorado and get back to St. Louis before New Year's. I'll be able to pay Grandma back then. I do have a job, and I'm doing it now."

"What?" Eddie was confused. "What job? You basically robbed our grandma, and now you have us heading out of the city. I have to get to work by seven tonight. I can't be out screwing around with you and your messed up life. You need to put that money back."

Travis reached over and grabbed the back of Eddie's neck with one hand squeezing it tightly and spoke in sharp staccato. "I. Told. You. Ed. I. Needed. Money." Travis saw Eddie's eyes start to glaze over at Travis' increasing grip on his neck. Travis let go and continued his excuses. "Grandma won't know I took it." Travis sat back in the seat and finally relaxed a little. "I'm giving you $100 to shut up and drive. You need to drive me to Colorado. I'll pay for your gas. I am doing a job for a guy, he'll pay me well when we get back."

"Travis!" Eddie shouted, "I have to be at work in a couple of hours. I don't want to lose my job. It's a good job that pays me, and I like working there. "

"Call in sick," Travis said flatly.

"I can't. I volunteered for the holidays. It's double-time. I'm up for a raise, too. I'm not going to leave them short-handed."

"Pigskin, you call in sick, or I'll make you so sick your next call will be for an ambulance," Travis threatened.

Eddie knew from the sound of his brother's voice that Travis was getting pissed. Travis was a lot bigger and older than Eddie, and Eddie knew Travis could pound him into pulp. Eddie was sure something was eating at Travis but wasn't sure what, but today Eddie wasn't going to simply be a doormat with his job on the line.

"Travis," Eddie demanded, "you need to explain what's going on right now, or I'll pull over and pitch the keys, and neither of us will be going anywhere."

Travis thought for a few minutes.

He finally sighed, drooped his shoulders, and began tiptoeing through an explanation. "Eddie....I'm in a real jam right now. I was having a few beers across the river at the Dumphole..."

"Oh shit," Eddie interrupted, "you went to that filthy sleaze-bar on the East side? What is wrong with you? You know that's a shithole filled with trouble, hookers, and ex-cons."

"Yeah, yeah," Travis pulled his ball cap down farther on his head and clutched the money. "What's done is done. I went there to meet a gal I met online. She never showed. Just a bunch of lowlifes there. They ganged up on me. After a few beers, I got mouthy. They took my money and wanted more. I told them I don't have any money. They threatened to beat the hell out of me if I didn't bring them money and a bag of pot. You know I don't do drugs, Pigskin, never have, but to get them off my back, I told them I'd get them some. Pot is legal in Colorado now. I figure I can buy a lot with Grandma's money, give it to them, and then I'm off the hook."

"Are you getting stupid or something?" Eddie was nearly screaming. "Do you think they are going to let you off the hook if you bring them a bag of pot? They'll never let you off. You'll be running pot for them until you retire. You are a patsy. P-A-T-S-Y!" Eddie spelled it out. "And if you haven't thought about it, bringing drugs out of Colorado through Kansas is called trafficking. It's illegal! We'll get busted bringing pot into Kansas, we'll go to freakin' jail! Those KHP's just WAIT for punk-asses like us to come out of Colorado and yank us right off the road!"

"I thought about that," Travis said. "I figure if we get there and back over the Christmas holiday, we'll simply look like holiday travelers and wrap the pot in Christmas paper. Like a present. They won't catch on."

"No way. You didn't think it through at all, again." Eddie was frustrated and getting frantic trying to get Travis to understand the gravity of the situation. "Do you think they have little pot stands across the border like farmer fruit stands or fireworks stands in July, with a complimentary gift wrap? No, we're going to have to go into a shop....a shop with security systems, and all of our identification clearly says we are not Colorado residents.

And add to that, back at Grandma's senior complex, it has video security. It won't take them long to piece together that you were there and didn't visit grandma and that you left with me in my truck, and Grandma's money is missing. And now you want to drive to Colorado to buy pot like there won't be a bulletin put out on us when they figure out you robbed Grandma. We have Missouri tags, and there will be a warrant out on us. We're dead men!"

Travis became very quiet and looked out at the road. He knew Eddie was probably right because he knew Eddie was smarter than he was. He hated Eddie for that. Eddie was a small guy, yet quiet and polite. Travis was much bigger and excelled in sports throughout high school. He tried to get Eddie interested in sports, but Eddie just wasn't natural. During a game of tag football, Eddie caught one of Travis' football bullets right in the face and it broke his nose. Travis jokingly called him "pigskin" after that because the football left an indentation of the football texture in Eddie's skin for weeks. Eddie hated it when Travis called him Pigskin, which made Travis use it that much more.

Although Travis excelled at sports, he was terrible in class and made up for that by being mouthy and arrogant. But now, Travis was looking to his little brother for an alibi.

He spoke softer now, realizing Eddie was probably right. "I didn't know what else to do in the bar, Eddie. They might have killed me. They had a freakin' knife to my throat and threatened my family if I called the cops, so I couldn't say anything to Dad. They held me while they went through my pockets and got my ID and know where we live. They are keeping my wallet with my driver's license until I get back with their pot." Travis hung his head and looked at the money in his now sweating hands. "If anything happens to Mom, it'll be my fault."

Eddie was speechless. He stared at the westbound traffic ahead, his brain blazing with too many bad scenarios to count.

Chapter 13

Eyeing Up I-70

The I-70 west of Kansas City is known as a very long, boring drive to Colorado. It can also be dangerous depending on the time of year a traveler has to drive that route. In Spring and Summer, violent winds and torrential rains can come barreling off the plains with nothing to slow them down, where wind gusts can easily reach fifty miles an hour or more. Those sudden broadside winds can rock a high-profile box truck or push around an eighteen-wheeler if it doesn't have enough weight to act as ballast. Summer heat and sun can play tricks on your eyes, and you might think you see a pond of water on the road ahead, but it's not really there. And if your car dies in the heat, there is a long wait for help. And of course, there is always the dread of tornados.

The fall season in open range country might have deer and elk crossing the highways during their rutting season. Many other critters are crossing the highway hunting food to fatten up for winter or looking for warm dens, each one a potential four-legged speed bump.

Every season can be problematic, but the worst time on I-70 is winter. Many times the interstate is closed by the highway patrol as it is simply not passable when the cold wind and heavy snows combine causing white-out conditions. In sub-freezing temperatures, there can be deadly patches of black ice that are impossible for drivers to see until a quick steering move sends them spiraling down the interstate. And there are snow squalls that blow in fast with no warning.

In some areas, there is no cell service, no GPS, nor satellite coverage, which catches many tech folks off guard. CB, or citizen's band radio, can only send and receive about a mile, so sometimes, travelers are surprised to find they are without any communication and caught in the unforgiving dangers of western Kansas' winter weather.

Unaware travelers should note that in winter's heavy snows and gusty winds when the road is already covered, drifts form in the medians and ditches, flattening out the landscape, making it nearly impossible to detect the paved roadways from the surrounding terrain. Even experienced drivers must be aware not to mistake flat, snow-covered surfaces for the roadway to avoid driving off the pavement.

With the many driving hazards that can happen in the heavy Midwestern snows, the most unpredictable of winter's harrowing arsenal of weapons against road warriors is the sinister Mega-Drift. Regular drifts are hazardous enough, but take heed, mega-drifts form when wind and snow creates an angry roiling curtain of white, obscuring all evidence of what it is building and shaping at its core. As a blizzard unloads its mountains of snow across the roadway, the massive Mega Drift strengthens, becoming the sole annihilator of all moving traffic.

These mountainous growing drifts of dense, impenetrable snow can form across all the lanes of the interstate and are nearly impossible to see during a daytime blizzard and become completely invisible when they loom in the night. They have been known to cloak entire overpasses in white oblivion, making them immediate, deadly vehicle blockades. In blizzard conditions when vision is obliterated by blinding snow, the mega drift is shrouded, lurking across the interstate like a treacherous, traffic-devouring snow mountain lying in wait to feed on the vehicles of unsuspecting travelers.

Among the locals and frequent travelers of the area, there is a foreboding fear of the mega-drifts. With no natural landscape obstructions across the vast planes to slow the blasting blizzards, the area has been called Blizzard Alley, where the mega drifts are sculpted by the Siberian Express weather patterns. The drifts form fast and unannounced. The only way to avoid the hazard is paying attention to the weather conditions, getting off the road, and finding a safe place to wait it out until the conga lines of plows can make their way across the counties, clearing the roads for safe passage.

Chapter 14

Where Are the Westbounders

"Breaker," Chuck chattered into his CB mike as he left Salina behind and settled a hot mug of coffee into a cup rack. He noticed that there was very little traffic on the eastbound lanes. Chuck had learned to read the road traffic just like an old fishing captain could read the ocean currents. Something was off with the traffic.

"Breaker one-nine, this is Cockroach leaving Salina looking for an East-bounder. Anybody got their ears on?" There was no response. Chuck repeated his message. "Breaker one-nine, this is the Cockroach looking for an Eastbound traffic report. East-bounder with yer ears on, go ahead."

Again, there wasn't a response. Chuck listened hard for any sign of communication, and finally he heard, "Hey Cockroach, this is Ten-Point westbound ahead of you. Not much traffic going east."

Chuck responded. "Yeah, ten-four, buddy, you got any info on that?"

Ten-Point responded in CB lingo, "Negatory, Mr. Roach, no news."

"Roger that," Chuck responded.

Chuck was concerned with the missing traffic, so he punched up his speed a bit to catch up with Ten-Point as the signal was growing weak. Chuck felt himself becoming a bit more aware of his surroundings. It was cold and a little windy, but nothing to worry about. Yet.

A few more miles and Chuck sent his request out over the air once more, and again he got no response. Only a car or two headed east in the opposite lanes that obviously didn't have radios. Chuck knew there should be more traffic this close to Christmas. This was strange.

Chapter 15

Jinga-bell-hey!

"Jingle bells, jingle bells, jingle all the way..," Jeff and Carol were singing, trying to get the kids involved as they drove the long, boring flatness of I-70. Christie had her face plugged into her phone, but when Nick tried to sing along, Christie would jab him in his thigh. Holly just kept saying "bells, bells, bells" and added an occasional "HEY!" while her parents sang.

"Can't you get anything on the radio?" Carol asked Jeff between songs in near desperation. After driving all day listening to children's CD's, Carol would have enjoyed listening to some adult talk radio for awhile.

"Nope. We're just getting too far away from radio signals. It's always been this way," Jeff said.

"DAMMIT!" Christie suddenly shouted from the backseat, startling the heck out of both parents to which both parents reprimanded her immediately.

"Christie! You do not use that language. Totally unacceptable. If I hear that again, you'll be turning in your phone," Carol scolded.

"Well, FINE, Moth-ER," came Christie's snide comment. "You can have my freaking phone. I can't get a signal at all now for a half hour. Bad enough I have to hear your off-key singing, now I can't even text Megan." And she threw her phone onto the front seat next to her mother. Christie scowled and sat back in her seat with her arms folded, staring out the window at endless fields in the fading daylight. Carol and Jeff looked at each other with that discouraged look that only frustrated parents can give each other.

Jeff tried to get Christie's mind off it. "I tell you what, let's play a game!"

"Oh Dad, for crying out loud, you can't fix everything with a freaking game!" Christie criticized.

"Okay, young lady," Carol interrupted, "that'll be enough. Just sit back and be quiet for a while. It's unfortunate that you don't like the circumstances, but you are just going to have to learn to deal with it and set a good example for your brother and sister."

Christie hated being told to set a good example for her siblings but knew she had to prove she was responsible if she expected to get her driver's license and permission to date in the next couple of years. So in her finest sarcasm, she turned to Nick, "Nick, sit up straight like a good boy," then stuck her tongue out at the back of her mother's head.

"I saw that," Carol said.

Nick was amazed. "How did you see that, Mom?"

"I was a kid once too. I don't have to see anything to just know it's there," she said.

Nick's eyes were wide with wonder that his mother had the secret parent knowledge. Christie was still scowling. Little Holly didn't care about all the squabbling and simply ended everyone's sentences shouting, "Jinga-bell, Hey!"

Chapter 16

CB Chatter

Another ten miles sped by when Chuck noticed some flurries blowing across his windshield and noticed a pretty stiff breeze had picked up. He chattered into his CB mike again. "Breaker breaker, eastbound, anyone got your ears on?" to which he got an immediate response from Ten-Point.

"Hey Roach, I see you coming up my back door. I'm back-peddling a bit. I'm empty and the wind is jiggling my rig. You'll be passing me up in a short."

"That's a ten-four," Chuck said into his mike. "I'm still looking for that traffic report from the eastbound side."

"I ain't heard anything since Salina," Ten-Point said.

"Me either. I'll keep trying. I'll radio back if I get anything, Ten-Point," Chuck radioed as he began to pass Ten-Point's rig.

"Yeppers. That's a ten-four," Ten-Point said as he flicked his rig lights to Chuck's passing truck. "I am probably going to park it at the next rest area and wait for the wind to die down, getting tired of fighting it."

"Okay, good buddy," Chuck answered. "Ten-four on the rest area. I'm heavy, the wind isn't playing tag with me yet so going to go through to Denver tonight."

"That's a roger," Ten Point radioed back. "Santa Claus will be coming up in a short and maybe he will pull off and we can get some coffee and shoot the shit until the wind gives out."

"Roger that. See ya on the flipper Ten Point!" And Chuck was out. He settled back in his seat, sipped his coffee and pushed on.

After a few more miles Chuck adjusted the squelch knob on his CB radio and listened hard for any distant chatter. Nothing but static. He radioed his message again and let the key up to listen. Finally, very faintly and breaking up, he could hear something. "Come back," Chuck called into his mike, "come back, you are fading and breaking up."

Another mile rolled by, and once again, Chuck heard the distant message a teensy bit better.

"This is KQZ-7797 base. Just south of McPherson stretchin' our ears out. I got your message, Cockroach," the voice on the CB said. "Haven't heard much of anything out of the left side of Kansas either, maybe its sunspots."

"Howdy KQZ-7797 base," Chuck radioed back. He was glad to hear a base CB station as they aren't mobile and have strong signals. "Ten-four on the sunspots. Appreciate the info. You got a handle?" Chuck asked.

"BaseBob. We be callin' ourself BaseBob," the voice on his radio said.

"Ten-four, BaseBob. Maybe I can catch you on the flipper. This is Cockroach, headed to Mile-High, then the left coast."

"Affirmative, Cockroach. We be having HAM capability, good buddy. Will fire that up shortly. Heard there was a snow squall coming in from the Dakotas and down through Nebraska, but didn't get anything from NOAA. So keeping our ears on. Will call out with information during the storm. Have a safe trip to Mile High."

"Roger that. Thank you, BaseBob. I'll have my ears on, wall-to-wall," Chuck said, "This is The Cockroach, I'm out."

"This is BaseBob at base KQZ-7797, out."

Chapter 17

Girl Talk

"Oh my God, Brittany, we've been driving for hours! Can we please stop someplace?" Tawnie whined. "I think I'm going to go insane if I can't get a Pepsi and stretch my legs soon."

Brittany frowned and turned down the CD. "Tawnie, I'm trying to save time. We have another seven hours to go. Every time we stop, we lose time. When we stopped in Kansas City I saw this truck go by, and now I'm passing it again.

"Um....correction Brittany," Delphia commented, looking at her laptop. "It's not another seven hours, it's nearly another nine hours, plus time for stops."

"Shit," Brittany said under her breath then pointed to Delphia's laptop, "how did it take us nearly seven hours to make a five-hour drive?"

"Well," Delphia began her explanation looking at her accumulated data, "you made a wrong turn out of St Louis that cost us going nearly fifteen minutes out of our way. Then we stopped in Columbia at Walmart for munchies and you wanted to buy a Mizzou sweatshirt. That cost us at least another half hour. We topped off the gas and got drinks in Kansas City, and a number of times you've let up on your speed and were driving sixty-two to sixty-five miles an hour while you were texting. And we hit rush hour traffic heading out of the city that slowed us and ate another half hour. So there you are."

"Damn," Brittany said. "I didn't think we'd run this far behind. At this rate, we won't get to Bryce's resort until way after breakfast."

"This is starting to sound like a very bad idea. Maybe we just ought to turn around and go back home. You can see Bryce when he gets back from their vacation. It's not like he's joining the army," Delphia recommended.

"No way, Delph. I've come this far, and just another nine hours and we'll be in good shape." Brittany put her foot into it and sped up a little. "If I drive a little faster, I can shave some time off."

"Yeah, and maybe we'll get pulled over and get a ticket," Delphia cautioned. "Driving over the speed limit like this will only buy you about thirty minutes."

"Oh girl," Brittany complained to Delphia, "you gotta run your numbers again, it has to be more of a time saving than that."

"No, it ain't," Tawnie commented from the back seat looking at a graph on her phone. "Delphia is right, maybe thirty minutes."

At that, Brittany put her foot into it and ramped her speed up. "Well then, if I buzz along at eighty, I'll be able to buy myself an hour."

"An hour," Delphia said flatly, "what are you going to do with an extra hour at three in the morning?"

"Shut up, Delph. Just leave it alone," Brittany snipped. I'm going to get there. If you want out, I'll let you out at the next town and you can get a bus back home."

Delphia was about to comment on Brittany's rudeness when they heard a cell phone ringing. It was Tawnie's. Tawnie looked at the screen. "Oh no!" Tawnie freaked. "It's my mother! She never calls me! Oh my God." Tawnie just looked at the phone screen.

"Answer it, you moron!" Brittany shouted. "If you don't answer it, she'll call my parents, then Delphia's mom, and we'll all be dead."

Tawnie swiped her phone and answered, "Hi Mom, what's up?" Brittany and Delphia couldn't hear Tawnie's mother talking, but got the gist of their conversation through Tawnie's responses.

"Yes, we're together. We are, um, headed out to get some pizza, then going to look at boots at the Fillay of Sole store, then probably go to the late movie." "Yes, we decided to ride together in Brittany's car." "Yes ma'am, we will be back at Delphia's by midnight." "Ok, see you tomorrow afternoon." Tawnie ended the call. All three of the girls looked at each other, Delphia and Brittany holding their breath.

"Jeez, Tawnie, what was that about?" Brittany asked. "Didn't you tell her you were spending the night at my house?"

"I told her we'd be spending the night at Delphia's. Mom thinks you are a bit wild, so I told her I'd be at Delphia's house instead. She said she saw my car at the mall parking lot. She expected my car to be at Delphia's not at the mall and wanted to know if there was a problem or a change of plan. I think I got it settled with her now."

Brittany looked at Delphia in near disbelief at the possible screwing up of her plan.

Tawnie asked once more if they could please make a stop as she needed a bathroom break. Brittany sighed, "Yes, Tawnie, we'll stop at the next rest area. But you gotta make it quick. And no more Pepsi for you. You pee too much!"

Delphia looked at Brittany in disbelief. "Seriously Brits, you can't be serious. If you plan on driving all night, then we're going to need some caffeine, either cola or coffee, and we will eventually have to stop to pee."

"I know, I know," Brittany sounded beaten, "We'll stop. You are right. If we get there at three in the morning, there's not much we can do, so we might as well make the drive decent. Maybe there's a truck stop ahead and we can get some coffee or hot chocolate." Delphia sat back smiling, as she felt she won that small battle. She looked back and winked at Tawnie, but Tawnie was furiously swiping her phone screen.

"What's up, Tawnie?" Delphia asked.

"I can't make my phone work now. I just talked to Mom five minutes ago, but now I can't get it to do anything," Tawnie commented.

Delphia looked at her laptop. She had no signal either. "Hey girls, we must be in a low area. I don't have internet. No Wi-Fi. Nothing."

"What low spot?" Brittany asked. "It's been flatter than a pancake for over an hour."

After some furious pecking on the keyboard, Delphia sounded concerned, "I can't even hook up to GPS."

"What does this mean?" Brittany asked.

"It means we are in the car....with no communication at all." Delphia frowned.

Delphia calmed herself, then thought logically and said, "I should have guessed that out where there is a small scattered population that cell companies wouldn't have towers and satellites aimed at the area like they do near cities." Delphia did more keyboarding with no response. "And I don't think we'll have any until we get nearer to Denver. I hope we have a map."

"We're on our own?" Brittany asked, quite seriously.

"Yes," Delphia replied and closed her laptop.

All three stared out the front window at the interstate and watched the dotted lines pass as they sailed around a blue 1963 Lincoln.

Chapter 18

The Wurst Radio

"Papa, are you getting tired of driving yet?" Wilhelmine asked, acting concerned and speaking sweetly as she watched a small car with three young girls pass them up to which her husband nearly shouted.

"Augustus Heinrich Buchbinder the Second does NOT tire of driving!" making Wilhelmine jump.

"Ja, okay, you stupid oldt man!" Wilhelmina snapped back. "I vas just trying to talk a little. This radio only plays noise they call music. No vonder kids today are angry, the music is angry, they drive angry." As she pointed to the girls disappearing ahead of them.

"I turn radio off then. There is no gudt radio this far from city," Auggie remarked.

"So how long before I go crazy listening only to car noise? Wind has been making vhistles around vindow for over an hour now," Wilhelmine complained.

"Vind vill qvit. You complain too much," Auggie said, to which Wilhelmine made a very mad face and tried the radio again. "Dammit Mina, I tell you, der is just notting but da crackling on radio. "

"Ya, radio ist broken in dis car," Wilhelmina muttered under her breath.

"I am oldt, not deaf Mina. Radio is not broke. We are too far from city antennas. Dexter from our building toldt me there wouldt be no radio out away from der city ven I vas packing the trunk. He gave me special radio. I threw it on the floor back dere." And Auggie pointed to the floor in the backseat with his thumb. "Maybe ve should try it."

Wilhelmine leaned over the armrest and saw the metal box with wires hanging out, a short antenna with another wire and a mike hanging off a coiled wire. "Dat?" She said. "Dat is radio? Dat look like junk pile from garage."

"Voman!" Auggie shouted, "You know notting! Dis is special radio. Radio like from the wartime. I get off at next rest area and show you vat it says." And Auggie put his foot into it, speeding up to nearly sixty miles per hour, eventually pulling into a rest area. "You go tinkle in the pot. I will plug radio in." Auggie said, suddenly interested in the metal box with so many wires.

Auggie remembered what Dexter told him and put the magnetic antenna base on the top of his car, cringing at possibly scuffing his wax job. He put it on and took it off three or four times, checking the finish with his flashlight. It seemed ok. He ran the wire into the back seat through a rear door and shut the door on the wire, then plugged the wire into the jack at the back of the radio, plugged in the radio's power jack into the cigarette lighter socket, and turned it on. He remembered Dexter telling him to turn it to channel 19 or was it 17? He dialed in 19 and adjusted the squelch....he didn't hear any music or talking. He picked up the mike and pushed the button thinking perhaps that activated the music. By this time, Wilhelmine had returned from the pit toilet.

"Ooof...toilet stinks," Wilhelmine commented, wiping her nose with a hankie. "Reminds me of oldt country, making in da barn."

"Did you go?" Auggie asked.

"Ya, I vent. But it stinks. You gonna pee?" Wilhelmine asked.

"Ja, I already pee," Auggie said.

"You peed? When did you pee? You been monkeying with junk pile," Wilhelmina argued.

"I pee in bushes while you go to toilet. Toilet stinks," Auggie said while he was trying to get the radio to work. Wilhelmine rolled her eyes and got herself situated in her seat looking at the metal box that now occupied her armrest space.

"Is dat box going to sit dere? Vhile ve drive??" Wilhelmine started sounding upset.

"Ya, box has wire to this mike, and box has to be close to us."

"I am not riding with box stuck in my side!" Wilhelmine demanded. "I have purse on seat for my Tums undt crackers."

"Shaddap. You don't need purse. No shopping here, nutting to buy," Auggie snapped back and grabbed her purse and dropped it on the floor of the back seat. "You will ride with box or you valk!"

Wilhelmine shot a comment in German and Auggie fired one back, and by then they were arguing back and forth quite loudly in German. Auggie was getting fed up with Wilhelmine and about to shake his fist when he fumbled the mike and it dropped to the floor which let up on the key, then they both heard someone talking.

"Hey, I don't know what language you are talking, but you are hogging up the air with your squabbles," the radio said.

Auggie and Wilhelmine looked at the box. It was talking.

"Mina, listen," Auggie whispered loudly, "box is saying something about hogging."

Suddenly Auggie got the gist of it, like radioing during the war. Mike key down to talk, up to listen. Auggie grabbed for the mike and held the key down.

"I am Augustus Heinrich Buchbinder the Second going to my great-grandson's baptism in New Mexico. I hear your voice, I know hogging. I am retired butcher!" And he let up the key. Auggie and Wilhelmine heard a little chuckle come back on the radio.

"Ok, Mr. Butcher Buchbinder," came a friendly response, "you are new to CB'ing. We'll help you get this figured out. First, you need a 'handle'...sort of a nickname so we know what to call you."

"I am Augustus Heinrich Buchbinder the Second. A retired butcher," he repeated, and he let up the key.

"Ok," said the friendly voice, "how about if we call you The Butcher?"

"Ja, I am da butcher," Auggie said again and shrugged his shoulders to Wilhelmine.

"Ok, Butcher, I am Cockroach and if you need some help, you press your key down on your mike and ask for me, and I will try to help you."

"I am talking vit a cockroach? We close our store once because of roach," Auggie explained.

Chuck was laughing but contained himself to explain, "No sir, Mr. Butcher, I am not a real cockroach, it is only my radio name. If you were in the war, you remember the signal corps and how those guys had code names. This is the same. Cockroach is my code name. Butcher is yours now."

"Ok, ja, I get it now," Auggie looked at Wilhelmine and shrugged his shoulders again. "So I do not get music on this radio, just call for help?"

"That's right, but you can also ask questions and talk about things. I am driving a big rig truck, is that you driving that '63 Towncar I passed a while back?"

"Ja. I've had her since she vas new. This is her first long trip," Auggie said into the mike.

"She's very pretty, Butcher. I hope you plan to keep her," Chuck said.

"I keep dis Towncar. I get rid of wife before I get rid of Towncar. It does not argue vit me," Auggie said, then smirked at Wilhelmine to which Wilhelmine grabbed the mike out of his hands and hollered into it, "He is a crazy oldt goat!" But she didn't have the button pressed in.

"So now you haff radio, Mina." Auggie was arrogant about it as he put the car into drive. "Now shaddap, I'm drivink!"

Chapter 19

Agnes' Midnight Truck Stop Diner

Matthew's radio never really worked in his Minibus so when he was out of range he didn't even realize it. He spent much of his drive time praying out loud. He prayed for each of his family, prayed for troubled people he remembered, prayed for the world. It kept him busy and mindful. If he felt sleepy, he'd sing church songs and once in awhile he'd sing "Proud Mary," a song he heard his parents play when he was young. He particularly liked "Proud Mary" and thought for sure it was from some revival event, probably a church full of joyful song because it was about poor people and how they coped with life on the river and he loved the phrase, "if you have no money, people on the river are happy to give." He thought more people should be that way.

It was now a couple of hours after dark and he was starting to feel a bit too cold as his fifty-some-year-old Minibus didn't put out much heat, and with the north wind kicking up, he could feel it push his bus now and then. He wanted to pray for more heat and the wind to quit, but he knew many people were too poor to have heat on this night and had to live with the winter chill. He thought it would be selfish to ask God to give him a little more warmth.

Looking for a truck stop to get a coffee to help him stay awake and warm up a bit he noticed that civilization was becoming more sparse as he drove into central Kansas and also noticed a few snowflakes beginning to blow around and thought it'd be pretty to have a white Christmas for a change.

He drove for quite a while before he finally saw a sign for a truck stop at the next exit, one mile ahead.

When the next exit ramp came into dim view he saw the name of the diner in large, lighted, red letters across the roof of the truck stop so it could be seen from the interstate exit ramps a half-mile away announcing Agnes' Midnight Truck Stop Diner.

He drove up the exit ramp to the short outer road then pulled into the bumpy parking area. There was an old fashioned marquee sign out in front of the parking lot with flickering lights, some of which stopped flickering years ago, and a few were totally burned out. A sign painted on the window saying "Truckers Welcome" and a blue neon "open" sign flashing on the door made it look like it walked off Route 66 in the1950s, time-worn but familiar.

Matthew parked next to a dumpster near the side of the place to help block the wind and left his motor running as he wrapped his coat tightly around his thin frame and headed to the diner.

Chapter 20

Heavenly Pie

Inside Agnes' Midnight Truck Stop Diner, it was warm, cozy, and filled with the smell of coffee, pie, burgers, and donuts, but at this late hour, it was only occupied by two truckers in a booth. Matthew sat on an old fashioned spinning stool at the counter, and the middle-aged waitress came from the kitchen and looked like she also walked in from 1950. Complete with hair net, pale aqua waitress dress with white collar and turned-up cuffs on her short sleeves with a white apron and well-worn nurse's shoes. She had her name tag on too, "Agnes." She asked Matthew if he wanted coffee.

"Yes, ma'am," Matthew said as he made fists and blew warm air into them.

"Pretty cold out in the wind tonight," Agnes said as she slid a paper napkin on the counter then sat a mug on it, adding hot black coffee from a coffee carafe. "You take anything in it?"

"Double cream if you got it. I'm not generally a big coffee drinker," Matthew explained.

"Lots of folks driving out here in the flatlands are not coffee drinkers, but most of 'em end up here having a cup to keep their eyes open. We got hot pie out of the oven, would you like some?"

Matthew looked at his cup and knew his funds were short, so figured he had to pass on the hot pie.

"No, ma'am. It sounds wonderful, but pie isn't on my menu tonight. Thank you."

"Ok, Reverend. Let me know if you change your mind," Agnes said.

Matthew immediately wondered how she could have known he was a minister when he was not wearing his clerical collar? He looked at her with a very puzzled look. Agnes, spending over thirty years waiting on travelers, had learned to size people up pretty quick. She picked up on his perplexed look.

"Oh, you have an angel lapel pin, the quilted bag on the counter is a Bible bag, you are wearing a bracelet of prayer beads with a crucifix hanging from it, you have a sense of peace about you, and you pulled up in that old Minibus, so you never had a well-paying job for a personable young man your age." She winked at him before turning to wipe the counters. The truckers overheard Agnes, and both nodded approval at her score.

Matthew smiled at her clever assessment as he wrapped his cold fingers around the hot coffee mug. "I guess we have something in common, ma'am," Matthew said with his slight Southern accent. Agnes looked a little surprised.

"What's that, Reverend?" she asked.

"We both help people that are tired of the dark to wake up and see the light." Matthew followed his comment with a laugh.

Agnes was amused and nodded at Matthew. "I guess you have something there, Reverend," and she went about wiping counters.

The two truckers got up and stood at the counter to pay their bill. One of them looked like Santa Claus with his ample girth and long white beard and white hair, or an old Harley biker.

"Cold night, Mr. Reverend," he said to Matthew. "You get any heat out of that bus?"

"Not much, sir," Matthew responded.

"You got a CB in that thing?" he asked.

"No. I'm afraid not. I guess I do my talking to God mostly," Matthew explained.

"Well, trust me, young man, the weather could get nasty if you are planning on driving through tonight. That Southern accent of yours and the red dirt on the back of your bus tells me you ain't used to the wild weather extremes Kansas can throw at you. I've been driving for nearly three decades, and I'm sensing this is going to be a bad night for driving. If it gets bad, you get yourself to a truck stop and stay there. No offense, but the crappy heater in that old bus isn't going to keep you warm enough if the highway becomes impassible, and you have to sit in it for a few hours parked on the shoulder. Nothing on the other end is so important that it can't wait. We'll keep an eye out for you.

"Our CB handles are Santa Claus and Ten-Point. We're kind of laying back a little and driving slow for a while to see what the weather is going to do. I'm seeing flurries now and then and not sure if it is going to bring in something bigger or blow itself out. It's been getting windier for the past couple hours, so I have concerns. Take care, Reverend." And with that, the trucker tossed a couple of bucks on the counter to thank Agnes for serving them, and they were both out the door letting in an icy breeze that Matthew felt on his legs.

As the door shut, Agnes brought Matthew a piece of hot apple pie.

"Oh," Matthew said as he looked at the gorgeous, golden, steaming piece of pie, "I didn't order pie."

"No, you didn't. Santa Claus told me to get you some pie, and he paid for it. Thank him in your prayers," Agnes explained.

Matthew smiled from ear to ear and thought, God doth provide! Then he stuck a fork into the point of the pie and pulled out a steaming chunk of apple and slipped it into his mouth, closing his eyes, savoring its sweetness. He wondered if there was pie in heaven.

Chapter 21

Make It Snappy

The two truckers climbed into their running rigs and adjusted their CB's so they could chat on their drive across Kansas. Over the years, Agnes learned to know the sound of their airbrakes, and one by one, she heard them rumble out of her parking lot.

Matthew was just finishing his pie and asked Agnes, "If it's no trouble, could I get another cup of coffee, please? It is really fine coffee."

"Sure, Reverend. It's hot too," Agnes said as she poured him another cup. She felt worried about the Southern Reverend and his Minibus. "You need to be careful keeping those hands warm. You don't want frostbite."

Matthew looked at the back of his hands, then turning them to see his palms.

"If you don't have an extra pair of gloves, get a pair of socks and pull them over your hands and up your arms. You got a pocket knife? Cut some holes for fingers. It'll help. And keep the legs covered. The big muscles need to stay warm. If you got a blanket or even an old sweater, just lay it over your legs. And get a hat on, young man," Agnes instructed. "Even if you have to use an old sheet like a scarf. Too much heat is lost from your head. Kansas cold is no time to worry about looking sensible or trying to make a fashion statement."

"Yes, ma'am," Matthew said as he added cream to his coffee. He always felt that God put angels in his path to teach him things to keep him safe. Maybe Agnes was one of His angels.

Agnes went to fix another pot of coffee when both Matthew and Agnes saw headlight beams bouncing all over the inside of the café. Matthew looked out the window to see a small car crashing over the broken asphalt as it nearly spun to a stop. A man got out donning a trenchcoat, then hurried up the stairs, threw the door open, then forced it closed behind him.

"Hey, anybody got some coffee in here? Can I get some coffee?" he demanded, nearly shouting.

"Keep yer shirt on pal," Agnes said as she came out of the back, wiping her hands on a towel and sized this guy up right away. Arrogant, she thought. "All I got is plain coffee. No latte or fancy stuff," she told him.

"Yeah. Regular coffee is fine," he said as he took a stool a few seats down from Matthew, "but make it snappy, if you don't mind, I'm running behind."

Agnes started to fume at being ordered around, but she got the guy's coffee and put it on the counter. "Anything else?" she asked coolly.

"You have anything to eat that's quick?" He sipped his coffee black as he put his cell phone on the counter and kept looking at it.

"Depends. Eggs are quick. Bagel. Toast. Sandwich." Agnes listed as she pulled a laminated menu from behind a napkin holder and slid it over to the man. Matthew wondered why she didn't mention the pie.

"I'll have a toasted bagel. You got cream cheese?" the man asked.

"Yes, the cream cheese comes on the side," Agnes said.

"How long is that going to take?" his words followed her to the kitchen.

The man sat there loudly sipping his coffee and looking at his phone over and over, then glancing out the window from time to time.

Matthew couldn't help himself. This man looked worried or troubled, so Matthew decided to try to engage the man in conversation.

"Is there anything I can help you with?" he asked kindly.

The man asked Matthew, "Is that your old Minibus out there running?"

"Yes," Matthew answered and glanced out the window to see it idling next to the dumpster.

"Well, you shouldn't leave it running like that. Someone will steal it." He went back to looking at his phone and seemed to be fretting.

"Well sir, if someone steals my beat-up bus, then they must have needed it. It would be God's will."

The man looked at Matthew in disbelief and shook his head and went back to his phone. Matthew noticed the man was very well dressed with expensive shoes. The man reminded him of his suburban church members that were more consumed with their own egos than the church, and Matthew considered just hitting the road, but Matthew didn't want to run away again.

Agnes brought the man's bagel, and he pasted some cream cheese on the edge and took a bite. For just a brief few seconds, the man seemed peaceful as he chewed his bite of bagel, then sipped his coffee. But once again he checked his phone and called at the waitress. "Excuse me, can you wrap this up and make it to go, and give me a coffee to go?"

Matthew could see Agnes getting irritated, so Matthew jumped in again. "You seem to be in a rush, sir. Is bad weather coming in?"

The man grew frustrated with Matthew's interruption and set his coffee down and turned to look at Matthew. "Look, I'm trying to get a call through. I have someplace to be, and I don't have time to deal with the weather. I'm headed to Palm Springs, and time is money." He dug in his pocket to get a business card to hand Matthew. "Here. If you need anything, like a lawsuit, call me."

Matthew glanced at the card and saw Mr. Tremont A Preston, Attorney at Law, Senior Partner, Connoiter, Rabinowitz, Aubuchon, and Preston Law.

Matthew addressed the man, "Mr. Preston, there were a couple of truckers in here a little while ago and commented on possibly some bad weather coming in. Your car is small and lightweight. Please drive safely. I will say a prayer for your safe journey."

"Oh, truckers," Mr. Preston's sarcasm escalated, "like they are meteorologists now?" And with that, he turned to Agnes and hollered out, "Is that order ready to go yet?" as he looked at his phone again then out the window at the light flurries. "I got to get going." He stood and dug for his wallet. "I didn't get your name, kid," he said to Matthew.

Matthew saw an opportunity to help the man realize what a jerk he sounded like, so Matthew said, "I am Reverend Matthew Zimmerman. I don't have a card to give you, but if you need anything, like a prayer, let me know."

Mr. Preston wasn't impressed at all. "Reverend, if you want people to respect your collar, you should wear it." He threw a twenty-dollar bill on the counter with a business card to Agnes as she handed him a coffee and a bag with his bagel and cream cheese. "Hope that covers it. Keep the change." And with that, Mr. Tremont A. Preston was out the door and quickly jumped in his car and was on his way out of the lot. Matthew and Agnes looked at each other and shook their heads as they saw his tail-lights disappear into the night.

"Take a lesson Reverend," Agnes said after she looked at the business card, "it takes all kinds to make a world, and usually, they never change. You have to take them as they are and try not to become like them. If you got an extra prayer, say one for that guy. Maybe someday, he'll take his heart out of his glove compartment and put it back in his soul."

"Yes, Ma'am," Matthew smiled at her remark.

Matthew was done with his pie, and Agnes refilled his mug with coffee and took his plate away. "Dollar, seventy-five, son," Agnes said. "Don't bother tipping me, I know you ain't got it. Save it. You might need more coffee later. The next truck stop is a couple of hours away near the Colorado border, and I'm hearin' on the radio that a storm might be cooking up in Nebraska and the Dakotas. You could be heading into that. Remember what I told ya about keepin' warm."

"Yes, Ma'am," Matthew said. "I think I'm plenty warmed up now, so I should be on my way after the little boys' room."

Agnes pointed him around the counter to the back while she filled a large foam cup with hot coffee and double cream for Matthew to go.

Chapter 22

Tech Support

Agnes had about five seconds of silence before the door to the café flew open again, and three young men piled in with the wind and flurries.

"Howdy ma'am," Joe said to Agnes, "you got hot coffee?"

"That's what we call it, black, hot, and nothing fancy," Agnes said.

"We aren't picky," Joe smiled, "just cold and tired."

Early had his computer notebook and swung himself into a booth, then clicked his game on and began working it. Barry took off his stocking cap, revealing his hat-hair that he tried smoothing with his hand while looking in the window reflection.

"Sit down, Barry. You're blocking my light," Early joked. Barry sat on the opposite side of the booth and picked up the laminated menu.

Without looking up from the game, Early said, "Pancakes. No point in studying the menu Barry, you always order pancakes with link sausage."

Barry continued studying the menu while Joe slid in next to Barry and held his hand out for the menu in no particular hurry. "Boy, it's cold and windy out. I didn't realize that the back end of that van would never heat up. I think we're going to have to rotate every hour, so whoever is in back doesn't get too cold. Either that or scoot a cooler up between the seats and sit up near the front."

"Yeah, I think that's what we're going to have to do," Barry said while handing the menu to Joe. "So now we need a weather report."

Agnes brought three mugs and a pot of coffee and sat it on the table with a few spoons and napkins. "You boys take anything in your coffee?"

All three thanked Agnes, and only Barry asked for sugar. Agnes pointed to the sugar jar on the table with the eraser end of her pencil, then readied it with the business end on her order pad. "What'll you have, boys?"

"I guess we'll have the pancake special, with sausage links."

"All three of you?" Agnes asked, and all three looked up and nodded to her like starving zoo animals. "Comin' right up."

As Agnes turned to go, Joe stopped her, "Ma'am? Do you have Wi-Fi here? We can't get our gear to give us a weather report.

"Well, son," Agnes explained, "I don't know about any why-fy thing, but we do have a T-V and A-M and F-M," and Agnes stopped and waited for the laugh as she thought she had teased them. But all three simply sat there staring at her.

She didn't explain the joke, "No, son, there is no Wi-Fi here. Sometimes we get weak cell coverage, depends on the weather. It'll be another year or so before they bring civilization out here. But I can tell you that tonight's five o'clock news, which is local, mentioned that a cold front is supposed to race through here sometime tonight and drop the temps twenty degrees. So it'll get windy and a lot colder. Just hope there's no snow, the reports have been mixed all day. If a storm is coming out of the Arctic and slamming into the prairie at breakneck speed, loaded with tons of snow, we call it a Siberian Express. They come fast, they come hard, and it comes with snow, a lot of snow, so much that they close the interstate. If it comes, we'll have people in the diner all night and well into tomorrow. I don't mind keeping the place open all night, that's why midnight is in the name of my place, I'm here all night. I hope I can catch a bit of a nap just in case this turns bad. It's been a long day."

"Siberian Express?" Early looked up from his game.

"Yes, son, it's a rapid weather change that is so dramatic that the temperature drops lickety-split." Agnes snapped her fingers for the speed effect. "We experience it as dangerously cold, sub-zero temperature drops, wind, and blowing snow. If it gets hooked up with a ton of snow, then it becomes a blizzard and will make driving next to impossible, and at times the roads become impassable."

"Thank you, Agnes, you have given me a brilliant idea." Early said as he turned off his computer and sat up. "I've been wanting to code a video game that is not about violence and killing, guns and hate, but about something that would still be exciting...your Siberian Express! What a cool idea!"

Agnes winked and held up one hand for a high five for each of the geeks, and one-by-one, they slapped skin with her. "Pancakes, coming up!" she said as she went back to the kitchen.

Early turned on his computer again and started furiously typing notes about the game he was going to develop. Barry sipped his coffee and stared out into the night, and Joe went to the men's room.

Matthew was still in the men's room just about done washing his hands as Joe entered. "Hey," Joe nodded to Matthew.

"Hey," Matthew commented back.

Joe stood at the urinal, and Matthew held his hands under the hand dryer. It stopped, and Matthew pushed the button in again. Joe was done and arranging his junk and looked at Matthew curiously.

"Hands are cold," Matthew admitted and rolled his eyes at his own comment.

"I get what you are saying. We had to come in out of the cold because my heater doesn't keep up in the back of the van," Joe commented.

"Same here. I'm driving a forty-five-year-old Minibus, and it just doesn't put out much heat when it's this cold out."

"Oh sheesh, is that yours out there by the dumpster?" Joe asked.

"Yeah," Matthew felt embarrassed.

"Hey, that's vintage cool, man," Joe complimented him when he saw that Matthew seemed self-conscious about his little heap. "not only cool, but it's easy on gas. They don't make 'em like they used to."

"Now you sound like my Dad," Matthew smiled.

Joe started washing his hands, "So you going far in that thing?"

"No, not too far, I don't think. I'm headed up to the northwest corner of Kansas. I hope I get there by late tonight or early tomorrow, depending on the weather."

"You got family there?" Joe asked, wondering why a young man would be traveling by himself this close to Christmas out in the middle of nowhere.

"Well, um, no, not family, more like a flock," Matthew hoped to avoid the question, but Joe was looking at him in earnest. "I, um, have a new job to start there."

"No kidding? So you a sheep farmer?" Joe was still curious as he tossed his paper towel in the trash.

"Well, um....not really. Wrong kind of flock. I am....well, I am a reverend. Reverend Matthew. I'm heading up to minister to a new flock." Matthew pointed to his angel lapel pin.

"Oh, sorry about the sheep thing," Joe said.

"No bother," Matthew commented, "you know at some point, we are all like lost sheep."

Joe nodded. "So you are a man of the cloth," Joe respectfully acknowledged, "like Matthew, Mark, Luke, and John, eh?"

"Yes," Matthew chuckled as the joke has been mentioned many times, but he never got tired of hearing it.

Both left the men's room and went out in the diner together.

"Hey guys," Joe said to Barry and Early as he slid back into the booth next to Barry, "this is Reverend Matthew. That's his vintage Minibus out there."

"Hey man," Barry said, sticking his hand out to shake, "awesome wheels."

"Thanks," Matthew said, giving Barry's hand a hearty shake. "Have you found anything on the weather on that thing?" he asked, pointing to Early's notebook.

"Nope," Early said. "We aren't getting any connections out here, so all we know is just what Agnes has told us. It's concerning, but so far, just a lot of wind and some flurries. We are pretty sure we'll be okay driving through to Denver.

There's a computer convention the day after Christmas in Vegas that we need to be at."

Matthew picked up his Bible bag and took his coffee. "I hope to get to my destination sometime tonight. I thought I'd be there by suppertime but didn't count on some of the hills coming through Missouri that slowed me down to about forty-five miles an hour plus stopping to warm up when I get the chance."

"No kidding. It's damn cold out there," Joe said, then apologized for his language.

"Not a problem," Matthew laughed. "I've heard plenty worse." Matthew bundled up and thanked Agnes and wished everyone a Merry Christmas and left the diner.

The three geeks watched Matthew fight the wind in the parking lot to get to his bus, then fought the door to get in. As he drove off, the three geeks gave him thumbs-up, and Matthew flashed his brights, pleased that there were still people that were cordial and pleasant. He thanked God for the company, Agnes' help, the coffee, and of course, the pie.

Agnes came out of the kitchen with a large tray filled with steaming plates of pancakes and sausage and three little pitchers of hot syrup; maple, strawberry, and chocolate. The three geeks gave her a good-natured applause as she sat the plates on the table, and she added a little flair in setting the syrup pitchers down on separate little plates.

"Awesome, Agnes!" Early said. The other two agreed, Agnes was awesome.

"Thanks, boys. Dig in while the hotcakes are hot," she winked and asked if they needed anything else.

"Forks?" Barry asked. "Forks would be helpful."

"Oh, my," Agnes frowned, "where is my head. Forks, coming right up." And Agnes sped behind the counter to rustle up forks and knives and napkins too. "Sorry, boys, just not working with all cylinders tonight."

"Don't worry, Agnes," Joe said, "the pancakes look great. I can hear your weather radio in back, I presume you are more concerned about the weather than you let on."

"Guilty," Agnes said. "I just got a bad feeling about the weather. Wish you boys weren't headed out tonight. That reverend neither," as she tilted her head toward the last place they saw Matthew's bus.

"We'll be okay. We have a van full of Barry's magazines. We could burn them for a month for heat," Joe kidded.

"Whoa! No, ya don't!" Barry said as he dribbled hot strawberry syrup all over his pancakes, "I gotta sell those!"

"Keep your shirt on, Barry. I'm just kidding. Sheesh!" Joe said.

"Well, I still worry about you youngsters. You all think you are indestructible," Agnes said as she topped off their coffee mugs from the carafe then went behind the counter to make more coffee muttering to herself that she was going to need plenty of coffee tonight.

Chapter 23

Chick Chat

Another stream of headlights bounced around through the diner windows until the car came to a stop.

Three girls piled through the door, all talking at once as Agnes was taking another round of pancakes to the geek guys.

Barry sat up straight as he watched the girls walk in. He eyed them up and down. Joe saw Barry's attention turn to the girls and grabbed his arm, and pointed to their car outside, "Look, man, Missouri plates. Throttle your engine Barry, something isn't kosher with them. They look way too young. Jail bait, you know." Barry still studied them. They were cute gals.

"Maybe it's warmer in the back corner," Brittany said as she headed to the booth in the back corner.

"No, I think you might be warmer right here," Delphia said as she pointed to a booth about halfway to the back. "There's a vent up there, and it looks like it'll blow right here."

"That's Delphia, Miss Brainiac," Tawnie said to Agnes that stood behind the counter, shuffling mugs on a shelf.

The girls piled into the booth, and Delphia put her laptop on the table and tried again to see if she could get internet access. "That probably won't work," Agnes said as she approached their table. "we don't have that Wi-Fi or any internet here, sometimes you can get a cell signal, but doubt you'll get it in this weather. What can I get you, girls?"

Delphia closed her laptop. "Do you have tea? Unsweetened tea?"

"Yes, ma'am," said Agnes, "it isn't fancy, you get a hot cup of water and your very own teabag." Agnes winked at her.

Delphia smiled, saying that was fine and looked out the window at the fattening flurry flakes, "Have you heard anything about the weather tonight?" she asked Agnes.

"Well, I was just telling the guys over there," Agnes pointed with the eraser of her pencil again, "that this storm could be something or nothing. It's just hard to tell out here in the flatlands because sometimes weather fronts blow in so fast. Sometimes so fast that they blow themselves out. If I was going on my gut though, I'd say there's going to be snow. A pretty good one too, but so far, no confirmation on that from the weather service."

"I guess that's good to know," said Delphia. "Do you think we'll be okay driving to Denver tonight?"

"I can't make that call for you, girls. If it were me, I'd find a place to stay until morning. At least in daylight, you have an advantage. There's a small cottage inn about forty miles back the way you came. I know the owners for years, it's a good clean place and cheap. The Cedar Inn."

"Oh, I am NOT going back!" Brittany suddenly lit up like a bonfire. "We can drive through. Even if we get snow, we can drive slow. I have an extra hour to kill so I can drive carefully if it gets snowy."

"Well, just remember I warned you girls. What'll you have, Ma'am?" Agnes pointed to Brittany.

"Do you have hot chocolate?" Brittany asked.

"Yes, in fact, we have excellent hot chocolate!" Agnes said.

"I'll have cocoa too," Tawnie said quietly and looked down into her lap.

"What's the matter, Tawnie?" Delphia asked. "You look like someone just gave you bad news."

"Nothin'," Tawnie said, "I'm fine, just a little scared of the weather." Tawnie looked to Agnes sheepishly.

"Young lady," Agnes asked Tawnie, "would you like whipped cream on that cocoa?"

Tawnie brightened, "Oh, yes I would, ma'am."

"You too?" Agnes asked Brittany.

"Does it cost extra?" Brittany asked.

"No. It's on the house," Agnes said.

"On whose house?" Delphia asked. Agnes looked at her.

Tawnie started laughing, "On the house, Delph, it means free."

"Oh, yes, sorry. I knew that," Delphia blushed.

They heard the geek guys chuckling a few booths over between pancake bites and Brittany stuck an arm up in the air with the one-finger salute to the geek guys. "Hey, bite me, Nerdicus!" Brittany puffed under her breath, but it was loud enough that Joe heard it.

"Brittaneeey!" Delphia whispered. "What is wrong with you?"

"They were laughing at us," Brittany said.

"No, they weren't. So what if they were? Can't you let it go?" Delphia kept whispering.

Joe put down his fork and looked over at the girls. He figured right away they were pretty young, too young. He got up, wiped his mouth with his napkin and put it back on the table, then straightened his shirt hem over his belt, and approached the girls. Agnes was leaning on the back counter next to the coffee machine, watching what was going on, wondering if she'd have to step in.

"Good evening, ladies," Joe said politely, and by now Barry and Early were alerted that Joe was up to something.

"Good evening," Delphia said politely.

"Is that your car out there with Missouri tags?"

"What's it to you?" Brittany snipped, and Delphia glared at her nerve to be so pissy.

"Well, you don't have to prove anything to me, but I thought I would tell you that the weather could get pretty bad this evening and your car there, I know that model. It is an older one that historically has trouble with its heater. If you girls get too cold, find a piece of cardboard and open your hood. Then slide the cardboard down in front of your radiator. It'll help the heater core be warmer," Joe said, then looked at his watch, "It's ten o'clock, do your parents know where you are?"

Brittany started to fire back, but Delphia shot out one of her long slim arms and cupped her hand over Brittany's mouth. "Don't mind her. She's got boyfriend issues and is pissy lately," Delphia explained. "Thanks for the tip on the car heater, but so far, we haven't needed it."

"Well, we have quite a few boxes in our van, if you need a piece of cardboard, let me know and I can rustle you up some," Joe offered.

"Thanks," both Delphia and Tawnie said. As Joe walked away, Delphia removed her hand from Brittany's mouth, then Brittany managed to blurt out after him, "No. Our parents have no clue where we are. We planned this out in advance. I'm going to visit my boyfriend in Denver for Christmas. So there."

"Damn Brittany," Delphia said, "that was rude."

And Tawnie added, "And majorly childish."

Delphia stirred her tea, and Tawnie stirred her hot chocolate, both were quiet and momentarily disgusted with Brittany's attitude. Brittany sat there looking back and forth at her two friends, and after a minute she said, "I'm sorry. You guys are right, I was rude. It was uncalled for. I'm just a little worried about the drive, upset about Bryce, and concerned about the weather. I'm going to go apologize to those guys." Brittany got up and walked over to the geek guys' booth, flipping her hair this way and that while catching her own reflection in the diner windows.

"Hey," she said quietly as she approached their booth, "I'm, um, sorry for being bitchy before. It was uncalled for." Then Brittany hung her head in semi-serious fashion, feigning a pout and acting just how sorry she might be, waiting to be forgiven. She recognized the geekiness of the guys and felt superior. But Joe was not impressed, he had a little sister, he knew the drill.

"It's okay, ----," he said, leaving space for her to mention her name.

"Brittany," she informed him.

"It's okay, Brittany," Joe said. "you remind me of my little sister, I just want you to be careful and safe. This being out on the road this late is not like being in high school."

Agnes heard Joe and nodded in agreement to Delphia and Tawnie. Delphia knew he was right too.

"Well then," Brittany said as she flipped her hair over her shoulder again and turned on her young amateur flirting mode, "how do you think you can protect me?" She shrugged her shoulders this way and that and batted too many eyelashes. Barry and Early looked at each other. Her comment made Joe wince.

"Look, no offense, Brittany," Joe began, "but you are too young, and all I can think of is to tell you that you should head back home. This boy you are chasing, I bet he doesn't even know you are coming. Does he?"

Brittany didn't answer.

"He is with his parents, isn't he. If you show up with two girlfriends and no adults, don't you think his parents will see you, and if they do, you don't think they'll ask their son who the girls are, then call your parents? Or call the police about unattended minors?"

Brittany didn't know how to answer that, and Joe could see she was stuck.

"Does this guy know you are coming?"

Brittany shook her head no.

"So, you are going to surprise him?"

Brittany slowly nodded, yes.

"Brittany, this is not a good idea. I think you already know that. You are going to get him in trouble with his parents, and after that, he probably won't even talk to you again."

Brittany defended herself, "But he wants me, I know. He's just shy."

"It doesn't matter if he's shy," Early chimed in, wiping his mouth with his napkin. "You'll just push him away, especially if he's scared or shy."

"Yep," Barry added, pointing his fork at her, "worse if he's scared AND shy."

Brittany looked at the three geeks and decided they couldn't know what she or Bryce were thinking. "Well, thanks for the pep-talk." And she excused herself to go back to her friends.

Early slowly shook his head in disbelief as Brittany went back to her booth. "That's a train-wreck looking for a place to happen," Early said to the other two.

"Yeah, I know," said Joe. "It troubles me that those three high school girls are out here alone this late."

Barry and Early knew what he was talking about. Joe's little sister was grabbed out of her car one night on her way home from a football game with one of her friends. Her friend was only smacked around a little, but Joe's sister was beaten badly and dragged into a field and sexually assaulted by three or four young men. It was a horrible time for Joe and his family. They were never the same after that. And now Joe sees these young girls in the same situation, with no concept of what easy pickings they might be for someone bent on assaulting a young girl.

"Drink up," Brittany urged Delphia. "we can't sit here all night. If the weather is getting bad, then we need to get as much ground covered as possible. Maybe we can outrun it. Go pee while you can pee in a heated bathroom."

After returning from the restroom, Delphia spoke while adjusting her beret, "I don't know, I think I agree with those guys, we should turn around and go home. He's right, too, if Bryce's folks see you, you know they are going to ask him who the girl is."

"Don't worry," Brittany said, "Bryce will never rat me out. He won't want me in trouble. It's just that simple."

Delphia shook her head. She realized she had to stay with Brittany so she wouldn't end up in a bigger mess or in a ditch somewhere.

When Tawnie returned from the ladies' room, Agnes saw the girls getting up and buttoning up coats, so she rung up the bill at the register. Joe jumped up and said he'd take care of their tab. Delphia and Tawnie thanked him over and over, but Brittany was cool about it.

"Remember what I told you about your car heater," Joe called after them as they walked out the door. Delphia held up fingers to indicated "ok," and they were off into the night.

"She'll be okay," Agnes tried to assure Joe as she refilled their mugs again, "we don't get a lot of crime around here."

"Sure. Sure," Joe said but wasn't comfortable with it. "Let's get going guys, it looks like the flurry activity is picking up, maybe we can luck out and get around the storm."

"You guys be careful," Agnes said as she put the money in the register and made change. "There's not much between here and the state line. It's almost three hours from here, and that's in good weather."

"Thanks, Agnes," Barry said. "Pancakes are awesome. Maybe we'll stop by on our way back. Do you only work nights?"

"Oh no," Agnes said with a tired look, "I own the joint and I'm open 24-7. I work all kinds of hours. I have a cot in the back and sleep when I can. I do have a cook and a couple girls that come and help out during the days so I can get home and catch up on sleep. It's hard to find all-night help, so I cover it myself, that's why I added "midnight" to the name of the joint. Agnes is here for midnight travelers, that's me. I'm here when the cook comes in, and we get pies going and biscuits for breakfast, fire up the grill with sausage from a local pork producer. Best biscuits and gravy in Kansas, so we are always busy at breakfast.

My dad used to run the place. He called it 'Big Al's Truck Stop Diner' then, and I worked for him. He loved this place, chatting with people always going places. But he had a heart attack a decade ago, and I ended up filling in for him and eventually running the whole show after he passed on. I changed the name to 'Agnes' Midnight Truck Stop Diner.' I thought about some cutesy names, but I like the "midnight" part and kept "truck stop diner" in for my father, then only changing Al's to Agnes', that saved me having to buy a couple more letters. So chances are pretty good if you stop in on your way back, and it's after nine pm, I'll be here."

The boys filed out the door, and Agnes went back to wiping tables and straightening things when she heard an annoying familiar buzzing sound. It was the weather-radio alarm.

Chapter 24

Storm Alarm

Agnes went back to turn off the weather alarm and listen to the report. It sounded like furious winds were coming in the next few hours along with snow, a lot of snow. Agnes thought about all the kids out there driving right into it and hoped they'd get past the counties that would be hit hardest before all hell broke loose.

She was still listening to the report when she heard the tinkling bell above the door then felt the cold draft of someone coming in.

Agnes stepped behind the counter to see a handsome young man picking a counter spot to sit at. "I'll be right with you," Agnes told him as she went back and turned up the volume on the weather radio.

As Agnes came back, Ben must have had a curious look on his face. "Weather radio," Agnes said as she pointed to the back office. "I keep updated weather information for the travelers that stop in. You want coffee?

"That'd be great," Ben said. "What is the latest on the storm? This morning, I saw a cloud line on the horizon, and the color of the sky had me thinking a winter event was brewing."

"That's right. Although they've been talking all day that it was nothing, it looks like it's turning into something," Agnes said as she poured a coffee for Ben. "Anything in it?" she asked.

"Just cream," Ben said. "Well, if a big snow comes in, it'll be great for the ski season."

"True. But in my line of work, it really makes my day extra long. Some of the smart drivers sit it out here, making some very long days. I always hope I don't run out of coffee or have to deal with irritated travelers. Other drivers think they can muscle through it, and I hear a lot of frantic calls for help on the CB, but there's nothing we can do to help them unless they are very close to a farm and a farmer can get his tractor out to them. And you've seen the land here, farm houses are quite far apart.

"Yes, indeed," Ben agreed, "people don't understand how dangerous winter can be. I grew up on a maple syrup farm in Vermont and everything was about the weather. When I saw the cloud line on the horizon this morning and the color of the sky, I just knew a big storm was coming in. I was raised to respect the winter. I'm not out to prove anything."

"Vermont, eh? I bet it's beautiful. I've never been to the East Coast. Heck, I've never been out of Kansas. Do you want anything else with your coffee, Son?"

"No thanks, I'm fine. My aunt loaded me up with stuff to eat when I left, but my coffee has been cold since yesterday," Ben said as he stirred his coffee. Agnes put the coffee pot back in the machine and continued her conversation with Ben.

"I was just telling my last customer that my father built this diner in the 1940's before I-70 came through, and the joint was really small, but he knew the interstate system was being proposed. Around the '60's the highway was coming, so he enlarged the diner to serve more travelers but mostly catered to the truckers.

He used to have framed newspaper articles hung on the walls about storms that blew through here, and thankfully there have only been a few deaths from the really severe storms, and most of those are from people leaving their vehicles or farmers trying to get their critters into barns and sheltered."

Ben sipped his coffee and listened to Agnes with interest.

"I remember one article from 1886 the temperature dropped to nearly 30-below, it was so cold that a train froze to the tracks and people had to get off the train and were graciously hosted by the people of the small town nearby. I only remember two deaths from a 1979 blizzard where people froze in their car. There was a huge storm in 1987 that closed nearly 400 miles of I-70 and stranded plenty of motorists, but the highway department sent out planes after the storm to spot the stranded folks."

"Dang," Ben said.

Agnes continued, "It seems the big storms are coming more frequently in spite of all I hear about global warming. Believe it or not, there were big storms in 1987, 1997, and 2007. I remember that 1987 storm, we had people in here for two days, and the 2007 storm we got about three feet of snow, and some of the drifts across the highway were fifteen feet high. The last biggie was 2011, so the clock is ticking, and we are way overdue." Agnes' voice faded as she walked over to the windows and looked out into the dimly lighted parking lot and saw that what were flurries a little while ago had turned into some heavy, fat flakes.

"Dang," she said, "the snow is picking up. I hope this isn't going to be the next big one. And you are planning to drive to Colorado tonight?"

Ben was fascinated by Agnes' knowledge of the weather but Ben felt confident that he would be just fine.

"I'm okay. I have giant tires on my truck, and I have a very good ski suit and even a coat that heats up. So even if I get snowbound, I'm good for at least a day. And I will pull over if the other drivers are looking too reckless. I have lived most of my life in the mountains in Vermont, I think I'll be okay if I can get used to the flatness," Ben joked a bit.

Agnes smiled at the joke.

Chapter 25

Bunco Squad

Once more, Agnes saw headlights bouncing in the parking lot, but this time the vehicle had two sets of headlights nearly blinding Agnes. She saw the vehicle come so fast up to the concrete parking curb that she thought it might just crash into the building. It was a huge thing, but she couldn't tell what it was on account of the brightness of the four headlights. Just then, it bumped up and over one of the curbs but came to an abrupt stop. The vehicle just sat there, lights on. Agnes had a wary feeling about it and casually stepped behind the lunch counter to a far corner where she kept a loaded handgun under a stack of towels. She was never so stupid to think that working the place alone, that there would never be any trouble.

Shortly she saw the backup lights blink on, and the huge vehicle backed up over the curb again and settled in a parking space. The lights went out. Agnes felt a little relieved but still was cautious.

All four of the vehicle doors flew open at once, and four hunched-up humans piled out, slamming doors and hustling up to the diner door pushing each other out of the way to be the first one inside and out of the cold. Ben and Agnes shared a look.

As soon as the door opened, all Ben and Agnes could hear were women bickering about the weather and how someone cheated at their last Bunco night. The wind and blowing snow followed them inside.

Rita looked back at her reflection in the glass and started fiddling with her hair. "Oh, for crying out loud, Rita, it's late, you don't need to make a fashion statement at a truck stop. Nobody is going to care what your hair looks like. I thought you said you had to pee," Doris griped and pointed to the sign that said "restrooms". Rita looked at the handsome young man at the counter and hustled off to the restroom to make repairs.

"Jeez," Doris said in frustration as she yanked off her coat and picked out a booth.

"Calm down, Doris," Janet said as she headed to the ladies' room, "you know how she is, especially when she's been sipping from her flasks all day."

"I know," Doris said. "I just wanted to smack the crap out of her today. I don't seem to have the patience for her extra brand of weirdness after she's had a few."

"I think we should get her some coffee," Jackie said, trying to ease the irritation. "I know I could use some myself," she added as she shook the snow off her coat and laid it across the back of a booth.

"Yes, coffee," Doris said as she threw her purse onto the seat of the booth.

Agnes couldn't help overhear them, and asked, "Four coffees?" to any one of them.

"Yes, please," Jackie answered as she slipped into a booth and tucked a few of her wind-blown hairs back into her French twist and straightened her pearls. Doris scooted in next to Jackie, knowing Rita would have to sit on the other side. Jackie knew exactly why Doris sat next to her and jabbed Doris in the arm with her elbow and gave her a look.

Janet was coming back from the ladies' room at the same time Agnes was bringing four mugs and a carafe of coffee to the booth.

"Ahhh, hot coffee!" Janet said as she swung herself into the other side of the booth rubbing her palms together briskly.

"Is Rita still in the john? Is she okay?" Doris asked as she took one of the mugs.

"Oh, well, you know Rita. There's a 'man' on the premises," Janet said, pointing her finger to the handsome young man at the counter sipping his coffee, "and Rita is doing a complete overhaul."

"I should have known," Doris said, then yawned.

Janet saw the yawn, "Well, maybe we should call it a day and stay at the next decent place."

"Maybe you are right, Janet," Doris agreed. "I know the Black Diamond would go through most anything, but it's been exhausting fighting the wind that's slamming us from the side."

"Not to mention us riding. It's like being tossed by waves in a boat the past couple hours. That thing has zero aerodynamics." Jackie added.

"Ok, next decent place, we're done for the day," Doris concluded. Then she noticed Rita coming from the restroom. She'd managed to smooth out her hair over the rat pile and doctored her makeup quite a bit as though she was going clubbing. Rita smiled a sarcastic smile at the girls in the booth as Janet began to scoot over to make room for her, but instead of sitting with them, Rita picked up the empty mug and took it to sit at the counter one seat away from Ben. Doris just slowly shook her head in frustration. That was Rita....there was a pair of pants in the room.

They watched Rita coolly roll herself onto the seat, then shrug her coat off her shoulders, laying it on the seat next to her. She smiled at Ben, who politely smiled back. Even Agnes was watching this frighteningly thin, older woman apparently trying to hit on the good-looking young man.

"Where you from?" Rita asked Ben like a cat waiting to attack.

"Vermont." Ben was polite but didn't want to encourage the woman.

"Oh, Vermont. Where maple syrup comes from." Rita acted like she was a walking encyclopedia of travel tips.

"Yes, ma'am," Ben said again, trying not to encourage her.

"Oh, you don't have to call me 'ma'am'," Rita nearly sang to Ben, "you can call me LaRita," she said, heavily rolling the "r" as though she had suddenly become Spanish and batting her eyelash-less eyelids

"LaRita??" Doris whispered to the other girls as she pounded her forehead with the heel of her hand. "Where does she come up with that crap?"

Jackie, even though she was quite amused by Rita's latest performance, tried to keep things calm, "Leave it, Doris. Rita has been sipping booze all day, let's not piss her off right now."

Ben, having been raised by a sharp-witted older woman, was not to be baited by what he saw as being hit on by a shriveled, out-of-date, old lady.

"Very well," Ben agreed. "Nice to meet you, Mrs. LaRita," as though he didn't understand what she was asking of him. The girls in the booth heard him, and all started giggling at how he really got her goat with the "Mrs." thing.

Undaunted, Rita tried again. "Where are you headed?" she asked as she overly fluttered her slightly askew eyelids looking like she got sand in one eye. Then she rested her chin on the heel of her hand and tried to make a dreamy smile at him, but it only made her look sleepy.

"I am going to work," Ben said simply without looking at her and sipped more coffee.

"OH, work, that's nice." She kept it up. "I don't work now. But I used to work." She knew she wasn't getting anywhere, so spun on her seat and did a little figure eight between seats, so she was now sitting next to Ben. Even as small as she was, she managed to lean her shoulder over enough to touch elbows with Ben.

Ben was onto her every move. "Well, look at the time," he said without looking at a clock or watch. "I don't want to be late." Agnes picked up on what he was saying and handed him the tab. He was getting up and saw that Rita had managed to sit on a corner of his coat. Instead of politely asking her to move, he simply yanked the corner of his coat out from under her. He paid his tab and thanked Agnes. As he passed the booth of ladies, he told them to be careful in the snow and Merry Christmas, and Ben was out the door.

As the door shut and the few flurries that blew in melted to the floor, Rita came back to the booth with her still empty mug and scooted in next to Janet. "Boy, he was cute, yeah?" she said, pouring a cup of coffee.

All Doris could say was, "LaRita?? Where did you come up with that?"

Rita, unfazed, simply explained, "Rita is too old-fashioned. Girls today have sultry exotic names, so I updated myself, DOR-is. Does anyone even name a kid Doris anymore?"

Doris rolled her eyes. "Well, LaH-Rita," Doris said with acute sarcasm, "maybe you should consider updating your wardrobe too."

"Why?" Rita asked. "I look slim, and I like these clothes."

"Rita, don't you see that you look like a sixty-five-year-old, out-of-touch grandma that is trying to look like an NFL cheerleader?" Doris asked while Janet gave Doris a gentle kick in the shins under the table to stop trying to create a scene. In true form, Rita wasn't particularly offended by Doris' comment as all she really heard was 'NFL cheerleader'.

"What?" Doris looked at Janet for the kick. "Someone has to say something."

"Um, no, no, we don't," Janet said, gritting her teeth.

Oh, Janet, don't worry about what Doris says to me," Rita assured her. "I must look pretty young for my age because many people call me "Miss," and look at me and smile."

Doris was about to explode, wanting to say that isn't smiling, it's stifled laughter, but a hard glare from Jackie told Doris to clam up. The three watched as Rita took another small flask out of her purse and poured some of the liquid into her mug of coffee.

"How many of those do you have?" Doris asked Rita, referring to her flask.

"I don't know. Why?" Rita said, slowly stirring her brew.

Doris just shook her head.

Agnes was keeping an eye on the ladies and walked over to ask if they needed anything else. The three answered no thank-you, but Rita asked if there were any more young men hiding in the back, as though she thought it was a cute comment. Agnes played along, "Well, just the three or four I keep tied up to peel potatoes and do dishes." Then she walked away. Doris and Janet stifled their laughter.

The ladies sipped their coffee and chatted about a variety of things until Doris yawned again.

"We need to call it a day, Doris," Janet pointed out.

"Yes, I know. I am tired. I hoped the coffee would jolt me awake, but it just isn't enough. Besides, now, after all the coffee, I'm going to have to pee in a half-hour again."

Janet got up and leaned on the counter and asked Agnes where there was a decent place to stay.

"Well, I hate to bear bad news, but about the only decent place around here is forty miles back. It's an older travel place of cottages, but it's clean and reasonable. They will even make you breakfast if you tell them the night before. It's the Cedar Inn.

"Oh man, going back forty miles? Is anything up ahead?" Jackie asked.

"Not for about a hundred miles, and I can't vouch for how presentable it might be," Agnes said.

"I don't want to go back," Doris said to the girls, "let's just move ahead. Janet can drive if I get too sleepy. A hundred miles is only an hour and a half, and we could be there before midnight."

"Assuming they have a vacancy," Jackie warned. "After all, it is right before Christmas."

Agnes brought the check and another pot of coffee and topped off their mugs. "Here you go, ladies," Agnes said, "more coffee. You can pay me at the register when you are ready to leave."

Rita reached over and snatched the check. "My treat," she said. The girls shrugged their shoulders. "But you can leave the tip," Rita finished. The girls started rummaging through their purses for some change. They didn't have much change as most of their cash was still in large bills from the bank. Rita went to the register with her wallet and the check.

"A hundred dollar bill?" Agnes said.

"That's the smallest I have right now," Rita said.

"I don't know if I have enough change for you," Agnes lifted the drawer, and only two twenties were in the drawer.

Rita was about to dig for a debit card when the door blew open and two young men, clearly not dressed for the weather, came in.

Chapter 26

The Ladies Are Held Up For Awhile

"Men's room?" the younger of the men quickly asked
Agnes. She pointed and he rushed to the men's room. The
other young man stood at the doorway and cased the place,
pulling his hoodie up around his cheeks before slipping into a
booth in the back corner and slouching in the seat. Agnes
kept an eye on him, something about him didn't seem quite
right. She didn't like the way he looked, and tried to blow it off
but was still dealing with Rita's cash and trying to find enough
change.

Rita finally produced a debit card but made a snippy
comment on why this diner didn't have any change, to which
Agnes explained she hadn't made a bank run because of the
holiday. Rita keyed in the debit information when the young
man came out of the men's room looking relieved.

"Could we get some coffee, please?" he asked Agnes and
pointed to the booth with the other young man, "Two." Agnes
nodded while she completed the transaction with Rita, who
noticed the young men too and had to make her presence
known.

"What's are nice young men like you doing out here in the
middle of Kansas?" She purred.

The younger man was about to answer when the hooded
young man in the booth answered for him, "What's an old lady
like YOU doing out here in the middle of Kansas?" Everyone

heard the derogatory comment. Rita's friends turned around to look. Even the young man from the men's room turned to look at his brother.

"You Jerk!" Eddie said, firing off an angry look at Travis. What the hell is wrong with you?"

"It's none of her business what we are doing," Travis snipped.

"She was just making conversation," Eddie chastised.

Travis knew Eddie was right, so he folded his arms and slouched further down into the booth.

"Please pardon my brother," Eddie said to everyone. "He's had a rough couple days."

Agnes walked over to their booth with two mugs and the coffee carafe and arranged them with spoons and napkins. "Sorry, I didn't see you pull in. I usually notice people coming in this late. You'll feel better when you've had some coffee," she said to Travis. Travis made a face.

"We parked kind of near the back, ma'am," Eddie volunteered then made up an excuse, "we didn't want our lights blinding people having coffee."

"Okay," Agnes said suspiciously.

When Agnes walked away, Eddie whispered to Travis, "Come on, Travis, we need to blend into the woodwork. Knock off being an ass. There could be a bulletin out on you by now. We don't want any trouble, especially out here in the boonies. I'm sorry there wasn't a drive-thru handy, but I needed some coffee, I've been driving for almost eight hours."

Eddie noticed there was no menu in the booth and got up to get one from the counter. He walked over to the ladies and apologized again for his brother's remark and flattered the girls with an obviously corny compliment, "I don't know how he could make such a comment about you lovely young ladies."

Jackie smiled and thanked the young man. Doris was counting the change on the table to make sure the tip was enough. Janet was keeping an eye on Travis. But Rita was thrilled a pair of pants came to their booth to compliment her, she assumed it was her anyway.

"Oh, thank you, young man," she said. "What is your name?"

"My name is Edward, but everyone calls me Eddie," he said, glad that the women didn't seem suspicious at all. "That's my older brother Travis, he's just upset about everything and gets mad easily. With the wind on the road, the other drivers, the cold, he's just been really crabby today."

"It's okay," Doris said.

Just then, Travis came up and bumped his brother away from the ladies' booth and grabbed the laminated menu Eddie was holding.

"I hope my brother isn't bothering you," he said in an arrogant voice.

Doris instantly did not like his attitude but kept her mouth in check.

"No, he isn't bothering us. He was simply being cordial," Doris said with zero emotion but made very direct eye contact. She wasn't one to show weakness when feeling threatened.

"Cordial," Travis repeated as though he was looking for trouble, "is that supposed to mean something?"

"Yes," Doris answered as Jackie and Janet looked back and forth at them as though it was a ping pong match. "It means he's being nice. That simple."

Travis stood there for a minute processing the situation, then said, "Is that your big Dominator Maximus out there?"

Rita jumped right in with too much helpful information, "Oh yes, that's her tank," she said, pointing to Doris. "It's a big thing, isn't it? That's why I call it a tank. She calls it the Black Diamond."

"And I bet it can drive anywhere," Travis said, looking directly at Doris, "even over fields and across creeks and stuff."

Eddie started to become concerned at the direction the conversation was heading, so he grabbed Travis' sleeve and said the coffee was getting cold. But Travis violently yanked his arm free of Eddie's grasp and pushed Eddie back to a counter stool where Eddie obediently sat, knowing he was out-muscled.

"Oh yes," Rita schmoozed to the pair of pants. "It can do anything, I think. Doris' husband had a lot of customizing done on it. I am not sure what else it'll do."

"Is that so?" Travis said with an attitude.

Doris started to see an overly unsavory ending to the exchange they were having, considering how arrogant this young man was being. She decided to do some damage control and invented some instant baloney about the Dominator, hoping her line of bunk would logjam any kind of travel plan Travis might have about borrowing her vehicle.

Doris puffed up her chest and leaned back in the booth, schlepping one arm over the back of the seat and started talking like a Texas cattleman, "Yeah, it's a big thing, alright. It eats up a mess of gas but has military-grade GPS gear, and a tracking classification system hubby installed so he could follow me around. He's a mighty jealous man. If the tracker doesn't sense the co-decahedron card in a given time, the vehicle even shuts down. The doors automatically lock up, and it just coasts to a stop. Nobody in, nobody out. But as you can imagine, it doesn't coast far." Doris sniffed up her nose and continued, "hate to say it, but Hubby is so jealous he even installed a video-cam so he can peek in on me when he wants to make sure I'm not entertaining some young stud, such as yourself. And, you know, I am not sure if it's true, but Hubby said he put a remote option on it that he could either disable it or blow it up with some kind of a gas valve in the fuel tank if he saw me with someone else." Doris continued her high-falutin' tough-talk by wiping her nose on her sleeve. "Yeah, it's an animal, alright." Another nose wipe. "Hubby calls her Exterota, that's Latin for Terrorist Killer."

Travis was quickly digesting all that she had said about her Dominator-Maximus. He wasn't sure if it was all a bunch of bullshit or even if some of it was bullshit. He had thought of taking her vehicle and getting off I-70 and going cross-country but now wasn't sure if he might be a prisoner or a BBQ in it if what she said was true. Travis backed down.

"Well, nice truck. Enjoy," he said, as he walked back to his booth with the menu.

Doris rolled her eyes and sat back in the booth and let out a breath of relief. Janet quietly whispered into Doris' ear, "co-decahedron? Exterota is Latin?? What the hell is that? How do you come up with this ridiculous shit?"

"I don't know. I panicked," Doris whispered back. "I was thinking off the top of my head. It was a gamble. I hope it worked."

Janet just shook her head in amazement at how quick Doris could come up with hogwash and miscellaneous bull.

Agnes easily heard Travis' exchange with the ladies in the nearly empty diner. She didn't like that kind of trouble in her place, and it was still bugging her why the young men parked in the back, especially without winter coats. She began rummaging under the counter as though she were straightening things and worked her way to the back corner of the counter where she kept her gun. She slipped it into her dress pocket under her apron and took off the safety. Something about that boy in the hoodie she simply did not trust.

Eddie got off the counter stool to go back to his booth and tried to be pleasant again with the women, feeling like he had to make amends after Travis' pep-talk with them.

"So, where are you ladies headed on this cold December night?"

Rita jumped right in again. She was always so chatty when she'd had a few. "Oh, we go to Vegas every Christmas so we can gamble and maybe find a husband."

"That is quite a gamble," Eddie went on, "Vegas, eh. Do you often win?

"I do," Rita said, "but they don't usually. They don't listen to what I tell them about the blackjack tables, all they play are slots. But I also 'invest' more money than they do, so maybe that's why I win more."

"Oh, you invest more, eh," Eddie said.

Travis had only sat on the edge of his seat in the booth and was listening to Eddie's chat with Rita. He was intrigued at the ladies' plans. "Hey Eddie, he said loudly, "your coffee's getting cold. I'm sure the ladies have plans."

Eddie looked at Travis and could see Travis still had his bossy older brother look, so Eddie excused himself from the ladies and went back to his booth.

"I wish they would leave," Jackie quietly said to the other girls. "I got a bad feeling when that older boy was talking to us."

"It'll be okay," Doris said. "He's a kid. He sounded like he might want to borrow the Black Diamond, maybe joyride or something. I just wanted to give him some serious things to think about. Forewarned is forearmed, you know. Maybe he took it to heart. I hope what I said stuck. I wasn't interested in not having wheels."

Jackie looked up to see the boys down in the corner, talking quietly. "I still worry," she said.

Travis caught Jackie's glance and knew he was being talked about and said so to Eddie.

"No kidding, I wonder why," Eddie noted with great sarcasm.

Travis ignored him and whispered, "Those old ladies must have plenty of cash if they are going to casinos. You get my drift?"

"No, Travis!" Eddie whispered back. "We don't need the Kansas law on us too."

"Oh hell, who are they going to call now? The local deputy? You think Deputy Duh will be able to catch us? By the time they call someone, and they get here, we'll be in Colorado. Untouchable. Those old ladies must have at least a thousand in cash. And look, there's only one older chick running the diner. We can hit the diner too. One sweep and we're done. I can pay off my debt to Razor and be home free."

"You are freaking crazy, Travis!" Eddie was doing a screaming whisper now. "Let it go! We'll do things by the book. I don't want to go to jail for aiding and abetting. I can't leave you on the side of the highway in a stinkin' hoodie, or you'll die. Otherwise, I'd be thrilled to dump you in a ditch! Let's just have coffee and a sandwich and move on."

Travis gulped the rest of his coffee then adjusted his hoodie. Eddie was headed into panic mode. Travis slipped out of the booth and stood, but proceeded to the men's room. Agnes took the opportunity to get Eddie's order and maybe pick his brain a bit.

"Decide what you want yet?" Agnes asked.

"Um, just a burger and fries," Eddie said, still fumbling from the exchange with his brother.

"Your brother is a pain?" Agnes asked.

"I'm afraid so," Eddie said and looked tired.

"It'll be ok, son," Agnes said. "He has a few lessons to learn yet before he grows up, and he might learn them soon. I'll get your order going. Just stay put I'll catch up with your brother when he comes out of the john." Agnes cocked one eyebrow and gave Eddie a knowing look.

The women were all getting up and putting coats on when Travis came around the corner of the hall to the men's room and saw the ladies putting coats on getting ready to leave.

"Whoa, whoa, whoa," he shouted and started taking large quick paces. "Where do you think you are all going on this cold winter night?" And he rushed over to Jackie and grabbed the back collar of her coat and yanked it rudely down off her arms and threw it on the next booth. Jackie was horrified and scared.

"Just sit back down," he shoved Jackie. Janet and Doris were exchanging looks. Janet's was a look of concern, but Doris was pissed.

"Does your mother know where you are?" Doris snipped at him, and Travis shoved her hard back into the booth. She fell clumsily backward onto the seat, catching herself with her arm on the table.

Eddie started to get out of his booth to get involved, but he noticed Agnes looking at him slowly shaking her head "no", and gave him such a hot pissed look that Eddie sat right back in his seat, cupped his mug with his hands, and stared at his coffee afraid to look up.

"So you are all headed to Vegas, eh? So you got some cash. Get it out of your purses and put it on the table, you got that?" Travis demanded as he indicated to the women to look at his sweatshirt pocket, where he was sticking an obvious weapon into the pocket fabric at them. The four women just looked at him. "Move!" Travis ordered them like something he had seen out of a TV crime show.

The girls slowly got their purses and began to carefully dig through them, glancing up at Travis now and then. Rita thought she could distract him. "Oh my, what was your name? Travis? I do not like you very much acting like this," she said as she dug through her purse.

"Shut up," Travis demanded.

"Rita," Doris said, "knock it off before you make it worse. This guy doesn't care what we think about him. Don't you get that?"

By now, Jackie was in tears and sniffling. "What are you crying about, Jackie?" Janet asked.

"I'm so sorry, Mr. Robber," Jackie said sincerely to Travis, which made Travis wince. He'd never been referred to as a criminal. Jackie sniffled on, "but I don't have any cash, really. I was going to use my credit cards when we got there." Janet was looking incredulously at Jackie that she'd mention her credit cards.

"What's the matter with you?" Janet asked as she laid some cash on the table. Jackie pointed to the weapon sticking through the fabric of Travis' hoodie pocket. "He's going to shoot me because I don't have cash, and I saw his face."

Travis rolled his eyes a bit, "I just want your cash. Give me your cash, and there won't be any trouble," he demanded.

Rita put all kinds of hundred dollar bills on the table and dug out a pen to put her phone number on one of the bills.

Travis went crazy, "What are you doing!" he screamed. "Marking the money??"

Rita was matter-of-fact in her booze-stupor. "No, I'm giving you my phone number. Tell your brother to call me when you're in jail. He's older than twenty-one, isn't he?"

"WHAT??" Travis was confused. "I'm taking your money, this isn't speed dating!!"

"Well, your brother is polite and good-looking, I just thought maybe he might want to hook up with an experienced woman. If he's over 21, he can ride with me to Vegas. I can teach him to gamble and win money, not have to steal it. And I can teach him to be a man, not a jerk like his brother," Rita instructed.

Doris about flipped when she heard that last part and expected Rita to be shot on sight, but the comment really flustered Travis, and Doris was beginning to see that this guy probably hadn't done this before. Doris was just about to stand up to the guy when they all heard what sounded like a sub-human growl that stopped them all in their tracks.

"Was that a yeti?" Rita barely whispered as she turned to look out the window.

Then the ladies saw Travis freeze when he felt the barrel of a gun jammed hard in his right kidney, causing him to wince in pain. It was Agnes. She shoved her gun in Travis' back a little more and in a deep snarling voice said, "Look, Punk, we are going to walk back to your seat, and you are going to sit down in your booth and one dumb move, and I'll shoot out your kidney so you can experience a good hour of excruciating pain waiting for an ambulance and a thirty-minute bumpy-as-hell, back-road ride to a clinic where there may or may not be a doctor on staff. March!" Travis just stood there, thinking if he should retaliate somehow when he heard the pistol being cocked, and Agnes shoved it a bit farther into his side. Travis was pretty sure he'd been out-muscled or at least didn't want to gamble that Agnes wouldn't do what she said.

The ladies all stood there stunned as Agnes marched Travis back to his booth then shoved him in it just as he had shoved Doris. Agnes demanded Travis hand over his weapon as she aimed the barrel of her weapon at the very personal private space between Travis' legs. He didn't hesitate and sheepishly pulled a coffee spoon out of his pocket. Eddie sat there dumbfounded, and when he gathered his wits, he said, "You asshole." Then he looked at Agnes to see what she would do next.

Agnes clicked the safety and pocketed her gun under her apron. Then as though nothing happened, went behind the counter, picked up the coffee carafe, and asked if anyone wanted more coffee. She walked over to the ladies' booth and poured some coffee and told them they should sit and relax for a few minutes before hitting the road again. All four nodded their heads in agreement. Agnes asked if they wanted to press charges, but explained they'd have to stay there for at least another hour for a sheriff or deputy to arrive, and another hour to file reports. All four discussed it for about ten seconds deciding not to make a report and started gathering their money to put back in their purses. Janet said, "I guess no harm done, just a little rattled."

"I'll take care of him," Agnes said, nodding her head in the direction of Travis and Eddie. "Just another punk. There have been a few robbery attempts here because we are kind of desolate, so I've learned to handle most of it."

Agnes strolled back to the counter and stabbed the coffee carafe back into the machine and wiped her hands, glaring at Travis. Eddie was still staring into his coffee cup as though it melted parts of his head. Travis was slouched in the booth and staring out the window at the increasing snow that was now lightly covering the ground.

Agnes busied herself, making another pot of coffee, then brought a little plate of home-made chocolate chip cookies to the ladies. "On the house, ladies. Thank you for not making a scene, and I'm so sorry this happened while you were here."

"No harm done," Janet said, selecting a cookie.

"Yeah, we're just a bit rattled and maybe a bit wiser about not blabbing about our plans out loud," Doris said as she stared hard at Rita then took a cookie. Jackie was already taking tiny bites of one. Rita just sat looking at the girls enjoying their sugary treats disgusted that they didn't care about slapping that cookie fat on their thighs.

"I'm going to have a chat with that young man before he leaves," Agnes said. "My dad was a marine in WWII, and for some of that time, he was a drill Sargent, a lot of that rubbed off on me growing up. I will make a point with him."

"He probably needs it," Doris scowled in Travis' direction.

"I'll wait until you are out of here, so he doesn't have an audience," Agnes said.

"Or witnesses," Doris said.

"Enjoy your trip, ladies," Agnes said. "Hope the rest of it is fun and enjoyable."

"Oh, well, I knew this was going to be our lucky trip, old lucky seven! We'll have a great story to tell, one way or the other!" Rita commented as she dribbled a little more liquid from her purse flask into her mug as Doris, Janet, and Jackie watched.

Rita looked at the three gals looking at her flask and said, 'Want some now?" and all three held their mugs out to her.

Chapter 27

Agnes Knows the Drill

As the women left, all chatting about heading onward to find a place to spend the night and talking about their frightening experience, Agnes saw Travis starting to get up out of the booth. Agnes immediately took her drill sergeant stance and lowered her voice to mean business. She shot out her right arm, and using her middle finger with her palm facing the floor, stabbed it in Travis' direction and growled, "YOU SIT. I'm not done with YOU!"

Travis knew he could 'take' her, but he knew she still had that gun in her pocket, and something about her had Travis thinking he should not mess around with this Kansas born, corn-fed, beef-raised, middle-aged, and armed, waitress-woman. And maybe she was even an ex-marine. He slumped back in his seat.

Agnes stood in front of the coffee machine with her hands on her hips, listening to it drip and watching Travis behind her in the stainless steel reflection. When the coffee was done, Agnes grabbed the carafe and headed to Eddie and Travis' booth. She poured fresh coffee into Travis' empty mug and added to Eddie's. Then she parked the carafe on the next table and put her hands on her hips to address Travis.

"Look, you punk-ass," Travis was taken aback by her sudden vaulting of demeanor from warm and friendly Coffee-Pouring Lady to scathing Iron-Handed Warden. "Never come into my place and pull crap like that again," Agnes growled like a rabid pitbull, "because next time, you'll want a goddam ambulance." Then she added in heavy staccato, "Do. You. Get. My. Drift?" Then used that middle finger again in a cutting motion across her throat. Travis sat there, stunned and speechless.

Agnes wasn't done yet. "You think you are such a bad-ass? Well, pal, I will send the word out to the truckers that you tried to hold-up my place. They'll hunt you down on the road and drag you out of that truck and make you wish you were never born. Then leave you hours from civilization. You think you are so tough. Follow?"

Travis was momentarily looking dazed and nodded that he understood. Eddie was visibly shaken but still wanted to stand up for his idiot brother. "I know he's sorry, ma'am. He just doesn't think ahead. Fact is, he's scared of a gang in East St Louis..."

Travis interrupted, "shut up, Eddie."

But Eddie kept going, "....and he needs to fix the mess because they threatened to mess up our mother."

Agnes squinted at Eddie, "so he thinks robbing a diner would solve that?"

Eddie thought about how stupid it all seemed now and said to Travis, "She's right, a robbery would only add to the mess you are in, and now you are taking me down with you."

"And Mr. Big Huge Brain," Agnes asked Travis with much contempt, "how did you think robbing this diner would solve your problems with a gang in East St. Louis?"

Travis, without looking up from his coffee mug, explained to Agnes how he promised them drugs and money if they'd stop beating him up and let him go. They gave him five days to bring it to them. "So," Agnes asked, "why don't you have a job and work for your money? You aren't any better than them."

Travis realized she was right, but he took offense, saying, "I can't earn that much in five days. Besides, they took my wallet and ID as collateral. I can't get a job without it."

Agnes confronted him, "Oh, that's bullshit. You can get a....."

Eddie interrupted them both. "So, he took our grandma's social security money this morning."

"You what?" Agnes was stunned as she looked at Travis. "You, Shit!"

That made Travis fume, and he gave Eddie such a cold look for tattling that it should have iced up his mug of coffee.

"Oh, wait, wait...." Agnes said, as she was thinking, "I get it....you were going to rob me and those ladies, for cash to pay for pot in Colorado so you'd have the drugs and money to give to a gang? How close am I?"

"Nailed it," Eddie said sheepishly.

"You are digging yourself a much deeper hole than you'll ever get out of. Why didn't you report this beating to the police?" she asked.

"The cops there don't care, and the gang would hunt me down and make it worse," Travis said, looking at the table and picking at the edge with his nervous fingers.

"Our dad is a cop in St. Louis, and Travis didn't want our dad to know he was in trouble, it'd look bad for our dad," Eddie volunteered. Travis made another angry face at Eddie for sharing too much.

"Look," Agnes instructed, "the first place to put your trust is in your father. Tell him. He can work out the details and make sure this gang doesn't hunt down your mother. Cops can work things out with other towns. Sure he won't be thrilled that you were in a bad place, but not half as un-thrilled if you are in jail for armed robbery....or should I say attempted spoon-robbery." Agnes' comment made them both crack a smile. "Now....you both promise me you are going to tell your dad right away and head back home." Both nodded their heads reluctantly. "I'm not letting you off the hook that easy, Mr. Big Huge Brain." Travis looked up at her with concern.

"See the heavy flurries out there? Well, the wind is blowing them into my parking lot. You will go out there and sweep it from all the parking spots up here by the diner and make sure it's cleared from the sidewalk and doorway. Then you'll salt it. After that, you'll be delighted to mop the diner floor. Then you are free to go. If you leave before that, I'll call the sheriff and radio out to the truckers. Your choice."

Travis was about to mouth her back, but Eddie kicked him under the table and said to Agnes, "Travis thanks you for your leniency."

Travis scowled. A lot.

"Don't make a big deal out of it, young man. I don't expect free labor. I'll pay you if you do a decent job. The better the job, the better I pay. There's a stiff broom out back, and I have an old coat and some work gloves by the back door. You can wear that. By the way, wearing just a hoodie and a jacket in weather like this was a dead giveaway that you were running."

"What about a coat for me?" Eddie interrupted.

"You don't need a coat. Your job is going to be as a supervisor and make sure your brother is on task. You will sit and drink coffee and let me know if he runs off, although, on a night like this, he'd be good for about forty-five minutes before he'd freeze to death. From my diner, on foot, there's isn't even a house within an hour's walk. Make sure you keep your keys so he can't take your truck."

"Not a problem," Eddie said, a little delighted to see someone teach Travis a lesson.

Agnes pointed Travis to the back of the kitchen.

Travis took a deep breath and moved out of the booth, slowly shuffling to the kitchen as though he were going to the gallows. Agnes and Eddie watched him.

"Tough gig," Agnes nodded at Eddie, "tough gig."

It didn't take Travis even twenty minutes to do the useless chores Agnes gave him. There was barely any snow, even though it was beginning to get heavier. In another hour, there would be twice the shoveling. Agnes knew it was just busywork to make her point.

Travis swept the lot and quickly mopped the diner floor. When he was done, the boys got their burgers and fries, and Agnes paid Travis for the chores minus the cost of their meal. They were soon jumping in the truck and on their way. Eddie started to turn East on the interstate to head home, but Travis told him to go West.

"But we promised the lady at the diner we'd go home," Eddie said.

"Yeah, and we promised we'd tell dad about all this, but he'll kill me when he knows the whole story. He'll probably put me in cuffs himself. So back to the original plan. On to Colorado."

"This is a very bad idea, Travis," Eddie said.

"I don't care what you think, Eddie," Travis said, "now let's get going. We need to get this over with ASAP, so get back on the road and step on it. We have to make up some lost time."

And they went West onto the interstate, into the snow and darkness. Agnes saw their headlights turn onto the Westbound ramp and that they didn't take her advice, she shook her head and muttered to herself, "those boys are headed for trouble," and finished clearing their booth.

She checked the weather radio again, and news of heavier snow than they originally forecasted was coming, but they weren't sure where the main load of snow would hit because of wild and variable winds. It didn't seem severely critical to Agnes, yet. Still, she took the empty diner time to take a cat nap until the next patrons came. Sensing weird weather approaching, she knew it could be a long night at the diner.

Chapter 28

The Warning!

Before Agnes of Agnes' Midnight Truck Stop Diner headed for the recliner in her office, she needed to check the diner door to make sure the dangling bells would clip the top of the door when anyone came in. She could hear those bells dingle even in her sleep. She grabbed a fork out of the silverware rack and walked over to the door and made sure it was shut good so it wouldn't accidentally blow open, then used the fork to poke the bells. The bells dingled their little song for her.

She looked out the door window to make sure her neon "open" sign was on and blinking, and that no one was lurking in her parking lot. She noticed the snowflakes had gotten quite large very quickly, and it was coming down nearly sideways in the wind. The sidewalk was covered already and it hadn't been a half-hour since that Travis kid swept it.

She couldn't see the interstate from her diner but could see headlights using the on and off-ramps about a half-mile away. She didn't make out any approaching vehicles, so headed for her office for a few minutes of quiet.

Shortly after she sat in her recliner, but before she got comfortable with her lap quilt, the weather radio jumped to attention, buzzing its alarm. Agnes folded down the footrest and got up to shut the alarm so she could hear the message. It seemed to take forever for the announcement to unfold, but there it was, the warning she dreaded hearing, the warning of hell coming. BLIZZARD. Agnes listened to the report. It was for a wide area from Colorado to Nebraska, down to the middle of Southern Kansas. Heavy snows expected, twelve to fifteen inches, high winds, cold temperatures, totally whiteout conditions, remain in your homes if you don't have to go out.

"The Siberian Express," Agnes said in an uneasy whisper. "It's coming." Agnes turned down the radio thinking about the people that had been in and out of her diner tonight. They were now headed into a whiteout that could be deadly in so many ways. She stopped for a minute and said a prayer for them all.

Agnes knew what she had to do, as she usually did in emergency situations. She hustled to an old storage closet and dug out a dusty box that contained a bunch of old radio gear and pulled out a CB radio along with some wires and a microphone and assembled them on her desk. Her father had antennas installed years before cellular phones came into use and they had come in handy for a few emergencies, like a wildfire from some idiot tossing a cigarette butt out his car window, tornado warnings, and a few wrecks on the interstate where she was able to relay information to the sheriff's department from the truckers. Agnes wrangled the antenna jack and power wire from behind the desk and plugged them into her CB. The second she turned on the radio, she heard the familiar static of a badly tuned station. She fiddled with the knobs and tuned into Channel 19, typically the road channel. For now, there was no chatter. Maybe the drivers got smart and got off the road.

Agnes settled back into her recliner, one ear listening to the weather radio, the other listening to the CB, and a third ear listening for the dingling door bells. She adjusted the quilt on her legs once more then shut her eyes for a well-deserved snooze. If there is a blizzard coming, it would be a long night at the diner.

Chapter 29

Family Matters

Jeff was noticing the increasing amount of snow, and it was starting to stick on the sides of the roads. Although concerned since he knew he had quite a bit more driving ahead of him, he feigned delight at maybe having a white Christmas. "I'm dreamin' of a White Christmas," he began to sing his best Bing Crosby impersonation, "...just like the ones I used to know..." and he reached his hand over to touch his wife's hand and smiled when she looked at him. She knew Jeff loved Christmas and a white Christmas would be icing on the cake. "Hey kids, we could be in for a white Christmas if this snow keeps up!" Jeff was animated in his comments while hiding his concerns.

Nick sat up and looked out the window. "Wow!" he said, as only a nine-year-old boy could when confronted with the idea of a big snow.

"Yeah," Jeff teased, "we could be snowed in at Grandpa's farm for a week or more!"

"I'd rather be dead," Christie said.

"I hope someone will arrange that," Nick shot back.

"KIDS...knock it off," Carol told them. "It's Christmas, be nice."

Christie was curious enough to sit up a bit to peer out the window at the fat white flakes collecting on the windows on her side of the van. Nick was looking out his window too, but excited about playing in the snow. Carol was looking out her window and starting to worry about the driving, and Jeff was looking out the windshield noticing how the snow was coming sideways and starting to stick to the road and stack up on the van hood. His concern kept growing, but he hid it.

"Let it snow, let it snow, let it snow...." Nick sang quietly, knowing it would irk his sister.

"Shut up," Christie whispered at him. "We'll be stuck out on the farm if it snows too much.

"No we won't," Nick planned. "Grandpa has that old sleigh, we can hook it up to his tractor, and we can go anywhere."

"You idiot," Christie said. "You can't hardly see anything out there. The wind and cold will kill you when you can't find your way back to the house."

"Just because you live with that cell phone in your face, doesn't mean we all do. I know how to use a real compass. We learned it in scouts." Nick stuck his tongue out at Christie and she copied it back to him.

"Well, you are a jerk," Christie sneered.

"Yeah? So that makes you a pig," Nick volleyed back.

"Oh, and you smell like a pig," Christie fired back.

"Well, you smell like dog sh....," and Nick caught himself before it slipped, but Jeff and Carol knew where it was headed.

"Alright!" Jeff shouted. "Not another word! The road is getting slick, and I don't need any distractions from the back seat. Just shut it up!" Jeff was angry now and the kids knew it. It took a lot to get him fired up like this. They both sat in their corners, trying to look out their windows where the snow was beginning to collect.

After a few silent minutes, Nick asked, "Dad? Are we going to be able to get there tonight, or will we have to stop somewhere?"

"Don't worry, Nick. I've been driving out in Kansas boonies most of my life and have a lot of experience driving in crazy weather." He winked at Nick in the rearview but gave Carol a concerned glance. "I have to be cautious and slow down a little and pay attention to the gusting wind, but we'll be just fine. And if we have a total white-out, we can pull off the road and wait a bit. The white-outs don't last long. They put the plows out on the interstate first too, so we'll be just fine. Just fine."

Even though Jeff talked positive, he was getting worried. Driving alone in bad weather in his youth was very different than driving with his family. He was thankful that the roads were pretty straight with very few hills to navigate.

"You look concerned, honey," Carol said quietly to Jeff.

"Do you know about the Siberian Express?" he whispered back.

Carol slowly shook her head and made a very worried face. "No. What is it?"

Jeff didn't want to answer, all he could say was, "It's bad. Very bad." Then sucked in a big breath of air and steeled his grip on the wheel. Carol looked at him with her expression asking for more information.

Jeff explained, "I think this is one of them. I think this is going to turn into a Siberian Express. That is the worst kind of snowstorm because it comes with violent winds that bring with it sub-freezing temperatures and mountains of snow. I'm going to need to get out of the car and put something in front of the radiator before the temperature dives. A piece of cardboard, plastic, something."

"What? Now you want to get out of the car?" Carol asked.

"Yes. The radiator won't heat up the water enough when the temperature plunge sets in, and it's going to get colder, fast. Our antifreeze isn't designed for this kind of cold, not to mention the wind chill factor. If the water starts to cool, it'll affect our heat in the van. We need to make sure we can keep warm in case we have to pull over for awhile," Jeff said.

"I wish now we'd have stopped at that last truck stop we saw about a half-hour ago. At least we could have asked about the weather in these parts," Carol said.

"It wouldn't have mattered. They never really know, Carol. The reason it is so dangerous is that it comes fast and usually no warning. Growing up, we had winds up to sixty miles an hour, and temperatures got down to fifteen, twenty below in a hurry. Wind chills were sometimes thirty or forty below. We bundled up and had to get the animals in the barn, or they'd freeze to death in a short time. It's nothing to fool around with." Jeff noticed in his rearview that the kids were hanging onto his every word.

"Were you kids listening?" he asked.

"Yeah, Dad," Nick said. "This is going to be so cool!"

Jeff cautioned the family. "We need to be very alert and cautious. Roads can turn to ice in a hurry as salt doesn't melt the ice at the very low temperatures, and there are always snowdrifts to worry about. I think we can make it to the exit of the state road where we have to get off. There is a small gas station there. They will probably have a landline where I can call Grandma and tell her we'll probably be a little late."

"Oh, I know your mother, Jeff. She's no ninny. If she sees this weather, she'll know we'll be late."

"Yeah, but I don't want her to worry, she's got enough with Dad," Jeff said. "Just another hour or so, and we can get off the highway and call. Maybe the side roads aren't bad as the wind is blowing from the north, and it won't pile snow on the state road too much as it runs north and south. We'll just have to figure it out when we get there. For now, I want to find a place to pull off so I can shove a piece of cardboard in front of the radiator."

"You can have my comic book," Nick offered.

"That's stupid," Christie said.

"I need something a bit sturdier and a little bigger," Jeff explained.

Nick unbuckled his seat belt and crawled into the back of the van and rummaged through the suitcases and Christmas gifts.

"Nothing much back here, Dad," Nick said.

"Isn't there a box we can cut up?" Jeff asked Nick.

"Nope. Unless you want to unwrap some presents. I think this is a shirt box for Grandpa." Nick held up a wrapped gift and shook it. "Would that do?" Nick asked.

"There's nothing else back there?" Jeff asked in dismay.

"I don't see anything. Mom has everything stuffed in canvas bags."

Carol looked at Jeff with a sheepish look, "so I try to recycle and save trees."

"I spy something gray and plastic," Christie taunted. And all the attention turned to her.

"What is it, Christie? This is no time for screwing around," Jeff told her.

"Well," and she folded herself over and reached down to the floor and picked up a floor mat and held it up, "how about this?" she announced.

"That could work, I think," Jeff said. "I have to find a place to pull over, so we don't get whacked from behind by another car."

Christie smirked at Nick. Nick sneered back as he climbed back into his seat.

Jeff began to slow a little and turned on his hazard lights as he tried to see where the shoulder would be solid enough to pull off. Carol was leaning between the seats looking out the back window to see if she could see any oncoming headlights.

"Jeez Jeff," Carol said, "I can't see anything back there. It's like off the end of the earth."

"We'll be okay, this won't take me a minute," Jeff said. "Carol, I need you to slide over to the driver's seat and be ready to go if something happens if this goes sideways."

Carol made an anxious frown. "This better not go sideways," she ordered.

"Hey, if I get hit by a passing bus, just put it in gear and keep going. You and the kids need to be safe and get out of here A.S.A.P. You don't want to be stranded out in a snowstorm like this."

"You are making me worry, Jeff," Carol said, and Jeff could see she was getting distressed.

"Piece of cake," he said to reassure her and himself as well. "Here we go, here's a place to pull off. Christie, get ready to hand me that mat, Carol, get ready to slide over. When I put it in park, I'll pop the hood. Then I'm going to jump out and shut the door as fast as I can, I don't want the wind to catch the door and spring the hinge. Then I'll open the hood and slip the mat in behind the grille, shut the hood, then Carol, make sure you can open the door for me from the inside in case the door handle is frozen stuck on the outside. I'm going to be very cold because I don't have winter gear to wear and can't use gloves to open the hood. So watch for me. Everybody ready to do their job?"

"Yes," Carol said.

"Yes," Christie said.

"Hey, I didn't get a job," Nick griped.

"We'll give you one later, Nick," Jeff said as he clicked off the radio and released the hood latch. "Christie, get ready to hand me that mat when I open the door."

Jeff pushed his door open into the wind and snow and slid out, then reached in for the mat that Christie slapped over the seat into his hand. Jeff grabbed the mat and pushed the door closed with his butt, and it clicked shut behind him. He was face-first into the force of the blinding snowstorm and pushed himself through to the front of the van. Carol scooted over to the driver's seat and could barely see Jeff until he stepped in front of the headlights. He quickly released the hood latch and fought with the mat against the wind when a huge gust blew up and snatched the mat out of Jeff's cold fingers, and it blew across the interstate so quickly that in seconds it was out of sight.

Everyone in the car groaned like the gallery at a golf tournament for a missed putt. "Ohhhhhh."

Jeff fought his way back to the car door, holding his coat around his neck. He cracked the door open.

"NICK!" He shouted with the wind and snow blowing everywhere into the van, "Is there another mat on your side?"

"Yeah, DAD!" Nick screamed.

"Get me the mat, and hurry!" Nick was on it before Jeff finished his sentence. Nick had a lot of his comic books on the mat but was able to wrangle the mat quickly and flipped it over the seat to Jeff's cold waiting hand.

"Two hands!" Carol yelled to Jeff over the noise of the wind.

"I got it," Jeff shouted back, then closed the door. Carol watched Jeff fighting the wind and trying to hang onto the mat. She couldn't see him when he stepped in front of the van as the hood was open. She heard the engine sputter a bit, so she goosed the accelerator. This was not a good time for the engine to be taking a vacation.

"Where is Dad?" Christie asked as she leaned up between the front seats. "What's taking him so long?"

"I don't know, Christie," Carol answered as she kept one eye on the hood and the other on the rearview looking for approaching headlights.

Carol tried to see what was taking Jeff so long. Trying to peek through the small space between the hood and the car, she couldn't see much over the snowpack that slid down off the hood. Then she glanced into the rearview again. "Oh my God. I see a car coming in the distance. Come ON, Jeff!" Carol was ready to scream or get out of the car and drag Jeff back. So many unpleasant scenarios raced through her head as she looked into the rearview at the approaching headlights shrouded by the blowing snow.

Then she heard a huge bang, then BAM, BAM, BAM on the door window, causing her to jump from the sudden fright. It was Jeff. The door latch had frozen. She pulled the door handle latch, but it was difficult to open. Jeff was right. It had frozen that quickly. The two fought the wind to finally get the door open, and Jeff slid into the seat at the same time Carol scooted back to her side.

"Car coming!" Carol shouted, pointing out the back window. Christie and Nick were also staring out the back.

"Come on, Dad!" Nick was nearly screaming. "Let's go!"

"I see it," Jeff said as he started the Minivan moving forward, but so slow. He knew if he stayed on the shoulder that the oncoming car might think he was on the pavement and come up behind him hitting the shoulder, then fishtailing, causing a wreck. So Jeff was trying to speed up slowly, leaving his hazard lights on, and turning his van slowly onto the road of I-70. He also knew by the time anyone saw his emergency flashers and tail-lights through the heavy blowing snow, that they would be too close to stop. Now his back tires were spinning a bit as their weight packed the snow, so he shifted into low and let the Minivan crawl onto the interstate. He finally got moving so he could accelerate a bit before looking back in the rearview to see the oncoming vehicle. It was scary seeing it approaching. Jeff had his Minivan up and moving, but the headlights behind them were still gaining.

"We're going to get killed!" Nick said with excitement that only a kid could imagine as a thrill.

"Stop it, Nick," Carol ordered. "And get that seatbelt on, young man, now!"

Jeff had the Minivan moving about forty-five now, and the headlights behind them were still coming up but not as fast, and it appeared the vehicle was changing lanes to pass them. It appeared to be in a hurry.

As the vehicle finally began to pass, everyone breathed a sigh of relief.

Nick saw it was a large pickup truck with tandem back wheels, and he could see someone riding shotgun wearing a hoodie. As Nick was staring, the guy in the truck turned in Nick's direction and stared back. Nick put up his hand for a tentative wave, but the man in the hoodie turned away as the truck passed, stirring up a lot of snow in its wind drag.

"Too bad we don't have a big truck like that," Nick said. "I bet he's got four-wheel drive, and with those big tires, I bet it'd never slip."

"That's not always the case, son," Jeff explained, "when it's icy, it won't matter what he's got. The guy is really going way too fast. There's no point in blazing a trail in this kind of weather. It's not that the truck can't deal with the snow, it's that the driver can't see what is up ahead." Nick sat back and watched the tail lights of the dually quickly disappear into the blowing curtains of snow.

"What was taking you so long under the hood?" Carol asked Jeff when she finally caught her breath. "You said it would only take a minute."

"Damn cold wind, Carol. The warm mat bent in the wind, then chilled so fast it froze with a curl in it. I had to try to unbend it so it'd fit down into the space in front of the radiator. I was fighting the wind and the frozen mat until my fingers were getting numb. I ended up breaking off a corner of the mat. It's not ideal, but it'll do for now. See, the air from the heater is warmer already."

"Thank God," Carol breathed, "I'll be glad when we get to your folks."

Jeff took a long breath too. His hands were so cold they hurt, but he didn't dare take a hand off the steering wheel to warm them up.

Chapter 30

The Cockroach and The Butcher

"Hey Breaker one-nine," Chuck said into his mike, "this is the Cockroach out in the white stuff. Santa Claus, Ten Point, you got your ears on?" And Chuck waited for a reply.

A faint reply finally came in, "Hey Roachman, naw, me and Ten Point pulled over at a rest-stop. Gonna snooze and let the snow do its thing. Will go again at daylight. Olive Pit coming in now to park. You get off the road, Cockroach. It's not gonna be a good night for sledding in an eighteen-wheeler."

"You got that right," Chuck responded. "I'll be looking for a place in a short. It's getting bad, not many on the road. Gonna try to go a little more before they close the damn freeway. I still got some visibility."

The response Chuck heard came in breaking up, "Hey Cockroach, losing you.....(undiscernible).....back this way.....(garbled talk).....," then Chuck heard nothing but static.

Chuck spoke again, "Roger, Santa Clause, this is Cockroach, out."

Chuck put the mike down and concentrated on driving. The wind was shoving his trailer so hard that keeping the truck in one lane was tricky, but Chuck had plenty of experience. He was growing concerned about the snow starting to stick to the interstate. If it became too slick, the wind could catch his trailer squarely and slide it right off the road dragging his cab with it. Chuck slowed his speed, the weight of his rig kept a firm grip on the road so far.

Just as Chuck had implemented all his snow driving techniques and settled back to focus on the road, his CB jumped to life, "Hey Mr. Cockroach, calling Mr. Cockroach, dis here is Mr. Butcher Buchbinder calling you."

Chuck smiled and remembered the butcher and his wife and picked up his mike. "Hey, Mr. Butcher. This is Cockroach. I can hear you. Come back."

After a few seconds of fumbling with the mike, Auggie's voice came in on Chuck's CB. "Oh, Mr. Cockroach, I don't think I can come back. Looks like ve may get stuck out here. Dis is terrible snowings. Like lake snow ve get in Chicago. Snow is covering everyting. Wind is terrible too."

All the while, Chuck could hear Wilhelmine griping in German and English in the background. "You are crazy oldt man! Chicago? We don't come from Chicago. We come from Cleveland!"

Auggie still had the button down on the mike, and Chuck could hear them squabbling. Auggie was argued back to Wilhelmine. "Nobody heard of Cleveland, Mina. Everybody knows Chicago. Lake snows in both places. Shaddap."

Chuck was waiting on Auggie to let up on the microphone button when Auggie remembered what he wanted to know.

"Mr. Cockroach, do you know a nice place we can park? Dis snow is getting bad."

Chuck became concerned. He wasn't sure if the old Towncar was ahead of him or behind him now, and he wasn't really sure if there was a rest area anywhere close. He doubted they could even see a mile marker, so there was no point asking them to try to find one. All he could think of was to get the old people off the interstate and to a safe place.

"Mr. Butcher, can you tell me where you are?" Chuck spoke into the mike.

"Ya. Ve are on de interstate seventy," Auggie said.

"Okay. That is good. Do you know what the last exit you saw was?" Chuck asked, trying to get a fix on where they were.

There was no answer for a minute.

Then Chuck heard Auggie again, "I haff to show Mina to hold mike button down when I talk. I can't hold steering vheel and mike. Mina, take finger off button now."

Chuck considered that Auggie was at least trying to drive safely. "Mr. Butcher, do you remember the last exit you passed?" Chuck asked again.

"Nah. Ve don't remember, too much snow to see anyway. Let up button, Mina," Auggie said over the air.

Chuck answered back, "I don't know where there is a safe place to pull over, Mr. Butcher. If it gets too bad to see, pull over under an overpass and try to wait it out. Stay in your vehicle. If you have plenty of gas, keep your engine running until help comes. Leave your hazard lights on, so other vehicles and the plows can see you. I'm going to worry about you."

"Ach du Lieber! Ve don't vant anyone to vorry over us. Ve vill get off at next exit or hide under overpass. Augustus Heinrich Buchbinder the Second does not vant to make people vorry. Mina let go of button now."

"Okay, Mr. Butcher," Chuck answered. "If you run into trouble, try to call me back. Okay?"

"Okay, Mr. Cockroach. Over and out." Auggie smiled as he remembered ending radio messages with "over and out" back in WWII. "Let go of button, Mina."

Chuck was beginning to realize he hadn't seen an exit in a while. He'd seen a number of overpasses, though. Still, he was worried about someone plowing into the old couple or worse, them being hit by a snowplow. He knew he'd have to keep an eye out for that old Towncar. He especially didn't want to plow into them with his rig if they didn't get their big vehicle far enough off the shoulder.

Chapter 31

Matthew's Prayer Answered

Matthew was getting cold as his Minibus fought the wind and increasing snow. His heater just couldn't keep up with the cold. He'd even done as Agnes from the Midnight Truck Stop Diner had told him and put an old sweatshirt over his head tying the arms around his neck, even though he felt ridiculous. His legs and feet were the coldest as cold air leaked in around the clutch pedal. He did put a sweater over his lap, but he couldn't have sweater sleeves hanging over his feet while trying to use the clutch.

"Please, Dear Lord, let there be another truck stop soon so I can warm up," he prayed aloud.

He was thinking about his situation and hoped it wasn't his penance for leaving his posts at the past two churches. He finally felt relief when he saw a sign that a rest area was a few miles up ahead. He was trying to decide to stop and use their pit toilet in the freezing cold to unload his coffee, or simply "re-fill" his empty coffee cup while in the bus. He considered that his bladder might hold more than the cup, so he decided to stop and deal with the pit toilet.

As he pulled into the rest area, he saw a number of trucks parked in the darkness, all running their diesels, so he figured it would be no problem leaving his bus running too. He shifted his bus into neutral and set the parking brake then scrambled out from under his sweater to run to the pit toilet about 25 yards away. It was exceptionally windy and cold as he dashed along in almost total darkness, being lit by only one snow-covered streetlight in front of the little latrine building. He was shivering as he stood over the pit and was not succeeding at his personal task for as badly as he needed to pee, especially with his hands so cold and a freezing breeze now wafting into his pants. Finally, with plenty of concentration, he was able to relieve himself of the two coffees.

"Ahhh, whew. Thank you, Jesus," Matthew said, chuckling at his own little joke. He considered washing his hands but saw the faucet was only one handle, meaning cold water. His hands were so cold now he decided to forego "cleanliness being close to Godliness" for today.

He bundled up his hands into his jacket sleeves and ran back to his bus. It was still running. "Thank you, God," he gratefully shouted up to the sky.

Just as he was climbing into the Minibus, the wind grabbed the door from his cold hands and flung it wide open, letting the wind blow the snow inside with a flurry of fat snowflakes. Matthew fought with the door against the wind, and finally got himself in and pulled the door shut. It seemed like now there was no heat at all. He sat there revving the engine hoping to get a little warm air out of the vents while he bundled up again, tightening the sweatshirt sleeves around his neck and spreading the sweater out on the seat, sitting in the middle and pulling the sleeves up around his lap. He kept revving the engine over and over, hoping the little heat coming out of the small vents would help warm the Minibus a little. He caught himself revving the heck out of it, so he took his foot off the pedal and prayed for patience ....and some warmth.

He'd just said "Amen," and was about to get moving again when there was a startling loud pounding on his window. He jerked when he saw a frightening, very large, old man, wearing a disturbing hat with fuzzy ear flaps that Matthew had only seen in the movies. Matthew stared for a moment stumbling in his head for a prayer of help. The man was not smiling, and Matthew realized the giant old man, even though considerably older, could easily yank open his door and drag him out of his bus, and beat him as flat as a communion wafer in a split-second. He wished he'd have locked his door.

The old man knocked again and rolled a finger in a circle indicating to Matthew to roll down his window. Matthew obliged as he felt he had no choice but to comply.

"Hey, Reverend, did you enjoy your pie?" the old guy said with a gravelly voice.

It took only a second as Matthew remembered this man as the trucker with the white beard at Agnes' Midnight Truck Stop Diner. He was instantly relieved. He was the guy that paid for Matthew's apple pie.

"Oh, yes, sir. The pie was wonderful, and thank you...." Matthew started until the trucker cut him off.

"It's goddam cold out tonight, oh, sorry, pardon my language, Reverend. I know this old Minibus doesn't put out much heat, and I can see you are shivering. I think you should come sit in my truck for a little while and warm up. I just made a small pot of coffee, and you're welcome to some. The other guy I was with at the diner is in my truck too. We'd enjoy the company."

"Well," Matthew started, he really didn't want to get in this guy's truck, but he was so cold he felt this may have been an answer to his prayer for warmth, "okay, if you don't mind, just for a little bit."

"Leave this old four-banger runnin', son, if you got plenty of gas. Nobody is gonna take it tonight. Let's get going, so we both don't freeze our asses off. Oh, pardon my language again, Reverend."

Matthew wrapped his sweatshirt around his head snuggly and slipped out of his Minibus. The old guy slammed the Minibus door shut, and they both hustled across the parking lot, the huge old man blocking the wind for him.

"Down coat!" the old man yelled to Matthew through the wind and snow. "You need a down coat around here in winter. You won't regret it."

Matthew was too cold to respond.

They got to the the old guy's rig, and he opened the big door, nearly shoving Matthew up the steps and into the truck. Inside was another old guy with a shorter dark beard, but he was just as big. He clasped Matthew's arm and yanked him up into the truck, and the white-bearded man followed up behind him and shut the door. The truck rumbled inside, and Matthew didn't know where to sit, but it was good and warm.

"I'm Pete, the guy at the diner, my CB handle is Santa Claus, and you can probably tell why. This other big guy here, this is Big John, his CB handle is Ten Point."

Matthew smiled and nodded at Big John. "I'm Matthew," and he stuck a cold shivering hand out to Big John. When Big John shook his hand, he jumped a bit and said, "Jesus, Matthew, you are near frozen! Oh, sorry, pardon my language."

Matthew chattered back, "No problem. It's okay."

Pete leaned back and slid a door open behind the seats revealing a tiny living space. A bed, a small fridge, a little counter with a coffee pot, a little sink, and a few small cabinets. Pete squirreled himself between the seats to crawl to the back and shoved the bed up, folding it nicely to make a little sitting space, big enough for two. Big John sat in the shotgun seat and spun it around to face the living quarters. Pete invited Matthew to the back part of the rig patting the seat he'd just made, "Come on, Reverend, come sit and warm up. Your damn lips are nearly blue."

"Thank you," Matthew said politely as he climbed in the back. "God Bless you, I think I was freezing to death."

"Well, I wouldn't expect someone out of Georgia to understand this nasty cold out here on the plains, so we kept an eye out for you. It's a miracle you pulled in here when you did," Pete said as he yanked a blanket out of a storage compartment and wrapped it around Matthew, tucking him in like a burrito.

"God works in mysterious ways," Matthew said, shivering.

"Amen," Big John added from his shotgun seat sipping coffee out of an old vintage Thermos cup.

Pete opened a cabinet to grab a mug and filled it with coffee. "I got some sugar and a dry coffee creamer if you need it," he said as he was handing Matthew the mug.

"Creamer would be nice," Matthew trembled.

Big John was adding a little more coffee to his own cup from his Thermos. "I take mine black but sometimes put cocoa in it." And he smiled a sheepish smile that seemed out of place on this huge guy.

"This is really a nice compartment, Pete," Matthew complimented as he hesitantly blew over the top of his hot coffee, "I never knew trucks had all this. I thought they were all, well, trucks."

"Yeah, a few of us live in them cross-country. So we spoil ourselves, so we don't have to mess with cheap motels and end up covered in bedbugs," Pete said as he spritzed window cleaner on the little counter and wiped it with a paper towel. "It pays for itself over a couple years. But I will say, I rarely have company like this!" Pete broke into a laugh that sounded like, well, Santa Claus. He rummaged in a little in a box in his storage compartment and took out a small strand of multi-color twinkle lights and plugged them in, and tucked them into the ceiling trim. "Here ya go, party lights!"

"I don't know how I can ever repay you for your kindness Pete," Matthew said as some feeling began to come back into his fingers.

"No thanks are needed. We are road warriors, we look out for those that are in trouble. There is so much evil and bad in people of the world that some of us must work on the side of good," Pete said.

"Amen!" Big John said again from his shotgun seat.

"Amen," added Matthew as he sipped his hot coffee, "there can never be enough good in the world."

"Oh... one thing I could use is a blessing for my rig if you don't mind. And if you have one," he sheepishly asked Matthew.

"I can't say I've heard of blessing a semi before, but I'd be honored to give it a try," Matthew said, brightening up as he had something to offer in exchange for the kindness he received.

Matthew sat his cup on the tiny counter, cleared his throat, and bowed his head, Pete and Big John followed. "Dear Lord God, Our Father in Heaven, bless this rig and all its gears and motors, to be mechanically safe for its long journeys across the ribbons of highways, and bless it's driver, as he drives the long hauls, to keep his eyes open and mind awake, his hands quick on the steering wheel and his feet steady on the pedals. Bless the tractor to move through the wind, rains, snows, and dust, steady ahead, sticking well to the asphalt through the weather that pushes it to its limit. Bless the transmission and engine that powers the trailers onward and all it carries across the country for the benefit of our nation's family. And dear Father in Heaven, we ask in your name, for its safe transit, for now, and evermore. Amen."

"Amen," Big John said again.

"Amen," Pete said, along with a little sniff as he wiped a bit of a tear in his eye. "Reverend, that was beautiful. Thank you."

"It is the least I can do. I believe you may have saved my life tonight. If you hadn't dragged me out of my bus, I would have tried to travel on and probably froze to death," Matthew said very concerned and looked deep into Pete's eyes to connect that he understood the godsend of how Pete saved him. "I thought the miracle in my life was heading out to lead a flock of farm folks in northwest Kansas, but now I think my Christmas miracle was running into you, especially when you consider the odds of all the things that fell into place that lead me here tonight. So thank you."

"Merry Christmas, Reverend," Pete said and threw a giant arm around Matthew's shoulder and hugged him tight, squeezing Matthew's slight frame like a cheap accordion causing him to grunt.

Big John leaned back in the seat, stretching his arms out as far as he could and yawned, "Well, you know, He works in mysterious ways. And I better get back to my rig. I wanna catch some shut-eye before this storm settles in as I might be shoveling my rig out in the morning."

Pete nodded. "I appreciated the company, John. Nice to chat face to face instead of the CB. Thanks for the sandwich at Agnes'. I imagine if this weather gets much worse, we may have to get across the interstate and head back to Agnes'."

"Yep. Not sure of a crossing point, though. I guess we can work it out when it's daylight and see how bad it is. Olive Pit pulled in awhile ago and was getting some shut-eye too. So we can convene in the morning and decide. Maybe we'll get someone on the radio coming in from Colorado to see how it is out there. My cellphone coverage is out, so all I got is CB. The last time I head anything was from Cockroach, he was going to try to head on through to Denver with a full load. Hope he doesn't get sidelined. We'll give ya a holler at daybreak," Big John said as he opened the door and climbed down, letting in a lot of icy cold wind and plenty of snowflakes before slamming it shut.

Pete sighed, "Good people, that Big John."

They watched him jog across the parking lot to his rig. He waved as he shut the cab door behind him, and they saw his compartment lights go on.

Chapter 32

Creepy Socks

"Well, Pete," Matthew started, "I do appreciate your thoughtfulness and generosity, but I know you need to sleep, and I need to get out of your hair. I think I only have another hour before I get off I-70 and head north, so I should be in good shape."

"Like hell! Pardon my damn French, Reverend," Pete said, "but it's damn cold, and I don't think you can do an hour without getting frostbite. Besides, once you get off the interstate, how long are you gonna be driving to wherever you are headed? Can you manage a couple hours in your Minibus? What if you slide off the road? You can snooze in the shotgun seat here if you want. At least it's warm and safe. Lots of long haulers in here tonight. It's stupid to be out on the road in this," Pete pointed out the window to the increasing snowfall. "Besides, you ain't doing your flock any good if you are frozen to death."

"Really, Pete, I do appreciate your hospitality, but I really wanna get back on the road and keep going."

"You know, my trailer is empty. If I had a goddam ramp, I'd push that bus of yours into the trailer and make ya stay right here. It is truly suicide Reverend. Look, I got a mess of ready-to-eat meal packets here. At least hang here, have some hot supper, then consider the situation out there," Pete said, pointing to the snow piling up on the windshield.

"Ready-to-eat packets?" Matthew asked.

"Yeah, it's like for preppers or camping meals, you know, ready-to-eat meals. I keep a couple dozen on the truck. You just add hot water, and you get beef and noodles or rice and chicken with a little biscuit and cookie. It's not gourmet, but it's hot and filling."

Matthew considered his offer and looked out at the snow that was getting frighteningly heavy but felt uncomfortable with infringing on his new friend this long.

"Come on, Reverend," Pete persisted. "You know God set this up for both of us. I like to talk and have some company, you are freezing and look hungry. This was all 'made in heaven' for us," Pete said as he waved his arms, indicating his little compartment with the happy twinkle lights.

Matthew gave in. "Ok, Pete. But just for a little while. As soon as this lets up, I'll be out of your hair."

"Sure, Reverend, as soon as it lets up." Pete rolled his eyes where Matthew couldn't see as Pete knew this was no quickie snow squall. Pete filled a measuring cup with water and put it in the little microwave. "Chicken and rice or beef and noodles?"

Matthew and Pete ate their meals right out of the packets and talked about trucking and reverending and how they compared what they do as helping bring people what they need, Matthew helped their spiritual needs, and Pete helped their personal needs. Having a last cup of coffee while Pete tidied up, spritzing everything with window cleaner and toweling it down, Matthew watched Pete intently when Pete noticed. "Military," Pete said.

"Huh?" Matthew didn't get it.

"Military. I learned to be neat and detail things out. I grew up with a mess of a mother, so I liked the order and cleanliness the military taught me. And it stuck. So pardon me while I wipe everything down."

"No problem," Matthew said, "cleanliness is next to Godliness, you know." Matthew saw Pete stifle a yawn and knew Pete was getting tired. He also knew that his old Minibus was rear-engine, rear-wheel drive, and other than having a lousy heater, it was pretty sure-footed on the road in bad weather.

"Well, Pete, it's been great. You don't know how much I appreciate your saving my life tonight. But I really want to be on my way. I want to be at my new church for Christmas Eve midnight services. I hope you can understand," Matthew said.

"Well, I do understand wanting to get where you need to be. But I strongly advise against it and to wait at least until the snow stops," Pete warned.

"I know," Matthew agreed. "As much as I appreciate all you have done for me. I just have to get going. My bus has been sitting there burning gas for an hour...." and Matthew's comments trailed off as Pete got up and rummaged in his storage box again.

"Ok," Pete said, "then one last thing. Take these." And he held out a pair of horrible-looking army green socks, complete with nubbies and a hole in one heel.

"Um," Matthew didn't know what to say, and Pete could see the young Reverend was appalled at the sight of them.

Pete did his Santa laugh. "Oh, ho ho ho. Oh, I know these are so ugly that their own mother would burn them, but they are wool. Just take 'em. They are an old pair I was going to throw out, but I think they'll do you some good. Put them on over your socks, then pull the cuffs up over your pants. You'll be surprised at how warm they'll keep your feet and ankles.

Matthew took the socks with the tips of two fingers.

"They ain't gonna kill you. They are clean. Laundered after the last time I wore 'em. And I always wore 'em over my socks because I hated the feel of the wool."

Matthew took off his shoes and worked the big wool socks over his own socks, then up over his pant legs.

"You'll need to loosen the laces in your sneaks. You have to give your feet room to circulate blood to help keep warm."

Matthew complied and finally got his shoes back on.

"My feet look fat," Matthew said as he looked down.

"Yeah, well, weather like this ain't a place for a fashion show," Pete said.

"That isn't the first time I've heard that today," Matthew commented as he studied his feet.

"Get that sweatshirt back on your head too before you head out. You want to keep as much warmth in as you can." Pete took a ballcap from a little stack of ball caps that were in the corner. "Here, put this on first."

Matthew took the cap. "Jeeze, Pete, this is too much."

"We get those things all the time from warehouses, stores, business that we deliver to," Pete explained. "I stack em up until I get a pile then donate them. I have a couple I wear, the rest I don't need."

Matthew looked at the cap logo that was a lovely rainbow-colored shape like a big raindrop.

"What is this?" he asked.

"It's a paint store in Tulsa," he said. "You can probably guess why I don't want to wear it on the road."

Matthew chuckled at the shared joke. "It's okay, Pete. I bless everybody. I don't judge them, that's God's job. I don't recall Him giving anyone the authority to judge each other, so each human is just as important as every other human."

"Oh, I know, Reverend. But there are a lot of very conservative trucks on the long haul. I am not interested in being political at my age anymore. I just want to pass the time, help where I can, and look to retiring so I can go fishing."

"Thanks, Pete. Really. You've been like St. Pete to me. Thank you so much for everything, especially your company, coffee, and the creepy socks."

Matthew's comment made Pete laugh his Santa laugh once more, and Matthew could almost see a Santa Claus twinkle in his eyes.

"Good luck, Matthew, may God go with you. And thank you for blessing my rig," Pete said as he crawled over the seat to unlatch the door and help Matthew down out of the cab.

"Thanks again," Matthew said, "I'll keep you in my prayers." And Matthew climbed clumsily down onto the snowy parking lot and jogged through the couple inches of snow to jump in his bus. It was still running, and not warm inside, but at least not freezing either. Matthew knew when he started moving that it might get colder if the engine didn't keep up with heating the air. His feet did feel warm though, as he stomped his feet on the floor to knock the snow off.

"Yes, indeed," Matthew said out loud, "the Lord does work in mysterious ways." And he shifted into gear and started to creep slowly out of the rest area lot and back into the snowy night.

Chapter 33

The Ladies Are Getting Along

"Thank God she's asleep," Janet said quietly to Doris as she glanced back at Rita, who was asleep. Rita's head was cranked back in the corner by the door, her mouth hanging open a bit with a little drool piddling out of the corner of her mouth. "She'd been shittin' nine bricks to Sunday if she saw all this snow."

"I'm going to keep going and hope it's going to let up soon. This tank actually seems to be doing okay in this snow, and the highway isn't totally covered yet," Doris explained.

"The road sure looks covered to me," Janet said. "You can't see the passing lane at all, and this lane just has tire paths left. I don't think it's going to be long before it's totally covered. You can't even tell where the shoulder is right now. Not to mention, you can't see fifty feet in front of the car."

"I don't think it's snowing that hard, it just looks bad because of the wind blowing it around. Besides, I can only drive in one lane anyway, and there's no real traffic. I would assume if someone is stopping ahead of me for some reason, I'd see their brake lights come on. I figure it's probably a snow squall, and it'll stop soon. Or we'll drive out of it. So far, I'm not sliding or slipping."

"Those big gnarly tires your hubby put on probably help grab the road," Janet concluded.

"Yeah, funny too because we argued about the expense for a month. I'm glad we got them now. I'm also glad this heap weighs a ton, at least the wind isn't blowing us around as much," Doris said.

"Hey ladies," Jackie whispered while unbuckling her seatbelt, then leaning up, sticking her head as far up front as she could. "Are we going to keep driving in this mess? If Rita wakes up, she's going to have a conniption."

"We know," Doris said. "Just trying to keep it steady as she goes. Rita drank a bathtub of booze today, so maybe she'll stay asleep."

"Jeeze, Louise, how can you see?" Jackie commented quietly when she tried to look out the windshield.

Doris increased the speed of the wipers that were doing a decent job of pushing the snow off the windshield. "I can see the tracks of other cars. Something big ahead of us mowed down a lot of the snow. I just follow those. I'm keeping an eye ahead for tail lights, that's my only real concern. I sure don't want to whack a car with this behemoth. I'm not interested in killing someone."

"Will we get a pee break soon?" Jackie asked.

"Next place we see. Keep your eyes open for a rest area or off-ramp in case I miss something," Doris said.

"Crap, Doris," Janet said, "I can hardly see anything until we are on top of it."

"Well, let me know anyway. I don't see anyone behind me, so I can always back up a few feet if we pass a ramp," Doris said.

Jackie sat back in her seat and looked out her window at the collecting snow. It was quiet for a while as Doris concentrated on the road with Janet keeping extra eyes open when they heard Jackie let out a small, "Oh no!"

Doris and Janet exchanged concerned glances. Doris made an effort to calm her fears. "Jackie, we're going to be okay. It's only snow. This Dominator is like a tank, if we have to, we can go off-road, just like the guy in the diner mentioned."

"Oh, I know," Jackie said, "but there's something else." She whimpered a bit.

"What is it?" both Doris and Janet said at the same time.

"Um, it's Rita," Jackie could barely get out.

"What about Rita?" Janet said, cranking herself around in the seat to look in the backseat.

"I think," Jackie said, "I think Rita finally drank herself to death. I think she's dead."

"What?" Doris swerved the Dominator a bit while trying to see the back seat in her rearview.

"Oh dear," Jackie said, "I'm spoiling everything. I don't want to sit next to a dead body. Can I come up front and sit with you?"

"Oh, Jeezus, Peter, Paul, and Mary!" Doris said. "Are you sure?" As she stretched her neck to see Rita still stuck in the corner, mouth hanging open and that drool still there.

"I think so," Jackie said in between soft sobs, "I don't see her breathing, and she stopped snoring a half hour ago."

"Jackie, can you take her pulse or something?" Janet asked.

"Oh no, I can't," Jackie sobbed. "I'm not touching a dead body." And she broke down in real sobs.

"Can you touch her skin to see if she's cold?" Doris asked.

"NO!" Jackie whispered as loud as she dared.

Janet looked at Doris and rolled her eyes around, "Jeez Doris, what are we going to do? We can't get a cell call out to police or an ambulance, and there's no place to stop."

"I guess all we can do is keep going," Doris said.

"Please get me out of the back seat!" Jackie cried. "I don't want to sit here in the dark with a dead body."

Doris looked in her rearview and saw Jackie all scrunched up against her door as far as she could.

"Can we make room for her up here?" Janet asked.

"Yeah, but she'll have to sit on the console. No seatbelt though, which I don't condone in this kind of weather," Doris said.

"I don't care," Jackie whimpered. "I won't complain. I promise. If you crash the car and I die, I don't care, I'll be with my husband that way. Oh, I miss him so much," and Jackie cried more.

"I don't know how much I can listen to that," Doris whispered to Janet.

"Can we pull over for a second so we can get her situated up here, or maybe we can just put Rita in with the luggage?" Janet said with a tinge of morbid humor.

"Not funny, Janet," Doris said, but then cracked a smile. "You know it's just like Rita to drink herself to death on our big holiday. This will go down in my history book as a page right out the seventh level of hell."

"Or maybe our really Lucky Seven trip!" Janet joked.

Ok, I'll pull over on the shoulder, so we get Jackie up here," Doris said, slowing the vehicle. "No cars are coming that I can see, so let's make it quick. Janet, why don't you check Rita for a pulse while we are shuffling."

Doris hit the shoulder, and the Dominator-Maximus simply plowed over some soft shoulder ruts jarring them all. "We're ok, we're okay," Doris explained to the others as she slowed to a stop, "just a couple ruts under the snow."

Janet popped open the door handle to open the door when the lights came on, and a courtesy ding sounded.

"What are we stoppin' for?" they all heard Rita ask through a sleepy yawn, and Jackie let out a little scream.

Doris started to chuckle, then Janet followed. The more they looked at each other, the more tickled they got.

"What's going on, girls?" Rita asked again.

Doris tried to explain it but got to laughing so hard she couldn't finish. Even Jackie was laughing now, with her tears still in her eyes. Rita started laughing too but wasn't sure why, but everything seems funny when you've had a bathtub of booze all day. Finally, Doris was able to say, "Oh Rita, you were sleeping so hard we thought you were dead!" Rita had to think about that but got to laughing anyway.

They were all still laughing as Doris put the vehicle in gear and started creeping back onto the highway, glumping it over the ruts and back into the traffic lane. "Wow, look at that, not even a slip," Doris said in amazement. "Some vehicle!"

They were all calming their laughter down when Rita said, "girls, I gotta pee."

"We've been keeping an eye out for a place, Rita," Janet said. "There should be something soon."

"No," Rita said rather abruptly, "I don't mean pee later. I mean, I gotta pee now!"

"Now? You just went less than an hour ago at the diner." Doris looked at Rita in the rearview. "If I pull over, you think you are going to simply squat in the snow?"

Rita looked out the window and realized how ridiculous that was. "Well, I can't help it, I can't hold it, I gotta go now, and I don't wanna pee in your seat back here."

"Was that a threat?" Janet asked Doris across the front seat.

"Well, I don't have a potty for you," Doris said, looking at Rita in the rearview.

"Okay, gimme that cup then," Rita said, pointing at a plastic cup in the cupholder.

"Oh no, you don't," Doris said.

"Oh yes, I am," Rita countered. "It's either that cup or your seat."

"Jeezus, Rita, why don't you carry some adult diapers if you can't hold it," Janet scolded as she took the top and straw out of the cup and handed it back to Rita.

Janet and Jackie sat and watched as Rita unbuckled her seat belt and started taking her bell-bottoms off, revealing a sparkly thong. Janet and Jackie looked at each other, and Jackie made the gag sign by putting a finger down her throat. Rita squirmed out of her thong, slinking it on the seat next to Jackie, who made a face of disgust. Rita then twisted herself around until she had enough room to pinch the cup between her legs. Everyone was waiting. Nothing was happening.

"Is your ass too cold?" Janet asked, getting a full view of Rita's saggy everything.

"Well damn, Janet," Rita said, "it's not like this is comfortable."

They waited. They waited some more.

"What the hell is she doing?" Doris asked, not able to see what was going on in the rearview.

"For crying out loud, Rita," Janet said, "get on with it, we're waiting."

"I'm trying to concentrate," Rita said matter-of-factly. "I guess I have a shy bladder."

"Oh my god," Doris said out of disgust, hanging her arms over the steering wheel.

Jackie was sitting in her corner watching this horror show, first staring at the cup and its placement, then at Rita's face that looked really old in the dim glow of the dome light. And Jackie knew if Rita missed, she'd be sharing the back seat with a yellow aquarium.

Jackie put her hands up to her face so she wouldn't see any more of it, yet peeked through her fingers anyway.

"Oh, grow up," Rita said when she saw Jackie trying to hide behind her hands. "People piss, you know," then went back to attempting to complete her mission.

Janet sat there, shaking her head at the ridiculousness of it all.

While Rita was working on her personal mission, she glanced out the rear window down the interstate. She cheerfully announced to the group, "Hey, there's headlights in the distance, someone is heading this way." At the same time, they finally heard the waterworks dribbling away in the cup, followed by a big sigh of relief.

"So, what's that?" Janet asked, "you needed a spotlight to complete your mission?"

Doris laughed at that.

Rita took the cup and handed it to Jackie.

"No. I don't think so," Jackie said, putting her hands under her armpits.

"Look, I can't sit here without pants. Somebody has to hold the cup so I can get my pants on before that car gets up here. Anyone got a napkin or a couple of tissues?"

"Oh god, this is getting so gross," Janet said, rummaging in the door pockets for some tissues.

"I have tissues," Jackie volunteered. And she dug a few out of her purse and handed them by two fingers to Rita but yanked her hands back after Rita took the tissues.

"Wuss," Rita said to Jackie.

"Gimme the goddam cup," Janet volunteered, "I'm sick of this whole mess. I have the lid, I'll cap it up. Doris has some hand-wipes up here you can use."

"You aren't going to put that cup in my cup rack, are you?" Doris asked.

"What am I supposed to do, hold it in my lap? Throw the cup out the window?" Janet asked.

"Shit," Doris said. She thought for a minute and took her foot off the accelerator to let the vehicle slow considerably.

"What do you have in mind? Having the oncoming car bash in our rear end?" Janet asked, noticing the slowdown.

"I'm going to pull over again, at least dump the pee out," Doris said, snapping on her hazard lights.

"Check," Janet said.

Once again, Doris drove the Dominator over the uneven edge of the road onto the shoulder. And once again, Janet hit the latch to open the door.

"Can't you just roll the window down and dump it?" Rita asked.

"NO!" Jackie screamed before Janet did anything with the cup. "It'll blow back on my window and freeze, and I'll have to look at pee until we get to the desert!"

"Aw jeez, just open the door a crack and spill the pee out the bottom edge of the door," Rita griped.

"Crap," Janet said, "my arm isn't long enough to reach down that far."

"Give it to Rita to dump," Jackie bristled. "It's her pee. Make her get out and dump it."

"F- you," Rita whispered to Jackie so only she could hear.

"I got it," Janet said and pushed the door open against the wind and stuck her arm and cup out the door to slowly pour the pee out so it wouldn't splash back on the vehicle. Doris watched the rearview for the oncoming car.

"Let's go, Janet," Doris said, "we don't have all day." As the car closed in, Doris saw that it was a truck, and it was coming upon them in a hurry. "Get rid of the pee!" Doris was getting riled.

"Okay, okay," Janet said as the wind blew snow and cold into the Dominator. She had just tipped the cup to pour the yellow contents into the waiting snow when a wind gust filled the cup like a windsock and snatched it from Janet's fingers. The cup tumbled away, cartwheeling pee all over the shoulder and under the Dominator, then in front of the now passing truck.

"Shit," Janet said, "I lost the cup." She slammed the door and fixed the latch.

"You what?" Doris said, "you mean you littered?"

"No. You know I'm not like that. I wasn't thinking when I tipped the cup, and the wind caught it and just yanked it out of my fingers."

"I think that truck was those two rotten boys from the diner. That awful boy in the hoodie and his brother. I'm glad they had to drive over that cup," Rita said, "And it's just as well. You all were grossed out by a cup of pee, and now it's in the middle of Kansas, or hopefully frozen onto the side of their truck." Then she sat back, adjusted her bellbottoms, and buckled herself back in.

"Ick, where's the box of wipes?" Janet said as she rummaged in one of the door pockets.

"I hope they didn't see that cup," Jackie worried. "They might be angry and cause us more problems."

"I doubt it," Doris reasoned. "I don't think they are going to want to mess with the Black Diamond, and they know we know their names. They'll just be on their merry way."

"I hope you are right," Janet whispered.

"Me too," Doris agreed.

"I see headlights again," Jackie said as she had been watching out the back.

"Ok, gotta go, and not in a cup kind of way, gotta get rolling now," Doris said, starting the Dominator merging toward the interstate lane and looking at her rearview seeing the dim headlights in the distance.

"I can't tell how far they are with the snow in the way," Doris said. So she ramped up her speed a little as she got back onto the interstate.

It was quiet for a minute as Doris steered the Dominator into a traveling mode then announced. "We're back in good shape, girls. The vehicle behind us must be going slow as it's getting fainter now."

"Maybe it's just more snow blocking your view," Janet warned.

"Yeah. Could be," Doris said. "Okay now, here's the deal, NONE of us ever says a word about this to anyone. If Dave finds out Rita peed in his precious Black Diamond Coach, he'll sell it and buy a new one."

"Rita peed in his Dominator??" Janet said with a wry little smirk.

Rita got the joke and laughed a horse laugh. Doris started to give Janet a dirty look, but then it turned into a laugh. Jackie said, "I don't get it," as they all got to giggling.

"Ok, girls, we are looking for a place to get off here so we can all go to the ladies' room before it's "cup" time seeing how we don't have any more cups. It's been a very long evening."

"Yep," Janet agreed.

"Yes, it has," Jackie nodded.

"Well, I'm having fun," Rita snarked.

Chapter 34

Motor Home Mystery

"You've been driving for over four hours without a stop, Herm," Louise said. "I can tell you've been fighting the wind when it hits the RV broadside. You need a rest."

"I'm fine, Lou," Herman said, keeping a steady eye on the road.

"The doctor said you weren't supposed to be sitting still like that any more than two hours without stretching your legs. We have to stop so you can get the blood moving. We really don't need a problem with another clot in your heart."

"I'm fine, Lou," Herman repeated.

Louise was becoming frustrated with Herman's push to get as many miles under his belt as possible before throwing in the towel for the day. He'd already been hospitalized two years ago for driving ten hours without enough of a break, and a clot formed in his leg that lodged in his lung, and he nearly died. DVT, deep vein thrombosis.

"Herman," Louise said, sounding like a school teacher, "you know I can't drive this heap if something happens to you. Can we please err on the side of caution? I can fix us a little supper while you stretch your legs, then we can put our feet up and take a snooze and get back on the road in an hour or so. There won't be any traffic after midnight."

"There's no traffic now, Lou," Herman said as though he didn't hear any of her warnings.

Louise sat there fuming. She'd retired from a long career in nursing and always got irked at the people that felt they were above doctor's orders. There were always those that seemed to think they were the exception to the instructions. Those exceptions wanted to do their own thing once they were pretty sure they weren't going to die from their ailments. And Herman wasn't any different.

"HERMAN!" she finally shouted, causing Herman to jump a bit and made Twinkles yip, "Find a damn place to pull over right now!"

Still unfazed, Herman said, "Lou, Lou, Lou. I'm fine. I don't feel leg pain, and I don't need to eat anything. Besides, there's a layer of snow on everything, and I just can't pull over and hope the shoulder will be solid enough to support the RV. But I will try to find a place soon. There must be a rest area around here someplace." Herman flipped a switch on the dash that lit up two spotlights on the top of the RV and aimed them at the side of the road, looking for signs indicating the next rest area. It was difficult to see much of anything with the battering snow reflecting back the searchlights.

Louise breathed a sigh of relief that Herman seemed like he was going to find a place to stop. Although, he had driven by rest areas in the past if he didn't like the way they looked.

"Ok," Louise said, "and it's time for your heart medication too."

"My heart is just fine if you wouldn't shout at me," he said, not taking his eyes off the road. "I need to keep one eye on the road and the other on the weather. It's getting pretty cold," he said, looking at his gages on the dash. "It was seventeen degrees not long ago, and it looks like it's dropping down more. With the wind chill, it's getting dangerous out there and cold enough to have to start thinking about our water tanks."

"There's no place we have to be, Herman. We have everything we need right here to last us a week, even if we go off the grid," Louise reasoned. "We can take our time and be sensible."

Herman started a conversation, but it wasn't with Louise. This was something he always did after his brother died.

"Well, Howie, what do you think? Is there a rest stop ahead? Yes, I know I need to stop and stretch for a bit. Okay. I'm still using the search lamps you got for me," Herman talked to the air.

Louise didn't interrupt the chats he had with his imaginary ghost brother, but she was getting irritated that he'd do the bidding of an invisible brother, but not hers. "So, what did Howie think?" she asked Herman, wondering if he used Howie as an avoidance behavior.

"Howie agrees with you. This time," Herman said.

Louise was curious, "So, do you see Howie? Hear him or what?" she asked.

"Of course, I see him and hear him. He's right here," Herman waved a hand as though he was erasing a chalkboard.

"How can he fit in the seat with you?" Louise tried to get him to see reality.

"Well," Herman answered, "it doesn't work that way."

"No? Then how does it work? How do you think it's him and not your imagination?"

"That's the odd thing about it, Lou," Herman tried to explain. "I don't see him as a solid human, like you sitting there. He's sort of like, well, like those sheer curtains you put in the dining room. Like a spirit veil, I guess. I can see him hovering right near me, as though those sheer curtains were slightly moving in the breeze. Sometimes I just see his face, other times more, sometimes it's his whole body, sometimes near and sometimes away a bit and sometimes I only hear him, kind of in my head. I don't know how it works. I don't even know if it's really him or just my brain putting him there because I miss him so damn much. It's like he's still here. We talk, we joke, we even had some arguments. He's not there all the time, though.

It started a few months after he died when I was working on something out in the garage. It scared the bejeebers out of me at first. It was just a distant voice mention my name that I wasn't sure I even heard. Over the past couple of years, I've gotten used to seeing his image. He seems to be around more and more lately and carrying on conversations in my head."

"Well," Louise considered, "maybe you are just dreaming."

"Oh, well, that's the crazy thing, Lou," Herman said, "I don't see him in my sleep, just in my waking hours. I will say, I see him much more now than right after he died. I don't know Lou, maybe I'm losing my marbles. Still, it feels good to see him and talk to him."

Louise could see tears forming in Herman's eyes. She knew this was not a time to question his time with his twin brother, in whatever form he concocted.

Herman saw the look of doubt on his wife's face and tried to explain it further.

"You know, Lou, when I had my blood clot, and I lost consciousness that was really the first time I actually saw him, but that one time it was like in the flesh. It was like we were both real and warm and together. He wasn't saying anything then, though. Just there, smiling, making me feel welcome and very peaceful. Then his face turned sad, and he started to wave goodbye, and the next thing I knew, I was conscious and in terrible pain in the ER hooked up to everything. He came to me later in the hospital and showed himself as I was convalescing, and he indicated that I cheated him out of having his other half with him. I remember telling him that I wanted to be with my wife and kids for awhile yet. He understood. He said he'd stick around and wait. But I haven't seen him in the fleshy version since. I only see him in the filmy version. I don't know what it all means, but it seems to help me get through the deep sadness I feel. He only used to visit me when I was alone, but a few times recently, he's shown up when you are around."

"Weren't you scared at seeing sort of a ghost of your brother?" Louise asked.

"No, and yes. At first, it startled me something awful, but after a while, I've come to expect it. You know, like Twinkles coming to sit on your lap. I'll admit that there's a profound feeling of peace and warmth when he's around. There's no fear. So yeah, at first it scared me, but not anymore. Not even a startle. I can't explain it. Even when we argue about stuff, it's still a great feeling. He's gone now again." Herman sounded disappointed. "When I'm quiet and focused on something, that's generally when I hear him. He tells me I've done something good or stupid, or reminds me where I left my wrench or screwdriver. Kind of handy at times. And yes, I have wondered if it is my own manifestation. But I don't care, it feels good to see him."

Louise left it at that. She looked out her window, mindlessly petting Twinkles and watching the snow dancing up against her window and collecting on the big RV side mirrors.

"Do you want me to clear the mirror, Herm?" she asked.

"No, Lou. It's way too cold for you to do that. I tell you what. I'll ask Howie if he'll do it, and let's just see what happens," Herman said.

Louise smiled and shook her head. "Okay. Go ahead and give it a try."

"Hey, Howie? I really need my side mirror cleaned off. It's too cold for us, and we can't pull off the road right now. While you are at it, we could use a rest area to pull off for a bit. Thanks, Howie. Love you, man," Herm said.

Louise sat there, watching the mirror. Nothing.

Just then, she heard Herman fumbling for the knob to fan the searchlights around. "Look, Lou!! I think that's an exit coming up! Ah-ha! Thanks, Howie!!" Herman took his foot off the accelerator and let the behemoth slow down, hit his jake-brake to slow quicker. Louise sat up in excitement to finally see a place to get off the interstate.

But as they neared, they both saw it was merely an overpass. Louise didn't want to say anything. Herman was disappointed and started to accelerate a little to get up to speed again. "Well, I guess that was too good to be true," Herman said in defeat. Louise saw Herman's disappointment.

"It's ok, Herm. Maybe it's still up ahead," Louise said.

"Yeah," Herman said quietly.

A quiet minute passed when Louise noticed something. "Herm?" She said.

"Yeah," Herman said.

"Guess what?"

"What, Louise," Herman replied, sounding frustrated.

"You aren't going to believe it, but the snow and ice are gone off the side rearview," Louise said quietly and slightly dumbfounded.

"Are you kidding?" Herman replied, his mood bouncing back like a kid getting back on the trampoline.

"No kidding, it's completely clean," she said.

Herman couldn't really see the side rearview because there was no traffic behind them to light it up, so he flipped on the amber side-marker patio lights and got a good look. He could see the rear exterior corners of the RV in the cleared mirrors.

"Damn," he said with a spiritual tone. "Howie? Howie, did you do that?"

He waited a couple of seconds. "I don't see him, Lou. He's gone."

"Well, maybe he had to go outside to clear the mirror," Louise said, trying to humor him.

"Oh jeez, Lou. Do you realize that the mirror would not be cleaned off if Howie was my imagination?" Herm said.

Louise was thinking about it.

Herman continued, "even if it was a warm thermal that melted it off, maybe it's still possible that he, in some way, could control that."

They were both quiet for a minute. Finally, Herman heard Louise quietly say, "Thanks, Howie. Watch over your brother, will you?"

Nothing was said between them for a few minutes. Both were thinking about what just happened. Sure the wind may have blown it off, although not likely with the layer of ice under the snow. Still, the mirror was clear now, no denying that.

Finally, Louise spoke up, bringing them both back to reality. "Herm, I'm going to have to use the potty. Can you slow it down and hold it steady, so I don't fall?"

"Sure, sure," Herm said, slowing the behemoth down and tightening his grip on the wheel. "Holding her steady is going to be a crapshoot in this wind, though."

"Ask your brother to hold it down," Louise said as she made her way back through the RV to the bathroom with Twinkles following. "When I come back, I'm bringing your medicine and a cup of water."

Herman made a face but kept the RV as steady as he could.

Chapter 35

The Duly Appointed Dually

Travis and Eddie Get What's Coming

"Can't you go any faster?"

"Look, Travis," Eddie said, "it is slicker than snot on the road. Did you see those old ladies in the Dominator parked on the side of the road back there? If they were having problems in that huge hulk of a tank, then we will too, for sure. I don't want to end up in the ditch in the middle of nowhere when it's fifteen below zero out."

"Those old ladies don't know how to drive. Slow reflexes. I'll bet that's how they ended up on the shoulder. Your big truck with four-wheel drive can do a lot better than we've been doing," Travis needled.

"Maybe it could, Travis, but I can't see shit ahead of me with the blowing snow in my headlights. I'm doing sixty. That's fast enough. I don't want to hit someone that might swerve in front of me."

"We only see another car like every fifteen minutes, who can you possibly hit? With no traffic and it is so flat, we could spin around doing a dozen donuts and not hit anything. If we slide off the road, we simply drive it back on the road," Travis kept chipping away at his brother.

"Yeah, well, you do that if and when you ever own your own truck," Eddie said as he began to slow down.

"Now what? Are you slowing down just to piss me off?" Travis asked.

"No, I see headlights coming up behind me," Eddie said.

Travis looked back, and sure enough, someone was coming up pretty quick. "It looks like a four-wheeler," Travis noted, squinting to try and see through the snow.

"A car?" Eddie said, sounding slightly alarmed that a car would be going that fast in this awful storm. "Jeez, hope it's not the cops. Hide anything you got. Maybe the lady at the diner called the cops after we left, and they are coming to get us."

"Nah, they aren't flashing their lights. No cop," Travis figured.

"You moron, Travis. They don't use their lights when coming up on someone they want to arrest, they don't want us speeding away," Eddie said.

Travis thought about that for a minute. "Crap. Maybe you are right."

Travis took the cash out of his jacket and was looking for a place to hide it. He glanced back and saw that the headlights were gaining on them, so he started ransacking the truck looking for a place to put the money so the cops couldn't find it. He looked up at the headliner and started to pull the liner away from the trim near the windshield.

"What the hell are you doing!?!" Eddie screamed as Travis peeled a corner of the headliner out. "My truck isn't paid for!!"

"The cops won't look under the headliner," he said as he started to peel, glancing repeatedly out the back window.

The car was still gaining on them.

"Dammit, Travis, just eat it or something!" Eddie screamed, pointing to the wad of their grandmother's money Travis had clutched in his fist.

The vehicle behind them was near enough that Eddie could see it was doing a little swerving and fishtailing in the wind. Whoever it was, they meant business.

"Jeezuz!!!!" Eddie was still screaming. "They are still gaining on us. The only reason someone would be driving that fast is the cops wanting to catch someone that attempted armed robbery!"

Then Eddie heard a rip and saw that Travis's plan to peel back a corner of the headliner left an eight-inch long tear and still no place to hide the cash. Eddie was seething at the headliner dangling over the visor, and now Travis had his hands back on the headrest and pulled it off the stalks that held it onto the seat. He tried rolling the cash to stick it in the stalk holes. It wouldn't fit. All he had time left to do was to spread it on the floor under the floor mat.

Eddie could see by the dash lights that Travis was sweating and looking panicky when Travis demanded, "You need to put some foot into it and get this truck moving. I see the cop car is slipping a bit and we have four-wheel drive. You can outrun them. Get going! If it is cops, we might end up in jail if that truck-stop gal filed a complaint."

Eddie sped up a bit, but the approaching vehicle was still catching up. Just then, Eddie's truck caught a blast of wind that caused a little fish-tailing, scaring Eddie. He recovered and slowed then yelled at his brother, "This isn't going very well, Travis. They are going to pull us over. You got us into this mess, you'd better figure out how to get us out of it, and at least get ME out of it. And you'd better calm yourself big brother, you look guilty as hell."

The oncoming vehicle was nearly on top of them, so Eddie moved over into the slow lane to allow the cops to put on their lights and pull them over.

"What are you doing!" Travis screamed as he saw the vehicle catching up.

"I'm pulling over," Eddie calmly said, clearly giving in.

"Don't pull over, just step on it! You can outrun them," Travis ordered. Travis was pissed and scared. "This big truck with tandem tires, we could leave them in our dust."

"Maybe," Eddie said, still a little rattled about the fishtailing, "but we could also wind up dead."

Travis was looking to argue with Eddie, but just about when he expected to see the police lights, he saw that the car wasn't a police car. It was a sports car with a ragtop.

"Oh man, check this out!" Travis said as he looked out the back window. "It's not a cop. It's a freakin' Spectaculeer! Cops don't drive Spectaculeers!"

Travis didn't let on how relieved he was and continued to antagonize. "You ain't gonna let this asshole pass you, are you? You know only assholes drive Spectaculeers." Travis egged him on until he felt Eddie step on the gas a bit.

The Spectaculeer flashed his brights, indicating he was going to pass. But Travis kept badgering his brother not to let the sports car get around them, so Eddie sped up and eased his truck into the middle of the interstate straddling the now buried center line. He still had the passenger-side tires touching pavement in the tire path of the slow lane, but the gathering snow was quickly burying it all.

Chapter 36

Meet the Mega-Drift

Mr. Tremont A. Preston could not figure out what the problem was with this truck ahead of him. It seemed to be all over the highway, and now it was driving in the middle of both lanes.

"Maybe the idiot driving it is falling asleep at the wheel, and the wind is pushing it around," he said aloud to his car.

"More information needed for an accurate report," Lexie responded blandly.

With all its automated road condition sensors, his Spectaculeer was doing quite well in the storm, and he figured the sooner he drove out of it, the sooner he'd be on his merry way. But now, this big truck was blocking his passing. He wasn't sure if there was enough room on either side to pass as the shoulder of the road was no longer visible. He flashed his lights once more.

"Either speed up or get out of the way, you redneck moron!" Mr. Preston hollered out loud.

"Please define redneck, Mr. Preston," Lexie commented.

"Lexie, cancel." Mr. Preston was now wondering if Lexie was going to be a backseat driver like his ex-wife.

Mr. Preston noticed the snow getting much heavier, and he was becoming concerned about completing his journey across Kansas this night. The snowflakes were huge and were spattering onto his windshield, and his headlights were reflecting the white flakes back so he could see almost nothing up ahead. But he maintained his confidence that the car's sensors would calculate all the information around him and alert him if he was too close to a vehicle ahead or veering off the road. He could barely see the dually truck tail lights that were just a car length ahead of him. There was nothing at all in his rearview, nothing on the eastbound lanes either. Mr. Preston sped up to drive closer to the truck, he thought maybe they'd get the message that he wanted to get around them. He was close enough to the back of the truck now that he was sure the driver could no longer see his headlights, but he flashed his brights again anyway.

"You are tail-gaiting dangerously close, Mr. Preston," Lexie warned, and Mr. Preston felt his car automatically slow slightly, in spite of his trying to accelerate a bit.

Mr. Preston had enough of his car nagging and telling him what to do, and now it was attempting to drive his car for him, "Lexie, voice commands, off!"

"That is not advisable in adverse weather conditions, Mr. Preston," Lexie argued, "it may close down some sensors."

He was getting frustrated and angry. He knew he was tail-gaiting too close and that it was dangerous weather without his car's opinion to tell him that. He hadn't slid or slipped yet, so he felt he could control his vehicle.

"Come on, you jerk, get out of the way!" Mr. Preston demanded out loud to the truck ahead of him.

"Define 'jerk,' Mr. Preston," Lexie asked.

"Lexie, OFF," Mr. Preston demanded. "Off!"

"Off is not a pre-programmed command I recognize," Lexie said.

Meanwhile, in the dually truck, Eddie said, "Travis, I need to let this guy go around. I don't want to drive this fast. I can't see ten feet in front of my truck, not to mention the snow on the road and the wind making it all worse. You look out front, tell me what you can see."

"You are a chickenshit, Eddie. Nobody is out on the road tonight. Stay in the middle, and you won't run off the road," Travis kept badgering. He was becoming so consumed with his own spitefulness that he hadn't noticed that Eddie had already slowed some. Eddie simply wasn't comfortable not being able to see what he was driving into.

Finally, Eddie began to move his truck into the slow lane, deciding to let the Spectaculeer go regardless of what his older brother commanded. He clicked on his turn signal to scoot over to the right a bit, even though he wasn't sure at all where the edge of the road was. The pavement path was now totally covered with snow, and Eddie hadn't driven in a lot of snow in his young life.

"You are a wuss, Pigskin," Travis said.

"Tell ya something, Travis," Eddie finally had enough of his brother and fired off at him, "if you know so damn much, then as soon as I can find a place to stop, YOU drive. I'm pretty much ready to hitchhike home, and you go get killed if that's something you want. I don't! And if you call me 'Pigskin' again, you can get out and freakin' WALK!"

Travis was shocked by Eddie's sudden outburst, and since he didn't much want to be alone right now, he pulled his hood up over his head as far as he could and yanked down his ballcap. Then he sulked back in his seat.

Travis felt the truck moving over, and they both watched the Spectaculeer's light beam move to the left and flash its brights as it began to pass their dually.

Travis leaned over Eddie's back, resting his left arm on the seat behind Eddie to see if he could see who was in the

Spectaculeer. "Maybe some hot chick is driving that ragtop," Travis mentioned.

"Chicks don't drive in snowstorms, Travis," Eddie said.

The snow was so thick now that they could barely see the Spectaculeer passing them, but the interior lights revealed a man was driving. Eddie tossed a casual wave to the driver. What Eddie didn't notice was Travis' arm behind him on the seat, flipping the middle finger to the Spectaculeer driver. The Spectaculeer driver saw it, though.

Mr. Tremont A. Preston sure saw that finger in the window of the truck. "What an asshole," he muttered under his breath.

"Explain asshole," Lexie responded.

"Lexie, nevermind. I'm trying to drive!" Mr. Preston commanded, then turned back to the jerks in the truck. "I'll show YOU," he shouted.

"Show tunes. Would you like to hear a show tune, Mr. Preston?" Lexie asked and began playing "Wells Fargo Wagon" from "The Music Man."

Mr. Preston was focused on passing the damn truck, so disengaged the auto-pilot control from Lexie.

As he accelerated, Lexie stopped playing "Wells Fargo Wagon" and commented, "You are accelerating dangerously fast for compromised pavements, Mr. Preston." But he ignored her and was concentrating on returning his middle finger as far out toward the passenger window as he could extend his arm while he passed the truck. Then he continued increasing his speed to put the truck in the distance with Lexie nagging the whole way to slow down.

As snowy as it was, Mr. Preston's prominent, ring bejeweled, middle finger wasn't lost on Eddie and Travis.

"What the hell," Eddie said, "I moved over, what else did he want, a hot fudge sundae?"

"I told you those Spectaculeer drivers were assholes," Travis innocently said, as though he had nothing to do with it.

"I'll show him," Eddie said as he sped up to tailgate the Spectaculeer. He turned on his brights then turned on his ultra-bright xenon fog lamps hidden under the grille. Travis was enjoying seeing Eddie becoming vengeful.

Mr. Preston was startled by the obnoxious lights behind him and could barely see anything because of the glare. He tried speeding up to get away from the truck, but the dually only followed close behind. Mr. Preston slowed a bit and moved over to the slow lane hoping they'd be happy to pass him and leave him alone. It looked like the truck was going to go ahead and go around him, but the truck came up alongside.

"Slow down Eddie, I want to get a load of this guy," Travis said as Eddie's truck came up even with the Spectaculeer again, this time on Mr. Preston's driver's side. Eddie slowed to drive side-by-side as he was irked that the guy in the Spectaculeer had the nerve to flip them off, not knowing that Travis instigated it.

Mr. Preston considered that the rednecks might be up to some bad business, so once again, he accelerated so fast that he could hear his soft-top rattling. He knew it would be dangerous, but he was getting both pissed off and concerned that they might run him right off the road into the snowbanks building along the shoulder.

Meanwhile, Lexie was busy trying to do her job without access to the auto-pilot control, "Mr. Preston, the roads are icy and dangerous. The temperature outside is thirteen degrees, and ambient temperature in the cabin is sixty-eight." But Mr. Preston was busy trying to ditch the truck people.

"Can you see the guy?" Eddie asked as they drove alongside the Spectaculeer.

"Um-hmm," said Travis looking out his window.

"Well, flip him the bird too," Eddie said.

Travis didn't need to be told twice, so he stuck his hand in the window with his middle finger prominently displayed right on the glass. He saw the Spectaculeer driver look up at him. Then Travis stuck his other hand up in the window with the other middle finger displayed.

"What are you doing, Travis?" Eddie demanded.

"Well, you said, 'flip him the bird too'....so this is two," Travis teased.

"Shit. You know what I meant," Eddie said. "What if the guy has a gun?"

Travis' smile fell. He hadn't thought of that but didn't want Eddie to know he hadn't thought of it. So Travis thought hard for a few seconds then said, "He can't dig out a gun while driving in nearly white-out conditions, and he can't shoot us if we are a mile ahead, so let's get going or run the guy off the road."

"I'm not running the guy off the road. I don't want to kill anyone," Eddie said.

"You won't kill him, there's too much snow. He'll just roll to a stop, that'll be enough time for us to get way ahead," Travis reasoned with his excruciatingly small brain.

"You are amazingly stupid, Travis. It is below freezing out, if he gets stuck out there, he'll freeze to death in a few hours. You know there's no help coming. You drove a snowplow one winter. You know they don't come out this far before the blizzard quits," Eddie explained.

Travis looked back at the Spectaculeer driver, who now had another hand signal in his window. It made Travis bristle.

"What the hell is that??" he shouted. Travis thought he'd seen that hand signal before but didn't remember what it meant.

Eddie tried to lean way over to see what Travis was talking about, but couldn't lean far enough to see down to the Spectaculeer's window. So he stretched way over to look, accidentally pulling the steering wheel just a bit, causing his truck to veer quickly toward the Spectaculeer.

Mr. Preston saw the front of that huge truck coming into his lane and knew he didn't dare swerve away on the snow-covered interstate, so he held the wheel loosely and hoped Lexie would make the necessary evasive moves, but he'd forgotten that he disengaged the auto-pilot program.

Eddie felt his truck veering and jumped back to the wheel, but his youthful inexperience had him overcorrect slightly, and he began to fishtail. Travis started to scream at him, and they both saw the little Spectaculeer moving ahead. Eddie was gathering his wits to slow when they saw the Spectaculeer suddenly vanish in the night. Just a second later Eddie and his brother saw the left front-quarter of their truck disappear into a wall of white, and they both felt the jolt of an absolute stop that was so abrupt that the back end of the truck lifted up a few inches where the wind caught it and swung it around a quarter turn before the rear slammed back down on the road. The truck was not moving and still in drive, the tires spinning, going nowhere. The entire driver's side was buried into an enormous snowdrift piled across the highway.

Looming nearly seven feet high in front of an overpass and spanning both westbound lanes of the interstate, it had formed in the dark, *a mega drift,* where blowing snow had shrouded the mountainous drift making it invisible in the night.

And now it had claimed its first two vehicles.

Chapter 37

Get My Drift?

"You ok, Travis?" Eddie asked as soon as he could rationalize what happened.

"Yeah, man, let's get out of here," Travis said even though his adrenalin had him shaking. "You drive like an asshole, Ed," he rudely said.

"No man," Eddie said, "it doesn't make any difference, we couldn't see this thing until we were already in it. That little swerve back there didn't have anything to do with plowing into this drift."

"You leaned over the seat and lost control," Travis scolded.

"You were asking me about that guy's hand sign, which, I believe, is the universal sign of peace, you moron. It's a "v" with two fingers, peace man. He just wanted to drive in peace," Eddie lambasted him.

"Ok, ok," Travis said, "let's just get out of here. If a big truck comes and doesn't see this, we'll be pancaked. Back this thing up and let's get going."

The engine was still running, so Eddie did as Travis said. But after shifting in reverse and trying to get the front corner of his truck out of the drift, his truck simply wasn't moving even though the tires were spinning. Eddie tried a few other maneuvers, rocking the truck out, attempting to move forward and back, but the drift would not let go.

"Shit Travis. This truck isn't going anywhere," Eddie announced. "We'll have to dig it out."

"Put it in four-wheel drive, it'll go over that drift."

"It's been in four-wheel drive since we left the diner," Eddie informed him. "And it won't go over this huge drift. I can't see either end of it and considering we can barely see the top edge, it's gotta be five to six feet high where we hit. All I can see is the snow swirling over the top. I think there is probably an overpass behind it, we have to get out of the truck and get under the overpass fast," Eddie started to rant. "Traffic will come, and if they can't stop, they'll plow into my truck, and we'll be creamed."

It took a few seconds to click with Travis, but when it finally sunk in, Travis was opening his door and trying to get out.

"Wait, man!" Eddie yelled, "you can't go out there in that hoodie. Where's your jacket, get it on! The wind chill will freeze you in five minutes!" Eddie instructed and tossed Travis his jacket while he got his own pea-coat buttoned-up, pulled his ballcap down tight, and grabbed an old pair of work gloves and a flashlight he had stashed under the seat.

"Damn it. I didn't see this coming. We don't have winter gear," Eddie griped as he scooted across the seat to follow Travis out of the passenger door.

The wind was howling, and snow blew in their faces and down their jacket necks. The snow was deep to tromp through and too cold to think about. Not far from them and half-buried in the drift, they could see only a bit of the trunk and the tail lights on the rear end of the Spectaculeer that was still running.

Eddie shouted over the wind and snow, "That guy really

plowed into the middle of the drift. I think we should check on him."

"Not me. I'm not having some tractor-trailer come slam me into muck on the back end of that Spectaculeer. I'm going to get around this snow trap and get under the overpass." And Travis began trudging through the snow to get around the drift.

Eddie wasn't comfortable leaving the guy. "My truck is going to be hit before his sports car," Eddie tried to yell at Travis, but Travis never looked back.

Eddie jammed his hands in his gloves quickly. With the flashlight tucked under his armpit, he pawed at the snowpack on the rear window of the Spectaculeer. He needed to clear a place to peek in and check on the guy. Maybe the guy was dead. He finally cleared a small space in the rear window, and he could see the guy in his car, struggling to get a door open, the dash lights still on. The guy just couldn't budge his door open with the snow piled against it. Eddie pounded on the rear window to get the driver's attention, then pointed to the driver's door and shouted that he'd try to get some snow pushed away enough so he could hopefully squeeze out the door.

Mr. Preston rolled his window down a tiny bit, "Hi, thanks for the help. I'm trying to call for a tow truck," he calmly said over the blowing snow.

Eddie could hear a woman's voice in the background saying, "This vehicle has come to an unexpected abrupt stop, Mr. Preston. There is some damage to the front bumper, but I will not set off the airbags as it appears your seatbelt has held you safe."

Eddie didn't see a woman in the car and told the driver, "I'll try to get the snow dug away so you can get out. Gotta work fast in case the next car doesn't see our lights," Eddie said. "You won't get a call out here, no cell towers."

"OK," Mr. Preston said, ignoring Eddie's information on cell phone towers and still trying to get a call out while he gathered his leather briefcase, gloves, scarf, and cashmere coat.

Eddie dug and dug, and there was nowhere to put the snow other than dig like a dog and push it between his legs with both hands, back up a little, and dig it out more.

Mr. Preston rolled his window down an inch again. "Don't you maintenance people usually have a shovel in your trucks?" Mr. Preston said.

Eddie stood up and looked at him in disbelief. But Eddie was quick and replied, "Don't you rich people usually have a chauffeur in your Spectaculeers?"

"Touché," Mr. Preston said, even though Eddie wasn't sure what he meant.

"Touché is a French term in fencing," Lexie said, talking to herself.

"Look, Mister, if I see any headlights, I'm taking off, you are on your own. My best suggestion then would be to lay on your front seat as flat as you can make yourself. If it's a big heavy truck, it'll do some serious damage," Eddie said, now heavily huffing and puffing from pushing the snow so hard and fast.

Mr. Preston tried to wedge the door open again. He could only get it open an inch or two.

"The driver's door is ajar, Mr. Preston," Lexie advised him.

He glanced out at Eddie feverishly pushing snow, when a glimmer of light out his back window caught his attention. Mr. Preston well understood the gravity of the current situation. Eddie saw it too.

"Look, Mister, I can't move all this snow fast enough. This is a ragtop, I got a fillet knife in my truck. I can cut this open...."

"NO!" Mr. Preston yelled. He could not fathom having his new Spectaculeer cut up. "Can't you dig faster?" He had no problem ordering Eddie.

"Look, mister, you have less than a minute and a half to decide to let me slice open that top and get you out, or you are going to have to kick out the rear window with your feet and crawl out, or stay in your precious Spectaculeer and get smashed.

"Ok, ok!" Mr. Preston was agitated but gave in. "Get your knife, cut me out!"

Lexie responded, "Mr. Preston, if someone is threatening you with a sharp object, would you like me to call 911?"

Mr. Preston finally cancelled Lexie and turned off his engine, grabbed his keys, and set his emergency flashers on while Eddie went to get his knife.

Eddie trudged out of the drift to his truck and quickly got his filet knife from under the seat and was about to climb up on the Spectaculeer with his knife when he saw Mr. Preston's pained face.

"You sure about this, Mister? You aren't going to sue me later?" Eddie asked.

"Cut the goddam top!" Mr. Preston yelled as he saw the headlights getting closer.

"Back away," Eddie said, as he took charge and raised the filet knife up over his head with both hands and jammed the point down into the custom convertible top and began trying to make a slice across the top. He was able with great difficulty to cut a cross into the fabric.

Mr. Preston was shoving his briefcase out the hole before he pushed his head through, and Eddie helped fish him out of the hole. They quickly climbed down and jumped into the snow, both watching the approaching vehicle. They had to trudge hard by the light of Eddie's flashlight as they worked their way across the edge of the drift to get around to the protection of the overpass. In the distance, Eddie could hear Travis hollering for him. It was so faint in the blinding snow and wind that Eddie didn't bother to answer.

"RUN!" Eddie heard Mr. Preston shout as he was pulling his legs out of the snow as fast as he could as the oncoming vehicle did not look like it was going to slow down at all. They followed the edge of the drift all the way to a steep embankment off the right shoulder before they found a place protected where they precariously slid down into the roadside ditch to get around the drift.

They were both trying to run hanging onto each other when they heard the sickening crash of metal, muted by the blizzard wind and the massive drift of snow.

"Jeezus," Mr. Preston shouted over the gale-force wind, "They hit hard, I hope they didn't hit my car."

"Maybe we should go back and see if they need help," Eddie shouted back over the wind.

"Look!" Mr. Preston took Eddie by the shoulders and pointed him toward the oncoming traffic. "Two more vehicles are coming. We'd better get up under the bridge, now!"

They were just getting up under the overpass, and Travis stuck out a hand to help them up the snow-covered berm when they heard two more crashes.

"Oh shit," Mr. Preston shouted over the wind, "this is going to be bad."

"Very bad," Eddie added.

"Thanks for getting me out," Mr. Preston heard himself say to Eddie.

They couldn't see much over the drift other than the top courtesy lights on Eddie's truck cab, but they could see the glimmer of at least one headlight through the blowing snow.

"I don't hear anyone hollering for help," Eddie fretted.

"Why would you yell out here? Ain't nobody gonna hear you," Travis yelled into the wind.

They saw another pair of headlights in the distance. "That's a truck!" Eddie shouted over the wind, "I can see the marker lights on the top of the cab."

"You mean a tractor-trailer truck?" Mr. Preston hollered back as he fished through his attaché case for a small penlight.

"I hope not," Eddie yelled back. "A loaded semi can weigh as much as eighty thousand pounds. If it's coming at a good clip, it could push that whole drift, your car, and my truck right up to our necks!"

Mr. Preston aimed his penlight to stare at Eddie's face.

"I'm not making that up," Eddie told him under the little spotlight that the LED made on his face.

Mr. Preston scrunched himself further up into the corner of the bridge decking.

"Ain't gonna do you no good, Mister. If that is a semi, the cab will hit that drift and cut the speed to near nothing, and that trailer could whip around on this snow and clean everything off above the underride bar. Which way it'd go, I don't know. And if it goes to the left, it could take out part of the bridge support."

"I think you are scaring this man," Travis yelled to Eddie.

As the lights of the oncoming truck loomed closer, Eddie wiped the snow out of his eyes and squinted at the pattern of the lights, they looked familiar.

"I don't think that's a semi," Eddie said, "it looks like a seriously dressed up dually. Way more than mine."

They watched the big dually suddenly hit its brakes and fishtail into a spin and heard the muted crash into the accumulating piles of ice, snow, and vehicles.

"I don't see anyone else coming. We should go down and see if anyone needs help," Eddie called back to Travis and Mr. Preston.

"I can't, man," Travis chattered back through the blowing snow. Dressed only in only a hoodie sweatshirt and light jacket, Travis was nearly begging, "I'm freezing my nuts off. You got another jacket or something in your truck?"

Mr. Preston shined his penlight at Travis. "Your lips do look like they are turning a bit blue, kid."

"I think I got a tarp in the back of my truck. But my legs are nearly freezing from the snow we walked through," Eddie said.

"Well," Mr. Preston added, "we need to figure out how to keep warm. We won't survive another half hour out here without going into hypothermia."

"Okay, I'll go down and check my truck and see if anyone else needs help," Eddie volunteered. Travis suddenly felt the slightest smidgeon of pride that his little, useless, non-athletic brother was tougher than he thought.

Eddie slid down the embankment. Trying to cover his face from the blowing snow, he hunched up the wool collar of his pea coat, and he stumbled through the uneven edges of the ever-growing drift. There was an edge that diminished some off the shoulder of the roadway, so Eddie used it, backing himself down the steep embankment and continued plodding through the snow and up the other side toward the pavement.

He hurried as fast as he could, pulling his legs out and tromping down the next step, their previous footprints nearly covered by the blowing snow.

He came around the drift and saw a big blue dually slid sideways into his dually but not hard enough to do a lot of damage. Both were together side by side like a parking lot and apparently had overlapped bumpers. The driver couldn't jump his truck free. Eddie rapped on the window of the passenger's side, which made the driver jump. The dually's engine was still running, so the driver unlocked the door. Eddie opened it, jumped in, and immediately put his legs and hands into the heater air under the dash.

"Hey man, I'm Eddie. We gotta get you out of here before the next vehicle comes. If it's big, you could get hurt."

"Damn," Ben said. "I saw the tail lights right there in the snow but just couldn't quite get stopped on the road before hitting this guy's truck."

"That's my truck," Eddie said.

"Oh, sorry, man. No offense. My tires just couldn't get a grip on the road anymore with the snow piling up," Ben explained.

"No offense taken," Eddie said, "but we gotta get you outta here. It's freakin' cold out there. Until we get help, we gotta stay off the road."

"Check," Ben said, "I have ski gear," and he reached back into a duffle bag and pulled out a ski mask, polar gloves, boots, a battery-operated heated jacket, and heated gloves, putting things on as quickly as he could.

"I gotta get a tarp out of my truck and get it up to the others," Eddie said. "I heard two other hits, can you check to see if anyone else needs help?

"Yeah, I'm good for at least 20-below in this. I have an extra heavy sweatshirt here if you need it. I'll check the other cars until I see headlights coming. Here, here's a hand-warmer pack, put one in each pocket."

Eddie looked at the little packets. "Amazing what they come up with these days." Eddie put a warmer pack in each pocket, squeezing them to activate the contents then said with his hand on the door handle, "Thanks for the sweatshirt and packs, my brother is up under the overpass freezing to death, he'll need this sweatshirt. I hate going back out in the cold but gotta get my brother and another survivor some warmth under the bridge on the other side of this drift. I hope I still have the tarp in my truck."

"Check. I got a quilt and a down sleeping bag, I'll grab that, and I'll see what else I can find smashed into this mess."

Eddie's truck headlights were now buried in the snow and useless, but one of Ben's truck lights at least lit up some of the drift and pile of cars.

Eddie was thrilled that he still had the tarp in his truck and headed back to the bridge with it while Ben walked around and saw a car nearly two-thirds buried into the drift. Ben pounded on the trunk lid to see if there was any movement inside the car.

A rear window rolled down a crack, and Ben could see a young girl crying, "Please don't hurt us. Please help us!"

Ben realized his face mask might cause concern for a young girl. "I'm here to help, just wearing a ski mask for warmth," he assured her, "are you okay?" Ben shouted over the wind. "Is anyone injured?"

"Yes." Tawnie tried to hold back her tears. "Brittany hit her head pretty hard on the steering wheel and has a big cut, and she passed out. Delphia said she isn't dead."

"So, there's three of you in there?" Ben asked.

"Yes," Tawnie said, trying not to cry. "Delphia is holding a t-shirt on Brittany's head to stop the bleeding. Can you call for an ambulance?"

"Oh, I'm sorry," Ben said, "there's no cell service out here. Even if there was, no one is going to come out this far to help in this storm." Ben heard Delphia in the car telling Tawnie, "I told you that already."

"We should get you all out of this car, if a big truck comes up here fast, it'll smash your car into smithereens and you with it. Get your coats and everything else you have to keep warm, and we'll get you out." Ben moved to the sheltered side of the car and started moving snow away from the back door. Inside, the girls were putting on everything they could find. Delphia had put on Brittany's new Mizzou sweatshirt and was trying to get a coat on Brittany.

Ben finally got their rear door cleared enough to get it opened enough to stick his head in. He saw the three terribly frightened and shocked high school girls. Tawnie was small enough to slide out of the semi-open door and stood in the snow, waiting for her friends. Delphia tried to push Brittany up and over the seat while Ben moved more snow to get that back door open so he could help Delphia get Brittany out of the car.

"Hey, what's your name?" he hollered over his shoulder to an already shivering girl.

"Tawnie," she said.

"Well, I'm Ben, Tawnie. Your job is going to be keeping an eye on the road behind us. You tell us the minute you see any approaching headlights."

"Oh god, no," Tawnie began to cry again, "I don't want to die."

"You aren't going to die," Ben said, "as long as you tell us if you see a car coming."

Ben went back to digging snow away from the door, and soon he was able to push enough snow away to squeeze himself in. He and Delphia struggled with Brittany, but Brittany was dead weight. Ben stopped to gather his wits.

Tawnie stood her post and barely blinked, squinting through the swirling snow, looking into the inky blackness back down the highway. She was shivering and held her arms folded, but never looked anywhere but for headlights. She suddenly felt a hand on her shoulder, and she expected to see Ben, but it wasn't. It was a young man with a sweatshirt tied around his head.

"Are you okay?" he asked.

With all the fear and shock, Tawnie couldn't answer.

"It's okay young lady. I'm Reverend Matthew. I wrecked my Minibus over there. I saw the taillights on that truck and slammed on my brakes and downshifted, but the wind caught my bus broadside and spun me off the road. That's it, laying on its side." Matthew looked, but the snow and darkness obliterated most of the view of his Minibus.

"You okay?" Tawnie finally got out.

"Yeah, just some bumps and bruises. Here, you look cold." And he took the blanket Ben left sitting on the trunk of Brittany's car and wrapped it around Tawnie's shoulders. "Why are you out here?" he asked as he adjusted the blanket on her. "Whose blanket is this?"

"I'm watching for cars coming. My friends are stuck in the car there." Tawnie pointed to the back end of their car.

Matthew tromped through the snow and looked inside, and saw Ben and Delphia struggling with Brittany.

"Scoot over, man....let me give you a hand," Matthew said. "Is she dead?"

"No," Delphia said, "she's just out cold from whacking her head on the steering wheel. She still has a pulse."

The three of them were able to wrangle Brittany's body up and over the seat, and while Ben and Reverend Matthew struggled to get Brittany out of the car, Delphia saw that she had no shoes on. Delphia fished the front seat looking for her shoes. She thought Brittany had brought boots to show off for Bryce at the ski lodge, but she couldn't find them now. As Ben and Reverend Matthew lugged Brittany out of the car, the cold wind hit her face, and she moaned a bit.

"Take it easy young lady," Reverend Matthew said, "we're going to get you help."

Ben gave Matthew a look of serious doubt. Matthew shrugged it off.

As Delphia climbed over the seat to leave the car, she saw Brittany's boots in the back seat and grabbed them. Ben saw Tawnie already wrapped up in his quilt and was still shivering. The five of them began to trudge through the snow.

"Where are we going?" Delphia asked. "It's getting very dark away from the headlights."

"The guy from that other truck said they were hiding under the overpass on the other side of the drift. We have to stay out of oncoming traffic and out of the wind," Ben said.

Delphia didn't answer. She was quickly working things in her head to figure out a way to remedy their current pitiful situation.

The five started to follow Eddie's tracks back to the overpass, but it was tough going for Ben and Matthew having to carry Brittany. She was still out. Ben told everyone to wait a minute, and he tromped back to his truck and grabbed his down sleeping bag and his flashlight. "We'll need this sleeping bag for that girl." He indicated Brittany. "She'll need to be kept warm, it'll be best if we can pack her up in it." Delphia stuck her hand out, offering to carry the sleeping bag and snuggled close to Tawnie sharing the quilt, but the wind was blowing so hard that the quilt wasn't doing much but flapping in the wind.

"Good idea to bring a blanket, Tawnie," Delphia said as they tromped through the snow. "We could use a couple of them now. Wish we would have listened."

As they got to the edge of the drift following Eddie's path to slide down the steep embankment next to the thicket of bushes, they could barely see the one headlight of Ben's truck that wasn't buried in the drift. They had very little light other than Ben's flashlight and the faint glimmer of the headlights of Matthew's sideways Minibus as the battery was quickly dying. Eddie was waiting with his flashlight near the back end of the drift to show the way. As they met up, they trudged along until they all came under the overpass. Mr. Preston waved his penlight at them as he and Travis held their hands out to help the newcomers up under the bridge.

Eddie tossed the extra sweatshirt to Travis. "This is from the new guy," and indicated Ben. "And I got the tarp," Eddie shouted. "I think it's big enough that we can all get under it and hold the edges down.

"Good idea," Ben said. "It'll help keep the wind out and hold our heat in."

They fought with the canvas tarp in the wind, and eventually, they'd worked their way to sitting under the tarp with the edges pulled down over their backs, and they either sat on or held down the edges. It helped some, as the snow was no longer blowing in their faces and down their necks, but it was still very cold.

Delphia and Ben situated Brittany in Ben's sleeping bag. It was a stressful situation so, Delphia was thankful for the thoughtfulness of the man with the ski mask. Delphia still held Brittany's head in her lap and was holding the blood-stained shirt on Brittany's head.

"Too bad we can't build a fire in here," Travis said. He was still cold, but thankful the wind wasn't blowing on him and grateful for Ben's maple leaf sweatshirt as he sat sandwiched between Eddie and Ben. Delphia and Tawnie shared Ben's blanket between Mr. Preston and Reverend Matthew. Matthew was clearly cold, so Tawnie offered him a corner of the quilt.

Ben spoke up, "That's my Aunt's handmade quilt," he told Delphia as he took off his ski mask. "My Aunt forced me to take the quilt, but now I'm glad to have it, and I know she'd be happy to know it came in handy. Let's have some introductions since I think we could be here for a while. I'm Ben. I was headed to Colorado to take a job as a ski instructor. I'm from Vermont and got this far." Delphia could barely see anyone's faces with only the penlight and flashlight for light, but she couldn't help notice that Ben seemed to be quite an attractive young man.

Eddie used his flashlight to shine in his own face, "I'm Eddie, this is my brother Travis. We were heading to..." Eddie then saw Travis glaring at him that he was about to blow their cover, but Eddie saved it, "....heading to Colorado to visit relatives for Christmas. We're from St Louis."

"I'm from St Louis too," Mr. Preston said. "My name is Tremont Preston." Mr. Preston wasn't that interested in being in a casual relationship with this ragtag group of storm refugees, but at least he had come to realize his situation and knew the boys had probably saved his life. "I just got that custom ordered Spectaculeer a few weeks ago. I was on my way to a golf tournament in Palm Springs."

"What do you do for a living?" Matthew innocently asked as if he didn't remember the snippy lawyer from the diner.

Mr. Preston hung his head and sighed, "I'm a lawyer."

Eddie and Travis exchanged worried glances. Ben and Reverend Matthew chuckled a bit.

"I believe we met earlier this evening at the diner," Matthew said. "You were in a rush."

"True," Mr. Preston said. "I guess this is my reward for trying to drive to Palm Springs to show off.

"Well, if we want to sue Mother Nature in this storm, we got the guy, eh?" Matthew teased.

Mr. Preston smiled a small smile.

Delphia jumped in. "I'm Delphia, this is Brittany," Delphia said as she lifted the bloody shirt off Brittany's face. At least the bleeding had stopped.

"I'm Tawnie. We were heading to Colorado so Brittany could see her boyfriend for Christmas," she confessed.

Mr. Preston raised an eyebrow figuring no parent would allow his teenage girl to go traveling that far for Christmas, so he asked, "Do your parents' know where you are?"

Neither of the girls answered right away. Delphia finally confirmed his suspicions. "No, sir. Brittany didn't want our folks to know. They would never let us do this, and she knew it. She talked us into this stupid trip and said we'd be back home the next day, and our parents would never know."

"I guess this is going to put a wrinkle into that plan," Mr. Preston said, as he looked at Brittany, thinking she could well be his daughter and wondered if his own daughter would sneak off like this without telling him. He was thinking about how often he pushed her away, and perhaps he should be more available to her.

"I'm Matthew," Matthew said. "I've already met Mr. Preston at the diner. But nice to meet everyone else. I'm a Protestant reverend from Raleigh, Georgia, headed to Victoria, Kansas, to minister to a new flock of farmers."

Matthew wasn't saying it, but he was plenty scared when he considered the situation from what the truckers and Agnes had mentioned to him only hours earlier. He also knew it was his job to tend to the spiritual needs of everyone huddled under the bridge. And if any of them should die of injuries or cold, it'd be him to tend the dying. He began to have some conflicting issues with telling people the truth that there was no help on the way and there wouldn't be any until the storm ended, or if he should try to bolster everyone's hope by encouraging them with positive messages that he knew were lies.

While Matthew was going over all this in his head and everyone was chatting, Matthew decided to encourage hopefulness among the survivors and interrupted, "I don't know everyone's faith requirements, but I will help you with your spiritual needs if you like. If you allow me, I'd like to say a prayer of thanks to our Heavenly Father that we are all pretty much okay, and to find us some help."

Everyone except Travis nodded their heads in approval, even Mr. Preston bowed his head.

"Dear Heavenly Father," Matthew shouted over the wind with his eyes closed, "we thank you for sparing us this day and ask your blessings to help us find help, help us stay warm, and for us to help each other. And please, if you can, end this blizzard. Amen."

Matthew heard a couple of amens from the group. It was short and sweet.

Then Mr. Preston spoke, "Do you guys with those big trucks think one of them is moveable? If we can get it out of the drift, can it be driven around the drift and maybe keep going to get help? Or, if nothing else, drive it into the field off the road? At least we could sit in it with the heat on and not get smashed by the next oncoming car."

Eddie spoke up, "I might be able to move my truck out. But the cab is small, if we jammed ourselves in it, we wouldn't get all eight of us in it. What about your truck, Ben?"

"I don't know," Ben shouted back, "I have a back seat, we might all be able to get in, but I think my front bumper is wedged under Ed's truck. If we can get it out of there, I might be able to get around the other edge of the drift, where it might have diminished amounts of snow. Maybe I can squeeze between the overpass pillars, and maybe I can park under the overpass to provide a bit of protection. Maybe, maybe, maybe," Ben shrugged.

"If you can get unhooked, maybe you can drive back for some help," Travis said.

"There's no point in trying to drive for help," Ben explained. "The way this is blowing there will be more drifts ahead, and with no snow fences in the open range areas, it will look like one flat expanse of snow. You can't tell where the road is, and you could easily drive off the road and end up down a ravine or into a bridge rail. There's a smaller drift forming just beyond the other side of this overpass, and this storm is only going to get worse, based on what I know about blizzards. Going for help right now would be a gamble. It'd be best to shelter in place until the storm calms a bit."

"Well, if we don't try to do something, we'll never survive like this. We'll be frozen in an hour. And this girl, her lips are turning blue," Mr. Preston pointed out with his little LED penlight.

Tawnie started to cry. "Oh Brittany, come on, girl, you'll be okay, just wake up."

Delphia calmed her, "She'll be okay Tawnie, this cold will help keep her from any brain damage in case there is bleeding inside her skull. As long as she's out, at least she's not feeling pain."

"But she also can't tell us that her legs are freezing off!" Tawnie continued to cry softly.

"The down sleeping bag will keep her legs from freezing off, Tawnie, I think, so she's not going to die," Delphia continued to be reasonable, yet she too was concerned.

Ben considered the situation. He was well dressed for the cold, but he couldn't watch these people freeze to death. "Eddie, you and me, we'll go try to untangle our trucks. If we can get them both loose, we'll each try to get around the drift in four-wheel drive. Do you have chains in that thing?"

"No," Eddie said, "no chains. We don't get a lot of snow in St. Louis. It wasn't worth the expense. I wish I had them now."

"I don't have them either," Ben said. "My truck was parked in a barn for two years, and it didn't even get wet. But I think we should try to move to a sheltered place. We'll have to watch for oncoming traffic, and as soon as we see headlights, we are going to have to abandon our trucks and make a run for it."

"I'm going too," Mr. Preston said. As soon as he said it, he was surprised that he volunteered. "If something happens, at least you have another pair of hands. At least I have some gloves and a coat. That'll leave Reverend Matthew and Travis to keep an eye on the girls."

Just about then, they heard another crashing sound like metal to metal. "Holy shit!" Eddie said. "Oh, sorry, excuse me, Reverend."

"You're okay," Matthew said. "Sounds like someone else added to the pile."

"I hope they don't hit so hard to rupture a gas line or a gas tank and cause an explosion," Travis said. Eddie frowned at his brother's drama.

"Well, I also hope the other vehicles didn't wedge us in so we can't get a truck out," Ben said. "We'd better get going before this gets worse."

"Mr. Preston," Matthew said, "here, take my sweatshirt and wrap it around your head. Your ears can get frostbite pretty fast in the wind, and it's very painful."

Mr. Preston looked around for his cashmere scarf that was now missing. "The wind must have taken my scarf," he said, "I don't remember it taking off." And now Mr. Preston looked at the overly worn, pilled, ratty sweatshirt, and was considering the options when Travis spoke up, "Look, Mr. P, no offense, but this is no time for a fashion show. Suck it up and wrap that around your head. We don't need any more casualties." Eddie was surprised that his brother actually made some sense for a change and sounded human rather than like his usual arrogant self.

"He's right. This no time for a fashion statement," Matthew said slightly amused that this was at least the third time he'd heard that today.

Mr. Preston put the sweatshirt over his head and tied the arms under his chin and gave everyone a cheesy grin. Then as they began to crawl out from under the tarp, Mr. Preston half-joked, "Ah'll be bahk!" in a terrible Schwartzenegger accent. There were a few groans.

The three men left Travis, and Matthew huddled up next to the girls, all sharing the big quilt. Tawnie was still chattering both from the cold and from her fears while Delphia tended Brittany, alternating rubbing Brittany's arms and legs through the sleeping bag to keep the circulation going.

Chapter 38

Helping Hands in a Blizzard

Eenie, Mina Minus Snow

"I think this freaking storm is getting worse!" Eddie shouted, clutching his coat around his neck as the three trudged down to the front of the drift to check the trucks. It was a couple inches deeper now as they tromped in the snow.

"Try to walk in my footprints," Ben shouted back to the other two. "It'll save your energy."

They finally came around the drift to where their flashlights could see the roadway and the conglomeration of askew vehicles. A couple of motors were still running and a few with lights still on. The girl's small car was dark and quiet, and the Minibus was off the road laying on its side, it's dim headlights looking like the battery was just about done. They could also see on the inside lane up against the guard rail was a newcomer, a large, blue, older Lincoln.

"You check on the Lincoln," Ben told Mr. Preston, "Ed and I are going to try to get our trucks loose."

"Check," Mr. Preston said and started to trudge over to the Lincoln. As he got close enough, he could see people moving in the car. He knocked on the passenger window, startling the person inside. There was a lot of movement in the car before the window rolled down about an inch.

"Are you okay?" Mr. Preston asked, clutching his coat around his neck in the wind and snow. "Anyone hurt?"

"I told zis schmuck he vas driving too fast!" Wilhelmina nearly screamed out the window at Mr. Preston, but he understood she was both scared and angry.

"We need to get you off the road right now," he said to her. "Do you understand?"

"Off za road?" Wilhelmina asked.

"Yes, in case a big truck comes. It could hit your car and kill you. Or cause an explosion of gas tanks. There are already five cars piled up here."

Auggie leaned over, "I am not leavink my Lincoln. I can get it un-stuck."

"It won't make any difference, Sir." Mr. Preston was trying to get him to understand the situation. "There is a huge snowdrift over the road, you cannot drive through it. We are getting everyone out of their vehicles and off the road."

"I haff radio!" Auggie announced like he just invented the fly-swatter, shaking his microphone at Mr. Preston. And he started to try to talk on the radio when Mr. Preston realized being nice wasn't going to get these elderly people out of there. He saw Wilhelmine's fur coat draped over the back seat and commented on it.

"Nice fur coat," he said, pointing her mink, then deliberately mumbled some other stuff so Wilhelmine would have to roll the window down a bit more to hear him. Then he quickly stuck his arm in the window space and unlocked Wilhelmina's door, swung it open, and told her she had to get out.

"Is cold!" she said. "I stay with Auggie. If we die, we die." And she folded her arms in defiance.

Mr. Preston appealed to her common sense. "Ok, you wanna die fine, but what if you only get half-smashed. No ambulance will come out in the snow like this, and it will ruin that lovely fur coat." Wilhelmina thought about that for a couple of seconds, looked at Auggie, and said, "I go now with zis man. I don't vant to be half-smashed potato pancake and don't vant to ruin mink."

"You go, voman!" Auggie shouted. "I get help on radio, and I vill get Lincoln out of trap here. Dis Lincoln like a tank, not like plastic cars dey make today."

"You can't make dat crazy Kraut do anyting," Wilhelmina told Mr. Preston. "Oh, and nice hat you got," she said, shaking her head at Mr. Preston's ratty sweatshirt hat. She got out of the car and opened the back door and grabbed her mink. "You should have mink too," she pointed at Mr. Preston's coat, "you got nice cashmere but never as warm as mink." And Wilhelmine slipped her arms into the fur. "Dis mink old now, but mink still warm. Auggie got me dis for our 50th anniversary."

"Oh, that's nice," Mr. Preston entertained her. "Nice to be married that long, my marriage only lasted ten years."

"Dis coat not for wedding anniversary, it vas for 50th anniversary of butcher shop! Eh, only ten years you gave your marriage, you just getting to know each other," she chatted as Mr. Preston led her away from the Lincoln.

Eddie and Ben couldn't separate the trucks as easy as they hoped by attempting to jump on the bumpers to bounce them apart. They decided to try one last Hail Mary. Eddie would rev up his engine and kick it into drive, and Ben would rev up his and kick it in reverse, and both would drop their trucks in gear at the same time, hoping they'd separate them by jumping them apart or ripping the bumpers totally off. Ben sat with his truck in neutral with one foot on the gas, winding up his engine with his window down, listening to Eddie rev up the RPM's in his truck until he thought one of the motors would throw a rod. They shouted to each other, "On three." Eddie nodded to Ben, then shouted, "One, two, THREE!" and both shifted their trucks into gear and let their feet off the brakes. Sure enough, the front end of Eddie's truck reared up slightly as it tried to lurch forward, and Ben's took just enough of a bounce down in reverse to unhook the bumpers. Ben's truck was free, but Eddie's was still jammed in the snow even farther now. Ben hollered to Eddie, "You want me to see if I can push the bed of your truck around to wedge it out of the drift? I think there's enough packed snow under it to be able to slide a little."

"I guess so," Eddie said, hating the thought of his truck being smashed up. Ben was thinking the same thing about his Blue Bomb but knew his Uncle Willie would always do something to help people in trouble.

Ben pulled his truck around and aimed the front end of it perpendicular to the side of Eddie's truck bed and ever so slowly closed in until they touched. Eddie put his truck in neutral, then Ben put his in low then slowly pressed the accelerator, trying to push Eddie's truck around to free the truck's front end from the weight of the ice and snow of the drift. After some engine revving and pushing, it looked like Ben was only pushing Eddie's truck deeper into the drift.

Ben got out of his truck to look at whatever damage he may have caused and saw Mr. Preston escorting Wilhelmina along. "What 'cha got there?" he asked Mr. Preston about the fur-covered old woman on his arm.

"An old couple in the blue Lincoln. The old man thinks he can move that thing. He says he's got a radio and is trying to find help."

"Oooo-kay," Ben said with some skepticism. "Put her in the back seat of my truck, so she's not freezing."

Mr. Preston led Wilhelmine to the back of the big blue dually shining his little flashlight so Wilhelmine could see where she was going. "Nice color dis truck," Wilhelmine said as he opened the door, but it was a few big steps for her to get in, and she was having trouble getting a foot up on the running board.

Suddenly Eddie came scrambling around the back of his truck, "CAR!" he started screaming, "CAR!!" Mr. Preston looked up to see another pair of headlights in the distant blowing snow. Ben came around the other side and shouted over the wind, "Time to go. I think we're unhooked. Get in, now!"

Wilhelmine's foot kept slipping, and Mr. Preston watched the oncoming car closing in. "Come on, ma'am. Just put your foot up here...." he said.

"This foot is having trouble..." she said as she struggled.

Mr. Preston looked up again, and the headlight halo was much closer. They were out of time. "Sorry ma'am, no time left for pleasantries," and he took her purse from her and threw it in the truck, then put his hands on her rear end and gave a big shove sending Wilhelmine and her mink nearly airborne like a fat, flying squirrel up into the back seat of the truck, her face landing comfortably on her needlepoint purse. Mr. Preston scrambled in after her. Ben was already in the driver's seat, and Eddie was shutting the passenger door, "Go! Go! Go!" he shouted, pounding his hands on the dashboard.

"We're in!" Mr. Preston hollered while slamming the door shut. "Let's go! Get us out of here!" he shouted at Ben.

Ben didn't bother to reply to the obvious, he was already in reverse and trying to rock his truck over the snow that had piled under it. Everyone in the truck was helping as they kept looking back to see the proximity of the oncoming car.

Wilhelmine had finally righted herself and was trying to look out the window to see if Auggie was coming, but she couldn't see much of anything out in the dark except the headlight halos through the snow. Finally, they all felt the truck drive backward a few feet then a few more, and everyone applauded as Ben got his truck moving. He backed up, and his backup lights lit enough behind them that he could see the big Lincoln still up against the guardrail next to the median with its lights on. Ben hoped the Lincoln would be far enough out of the line of fire of the oncoming vehicle. "I'm going off-road now, so hang on. There's a pretty deep ditch under the snow, then I'll try to get around this drift to the backside and under the bridge. My undercarriage is high enough, I think I can plow through it."

"I don't know if that's a safe enough place, Ben," Mr. Preston advised. "Eddie mentioned earlier, if a loaded 18-wheeler comes in here with a tired driver, he'll plow right through that drift and right into us or hit the bridge supports and collapse the bridge on top of us. Maybe we'd be better off out in the field."

There's no shelter in the field," Ben said as he slowly moved the truck off the interstate and slowly down the shoulder to the steep ditch that ran alongside the road. "I think we'd be better off staying on the road so we can be found....just in case things go sideways."

"At least it's warm in here," Eddie said, putting his hands and feet down in front of the heater vent.

"Ist my Auggie going to be alright?" Wilhelmine asked, still looking out the windows.

"His Lincoln is pretty tough. He will probably be okay," Mr. Preston said as they bounced around down the steep embankment into the ditch to get around the drift.

"By the way, I am Tremont Preston," he stuck his hand out to her.

"I am Vilhelmine Buchbinder, the butcher's vife!" and she lightly shook his hand. "Everybody calls me Mina."

Chapter 39

Military Mode Mayday

Auggie's Towncar Tank

Auggie saw the oncoming lights in the distance but needed to get a message out to that truck driver about this pile-up on the interstate. Auggie slipped into military mode, his mind going back to when he was a marine in WWII, the bombs going off around him, and guns shooting over his head. He got the feeling of the foxhole adrenalin and knew his unit depended on his getting a message out. He grabbed the mike and pressed the button and shouted into it.

"Mayday! Mayday! Mr. Cockroach, this is The Butcher, Mayday!" In the adrenalin rush, the memories came back of radio signal corps, so now he knew to let up on the mike button. Auggie listened but heard no answer. He repeated his message again as the distant headlights kept coming. Still, he got no answer. He knew in another thirty seconds there was going to be a collision, but he wasn't about to leave his foxhole. Once again, he pressed the button, "Mayday. This is The Butcher. Big accident on highway in snowdrift. Slow down. Mr. Cockroach, Mayday!!"

Auggie saw the headlights closing in on the pile-up when suddenly the lights veered to the right, away from him, then the tail lights swung around, and again the headlights came back around. This oncoming vehicle was spinning. "TOO FAST!" Auggie shouted at them, even though they wouldn't hear him. He saw the Minivan spin around once more before it skidded onto the shoulder on the other side of the road. He saw by its lights that it missed the guardrail then slid down the steep embankment, tipping over on its side and sliding to a stop.

Auggie watched in horror for only a second before he was back on his radio. "Mayday, dis is Augustus Heinrich Buchbinder, there is big accident on seventy highway. One roll-over, a snowdrift, some stuck cars. Please send help. Mayday." Auggie let up on the button and held the mike to his chest and prayed for an answer.

"This is the Cockroach," Auggie finally heard crackling distantly through the static. "What's your twenty?"

"Mr. Roach, this is Auggie, the Butcher. Big accident."

"Do you know where you are at?" Chuck asked.

"On interstate seventy, someplace in Kansas," Auggie answered.

"Well, Mr. Butcher, I don't know if I'm ahead of you or behind you," Chuck answered back. "Do you know what mile marker you are around or what the last town sign you saw?"

"I don't know mile markers. Last time we saw a sign, it was truck stop. I tink it was Midnight something," Auggie said.

"Was it Agnes' Midnight Truck Stop Diner?" Chuck asked.

"Ya. I tink so. We did not stop. We went to rest area after dat, maybe three-quarters of an hour after passink diner. Mina did not have to go when we saw diner."

"Okay, Auggie, is your car drivable?" Chuck asked.

"I don't know. I cannot talk on the box and drive," Auggie answered back.

"Well, find out. If you can, get your car as far off the road as possible, so the next car coming doesn't hit you.

"Next car coming already happen. Looks like Minivan, they go too fast, they spin and fall off da road. Van on its side now, but looks like someone trying to get out of da back hatch."

"There won't be any help, Auggie. Our radio signals don't send far enough for highway patrol or sheriff. See if you can help them," Chuck suggested.

"Ok," Auggie said.

"I am going to try to radio someone on another station. So see what you can do to help the people in the Minivan. I'll try to get back with you in a short," Chuck said.

"This is bad time of year to wear dem shorts, Mr. Roach," Auggie told him.

"Um, yes, I know," Chuck said, shaking his head and smiling. "Over and out."

Auggie put the mike down and put his car in reverse to try to pull away from the guardrail he'd slid into to avoid crashing into the drift. He heard the metal to metal scraping of the guardrail and the side of his car. But Auggie was still in marine mode and knew he had a job to do. He jammed his transmission down into low and slowly backed away from the guard-rail, scraping down the whole side of his beloved Lincoln. He moved away enough to drive across both lanes of traffic, shining his headlights on the Minivan laying on its side. The back hatch was now open, and a young man was helping two children out into the snow.

"Oh cheeesh," Auggie said under his breath. "Das kinder. This is not good for dem." Auggie turned his brights on and put his car in park. He opened his door and stepped out and shouted through the wind, "Are you okay?"

The answer came back, "I think so," as a young woman crawled out of the hatch. She had a toddler in her arms that was clutching her mother as tight as she could.

"You must get in my car. You vill freeze children! Ve must get off highway before more cars come," Auggie shouted, the frozen air making him cough. He got back in his car and watched the family of five trudge through the snow, slowly climbing up the embankment of the shoulder, slipping now and then, and hanging onto each other.

Auggie was still coughing when Jeff opened the passenger door.

"Are you sure this is okay? Jeff asked Auggie.

"Ja," he coughed more. "Yust get in." Carol and the three kids opened the back, and Carol had to stack a few of Wilhelmine's bags and boxes, but there was plenty of room for the four of them.

"Wow, cool, dad! This car is so big!" Nick said.

"We haff to get off dis highway," Auggie said between coughs.

"Are you going to be all right?" Jeff asked Auggie again, concerned about the coughing.

"Ya," Auggie coughed. "I was marine in WWII, dis snow is notting compared to bombs going off!"

"How are we going to get off the road?" Jeff asked. "That is a pretty big drop into the ditch." Jeff pointed to the side where his van rolled down. "That's how we ended up on our side, just too much angle down that ditch."

"Ya, I see dat," Auggie said. "I tink I can go on other side of drift. Maybe median isn't such a ditch." And Auggie backed up his car and turned to go to the left around the mounting drift. He aimed for the guard rail again and pulled up parallel to it, shifted into low, and pressed lightly on the accelerator. "Dis car like a tank, I push the snow away and hope drift is small, and no one coming dis way."

Jeff didn't know what to say. But with his van laying on its side, he didn't have many other choices. He saw the burgundy dually truck's tail lights with the front buried in the drift and a conglomeration of other cars sticking out.

Auggie was determined not to abandon his post to help this family to safety. He slowly guided his Lincoln along the guard rail, scraping the driver's side more.

"I'm sorry about your car," Christie said.

"Is only car, young lady," Auggie said. "No car is important ven it comes to family."

"Oh, but we aren't your family," Christie corrected.

"Not mine," Auggie said, "but you are A family. Togedder. Notting more important dan that!"

Carol winked at Christie, she knew the old man was right.

Auggie kept moving forward and pushing snow with the giant Lincoln grille.

"Hope metal rail end soon. I don't tink car is going to push much more snow," Auggie said.

Just about the time he said it, the scraping sound ended, and Auggie could steer his landship a little farther toward the median where the drift had waned into about a foot of snow. Auggie goosed the big V-8 engine, and the car plowed up and over the mound of snow. The Lincoln was finally free. Auggie was relieved he didn't have to cross the median, and only had to get over the tail end of the drift.

"Ahh! Now we roll!" Auggie said, attempting young people slang.

Everyone was sighing relief, and Auggie was beginning to move along when the car banged to an abrupt stop. Auggie's lap belt kept him from whacking his head. Nick had fallen onto the floor of the backseat, and Carol was hanging onto the back of the front seat clutching Holly. Christie was okay, and Jeff managed to catch himself on the dashboard. Auggie was muttering something in German, and it didn't sound nice.

"What happened, Dad?" Nick said as he collected himself from the floor of the Lincoln.

"Looks like we found a bridge support," Jeff said. "I'm so sorry about your car. Are you okay?" he asked Auggie.

Auggie was coughing again. "Ya, ya, hitting bridge vas easier than takink grenade. Yust happy ve vere not going fast. I tink I got ding on car grille," Auggie said as he shifted into reverse and slowly pulled away from the bridge support, then puttered around it and under the bridge. There they saw Ben's truck lights. "Look," Auggie said, "odder truck from drift. They took my Mina. Hope she is ok."

"Stay here," Jeff told them all when he saw Ben get out of his truck. "Let me find out what is going on." And Jeff jumped out of the car and met with Ben.

As they shook hands, Ben said, "We have three young girls and two guys up under the bridge yet. I have another two guys and an old lady in my truck. I can maybe squeeze in one or two more to keep warm. How much room in that old Lincoln?".

"There's six of us in there. Maybe we could squeeze in one or two more because three of ours are little kids," Jeff explained over the wind and snow. "If anyone else piles in here, it's not going to be good."

"One of the girls is knocked out. She hit her head pretty hard on the steering wheel. She's going to need medical help," Ben said. "Nobody's phone works out here, no Wi-Fi, nothing."

"The old guy has an old portable CB radio, but even if he could call someone, no one is going to be able to come out here and get us until this stops," Jeff said. "I grew up about 100 miles from here, and there's really nothing around, even if it's a nice day, you won't get cell coverage until you get closer to Denver."

"What we need is a better radio," Ben said.

"What we need is a warm place for everyone," Jeff said.

"Yeah, let's get that going before someone ends up with frostbite," Ben said. He opened his truck and told Eddie to go up under the overpass and get his brother, Matthew, and the girls and get them into one of the vehicles. Jeff went back to Auggie's Lincoln and got in.

"My name is Jeff, and this is my wife Carol," Jeff introduced himself to Auggie.

"I am August Heinrich Buchbinder, a butcher from Cleveland, but you call me Auggie," There were light handshakes all around.

"I'm Nick!" Nick said. "And this is my sister Clementine."

"Nick!" Christie shouted. "My name is not Clementine, it's Christie," she explained to Auggie.

"Ahh, da kids," Auggie said. "My brudders did da same to me. Alvays teasing." He smiled at the memory.

Chapter 40

Sardines

The six in the Towncar were all adjusting to the available space, repacking Wilhelmine's bags into a smaller space when there was a knock on the passenger window. Jeff rolled the window down a couple of inches. It was Mr. Preston again with a large fur-covered woman.

"Hey, Mrs. Lincoln here wants to sit in her own car," Mr. Preston told Jeff. "There's not much room left in that guy's truck anyway. We have eight of us packed in there now."

Jeff glanced around the interior of the Lincoln, "We'll have to squash Mrs. Lincoln in, but it's do-able." With that, he started to pick up the CB radio on the center armrest when Auggie shouted at him.

"Don't move radio! I call for Mayday help. Waiting for answer from a cockroach."

Jeff looked at Mr. Preston. Mr. Preston shrugged his shoulders.

"Ya, he talk to roach on that ting," Wilhelmine volunteered.

"Cool!" Nick said to his sister, "A mayday call."

"Are you out of your mind?" Christie reached over and poked Nick in the arm.

Nick pushed back. "No, you moron," Nick said. "Mayday is a call for help. He must have talked to someone on his CB radio. Is someone coming?" he asked of Auggie.

"I hope so," Auggie said. "I talk to da cockroach and say mayday, big accident on seventy highway. He radio back to try to help. Told me to get far off da highway, so we don't get smashed."

"Well, we have to make room for your wife, Auggie," Jeff said. "Your back seat is full, and the only place left for your wife is the front seat here. That truck over there has eight in it now."

Auggie frowned and looked at his CB, then at his wife standing in the swirling snow.

"Mr. Auggie," Nick chirped in, "if you hand that radio back to me, I'll hold it. I know how to talk on a CB for help. We learned it in my junior Civil Air Patrol meetings."

"You can use dis?" Auggie asked, looking in his rearview at young Nick.

"Yes, sir!" Nick said and saluted Auggie. Auggie relented and carefully began to gather the wires and hand the equipment over the seat to Nick. Nick was nearly aglow with joy to be able to use the CB.

"Alright!" Nick gushed. "I need a CB handle!" And he started thinking about a cool name.

Christie gave him a dirty look then said to her mother, "Are you telling me that our lives are in the hands of HIM?" she said, pointing to Nick and the CB.

"Well," Carol sighed, "do you know how to use a CB radio, Christie?"

Christie didn't respond. She just folded her arms in disgust and fell back into the seat, staring straight ahead, then mumbled, "We're all going to die."

Carol gave her a dirty look.

Jeff got out of the car and helped Wilhelmine to get in, but she wanted to take her mink coat off first, so there was some fumbling around laying her mink over the seat so she could sit on it. Mina finally got into the car and scooted to the center with great movements like a harp seal lugging itself out of the ocean onto a pier. Before Jeff got back in the car, he looked at Mr. Preston and asked, "How long do you think this storm will last?"

"I don't know," Mr. Preston said. "The snow guy in the truck mentioned that it's heavy and strong and doesn't look like it's weakening. I hope the gas holds out until we get help."

"Good point," Jeff said, then got back in and closed the door, and Mr. Preston went back to Ben's truck.

Chapter 41

Technical Difficulties

Joe was back in the driver's seat of the geek's van after Barry had given him a break. Joe was having a lot of trouble with the broadside winds hitting the van causing occasional sliding.

"We really should find a place to stop," Barry said. "The snow is so heavy I bet we won't be able to see tail lights of cars ahead of us until they are twenty feet away."

"I've already dialed us down to forty miles an hour," Joe said. "This thing is too light-weight to drive any faster and not get blown off the road."

Early had already done the math in his head. "Twenty feet at forty miles an hour? That gives you one-point-five seconds to stop from the time you'd see a stopped car ahead."

Joe frowned, then let up on the gas and dropped his van down to thirty-five miles an hour. "Yes," he said. "We gotta get off here."

"If we stop," Barry asked, "will the heater still work?"

"Enough that we won't freeze," Joe explained, "but I don't have a full tank of gas. I only have a little more than half. If we stop, that might keep the engine running for a couple hours so the heater will work, but after that, we're screwed."

"Well, how about if we pull off for an hour. Then decide if the snow is going to let up or not. We can make a call then," Barry advised. "There's no one on the road, not even truckers. I haven't seen anything on the other side, either. I think that's a sign we should be off too."

"What if the snow piles up during that hour and we get stuck and can't get the van out? At least if we are still moving, we won't get stuck, well, unless we slide off the road. We should find a truck stop or rest area to park where it's safe. I'm sure other travelers are hunkered down someplace," Joe said.

"Oh sure." Early said with much sarcasm, "Let's keep driving when there's always that chance you might drive right off the road into a ravine, and we'll roll this tub and get killed by Barry's magazine boxes beating us to death like rolling in a dryer with a bunch of hammers. Then we'll be frozen like pork chops until somebody finds us in Spring and opens this van like a canned ham to thaw out our bodies."

"Cartoon visuals and point taken," Joe grumbled and slowed his van even more. The snow was blowing so hard now that they could hear it scratching at the outside of their van and whistling through the loose passenger window. That, and the occasional steering corrections to accommodate the wind that pushed them sideways from time to time, was making for a worrisome ride. Joe turned his right turn blinker on.

"Are we getting off?" Early asked as he leaned up between the seats.

"Not really," Joe answered. "It's just a precaution. I'm slowing. If anyone comes up behind us, hopefully, they'll see the turn signal and think we're slowing to turn."

Joe was still looking for a decent place to get off when suddenly Barry shouted, "Holy shit!! I can see car lights off the road out there." And pointed out his window to the side of the road. They could see weak headlights and could tell by the arrangement that the vehicle was on its side. Joe tapped his brakes and slowed more.

"We should stop and check it," Joe said as he continued to slow.

"Oh man," Barry said, peering out his window through the accumulated snow, "I think there's two cars off the road on their sides."

As they were trying to see the vehicles on the side of the road, Joe was not paying close attention to what was ahead. When he finally glanced up, he shouted, "Hang on!" as he plowed his foot hard into the brake pedal, and the van began to slide. Joe saw almost too late the faint tail lights still lit in the vehicles jammed in the drift. "Incoming!" he shouted, just as they crashed into the other cars buried in the drift, coming to an abrupt stop.

Barry and Joe were belted in and were whiplashed a bit, but Early was laying back on the makeshift seat of boxes. He was thrown hard up against the front seats and bruised badly by the abrupt shifting of boxes using him for a shock-absorber.

"Oh shit," Joe said after the initial adrenalin rush passed. "Are you okay, man?" he asked Early. Early could only groan, and Barry was already unbuckling his seat belt to get the boxes off Early.

Joe was relieved that his engine was still running, so he moved his van into a position over to the side of the road where it wouldn't be as likely to take a hit from another oncoming vehicle. Meanwhile, Barry was tending to Early.

After parking the van, Joe helped Barry re-arrange the boxes and fixed up the couch-like seat again, packing it with the sleeping bags. The two struggled to get Early off the floor and onto the makeshift bench covering him comfortably with one of the sleeping bags. They noticed he was developing big bruises on his face.

"Man," Joe said to Barry, "we need to get him some help."

"I'm okay," Early whispered then groaned.

"Yeah, you're okay, man," Joe said but gave Barry a worried look.

"Face it," Early whispered again, "this interstate is going to be closed for two days after the storm ends unless there is a sunny day in the 70's. I caught a glimpse of that massive drift that's eating cars. This is the Siberian Express the waitress told us about. No one in, no one out."

Barry and Joe looked at each other with dismay.

"And I know," Early whispered until he groaned and faded out, "there's no communication for help, no one is coming."

"We gotta do something," Joe said.

"Like what? Call Uber-Tom for a ride?" Barry said.

"Nah, first we need to check on those cars out there and see if someone is hurt," Joe said.

"What good is that?" Barry asked. "Early is hurt, and we can't do anything for him. What can we do if someone is really hurt?"

"It doesn't matter," Joe reasoned, "we have to try."

Barry conceded. They didn't bring a lot of winterwear as they were planning on being in the desert after two days of driving, but they did have coats, and Barry had the scarf and gloves his mom made him pack. Suddenly he didn't think his mother's over-protective nature was so bad and wished he'd have brought the boots too. Barry grabbed Early's Faraday flashlight and started cranking. Joe looked at him cranking the crank like crazy.

"Who knew we'd need this?" Barry said.

The light slowly came on and got brighter as Barry furiously cranked. The faster he cranked, the brighter it got. Joe looked at the crappy light and said, "Knock yourself out Barry," as he took a compact LED flashlight out of his pocket and clicked it on, and it brightly lit up a significant area outside the van. Joe jumped out into the snow. Barry frowned at his flashlight and followed Joe out on the shoulder and landed into nearly a foot of snow. Joe shined his flashlight on the faint ruts still visible in the snow from the two vehicles that went off the road.

"The hatch is open on the Minivan," Barry hollered over the wind storm. "They must have gotten out." They both slid down the embankment and approached the Minivan looking it over with their lights. A back seat was pushed forward, so it was clear whoever was here left through the back hatch.

"There's a kiddie seat in there, and look at the bags of wrapped presents. Where the hell does someone go in a storm like this with kids?" Barry shouted to Joe.

"They find shelter of some kind or freeze to death," Joe shouted back, and he flashed his flashlight around to see if he could see people anywhere or where they went, but only saw the drift ahead and mangle of cars. They went over to the other vehicle on its side with the fading headlights.

"Hey, this looks like the preacher's Minibus that we met at the diner. I doubt there would be two of them headed in the same direction at the same time. We gotta find him and see if he's okay," Barry shouted.

"Where could he possibly go? Joe said, looking out at the darkness.

"Maybe his angels came and picked him up," Barry supposed.

The two guys left the abandoned vehicles on the side of the road and made their way back up the embankment to the demolition derby mashed into the drift. "Damn, they hit hard. We were lucky I was driving so slow, or we'd be mashed in there too," Joe said. They looked into the little car that still had a rear window slightly open and could see blood on the seat and steering wheel. But no people. They could barely see the glimmer of the Spectaculeer's rear emergency flashers buried in the drift, but the little car was too far into the drift to see inside. They checked in the dually truck.

"Nobody is here," Barry hollered to Joe.

"Maybe someone picked them up," Joe shouted back over the wind. "People just wouldn't walk away from their only shelter in this weather." Joe swept the area with his flashlight, first high, then swept his light beam around low.

"Hey Barry, check this out," Joe yelled and pointed to what appeared to be very faint tire indentations already covered with snow. "Looks like someone headed south, maybe they drove around the far side of this drift."

"Maybe those tracks are from one of these wrecked cars if it came fishtailing across the road," Barry shouted back.

Joe tramped through the snow, then bent down and shined his flashlight just across the top of the snow again. He could see the trace of tracks easily in the shadows, and it sure looked like someone drove around the southern end of the drift, half on the shoulder and half in the median. He wondered if maybe they got around the drift and kept on going. "This drift is piling up high, but it can't be piled up under the overpass. With the bridge supports and guard rails affecting the wind, there's probably hardly any snow on the back of it. I think someone drove around it on the south end." Barry yelled back to Joe.

"Maybe we could get around too, and keep going," Barry suggested. Or turn around and go back to that diner where the lady can call for help for Early."

"I don't think it'd be smart to try to get across the median to head back. I think the snow might be too deep in the middle," Joe called back. "There is usually a ditch in the median, and it'll be hidden by the snow drifting over the top of it. If it's too deep and steep, my van might tilt over. I don't want to gamble with our only source of protection since there's nothing around here."

"So what do we do? Sit here and freeze and wait for plows?" Barry pointed out. "Early said they would probably close the interstate and they won't be looking for us. He's right, you know."

"Yeah. I know. Let's get back to the van, I'm freezing my face off," Joe said.

They got back to the van and knocked off as much snow as possible, then shut themselves in the relative warmth of the van.

"Whew. Jeeeez, it's cold," Barry said. "Come on heater, do your stuff."

Joe revved the engine a bit to hopefully warm up the heater a little more.

Early groaned again.

"We gotta do something about him. Can they bring in a chopper in a storm like this?" Barry asked.

"Doubt it," Joe said. "If we could get a message out, chances are we'd get help as soon as someone could move, but it's not going to happen if we can't contact anyone. Wish we had an old CB radio or better yet, a HAM set."

"That's funny," Barry said. "We learned about those old tube radios in tech class, and we all laughed at how simple they were. And yeah, with all our high tech crap, we are useless in this blizzard."

Joe pushed his seat back and put his feet up on the dash vent to warm his now wet feet. "Get your wet socks off, and your feet will warm up faster if they are dry." Barry complied, and both were sitting with their feet up on the dash.

Early groaned again and tried to lift his arm to get Barry's attention.

"Barry," Early's quiet voice spoke slow and softly, "Barry?"

"What, man. I'm right here," Barry answered.

Early spoke with barely a whisper, "The magazines. Was there ever an article on building a two-way radio?" Barry raised his eyebrows at Joe. Early continued softly, "You said wrecked cars, maybe you could get enough parts to build one."

Barry brightened up at the idea but immediately darkened down. "Tools. We'd need tools for that. Even if we found a radio recipe, we'd still need tools."

"I have a tool kit under my front seat in case the van had a breakdown," Joe said. "It's a couple of wrenches, pliers, and nut drivers, it won't do any good with electronics."

"Tools," Early scratched out of his throat, "in my duffle bag."

"Good man," Barry said, patting Early's shoulder.

Barry looked to the back of the van and saw all the boxes of magazines strewn about from the breakneck stop in the drift, not having a clue where to start looking for radio articles without a computer search. Joe turned on the dome light, it was crappy but good enough to look through the magazines.

Barry climbed between the seats to pick out a box and lugged it upfront for Joe. "Start looking," Barry told him. "Anything that sounds like a two-way radio."

Barry sat on a couple of boxes in the back of the van and opened a box of magazines, and he could smell his grandpa's cigarette smoke that transported him back to his grandfather's basement workbench, and the many hours they looked at the magazine articles deciding which project to tackle.

"Ok, Grandpa," Barry said as he dug into the magazines, "I hope you have something here for me. People need help, and we need a radio."

Chapter 42

Help Anyone

"Breaker, breaker, one nine, you got Nick the Quick looking for a cockroach," Nick said like a professional disc jockey into the CB mike. "Breaker. We got a 10-33 on the I-70 in the westbound lane, a lot of cars stuck on the road. Anyone got their ears on?"

Jeff turned around to look at Nick and smiled.

"Where did you learn to do that?" Jeff asked him.

"Old movies," Nick explained.

"Old movies?" Jeff asked.

"Yeah," Nick said, "some old movie about a race. Something about cannonballs."

"Cannonball Run?" Jeff asked as he glanced at Carol.

"Yeah. I think so," Nick said. "They raced a lot of big old cars and talked on their CB radios. It was pretty funny."

Carol started to chuckle a little and winked at Jeff.

"What's funny?" Nick asked.

"Those cars were new when I saw that movie," Jeff explained.

"Ew," Nick cringed. "You drove those creepy old cars?"

Auggie interrupted as he patted the dashboard, "Dis car older than dat Burdt Reynold's car."

Jeff and Carol looked at each other surprised that Auggie knew of the movie.

"Your car is big and pretty and looks nearly new," Nick complimented Auggie, "and I'm sorry you got it banged up on the side."

"You do gudt job on radio, kid. Hope you can find Mr. Cockroach and maybe get some help. Ve ain't going no place wit-out help."

"Vat if ve haff to go to da batroom?" Wilhelmina asked.

"What ist mit you vomen and batrooms? You vill pee outside. Like ve didt back in the oldt country," Auggie told her.

"Ya, but ve had pots to piss in back den. My mutter trew dem pots of piss out da door ven it vas such snowing," Wilhelmina reminded him.

"We did the same when I was a kid on the farm," Jeff said. "Mom threw the pee out the door into the snow."

"You had gudt mudder!" Wilhelmina said and patted his knee. "Hope she toldt you not to eat yella snow."

Everyone in the car was giggling about the yellow snow, except Christie, who was holding her hands over her ears.

Even though there was a bit of joking going on, Jeff and Carol were still worried about not getting help in time. What if the cars ran out of gas, or if they were buried in snow. They both realized they could all freeze to death but didn't want to frighten the kids or the old couple.

"I'm going to get out," Jeff said as he shuffled around, buttoning up his coat.

"You what?" Carol exclaimed. "I don't think so, pal. You just stay in the car with the rest of us."

"Wait, Carol, let me explain," Jeff said as he wrenched himself around to look at her using his hands to demonstrate. "If the snow piles up and packs down on the exhaust pipe, it'll back carbon monoxide into the car, and you know what happens then."

"Yeah," Christie piped up. "Hopefully, we die," she said with her teenage sarcasm.

"Now Christie, you just lighten up," Carol sternly told her. "We do not need your pessimistic attitude right now. This is an unpleasant situation, but compared to what many of the people in the world have to live with, this is nothing. We'll just wait it out, and we'll get help."

Unfettered, Christie snipped back her assessment of their situation, "Sure, Mom. Good idea. Nobody knows we're here. We're miles from any signs of life, there's no traffic on the other side of the highway, the snow is blowing so hard you can't see two feet, it's dark as hell, and we can't even get a radio call out. On top of that, it's freezing cold, and eventually, we'll run out of gas!" She folded her arms and sank back in her seat, trying to hide the forming tears of her fears.

Everyone was silent. They all knew she was right. Jeff opened his door and got out quickly and slammed the door. They all watched the snow blowing in his face as he made his way to the back of the car.

He was out of sight as he bent down to clear the snow away from the tailpipe. When he emerged, he knocked on Carol's window and pointed to Ben's truck, and he ducked his head into the blizzard and started his trek over to the truck to explain that the drifting snow around his tailpipe might cause his exhaust to back up too.

Jeff knocked on Ben's truck window, startling Ben and everyone else in the truck. Ben rolled his window down, and Jeff shouted across the short space between himself and Ben's window. "You know you gotta keep snowpack off your tailpipe?"

Ben made a face. He didn't know. He hadn't driven in the snow much back at the maple farm and had never been stranded. If it looked bad, they used skis or a snowmobile. Ben zipped up his coat, pulled a mask over his face and pulled his hood up, then got out of the truck with Jeff. They both walked back against the raging weather to check his tailpipe. It was okay for now.

"Whaddya think?" Jeff shouted over the roaring wind.

"I don't know. I don't know how Kansas operates in a snow emergency. This wouldn't be too awful if it were Vermont, there'd be people out on snowmobiles as soon as it lets up. I don't know about here."

"We're kind of out in the middle of counties, I think. If it clears up and we get daylight, they might send a plane to see if there's any trouble. But we're under an overpass, they'd never see us from the air. If we can get word out, they'd know to look for us. We have no communication, only a CB in the old guy's car, and they haven't been able to hail anyone," Jeff explained.

"Maybe the CB is weak or something. I don't know much about those old CB radios. I use my cell phone for everything. My biggest worry right now is this could turn serious in a big hurry if I run out of gas. We'd only be good for a couple of hours before frostbite sets in on extremities. And that girl is still unconscious, she needs medical help. The best we can do for her is to keep her wrapped up in my sleeping bag. I haven't heard any more crashes on the other side of the drift, but the storm is so loud, I don't know if we'd hear it anyway," Ben shouted over the wind.

"Yep, I thought about that too, but I don't want to scare my kids. We're lucky we don't have anyone dead," Jeff said. "I think we'll be good for a couple of hours. Maybe then the storm will let up. We can probably figure a way to get gas out of the other cars if it wasn't blowing so hard, and that would buy us some time until the plows get through. Wish now that we'd have stopped at that truck stop we saw a few miles back."

"I know. I stopped there, and the lady warned me to stick around for a while, but I wanted to keep going. I'd rather be sitting there sipping coffee instead of stuck out here," Ben said as he looked in the back of the truck and saw his ski gear. "You need to get back to your car before you freeze, you aren't dressed for this."

"Okay," Jeff said. "Check back with you later, man."

Jeff turned to quickly shuffle back to the Lincoln, and Ben patted Jeff on the back. "See ya." And Ben looked again at his cross-country skis and got an idea.

Chapter 43

Ski Trip

"No, no, no! And hell, no!" Mr. Preston said after Ben told the group in his truck that he was going to go for help. "That is a bad idea all the way around. You'll freeze out there alone in the dark, or someone will drive over you. Bad, bad, bad. Just stay with us in the truck, we're okay. Someone will find us. It's not like we're on a back street someplace, we're on an interstate, it'll be plowed soon to keep traffic moving."

"I can deal with this kind of weather," Ben countered back. "That truck stop back there is only maybe twenty or so miles. I can make it in an hour or two, depending on how much is downhill. I have very good gear for the cold, down to twenty-below." He held up his special ski gloves that had a battery operated warming pocket in them.

"I think that truck stop is more than any twenty miles," Eddie said quietly. "More like forty." On one hand, Eddie wanted to be rescued. On the other, he kind of looked up to Ben, a nice guy, and didn't want him to leave the group.

"Someone has to do something," Ben said. "There are seven people in that car, and we have eight here. I can't sit here and maybe watch fourteen people die from exposure if we run out of gas when I know I can probably make it back to the truckstop and get us help. There are little kids in that car, they can't last long in the cold."

Mr. Preston watched the snow piling up on the hood of the truck. "I vote no," he said quietly. "Why can't we go back around the drift and drive back to the diner?"

"I think by now it's possible that every overpass would have drifts, not only that but flat drifts in the low-lying areas could be deep enough to maroon cars in the middle of the interstate. I think it'd be very risky to attempt a drive right now. That's why they close interstates, so people aren't out there finding ways to drive off the highway and into creeks, fields, bridges, or road signs. We'd end up the same way in a different place. At least here, everyone is in one place. I'm light enough and fast enough to skim over the top of the low-lying snow and flexible enough to go around any other drifts piled across the roadway. It just makes sense," Ben explained to Mr. Preston.

"I think Ben is right," Delphia said as she looked to Ben. "If he has well-insulated gear, his body heat can keep him functioning. Just like the people that climb Mount Everest, they don't usually die from the cold, they die from oxygen deprivation, and that shouldn't be a problem for Ben. He's used to snow, and no doubt he knows how to shelter in place if he's spent most of his life outdoors."

"Yes, Delphia. That's right," Ben confirmed as he winked at her causing her to blush and look away. "I think I can do this, and I need to try. I can't sit here and do nothing and jeopardize everyone else."

"You young people don't think. It's pitch black out there, and once you get away from the car headlights, you won't be able to see your hand in front of your face, not to mention your face in the blinding snow. You'll get turned around and wind up wandering in a field someplace, or exerting yourself, or possibly dehydrating and who knows what else." Mr. Preston ranted.

"Well," said Ben as he pushed up a sleeve displaying his watch, "this watch has a compass on it, and I know how to use it. I know I have to go back East, I think I can stay on the road. The powder collecting is near perfection for cross country. There are things I can watch for, highway marker signs, road signs, the ditch on either side of the pavement, even the guard rails. I have poles. I can stick them down and feel if it's pavement, snowdrift, or field. I can make about seven to ten miles an hour depending on the wind resistance, and I can double that speed on downhill grades. I have a flashlight to use to signal someone in case someone else is coming on the road, and I'll have plenty of time to get out of the way, just 'schuss' down into the ditch on the roadside. Besides, the girl here needs medical attention."

Delphia looked at Brittney's now pale face then back to Ben. As concerned as she was for her friend, she couldn't help being intrigued with how good-looking and sensitive Ben was.

Mr. Preston thought about it all when Ben continued, "The only problem I think will be is if I have to pee. I don't want to freeze my dick off." And that made Mr. Preston and everyone else laugh.

"Ok, Ben," Mr. Preston said, "it's your life. You missed your calling, kid, you should have been a lawyer. You have a gift for arguing your point."

"I got it from my Aunt Kate, blame her," and he winked at Delphia again, making her look away and feel shy. She hated seeing him putting on his ski gear, knowing he'd be leaving the group, but she realized it might be the only way they'd be rescued. "I'll go for about an hour. That should get me seven to ten miles, at least. If something doesn't look right, I'll head back this way. I figure there should be a sign someplace on the east-bound lanes saying where the truck stop might be. If I can find a sign about the diner, and it is way out of range, I'll come back, so don't spazz if a frozen snowman knocks on the window."

"Good Luck, Ben," Delphia said, obviously developing a crush on him, infatuated with his good looks, good nature, and he was smart too.

Ben turned to look at her. "Thanks. You know, Delphia, this isn't about luck, it's about testing my lifelong skills at being out in the snow and my cross-country ski ability. I'll be okay. I'll see you later, promise. Here, hold this until I get back." He dug a little box out of his backpack and handed it to Delphia, the little box with a picture of a cow on it, and he winked again at her as he opened the door and pushed himself out into the blizzard.

"I'll pray for you!" Matthew shouted as Ben left the safety of his truck.

They watched him through the flying snow as he checked his flashlight and stowed it, got the gear out of the back of the truck and fitted the skis on, grabbed the poles, put on hand gear, and wrapped his extra-long scarf around his neck twice. He held up a hand to wave goodbye as he pushed his skis over the snow to the Lincoln.

Jeff rolled down his window. "What the hell are you doing??" Jeff asked when he saw Ben bundled up and had skis on.

"We've been sitting here for over two hours, and I have less than half a tank of gas left. I'm going for help. I can't sit here and do nothing. I'm going to try to cross-country ski back to that diner. I think I can do it. They should have landlines to the sheriff or highway patrol. If nothing else, they can alert the plows not to plow over us all."

Jeff didn't want to see Ben go, but Auggie had only a bit more than a quarter of a tank of gas left and knew Ben was right, someone should do something other than sit and hope the gas lasted longer than the storm. Jeff stuck his hand out the window, and Ben shook it. "Good luck, man."

"May Godt go vit you!" Wilhelmina added.

They all watched as Ben schusshed into the darkness and out of sight.

As Ben skied toward the south end of the mega drift and into the median to go around the drift, the wind hit him full force. He hadn't realized just how bad the wind was wailing across the plains of Nebraska and Kansas, nothing to stop it, nothing to slow it down. He was struggling to keep the wind from pushing him backward and sideways across the median. He'd finally worked his way across to the front of the drift in when he saw the older white van parked on the side of the road. It had some front end damage but still had its lights on. Ben approached it and heard the engine running as he tapped on the window.

Joe jumped from being startled then nearly jumped for joy! "Thank God!" he shouted at Early and Barry. "We're being rescued!!" And he rolled down his window, nearly shouting at Ben, "Thank God, Thank God someone came to rescue us! Is everyone else okay?" he asked as he pointed to the pile of cars barely visible now in the mega drift.

Ben pulled up his face mask, "Sorry to disappoint you, but I'm going for help." Then he explained to the three techies about crashing into the drift, and how there are fourteen people packed in two vehicles on the other side of the drift with a tiny bit of protection under the overpass.

Joe's face fell. Ben went on to explain that he was going to try to get back to the truck stop a few miles back. Joe told him he thought it was a bit farther than one or two miles, like at least thirty, but Ben explained that he felt he had to try. Joe and Barry understood. Joe told him to mention that Early had hit his face pretty hard and was kind of screwed up, probably needing some medical help.

"One of the young girls in my truck on the other side of the drift has been in and out of consciousness. So we have two that need medical attention. If you can drive this thing, you might try to get it around the south end of the drift before it piles up so high that it isn't passable. Get behind it so the snow doesn't bury you or something big come down the highway and not see you," Ben told Joe. "You all will be easier to find in a group."

"Check," Joe said.

Ben waved as he skied away from the van, and Joe hollered good luck to him and rolled up the window. Joe looked to see if his socks were dry yet on the vent. Not only dry but warm and dry as he put them back on. "I think the guy is right on both accounts, Barry, someone needed to go get help, and we should try to get the van behind that drift."

Chapter 44

Moving Van

"Ok," Barry approved. "Let's get this thing on the other side of the drift if we can, just be careful, so you don't knock my piles of magazines over. I've been through all these so far, and I don't want to mix up the seen and unseen ones. I don't want to miss an issue that might be able to help us out."

Joe goosed the accelerator a bit and then shifted into low as he began to inch the van out of its spot on the side of the road. The tires were slipping as Joe tried to tease it out of its parking spot, but the wheels kept turning, and they were going nowhere. Over and over, Joe tried everything to get the van moving, rocking it out, inching it out, gunning the engine. It wasn't moving. Joe put it in park. "All I'm doing is wasting gas we might need. I seriously doubt that guy is going to be able to go all the way back to the café to get help so I'd be more comfortable not wasting gas. We're screwed." And he crossed his arms over the steering wheel and stared out at the blinding snow.

Barry looked at the stack of magazines he'd already looked through. He knew they'd bring good money at the trade show even though he was slightly reluctant to sell his grandfather's collection. His frail frame slumped as he realized what he had to do. He closed his eyes and spoke to Joe, volunteering his magazines to rip up and put under the tires to get some traction.

"You don't have to do that, Barry," Joe said quietly. "We can wait awhile yet."

Barry realized the situation and knew there would be no help for a long time yet. "Look, Early needs some help, and we'd be a lot better off like the guy said, and get with the others behind the drift and have a little protection from the overpass. He sounds like he knows the outdoors."

Joe drummed his fingers on the steering wheel and thought about it. "Okay, you are right, Barry. I'm sorry about your grandfather's magazine collection."

"I know. But they won't do me any good if I'm frozen to death," Barry said as he began stacking up the magazine boxes over the back axle. I'm going to pile these here to hopefully put a little more weight over the rear wheels.

"Yeah, good idea," Joe said as he left his seat to help redistribute the boxes. Maybe we could move Early to the floor and use the weight in those boxes too."

They both heard Early groan. "Can he hear us and understand us?" Barry asked.

"Beats me," Joe replied. "I hate to lay him on the floor, I think it's too cold with the wind blowing under us.

"Well, I think this is an emergency, we can put a couple sleeping bags on the floor first, and cover him with the third one. We can fix up his box couch again if we get this heap out of the snow and moving again," Barry reasoned.

Joe helped Barry move their friend to the floor and situate him with the sleeping bags, then they lugged the boxes to shift the weight over the rear axle.

"Good job," Barry said after the boxes were all stacked up, and he started to button up his coat and put on the scarf and gloves his mom made him take. He grabbed an armful of magazines off the stack he'd already looked through and slid the van door open. "Start it up, Joe. I'll bang on the side when I get magazines down under each tire, just keep moving once you're free, I'll catch up."

Joe nodded and shifted the transmission down into low gear, Barry jumped out into the storm and slid the door shut.

He fought the wind, trying to hold the magazine stack while trying to open one at a time and jam it into the snow under the tire. He folded another under the first magazine to extend the length of the small magazines. He repeated it for each tire, then banged on the van. He could hear the engine noise groaning, but the tires still spun. The back tires spun on top of the magazines, and the tires shot the magazines out the back, and the wind quickly carried them away. Barry banged on the van and told Joe to wait, then he did the same thing all over again for each tire, but adding a few more magazines, stomping on them wedging them down into the loose snow, then pounded on the back of the van again.

Joe carefully touched the accelerator and very slowly tried to nudge the van to drive just a half-inch at a time. The tires began to turn and moved the van slightly. Barry was just about to shout for joy when the wheels started to spin again. Snow collecting on the magazines created a very slick surface causing the tires to easily spin smashing some magazines down into the snow and shooting others out to the wind.

"The magazines are too damn slick!" Barry cussed as he opened the van door and grabbed another armload of magazines. "One last try, Joe," he said as he slid the van door shut and started ripping pages out and crumpling them this time and jamming them into the snow in front of each tire. He crumpled and jammed a couple of years of his grandfather's magazines under the tires. In addition, he decided he'd get behind and push. He pounded on the back door of the van to go, and Joe started to once again slowly nudge the van forward. At first, the wheels started to move a tiny bit, but Barry saw the crumpled pages begin to slip and slide. He was getting worried and was upset at wasting the precious magazines for nothing. "This has to work!" he muttered into the cold, then he hollered into the stormy night up to his grandfather, "Let's give it all we got, Grandpa!!" and Barry put his shoulder into the back of the van and gave it a mighty shove as Joe touched the accelerator and just like a miracle, the van tires began to roll a tiny bit finally gaining a bit of traction. As the van moved forward an inch at a time over the crumpled magazines, the wind and snow ripped the loose ones away and into the night. But the van was now moving.

Barry tromped after the slow-moving van pounding on the side, "Wait, wait...!" But as he reached for the door handle on the side, he slipped and fell, luckily he didn't fall under a rolling tire. Joe kept the van moving slowly as Barry finally caught up, slid the door open and jumped in, knocking the snow off his pants and shoes, then watched the pages of magazines in the red glow of the taillights take flight up into the air, as though his Grandfather was collecting them for another read. He slid the door shut and sighed.

As Barry got back in his seat and put his seatbelt on, he looked forlornly out the window as he watched the last few crumpled magazine pages zip off into the dark.

"Sorry about the magazines, Barry," Joe said, "but your grandfather's magazines really saved the day for us. That ski guy was right, another vehicle could come along and plow right into us, or the snowplows could come and scrape us off."

Barry sat in melancholy silence, thinking how he'd forsaken his grandfather's magazine collection. He hoped it wasn't totally wasted, and now they'd be able to get across the road and hopefully behind the drift where there were others.

Slowly Joe drove the van across the highway toward the center median following the previous tire tracks that were now nearly hidden in the snow. The right tires had to climb up the snowdrift a bit to get around, which tilted the van precariously to one side for a frightening moment, and they bumped the guard rails a few times, but they were getting around the drift.

The van began to level out as they passed the edge of the drift.

"That's about a thirty-degree angle," Barry figured.

They could see as they rounded the drift that the wind and snow were a teensy bit less, and that could be enough to buy them the additional precious time of not freezing to death. Joe saw the car lights of the Lincoln and the truck and pulled up next to the Lincoln. Barry rolled his window down as Auggie rolled down his.

"How you like dis snow?" Auggie shouted out at Barry.

"Not so much. How are you?" Barry asked.

"We doing okay. We sent someone for help. Hope it comes soon," Auggie said, looking at his gas gauge.

"Yes, we saw that guy. He told us to drive around the drift here for some protection from the storm," Barry said.

Then Barry heard Nick calling out on the CB radio, "Breaker, breaker, one nine, anyone got your ears on? Nick the Quick here, MayDay on I-70!"

"You guys have a radio?" Barry yelled across the space between the vehicles.

"Ya," Wilhelmina replied as she leaned over Auggie, "and it only play awful music of noise and pounding." And she shook her fist at the dash, then at Auggie.

"No, no!" Barry said, "I mean, do you have a two-way radio?"

Wilhelmina didn't give up, "Ya. No "two vays" aboudt it, radio ist crap."

Jeff intervened and leaned over both Wilhelmina and Auggie, "Yeah, the kid has a small CB radio. But he hasn't been getting anything for over an hour. Just static."

"Antenna isn't enough," Barry said, looking at the magnetic antenna on top of Auggie's Lincoln.

"What do you mean?" Jeff asked.

"It's a short antenna. You need a longer antenna, it'll give you a bit more radio distance," Barry explained. "Those little portable units aren't very strong. They're okay for a mile or so, but in weather like this, that huge drift, the overpass, I doubt you can even get a mile out."

"You know someting about dis radio werks?" Auggie asked.

"Not much. Just a little," Barry said. "Our friend that knows a lot about it, he's been injured when we ran into the pileup."

"Oh my God," Carol said and put her hand over her mouth.

"Don't worry, Mom," Nick said. "We'll get through to somebody." And Nick called out again on the CB.

Chapter 45

Early Warning

While Joe and Barry were shouting out the van window to the people in the Lincoln, they didn't notice Early trying to get their attention by opening and closing his palm that was resting on his chest. Finally, Joe noticed the movement.

"Oh man, you cold buddy?" Joe asked him. Early only groaned a bit. "Come on, Barry, we gotta get him off the floor."

Joe pulled his van in front of the Lincoln, its headlights helping him see the magazines a bit better, and parked. Joe and Barry shuffled boxes once more. They packed up most of the magazines that didn't have any useful help back into the boxes and used them to arrange a pallet off the floor for Early using all three sleeping bags to insulate him from the cold. Early groaned loudly as they hauled him off the floor and onto his new banana box arrangement.

Joe could hear his name faintly being called by Early, so he knelt down and asked him what he wanted.

"Antenna wire ...from CB to antenna... make it eighteen feet," he barely whispered. Joe looked up to Barry, who also heard the message. Early was saying something else, but they couldn't make it out, then Early was out again.

"Eighteen feet of wire? Where are we going to get eighteen feet of wire?" Joe looked at Barry.

"We could yank plug wires from the other cars," Barry suggested. "Each car would have four to eight of them. After cutting the business ends off, each one would be at least a foot." Barry felt like he'd solved all their problems.

"Nah," said Joe. "The cars are buried into that drift, you can barely see the back ends, we'd have to dig out an entire car to open the hood and hope it's not mashed up in the front, so the hood latch still works. Too much of a gamble to go back around the drift to dig."

"Ok, you're right, I guess," Barry sounded depressed now. "I'll go ask if any of them have any ideas."

Barry pushed his door open against the wind once more and slipped out into the snow. It wasn't as deep here as it was in front of the drift, but still blowing blizzard conditions. He trudged the few steps over to the Lincoln, and Auggie rolled his window down.

"We need eighteen feet of wire for the CB to work better. Anyone got something?"

There were no positive answers. Barry trudged over to Ben's truck and was surprised to see Matthew and asked about his Minibus. Matthew confirmed he slid off the roadway, trying to avoid the other vehicles. Barry also recognized the young girls from the diner, and Delphia explained about them crashing into the drift. Barry introduced himself to the others and detailed what he needed, but no one had anything there either. Barry looked in the back of Ben's truck too. There were only a couple duffle bags and some other ski gear. As the group in Ben's truck watched Barry, Eddie mentioned to them that jumper cables have a lot of wire, and sometimes people have them in their trunks. He asked everyone if they had a set in their cars, but it was all negative again. Mr. Preston rolled down the window, "Hey, kid!" he shouted at Barry through the snow. "Hey, kid!" he shouted again as he slapped his palm loudly on the door so Barry would look up. Barry heard it and stepped up to the window. "Ask the people in the Lincoln if anyone might have jumper cables in their cars. If so, you're in luck."

Barry trudged back to the Lincoln and was starting to chatter in the blinding wind and snow. He tapped on the window again, and Auggie rolled it down. "Any of you have jumper cables in your cars?"

Carol got excited, "I do! I have jumper cables and an emergency pack in the back of my minivan. It's got a couple of flares, a couple of those foil blankets, a couple of those triangle warning signs...I don't know what else. Maybe something that can help."

"Is your car the one on its side near the Minibus?"

"Yes! The hatch is open, and the box is up against the back seat. Jeff can help you," Carol said.

"Shit." They all heard Jeff say under his breath. "Don't bother," he said. "I took that box out of the van when I was loading it with Christmas presents, luggage, and the coolers. I left it on the garage floor."

"You ass!" Carol muttered under her breath.

"I didn't think anything was going to happen," Jeff said.

"That's the idea behind an emergency pack," Carol admonished, "you don't know when something is going to happen. That's why they call it an *emergency* pack."

"Nice move, Dad," Christie said, looking out the window so no one could see tears of concern forming in her eyes.

"Ho-kay." Wilhelmina said as she felt the anger in the car building, "We haff problem, we have gudt minds, we solve problem. We must tink. Young girl," she pointed to Christie, "hand me big blue bag from back."

Christie mindlessly grabbed the bag and handed it over the seat to the old woman.

Wilhelmina dug her arms down in the bag and rustled the bag for what seemed like forever until she popped up with a package of crackers and a few boxed drinks.

"Don't have many. But vill share mit other travelers." She motioned to Auggie to hand some crackers out to Barry and some boxed drinks and told him to share with the people in the other truck.

"She ist feeding people to make dem happy," Auggie said as he sheepishly handed the food supplies out the window.

"Thank you, Mrs.....uh....Mrs.??" Barry said.

"You call me Mina. My name is Vilhelmina Buchbinder."

And Auggie put in his two cents, "The butcher's vife!"

"Nice to meet you, Mina. My name is Barry. Thank you for the snacks. I'll take some over to the other truck."

"Ya. Dose young folks need energy to tink!" Wilhelmina instructed.

Barry stopped at Ben's truck and handed over two of the drink boxes and some crackers, explaining it was from Mrs. Buchbinder.

Matthew said, "God bless, Mrs. Buchbinder!" and "Thank you!"

Mr. Preston commented, "We have one of Ben's coffee cups here, and we've been melting snow to drink, no point in dehydrating."

Travis wisecracked, "Yeah, it's that much less snow to bury us in." Eddie punched him in the arm.

"Be thankful you useless sack of...sack of...." Eddie stalled and quickly glanced around seeing Matthew's angel pin, Mr. Preston's distinguished aura, and the young girls worried faces, so Eddie chose "...sack of birdseed!"

"Nice save," Matthew said. The girls chuckled, and Mr. Preston smiled in the rearview mirror at Eddie.

Barry hustled back to the van, sliding the side door open and hopped in. "The old lady in the Lincoln gave us a couple of juice boxes and some crackers. Gotta share. Not enough to go around," he said.

"That's nice," Joe said. "Maybe we should save it in case Early needs it."

"Okay," Barry agreed. "They are melting snow in coffee cups, so they have a little something to drink. You got something here?"

"Just a foam cup from the diner. But better than nothing." Joe opened his door and leaned down and scooped up some snow and pushed it around in the cup to clean out the coffee residual, then packed it with clean snow. "There. It'll take forever in a foam cup, but we could be stranded here for quite a while."

Barry was already in the back going through the magazines again. There had to be something in them, somewhere.

Chapter 46

Ben

The Snow Man

Ben had been schussing for almost an hour, and so far, all he saw was snow in his face and endless blackness. Not a farmhouse with lights on, nor an outlying street light. Nothing. It was like being on a distant planet. He figured he should have seen a road sign by now, a gas sign, a rest stop, a town sign, an exit sign, but there had been nothing.

Ben was determined to keep going. What he hadn't figured on was how tiring it was pushing against the relentless wind, and the constant snow blowing into his face. He was also starting to feel a bit of the chill from the blinding persistent blizzard conditions. The batteries in his warming gloves were only good for a couple of hours, so he was more than mindful of the time he'd been moving. He kept hopeful because he really didn't want to give up and go back.

He didn't have a clue how far he'd gone because some of the strong wind gusts pushed him around on his skis no matter how hard he dug his poles in. It was a struggle just to stay on, what he hoped was, the road. He tried not to let the darkness and snow wear him down. He knew his aunt would never give up and so he concentrated on thinking about her.

Finally, he'd come to a slight downhill grade and was able to slowly coast using his flashlight to see if he could see a road sign, a mile marker, or maybe a guard rail, but there was nothing. He became concerned that he just might have skied off the interstate and was now in a field somewhere. As he skied to the low point of the grade, he stuck his pole in a small pile of snow, and it clunked. It was something hard, so he pushed the snow off, revealing the edge of a concrete railing. He shuffled sideways to the other side of the road and poked his pole around until he found another concrete railing. Two sides. He was relieved and felt sure he must be over a creek and still on the roadway. He shined his flashlight over the edge of the rail to see below. He wasn't high enough to be on an overpass for a train or farm road, so it had to be a creek. He followed the rail hoping for a sign naming the creek, but there was none, perhaps it was a culvert.

He checked his compass, and he was still headed easterly and was satisfied that he was still on the main interstate. There had to be a sign soon so he could figure out where he was and maybe where the diner was. That diner didn't seem to be this far that he could remember, so he kept moving.

Chapter 47

All Kinds of Short and Odd Passages

Herman was driving his beloved RV about twenty-five miles per hour now. He could barely see anything, and his determination to make it past the storm wasn't giving up. Louise had quit asking him much of anything as he was just becoming crabbier at losing time in the weather. She was white-knuckling the drive now and praying he'd get tired and pull over, but so far, she had to admit, there was no place to pull over. A huge heavy RV could bog down on the soft shoulder, and they'd be stuck for days until they could get a giant trucker's tow out to them. They both knew that stopping in white-out conditions could result in a terrible pile-up, so they kept a slow pace. Herman was watching his mirrors like a hawk, and Louise focused on trying to see if anything was in front of them using the spotlight to look for signs along the roadside indicating a rest stop that they could pull into for awhile.

Louise knew it was way past time for Herman's blood thinner medication and dreaded saying anything as he despised taking medications and despised Louise mentioning it twice as much. She got his pill and tried to get a cup of water, but the wind was rocking the RV enough to slosh the water out of the cup. Even Twinkles stayed in the seat rather than following Louise around.

"Herman, here, take your pill," she loathed mentioning it.

"Can't you see I'm trying to drive in a goddam blizzard, Louise!" he snapped.

"Take your pill."

"I'll take it later, set it down," he argued.

"Please take it. Then I'll shut up," Louise kept at him.

Louise's nursing skills were taking over, and she was ready to strong-arm him into taking his pill when he eased up and said he'd take it as soon as he could pull over as he didn't want to take a chance on a momentary lapse of vision on the road. Louise gave in and set the water in his cup rack and dropped the little pill in the change cup, and situated herself back in her seat with Twinkles.

Louise had concerns that she hadn't heard a peep for over an hour on the CB. Truckers usually kept good tabs on bad weather and kept information flowing for the other truckers that were heading in and out of a storm. But now, nothing but silence. She adjusted the squelch a bit more but got nothing but static.

"You know, it's always tough to get a signal in all this snow, Lou," Herman said as he could tell his wife was starting to fret and wanted to calm her. "When it lets up a bit, we'll get contact."

Louise knew he was full of it and that he was trying to calm her, so she let it go and continued to stare out the window hoping for a sign of a truck stop or rest area ahead.

*   *   *

The Go-Go Girls Gotta Go

Jackie leaned over the seat, "Girls, I hate to bring this up as it's only been a little more than an hour, but I gotta go again. I thought I could wait, but I think the coffee and stress are playing tricks on me. I don't want to have to pee in a cup."

"I know," Doris said with concern. "I gotta go too, but there just hasn't been any place to stop."

"I haven't seen anything either, and I don't plan on squatting in the snow," Janet added.

"I know. But I gotta go, and it's starting to hurt," Jackie complained.

"You'll change your mind about that cup real soon," Rita told Jackie. "We should have kept that dam cup."

"Okay," Doris said with some frustration. "I'll speed it up a little faster, and maybe we can find a rest area and get off here."

Since there was no response from the peanut gallery, she sped up a bit and asked Janet to keep a sharp eye out for a rest area sign or even an exit, just to get off the interstate. "Five more minutes, or we'll all need a cup," Doris muttered to herself, knowing there were no more cups, dreading all of them trying to use her husband's Dominator-Maximus as a bathroom somehow, or worse, squatting out in the blizzard.

Doris kicked the speed up, and the heavy, sure-footed Dominator was managing the snow-covered road pretty well even though it was slow going. After a few minutes passed, Janet shouted and started pounding on the dashboard, "Tail-lights up ahead! A truck! Careful, Doris!" Doris ever so slowly moved out of her lane and into the passing lane.

"That dam truck is driving about twenty miles an hour!" Doris exclaimed as she steadied her hands on the wheel, getting ready to pass. "I don't like this. If the wind broadsides his trailer, it'll swing into our lane and clip us."

"I'm sure he's a professional, he'll keep it in his lane," Janet encouraged.

But as they caught up to the tail-lights, they saw it was not an eighteen-wheeler but a huge RV. Doris steadied her steering, flashed her headlights that she was going to pass, and clicked on her blinker.

*   *   *

RV Gets a Pass

"Some jerk is going to pass us, Lou," Herman announced. Louise leaned forward to look in his side mirror and saw the headlights.

"Be kind, Herman. You are barely driving twenty. Maybe they need to be someplace. Maybe it's a doctor." Louise tried to make it seem okay that someone was passing them in this weather.

"OK," Herman gave in, "I'll slow some more so he can pass us quicker." He eased up on the gas, and the RV began to slow a bit to allow the passing vehicle to pass quickly and move on without the wind blowing his RV into them.

*   *   *

Careful

As the girls began to pass the RV, Janet commented, "There's a good deal, you know, I'll bet they have a bathroom on board. They don't have to hunt one down."

"Too bad we can't get them to stop so we can use it," Rita said, looking out the window up at the huge RV.

Doris wasn't talking, she was focused on carefully steering the wide Dominator past the long RV and slowed so she'd be more confident of passing and not sliding into it. She watched the side of the RV like a hawk making sure she was staying a safe distance. She could see the driver of the RV in his big side mirror and saw that he was glued to his mirrors too, making sure there was enough room between both vehicles.

*　*　*

Napkin Note

The Dominator was just about ready to clear the front of the RV when Herman shouted to Louise and started to laugh. "Lou! Lou!! Come see this!!" Louise got out of her seat to lean over his side to see what was so amusing. She saw the massive Dominator all decked out with lights looking rather commanding and indestructible, and yet someone was holding up a little sign against the back window written on napkins, "Gals have to pee! No rest areas. Can we use your potty?"

Herman thought this was hilarious. He expected a bunch of hunters or drug dealers in the Dominator, not four older, apparently incontinent, ladies. Louise didn't think it was too funny, being a nurse, she knew the issues revolving around older women and weak bladders. They simply couldn't hold it like young girls. "They're right, Herm," Louise said. "There hasn't been a rest stop for a long time."

"Wait...what?" Herman said. "You think we should stop like we're a traveling portable potty for total strangers and gamble with getting stuck or stabbed and robbed?"

"Well, jeez, Herman, you know what it's like to have to go. They're older women, they aren't going to rob us. There's been no traffic for an hour, maybe we can stop half off the road, let them run in and quickly use the john then get going again. Shouldn't take five minutes."

"You are crazy," he told her.

"Yes. But this is an emergency, and the weather is severe. Besides, you can use the time to take your med," Louise calculated.

Herman sighed and sat back in his seat. "Okay." He turned on his cabin light so the girls could see him, and he waved a come-on wave and turned on his blinker for a right-hand turn. Then he saw the girls in the back seat waving madly at him then high-fiving each other.

*   *   *

Pit Stop

"DORIS!" Rita shouted, "Pull over behind the RV!"

"What?" Doris asked as Janet looked at what was going on in the back seat. Jackie held up the sign so Janet could see it.

"Aw jeez, are you kidding me?" Janet asked.

"What??" Doris asked again.

"They made this sign on napkins," Janet grabbed it and read it to Doris, "it says, 'Gals have to pee. No rest areas. Can we use your potty'?"

"Well, it does look like they are going to pull over," Jackie said.

"My idea!" Rita beamed.

It took forever for the RV to come to a stop with its right wheels as far to the edge of the road as Herman dared, and the left side still hanging on the interstate. Doris pulled in front of the RV's headlights so the older couple would see that they weren't ax murderers.

"Let's go two at a time, I don't want to leave the car unattended," Doris said. "Jackie, you and Rita go first. No socializing, we gotta get this done fast before someone comes."

It didn't take Jackie long to get out and tromp into the snow and hustle to the RV door. Louise was waiting with Twinkles at her ankles and opened the door as the steps rolled down into the snow.

"Oh my God, thank God, thank God," Jackie was saying all the way into the RV. Louise sensed the urgency.

"Come this way, no time to lose," Louise said as she and Twinkles showed Jackie back to the bathroom.

"So," Rita said as she tried to make conversation with Herman, "you live in this thing?"

"No. We're headed to San Diego for the winter," he said.

"Nice," Rita said. "We do appreciate your stopping for us. I know this is ridiculous, but we just weren't able to find a place to get off. This storm is terrible. Your RV seems to handle it."

"Yes," Herman said.

"Have you been in the sun lately?" Rita asked.

"No," Herman said as he looked Rita up and down as he thought she looked like an old hooker.

"Oh. Well, I just thought you looked sunburned. I'm hoping when we get to Vegas that I can put my bikini on and get a little sunburn myself."

Herman could not fathom this awfully skinny, wrinkled woman in a bikini and tried not to think about it when Louise and Jackie came forward with Twinkles running ahead, thrilled for having company and new things to sniff. "Oh, thank you, sir," Jackie said graciously. "I cannot tell you what a blessing you are." Jackie was truly gracious, and Herman seemed to appreciate her classiness. "I don't know how I can ever thank you folks."

"Just drive safe," Herman said, wondering what a classy gal like this was doing with the hooker. Louise took Rita back to the bathroom, and Jackie could hear Rita remarking on the RV and how nice it was inside as Twinkles ran along.

"I'm so sorry we had to stop you," Jackie said shyly. "I just didn't know what to do. We must have missed a rest area back there someplace, they usually have one every hour or so. I hope this isn't too much of an imposition," Jackie kept apologizing.

"It's okay," Herman said, looking out at the snow and monitoring his mirrors, "just move it along quickly."

Louise came back with Rita, and when she opened the door for the two gals to leave, with all the excitement going on, Twinkles ran out the door thinking it was all such fun. Louise yelled, terrified that Twinkles would take off in the darkness and snowstorm. Jackie was quick and jumped out and was going to grab the little dog when she saw the dog squatting. When Twinkles was done, Jackie picked her up and handed her to Louise, who breathed a sense of relief. Rita was amused by all the activity and said, "Well looks like we're all relieved now!"

Herman stifled a smile and kept his smirk firmly in place.

Jackie headed back to their vehicle, all the while waving and apologizing to Louise and Herman.

"It's okay," Louise kept saying. "I understand. I'm glad we could help. It's very bad out tonight, hope you can get off the road soon."

Rita and Jackie hoofed through the snow while Doris and Janet passed them stepping as quickly as they could through nearly a foot of snow in places.

"Oh my God," Doris said, as Louise helped her up the steps, "you are a lifesaver. I don't know what those gals would have done without you. I know this is a terrible imposition from total strangers."

Louise led Janet back to the bathroom, telling her it was okay and that she understood the lack of rest stops and the terrible snowstorm.

Doris stood just inside the door and looked around. "Wow. This is some setup. I'm Doris, by the way."

"Herman," he said, not offering to shake hands.

"Well, Herman," Doris said, digging in her pockets, "I'd like to offer you something for your time."

"Don't need anything," Herman said. "Put it back. Got everything we need, and apparently something you need."

"Funny guy!" Doris appreciated the dry sense of humor as she pulled her hand out of her pocket.

"You like that thing you drive?" Herman asked, curious about the Dominator.

"It's my husband's. It's like his second wife," Doris said, "he had me drive it as he said it'd be safe if we ended up with bad weather. He's right. It's really been solid so far."

"My wife says my RV is my second wife too. I'd probably like your husband," Herman commented.

Louise came back with Janet and led Doris back for her turn.

"I'm enjoying your brief company," Louise told Doris. "It's a nice break. Herman can be such a pill sometimes. Which reminds me, he needs to take his pill."

"Well, we don't want to keep you. We know it's dangerous driving tonight. We are just trying to find someplace to stop until the snow quits," Doris told her through the bathroom door.

"Well, I hope it quits too. Herman just likes to prove his RV is like the road gladiator or something and doesn't stop for anything. He's been driving way too long today."

"Me too, but we just can't pull over on the side. I can't even get a call out for information," Doris said.

"You won't. Not around here. Too far from cell antennas and anything else. You can get some AM radio stations, maybe, that might help with the weather situation. We're from up north, these snowstorms can last for hours and hours. I hope we can find a rest area soon so we can pull over until this stops," Louise explained.

"Well, first chance we get, we're off the road too. I don't care if it's a rest area or the Hilton, we're stopping," Doris commented as she washed her hands.

"Us too. We just can't see far enough to read the signs or see if there's an off-ramp," Louise said.

"We'll keep our eyes open. Maybe we can signal you if we see something. Like run our emergency flashers or something," Doris suggested.

"That'd be nice," Louise said, realizing that her brief chatting with the talkative gals was about to end.

"Thank you so much for stopping for us. You guys are angels, you know. It could be five minutes or hours before we found a potty stop. I feel like a jerk using you this way. I hope we can help you find a place to pull off too," Doris said, feeling lousy about asking to use someone's bathroom.

Louise led Doris up front and opened the door, so Doris and Janet could run back to their vehicle. Doris hugged

Louise making Twinkles yap at the hug, "Thank you, dear. I'll never forget this."

Herman and Louise watched the two gals tromp through the snow and get into their vehicle. Louise waved as the girls waved back. Herman turned the cabin lights out and revved up his diesel engine and waited for the girls to start moving their vehicle.

As the Dominator started to move, Herman stepped on the gas, but Louise yelled at him to stop. She yelled so loud that Herman instinctively hit the brake.

"What?" he asked.

"Your pill. You WILL take your pill now," Louise was adamant, so Herman gave up and took his pill.

"Thank you," Louise told him, "now you can go." And she patted him on the head, then plunked in her seat, patting her lap for Twinkles to jump up, and they were ready to roll again.

Herman saw the Dominator pulling away slowly and had barely gone fifty feet, and even with all its specialty lights, it was nearly invisible already.

*   *   *

Making an Adjustment

"Wow, was that something!" Doris said. "Using a total stranger's bathroom on the interstate. That'll be one of those stories we can tell for years."

"Yeah," Rita said, "if we survive."

"Oh pooh," Jackie said, "this must be part of our Lucky Seven trip, we were lucky enough to use a bathroom in the middle of the interstate."

As Doris got back on the road, she had trouble seeing. "Oh man, that RV is behind us, and those huge lights are nearly blinding. I was better off behind them so I could see. Not to mention that I'm the one blazing the trail now, at least when the RV was in front, it was smashing the snow down," Doris said.

"Well, slow down, he'll pick up speed, and if you stay in the left lane, he'll go right by on the right lane, and you'll be in good shape behind him," Janet said.

"Yeah," Doris agreed and slowly changed lanes but didn't use her blinker.

*   *   *

Making Contact

Herman saw the Dominator moving over to allow his RV to pass them. He considered that the Dominator might want to follow his RV as its tandem rear wheels would leave a decent path to follow. The road was covered with snow now, but there were faint tracks he was following. He turned on his searchlight once again to search the side of the road for signs or markers and to make sure he was over far enough to pass the girls' Dominator safely. Jackie and Rita were waving out the backseat, and Louise leaned over to wave back.

The Dominator began to fade back farther and farther. Herman watched them in his mirrors to make sure there wasn't a problem. He wasn't going fast, just creeping along and making sure they didn't miss an off-ramp while keeping an eye on the Dominator's lights that were nearly behind him now.

He turned on the rearview parking video and watched the Dominator settle in behind him. When he glanced back to the road ahead, suddenly his brother's image materialized in front of him. He was smiling brightly and holding his arms out as if to gather him for a hug. Herman looked at him for just a moment.

Louise was going to tell him to watch the road when she screamed at the top of her lungs, "STOP!!"

Herman was on the brakes, but too late, they were right on top of the drift and plowed into it in slow motion, pushing into the other cars, and throwing Louise and Twinkles out of their seat. Twinkles rolled onto the dash and up to the window while Louise fell forward and smashed her chin and shoulder on the large padded dash. The RV pushed into the snow up to the enormous windshield, cracking it before they finally came to a stop. Just as quickly, they felt a crash in the back that pushed the RV another half-inch into the giant drift. Herman watched the crack in the windshield continue across its width.

"Louise!" Herman shouted, "Are you okay? Louise!"

Louise coughed a few times but said she was okay and started to get up as the window crack extended a little more. They both watched the crack grow until it finally stopped just inches from the rim of the windshield frame.

"Those girls must have plowed into the back of us after we hit the drift," Herman said. "Get Twinkles, and we need to move away from the windshield in case it gives way," Herman ordered as he wrangled the keys and grabbed his wallet and CB mike, stretching the cord as far as it'd go and tying it around the arm of the couch.

Louise was slow getting up, but she managed to hang onto the seat and the dash to push herself up off the floor. Twinkles was stunned and didn't want to move, so Louise picked up the shivering pup, and headed back to the sofa and sat with her, trying to shake off the shock.

"Now what, Herman?" Louise asked while trying to cuddle Twinkles to calm her.

First, I'm going to check on those girls behind us. Then I'm going to see if anyone is in any of the cars we just smashed into. It only looked like one or two. Still, I don't want to kill somebody. If the girls back there are okay, then I need them to back up some so I can back this thing up a bit to get the snow pressure off the windshield." He dug out boots, his down coat, and fur hat.

"You stay put!" he ordered Louise.

Herman opened the door and stepped out into the snow and trudged to the front of the RV. He saw that there was no obvious way to get between the RV and the drift to check on those cars. He had to back the RV out, but the Dominator was behind him. He trudged to the back of the RV through a foot of snow, foot by foot. He wasn't used to pulling his feet up so high, and he was out of breath by the time he got to the Dominator. Doris was out already looking at the front of her Dominator when she saw Herman.

"I'm so sorry!" she shouted over the wind. "What happened?"

"It's okay, we ran into a giant snowdrift that's piled up across the interstate. It's really monstrous. At least we weren't going that fast thankfully. Are you girls, okay?" Herman asked as he held the collar of his coat tightly around his neck.

"Yeah, I think we're all okay," Doris said, looking at the damage on the rear of the RV in her headlights. "We didn't hit hard enough to set off the airbags, and we all had our seatbelts on. Is your wife okay."

"Yeah, she fell, but she's okay," Herman coughed in the cold wind. "Looks like nothing but cosmetic damage on either of us. That Dominator is tough. Can you back it up about twenty or thirty feet? I'm smashed into that drift, and I think I pushed another car deep into it. I need to back out of it to see if anyone is in the cars. I don't think there's any damage to the diesel back here, so I should be able to move it."

"On it," Doris said, realizing the urgency.

*   *   *

Damage Control

"Gotta back up," she told the other girls as she got back in the Dominator. "Everyone okay?" She heard three yeses and saw Rita taking a sip from her flask in the rearview. Well, Rita must be okay. The Dominator was still running, and Doris easily moved her vehicle back about fifty feet. Herman waved to her that it was far enough. She watched Herman coughing a few times as he so slowly trudged back to the RV. He looked to be struggling to walk.

The girls soon heard the diesel engine grumble a few times, then the back-up lights came on, and the behemoth slowly moved back with the back-up beeping accompaniment. They heard a few exhausts of air, then it was relatively quiet.

"I can see the guy getting out again," Janet said, looking down the right side of the RV. "He's going up to the front with a flashlight, and I guess his wife is operating the spotlight."

"Yes, he told me a couple of cars were already piled into that drift, and he wanted to see if anyone was in one of them," Doris explained.

"Ew," Jackie said. "I wouldn't want to look. If they weren't dead before, I'm sure that RV would have done a lot of damage."

"Oh, don't be such a baby," Rita said, obviously having had a sip too many out of her flask.

"Knock it off, Rita," Janet said. "Let's just hope nobody got hurt. It'll be a miracle."

They waited and chatted about the weather and getting to Vegas for what seemed like too many minutes. Then suddenly, they heard the RV's diesel horn blasting over and over. Even in the howling storm, that horn was loud.

"What the hell?" Doris said.

"Something is wrong," Janet said. "That's not just having fun, that's a call for help. I'm going up there."

"Me too," Doris said. "Jackie, can you watch Rita while we go up there and see what the problem is?"

"I think I'll be okay," Jackie said.

"Honk the horn if there's a problem," Doris said, and they both were out of the car, hustling up to the front of the RV.

*   *   *

Tea for Two, Three, Four, Five

Louise saw them coming in the RV's rearview and opened the door before they got there. "It's Herman!" she shouted as the girls approached the door. "He fell in front of the RV, I can't pick him up." Louise met the other two as they went in front of the RV. There was slightly less wind in the alcove the RV made in the drift, and Herman was lying sprawled out in the snow. "Can we get him into the RV?" Louise asked.

"We can try," Doris said, noticing that he looked huge in his coat, hat, gloves, and boots compared to his smaller frame behind the wheel.

The three women grabbed his coat sleeves and feet and pulled him along the snow. They stomped down the snow down along the side of the RV so they could pull him easier. By the time they got to the door, they noticed how pale Herman was. Just a short time ago, he looked like he'd been out in the sun all day. The women struggled, lugging Herman back into the RV inch by inch. Doris didn't want to say anything, but Herman didn't look very good. Doris looked at Janet, and Janet gave her back a look of deep concern.

They got him in the door, then lugged him up on the sofa. While Janet and Doris plunked in the seats to try to catch their breath, Louise unbuttoned Herman's coat and took off his hat, then opened a drawer and took out a stethoscope. She listened to his chest, then his neck, and felt his wrist, then listened to his chest again. Then she slumped onto the couch next to him. "He's gone," she said.

"What?" Doris couldn't believe what Louise was saying. "Are you sure?"

"Yes, she's sure," Janet said and made a face at Doris for asking such a dumb question.

"I'm sure," Louise sighed, staring into space. "I'm glad you ladies are here, or I think I'd lose my mind if I was alone."

"I'm really sorry," Doris patted her shoulder as Louise started to make a few tears. "Can we get an ambulance or something?"

Louise shook her head no. "He was living on borrowed time, and we both knew it," Louise wept. "Just before we hit the drift, I heard him say 'Howie!"

"How what?" Doris asked.

"Shut up," Janet told Doris and punched her arm lightly.

Louise understood the confusion and explained about Herman's twin brother Howard and how close they were and how crushed Herman was when Howie died a few years ago. "Herman had been seeing Howie like a ghost for months. And lately, it had been more frequent to the point where Herman was talking to him off and on. I know he'll be happy to be with his brother. I think when he said 'Howie,' he saw his brother telling him it was time to go with him."

After a moment or two of uncomfortable silence, Janet asked, "What can we do for you? And where is your little dog?"

"I put her in the bathroom when I went out to check on Herman. She's fine there. I don't know what to do right now. It's not like we can call for help. I know you want to be on your way, but I'd sure like it if you stuck around for a little bit. I don't really know what to do. I've never driven this thing, much less in this weather," Louise said, sounding forlorn and deserted. "I can fix some tea."

Janet and Doris looked at each other. It was cold in the RV but nothing like outside. Hot tea? Sure, why not. They both said it'd be nice for a cup of tea.

Louise was mindlessly making tea while the girls sat in the little dining booth. Louise would glance at Herman from time to time as though she expected him to wake up. Doris was wondering if he might do just that.

"You know, I spent my life as a nurse," Louise rambled, "if I'd have been able to get an ambulance here, I might have been able to save him. I just didn't have a defibrillator nor a shot of epinephrine. I saw him fall, and by the time I got out there, there was such a look of peace on his face. He'd been having heart trouble for so long, and I know it worried him. I think he rushed through this drive, so we'd be at our winter home where there were doctors and hospitals he liked. We didn't see this storm coming." Louise shook her head lightly sobbing as she stirred the water in the pot unnecessarily.

"Nobody saw this storm coming," Janet said. "It is one of those things."

"You know, a lot of things fell into place for him," Doris said.

"What are you talking about?" Janet asked.

"Well, if Jackie hadn't had to pee so bad, and if Rita wasn't such an idiot drunk to write notes on napkins, and if Louise and Herman hadn't volunteered to allow us to use their bathroom, we'd have been long gone ahead of them, and we'd have probably hit that drift first, and the RV would have plowed into us and probably killed us all. He'd have felt awful if he'd have hurt us or worse, and if he'd have had a heart attack on top of that, Louise would be sitting here alone in a blizzard. Instead, here we are, so Louise has someone here to try to help her.

"I appreciate you ladies hanging here with me for a bit. This is quite an ordeal for me even though I knew his time was coming to an end," Louise said.

The three sat in uncomfortable silence while Louise prepared more tea.

Then they heard the horn of the Dominator blasting over and over. "Maybe we should be going now," Janet said as she elbowed Doris.

"Oh no," Louise looked at them both wistfully. "I just made tea. Oh, and I don't want to be alone right now. Can you stay a bit more?"

"Well, the other two gals are in my car," Doris said.

"They're welcome in here. If the generator isn't damaged, I can turn on some heat. I at least know how to do that," Louise begged.

"Oh...well, I am not sure this would be Jackie's cup of tea with your husband here like this. And Rita...uh, well, she's probably a couple sheets in the wind by now," Janet said as she elbowed Doris again.

"Oh my," Louise said. "You are probably right. It's a lot to ask someone to sit by a dead person. I've seen so much in my career. Would it be better if we moved him to the bedroom?"

They decided to lug Herman to the bedroom. Louise took his coat and boots off as they situated him on the bed.

The girls in the Dominator kept honking the horn, and it was irking Doris something awful.

Chapter 48

Tea Time

"Here comes Doris," Jackie fumed to Rita as she saw Doris stomp out of the RV and slam the door behind her. "You can lay off the horn now. You made your point."

Doris tromped through the wind and snow, holding her coat closed around her neck, and her eyes were squinted up because of the headlights of the Dominator or because she was pissed at Rita's endless blasting of the horn.

"What?!?" Doris demanded as she swung the car door open and jumped in. "This better be important."

"Well, it's taking you too long," Rita said. "We're worrying that something will come whack into the back of us too."

"Yeah, you're right," Doris said as she leaned over and pulled the keys out and turned on the emergency flashers. "Bundle up, you're coming up to the RV. Louise is making tea." Doris didn't elaborate on Herman.

The three trudged up to the RV and filed in, knocking snow off their shoes and all gabbing about the cold, the wind, the snow, and were simultaneously thanking Louise for having them in for tea. They fixed their tea in small foam cups, and Louise opened a tin of cookies as they talked about the places they were headed and the cookies when Rita piped up, "Where's your husband?"

Louise looked wide-eyed and looked at Doris and Janet. Janet jumped right in, "Oh, he's back in the bedroom laying down for awhile."

"Um, yes," Louise nodded as she caught the glances of Doris and Janet, "he drove a long time today, and this accident left him out of it."

The ladies continued with tea, talking about their children, grandchildren, and other topics avoiding the real issue, which was the huge drift in front of them and Herman's demise.

Rita must have sensed men's epithelial cells in the RV and couldn't leave it alone.

"So, your husband is napping? While the RV is half on the interstate? Was that his plan? Did he say what his plan was?" she asked as she sipped her tea, looking over the top of her cup at the wall of snow outside, then back into the darkness of the back of the RV. "He's not going to be able to plow through there, is he?"

They all looked at the wall of packed snow just ahead of the RV, lit up eerily by the RV's headlights.

Jackie chimed in too, "Did your husband find anyone in those cars? Was anyone hurt or...um...dead?"

Doris rolled her eyes and said as she sipped her tea, "go ahead, Janet. Answer that."

Louise dropped her fake smile, "I'm sorry. I have to level with you girls. I don't know if anyone is in those cars," she said, and the tears began again. "Herman never got to check them out. He collapsed in front of the RV. By the time I got my coat and got out there, he didn't have much of a pulse. That's when I came in and started blasting the horn. Janet and Doris helped carry him in, by then he was already gone."

"Gone?" Jackie innocently asked.

"Dead," Rita told her unceremoniously.

Jackie's eyes filled with tears as she went over to Louise to hug her. "Oh, I am so sorry. And you are so strong! Fixing us tea. Oh my, when my husband passed, I was useless for months."

Louise patted Jackie. "I have to keep it together because there's nothing I can do about it now," Louise sniffled. "Herman has had a bad heart condition for years and was lax on taking his meds, and I know this storm was causing him some stress. Then hitting the drift and worrying about the cars in front of us. I could tell his blood pressure was up, and I don't know if he was taking his pills or spitting them out. He always felt he could overpower any illness." Louise wiped her eyes with a tissue.

"Well, what are you thinking about doing?" Jackie asked. "Can you drive this back home?"

"I can't drive it, and I don't know what I'm going to do yet, maybe I'll just....." and Louise was cut off by a banging on the RV door that startled them all and set Twinkles to yapping and scratching on the bathroom door. Louise stepped back and let Twinkles out.

"Open up," a man's voice hollered, "we're freezing!"

Louise didn't even think it through as she opened the door. Two men stood out there not dressed well enough for blizzard conditions. One of them wore a simple winter coat with a hood, the other wore a ratty sweatshirt tied around his head, and really ugly socks pulled up over the cuff of his pants.

"Get in," Louise ordered them. As they knocked the snow off, Twinkles ran out of the RV again to welcome the newcomers, skipping down the steps and jumped down into a fresh patch of snow and nearly buried herself. Jeff reached down and grabbed her, and handed her back to Louise as they climbed up the RV steps. "Where did you come from?" Louise asked, looking out into the darkness.

"We belong to the cars in the drift, sort of," Jeff said. "We have sheltered behind this drift under the overpass. It breaks the wind a bit and gives us a little refuge. I'm Jeff, and this is Reverend Matthew. We heard the horn blasts, then lots of horn honking, and it sounded like someone needed help in a bad way."

Jeff and Matthew went on to explain how their vehicles ended up undrivable, both of them on their sides down the embankment. Then Jeff told about his family being taken in by the old people in the blue Lincoln. Matthew told about the girls, then about the guys in the white van, and that they had all made it behind the drift for a little protection, and mostly to avoid additional vehicle crashes. When they heard the RV blasting its horn, then another vehicle horn, they decided that they should attempt help. They gambled on driving Ben's truck as far around the lower south edge of the drift as they could manage without getting stuck or bouncing the unconscious girl around. When the truck started tilting too much climbing over the end of the drift, Jeff and Matthew got out to hoof over to see what the crisis was.

"This drift just seems to hide in the dark, then it suddenly consumes vehicles," Jeff said, looking out at the creepy wall of white.

Doris introduced herself and the girls, then explained to the two men about their experience with Louise's RV and about Herman. Jeff and Matthew took a few minutes to offer Louise condolences, and Matthew offered to give Herman Last Rites. Louise and Matthew went to the bedroom for a few minutes while the others sat quietly, listening to Matthew's prayers.

When they came back, Jeff explained to the ladies that they needed to leave the RV right away.

"You gotta get out of this RV," Jeff said. They have tanks of a hundred gallons of diesel fuel, even if you only have half a tank, that's still nearly fifty gallons. If something plows into the back of this, it's a possible explosion, not counting the tank of

LP gas. This RV is nothing but a big highway torpedo. Is your vehicle still drivable?" he asked Doris.

"Yes, I'm pretty sure. I didn't go far after I ran into the back of this thing, I just backed it up about fifty feet. It seemed okay," Doris said.

"Ok," Jeff said to Louise, "I advise that you take what you need for a while, and we all get into her car and get back under the overpass and wait this out. I think that the south end of the drift, where we came through, will eventually become impassible too."

"Say no more," Rita said as she patted Matthew's knee and smiled sweetly.

"Uh, Rita," Janet said, "the man is thirty years younger than you."

"That doesn't bother me if it doesn't bother him," she said casually as she wrapped her coat around her skinny body trying to pose like a runway model, an old, skinny, wobbly runway model.

As Louise wandered around deciding what to take, getting her coat and picking up Twinkles, they decided to write a note and leave it in the RV, explaining ownership, how to contact Louise, and explaining her husband in the bedroom. Louise turned the diesel engine off and fired up the generator, turning the heat down far enough that the water tanks wouldn't freeze, but cool enough that Herman's body wouldn't suffer until they got help.

Louise remembered Matthew's kindness as she gathered up Herman's coat, "I'd like you to wear Herman's winter wool coat, gloves, and his hat. You look like you could use a warm coat," she said, seeing Matthew wasn't dressed for the weather and wanted to repay him somehow for the last rites and prayers. At first, Matthew was hesitant, then Louise told him it'd be a blessing if he'd wear it in exchange for his blessing Herman. Matthew didn't argue long. He said a short prayer of thanks, then snuggled into the warm wool coat and fur cap. Herman's boots were too small for either of the guys, so Louise stuck her feet in them. They were too big but better than her sneakers. Louise wrote the note, left all the road courtesy lights on, then shut all the cabin lights. With Twinkles under one arm and her things under the other, Louise and the others piled out of the RV and trudged back to Doris' Dominator.

"Whoaa, those are some wheels!" Jeff commented when he saw the Dominator lit up and looking as though it was ready for battle, "It looks like it has all the bells and whistles!"

"Yes, my husband wanted it all," Doris said as she was struggling to open her door. At first, the doors on the Dominator wouldn't unlock as they'd frozen, but soon they were able to jiggle them enough to get the doors open.

As they were getting in, Rita said to Matthew as she patted the seat next to herself, "Here you go, you can sit with me and keep me warm with that big old coat." Matthew smiled politely while Janet yanked his arm and made him sit in the front between the seats. The other four packed into the back seat.

"Cozy," Rita said, irked that they had Matthew sit up front.

Doris started up the Dominator and revved the engine a few times and checked all her mirrors and ran the anti-fog and defrosters full blast. "We need to wait a minute, I can't see yet," she said.

Rita remarked, "You can't see anything anyway." Doris just shook her head and started to roll the Dominator forward, slowly inching alongside the RV and looking at the front end as they approached the intrusive depression the RV had made in the drift.

"Whoaaa. That RV did some damage to that drift," Doris said. "You never did find out if there were people in those cars. Maybe we should check."

"It's okay," Matthew said. "Everybody is out. That grey car almost totally buried, that's Mr. Preston's, there is a little blue car buried in there that belongs to three high school girls, that red truck, that's Eddie's. Jeff's van and my Minibus are on their sides, off the road."

"Jeez," Janet said. "How many people are involved in this thing?"

"So far," Jeff started counting on his fingers, "including you five, twenty-three, I think."

"Damn," Doris said as she continued to crawl the Dominator forward.

As Jeff directed her, they could finally see the rear of Ben's truck parked near the guard rail waiting on them. Jeff told Doris to follow it. They drove slowly toward the diminished south end of the drift, while all were swapping stories about how they ended up here.

Things quieted down as Doris slowly inched the Dominator to take on the rising angle of the far end of the drift. They held their collective breaths as it angled way up and over the snowpack. It did well, as Doris expected. As they came down around the back of the drift, they could see the immensity of the drift and how it changed the wind current to blow most of its mischief over the refugees hiding behind it.

"Damn," was all anyone could say.

Jeff showed Doris where to navigate between the bridge abutments and guard rail, then brought the Dominator to stope in the middle of all the other vehicles.

Doris parked it.

"So, what's the plan?" Doris asked. "What can we do other than sit and wait this out?"

"Well, we can't do much. There's no way to communicate. Cell phones don't work at all, even the GPS doesn't calculate here. Because we're under a bridge, even AM radio is nearly impossible to listen to. The guy in the Lincoln has a little mobile CB radio, but it doesn't get out far enough because of the bridge, the snow, the clouds, and the distance."

"We're all gonna die, you know," Rita remarked, still irked that Matthew sat up front.

"Why can't we just drive back to one of the truck stops or continue on?

Jeff explained just as Ben had mentioned that there would be more drift piles at other overpasses, not to mention the snow piling up in the ditches and medians making a flat landscape that was impossible to tell exactly where the road was, not to mention other possible pile-ups along the way. He went on, explaining, "If we miscalculate where the pavement is, we could end up sliding into a ditch and rolling, just as my Minivan did. Or we might slam into other cars that have stalled. I think trying to move would be near suicide. It's just better to stay put for now and stay together as a group, at least until the blowing snow ends. It won't last forever, maybe just a couple hours, I hope," Jeff said.

"Oh, so these things blow out in a couple of hours?" Rita cooed to Jeff.

"Well, sometimes. Other times they can rage for more than a day. I'm hoping this will blow out quickly," Jeff explained.

Doris and Janet looked at each other. Matthew caught the concerned glances.

Chapter 49

Planning To Relocate

Jeff and Matthew jumped out of the Dominator when they arrived at the back of the drift and knocked on the window of Joe's white van. Joe leaned over and rolled the window down.

"We just brought five more people back here," Jeff told Joe, pointing to the Dominator, "by the way, I'm Jeff."

"Hey, man," Joe said. "Tell them welcome to the overpass. I'm Joe, and that is Barry back there, and Early is the guy laying down. He got his face mashed up when we didn't stop quick enough to avoid the drift pile. He needs medical help, I think. Anybody got a plan?" Joe asked.

"No. One guy bundled up and had some cross country skis, he headed back to a diner for help," Jeff commented.

"Oh yeah, he stopped by our van on his way out. Hope he can find the diner. Nice gal runs the joint," Joe said, looking at the snow piling up on his windshield.

"Well, keep thinking. Maybe we can come up with something so we can be found," Jeff said, then quickly returned to the Lincoln.

"Wow. Nice coat," Mr. Preston said to Matthew as he got back in Ben's truck.

"Yeah, it's warm," Matthew said. "Got it from a guy driving an RV that plowed into the drift. The RV buried your car and the girls' car way into the drift. It's a good thing you weren't in it."

"Oh, dear," Tawnie fretted.

"So, are they bringing the RV around?" Mr. Preston asked.

"No. I don't think so. No one knows how to drive it," Matthew said.

"Oh, I can!" Eddie volunteered. "I got my trucking CDL over a year ago when I was going to get a job as a trucker. The RV should be about the same."

"When the hell did you get your CDL?" Travis looked at his little brother in amazement.

"I was making it my business to learn a trade," Eddie said. "I wasn't going to count on inheritance." Eddie emphasized the word 'inheritance.' Travis winced at the shot Eddie gave him.

"If we could bring a big RV back here," Delphia said while doing some calculations on her laptop, "it might be able to deflect the main wind tunnel speed that goes through here. It would stop the low-pressure area that is creating the high wind gusts blasting under this bridge, and it might reduce the snow piling up around us. At least if we have to climb out of here, it'd be easier if we weren't walled in on both sides by mountains of drifts.

They all looked at Delphia. She felt weird and shrugged and went back to her computer.

"Who owns the RV?" Mr. Preston asked.

"Uh, an older lady in the back seat of that Dominator," Matthew said.

"So how'd she drive it this far?" Mr. Preston pressed.

"Well, she didn't." Matthew had to explain what happened to Herman, Louise's husband. Delphia and Tawnie looked at each other with concern, both wondering how bad this whole trip could become. Now there was a death to deal with.

"Oh boy, that's terrible," Mr. Preston shook his head and was surprised he was actually feeling bad about the RV driver. He wasn't sure if this emotional reaction was a good thing or not.

"You know, if it's big enough, we could all pile in the RV and be sort of warm," Eddie said. It should have a generator if it's still working, and it'll run a heater.

"And maybe," Delphia added, "if the generator works, we could get some light and recharge our devices, oh, and maybe they have a first aid kit, so I can patch up Brittany's head."

"And maybe a little girl's room?" Tawnie peeped in.

Mr. Preston and Eddie looked at each other, nodded, then got out of the truck and plodded over to the Lincoln and rapped on Jeff's window.

"You got something?" Jeff asked as he rolled the window down.

"Yeah, maybe," Mr. Preston said. "Mr. Ed here has a CDL license and says he can drive that RV. If it runs and if he can maneuver it back here, we can probably ALL fit in it. We'd have some breathing room, heat, and even a bathroom."

"Yeah. Yeah!" Jeff got excited at the idea of some kind of plan. "I'm sure Mrs. Buchbinder here would like a bathroom break soon. We'll have to move vehicles to fit it under here. If we can get the lady's Dominator to take us back to the RV, then get the dually and that van positioned on the north shoulder, there will be room to park the RV. It'll give us a little windbreak too. It's taller than that Lincoln, so maybe we could get that antenna up on its roof. It might send a better signal too."

"Yeah, the smart girl in the truck already mentioned it'd help with wind thrust, or whatever she said. We need you to go with us, Jeff." Mr. Preston said. "I'll stay with Eddie in the RV when we bring it around, but we need you to ride in the Dominator to help the lady around the pile, there and back. We don't need anything going haywire."

"Sounds like a plan," Jeff said. "Tell Matthew to go explain what we're doing to the guys in the van now that it seems the reverend has a warm coat and hat that he can run an errand. I've been talking to Mr. Buchbinder about it, and we think he should turn his car around to aim his headlights west out from the overpass. We have considered with the mega drift on the one side and the smaller drift on the other side, this might look deserted if someone comes looking from the air. With the Lincoln's big old incandescent beams lighting up that smaller drift, we have a better chance of being found."

"Makes sense to me," Mr. Preston said and headed back to the truck with Eddie.

"Damn. It's cold," Eddie said, ducking his chin down to his neck as they walked back to Ben's truck to talk to Matthew and explain to him he would be coordinating moving the vehicles around to accommodate the RV in the space under their overpass.

The three guys got out once more, and while Matthew went to talk to the guys in the white van, Mr. Preston, Jeff, and Eddie tromped over to the Dominator. Eddie immediately had some concerns as he remembered the ladies at the diner had a Dominator exactly like this one. Mr. Preston knocked on Doris' window, startling Doris and the other ladies. Doris rolled her window halfway down, letting the snow fly in, and the cold air blow across her face.

"Can we trouble you to drive us back around the drift?" He shouted over the wind, clutching his coat collar around his neck. "And if you don't mind, whichever one of you owns the RV, we'd like to try to drive it back here so we can all use it for refuge until we get help. We also think that if we put that little mobile CB antenna up on top of the RV, we might be able to get a distress call out."

Rita saw Mr. Preston and didn't pass up the opportunity, "Wow, you are a looker! Are you married?" she said, pushing her head as far as she could between the shoulder harness and the headrest of Doris' seat.

"Keep your ponies in the stable, Missy." He smartly discouraged Rita with a whimsical Duke Wayne accent, then looked at the other ladies for their okay to use their vehicles.

"Putting the little CB antenna up on the RV probably won't help," Louise volunteered, leaning over the front seat. "We have a CB in it and a substantial antenna on the roof, and we weren't getting anything for quite awhile."

"Hm," Mr. Preston mulled that point for a minute. "Well, even if not, can we try to get it back here so we can use it for shelter, Ma'am?"

"Yes," Louise said, "but you do know that my husband is still in it."

"Yes," he said. "I heard. I'm so sorry. But this is an emergency, and I think he'd understand the situation. We'll do right by him," Mr. Preston promised.

Doris hit the door locks to unlock the doors, and Rita swung her door open, scooted as close as she could to Louise in the middle, and patted her seat for Mr. Preston to sit, but Mr. Preston pushed Eddie from behind to sit next to Rita. Eddie pulled his pea coat collar up around his face and pulled his ballcap down as much as possible. Mr. Preston and Jeff made their way around the Dominator to the passenger side. Janet opened her door, scooted to the middle, and Jeff sat shotgun up front, and Jackie opened up her door and stepped out so Mr. Preston could sit in her seat.

Eddie slumped himself in the seat as far as he could while the interior lights were on when everyone was getting in. He knew darn right well who these ladies were now. They were definitely the ladies in the Dominator-Maximus from the diner. Eddie suddenly didn't want to be recognized at all.

"We may have to double-up," Jackie was embarrassed to tell Mr. Preston as she stood out in the snow, realizing she'd have to sit in his lap. He nodded, glad he didn't have to have the old blonde gal sit in his lap. Jackie carefully got in and sat on Mr. Preston's knees, leaning as far forward as possible.

"I won't bite," he said, as he gently nudged Jackie back on his lap and leaned her against himself. "It'll be cozy and warm for a few minutes. Ok, we're ready to go," he said.

"Hope when we get up there that nobody else is in that mess," Doris said. "We don't have room for many more. And I hope there are no cars coming," then she put it in drive, checking her mirrors, only to see a demoralized Rita, sitting with her arms crossed between Louise and Eddie, not even giving Eddie a second look. Well, finally, a guy that is beneath her, Doris thought.

Rita slowly shifted her eyes to take a peek at the guy that got in next to her. "Don't I know you?" she said. "I never forget a face."

"She never forgets a MAN face," Jackie said, having overheard Rita's comment.

"I'm one of those guys that has a familiar look," Eddie muttered and turned to look out the window at the blackness and snow.

"Ok," Jeff said to Doris, "aim back around to the south side of the drift. Take your time, it's getting slicker with us packing it down with cars and trucks, but I think your nubby Dominator tires will be able to manage it."

Doris did as Jeff told her, but the ride was pretty rough as the left side of the Dominator rose up the snowpack to a worrisome angle as they crossed over the previous tire tracks keeping away from the guard rail. The bumpy ride made Jackie feel uncomfortably shy sitting on Mr. Preston's knees, bobbing about and leaning on the door until Mr. Preston put his hand under Jackie's elbow to steady her.

"I hope I'm not making you too uncomfortable," Jackie apologetically said to Mr. Preston.

"No," he told her. "No trouble at all. You are fine. Here, let me hold onto you, so you aren't rocking and rolling." And Mr. Preston put his hands around her waist to help stabilize her. "I think this'll help. Hope you don't mind."

Jackie felt her body heat up with this man's touch, even though it was through coats and gloves. "No, sir. It's okay," she nearly gasped. She was noticing how her face felt like it was on fire in spite of the cold.

"You don't have to call me 'sir,'" he told her quietly, "my name is Tremont." He found himself stopping to breathe in her air. "You know, you smell really nice. I like what you are wearing," he whispered to her.

Jackie felt her body heat smoldering and wanting to open a window. "Oh," she said in sort of a daze, "I didn't put on any perfume, just soap and water, I guess." Jackie blew out her breath, thinking it sounded like steam escaping from a locomotive. She felt more flushing coming on, realizing her comment sounded idiotic.

"Well, it's very nice," Mr. Preston said, trying not to keep embarrassing her.

*   *   *

Matthew Delivers a Message

Meanwhile, Matthew tapped on the window of the geek's van. Joe rolled his window down a bit again and remembered the guy from the diner with the Minibus, they shook hands and Matthew said, "I've been in the truck over there after I rolled my Minibus. They are going to try to bring a big RV back here that crashed into the drift. That was the RV horn blasting we heard awhile ago. We need to line up the vehicles and cars on the north shoulder of the road to block the wind a bit and get the Lincoln turned around, so his lights shine out west onto the piles of snow out there in case there's an air search."

"I'm glad someone has a plan," Joe said. "I saw your Minibus out there, glad you are okay.

"Dammit!" Barry said in frustration as he threw a few magazines up against the wall. "There's NOTHING to help us in these magazines!"

"What's he up to?" Matthew shouted over the blizzard wind.

"He's got about 50 years of old magazine subscriptions for mechanical and electronic stuff. He hoped he could find something that would help. He's been going through them," Joe explained.

"Is that your friend laying down?" Matthew asked.

"Yes, that's Early, he banged his face pretty hard when we came to a fast stop earlier," Joe explained.

"Is he okay?" Matthew asked.

"I hope so. Just maybe a concussion," Joe guessed. "As long as he's out, at least he's not feeling any pain. So we leave him be."

"Maybe there's something in the RV," Matthew hoped. "Anyway, I'm going to chat with the Lincoln and then move Ben's truck while the others are headed out for the RV, if you could pull your van up close behind the truck, that'd be great."

"Got it," Joe said and watched Matthew head over to the Lincoln until he was nearly obliterated from view by the dense blowing snow.

*   *   *

Travis Has Issues

Matthew had left Travis in charge of watching over the girls in the truck while he was letting everyone else know the plan.

Travis kept looking at the three girls left in the truck with him. Delphia caught a glimpse of him staring at them and wanted no part of him. He looked like a punk with his attempt at youth whiskers that reminded her of iron filing particulate matter in last year's science class. He left a thin, scraggly patch of hair on his chin to prove his manhood, but Delphia remembered an old Aunt with similar chin hair. Delphia continued to run calculations on her laptop, determining wind velocity and possible wind chill factors. Tawnie sat with her arms folded, looking out at the snow and worked at holding back tears of what will happen if they don't die and have to call parents to come get them nine hours away from home and deal with their punishment for lying. Dying seemed preferable.

"So, how old are you," Travis asked Delphia with an abrupt tone.

"Probably jail-bait for you," Delphia answered with no emotion, not even looking up from her screen.

"I wasn't asking for a date," Travis tossed back. "I was just making conversation." Travis felt her rile him. Delphia didn't flinch. She knew better than to add to his arrogance.

"I am working on a problem," she told him.

"Oh, that's rich," Travis needled her. "You know, you can't math your way out of this mess. You three made a bad call, and you'll have to answer to your parents for it."

"That's true," Delphia responded, and based on how edgy he was, she gambled about his situation and said, "I'd rather have to answer to my parents than the law." And she went back to her calculations.

That pissed Travis off. "Who said something?" He demanded, suddenly becoming overwhelmingly annoyed.

Delphia saw that he took the bait easily, "Nobody said anything," she said.

"That's bull!" Travis was working himself up more. "Did Eddie say something?" He continued his demanding tone to the point where Tawnie made herself as small as possible.

Delphia quietly folded her laptop, then turned and looked him right in the eye, "Look, you are the one that told me. You gave yourself away. It's called deductive reasoning. A simple matter of taking cues and assembling the results in a constructive, cohesive, substantive way. Mr. Preston is a lawyer, and he's been watching you like a hawk. I figure he's familiar with your kind in his line of work. He's learned to pay attention to the cues you give off. You have shown repeatedly that you are easily baited to attack when you don't have any data to determine your ability to overcome your opponent." She stared at him without blinking.

Travis couldn't make his eyes focus on her, and his eyes darted around the truck interior as though he was looking for a translator to explain what she said and give him a smart comeback, but he knew he didn't stand a chance in hell of verbally sparring with her. Even though she was young, she was miles smarter and way out of his league, and he knew it.

He could see that it apparently amused Tawnie as he could see her peering at him over her shoulder.

"Shut up," was all he could say as he sank back in the seat and pulled his hoodie around his face.

Delphia winked at Tawnie and opened her laptop again, and continued working offline.

*   *   *

RV Hunting

While the others were jockeying cars, the group in the Dominator had slowly moved past the south side of the drift with their plan to get the RV to put into service as a refuge.

"Looks bigger than before," Janet said as they slowly rolled past.

"I think it looks wider rather than taller," Doris commented.

"Wider, taller, who cares," Rita snipped.

Doris pulled around the drift, the Dominator still managing to keep moving even though the snow was getting pretty deep except for where it was packed down from the vehicles traipsing back and forth. It was still a significant hurdle tilting the Dominator at quite an angle, but not enough to roll it.

"Whew," Doris breathed as they came off the end of the drift. "I'm glad we didn't get stuck."

"You aren't the only one," Rita chipped, giving Eddie a dirty look.

Doris made her way to the front of the RV, her headlights shining into the space between the RV and the drift.

"Wow, snow is beginning to fill in where the RV plowed into it," Janet said.

Mr. Preston turned to Eddie. "So, you can drive this thing?"

"I think so," Eddie said, looking at the immensity of it.

"Thirty-eight feet," Louise told them.

"I should be good," Eddie said. "Some of the big rigs they had us drive were nearly sixty feet." Still, Eddie had some concerns about getting past the drift and between the guard rails and the bridge abutments. He didn't want to say anything to worry the women or draw any more attention to himself.

"The door is unlocked. There's a rocker switch right inside the door on the left, house lights," Louise said, looking wistfully at her husband's thirty-eight-foot coffin at this point.

"Let's go," Mr. Preston instructed, "the snow is only getting deeper."

"Yep," Eddie said, and he and Mr. Preston got out of the warm Dominator and trudged through the knee-deep snow, Mr. Preston taking a moment to knock the snow off the headlights of the RV.

Rita looked long and hard at Eddie, something about that guy looked awfully familiar. She took another sip from her flask.

*   *   *

Brotherly Love and RV Wrangling

The guys climbed in the RV and felt around for the light switch and flipped it on.

"Wow," Eddie said, "I've never been in an RV this big before."

"Me either," Mr. Preston said, as he walked back to see the cargo, they would be hauling along with them. He flipped on the bedroom light and saw the man lying on the bed, looking as though he was sleeping even though he looked somewhat gray.

While Eddie was trying to start the diesel engine, Mr. Preston came forward, concerned that it didn't start right up.

"Don't worry," Eddie told him, "diesel is hard to start cold." Eddie kept at it until they finally heard the diesel rumble slowly to life. Eddie sat back in the seat. "Whew."

"Okay. Let's go before it dies," Mr. Preston told him as the motor sounded uneven.

"Uh, no sir," Eddie said politely. "A diesel needs to run for a few minutes to build up pressure in the air lines, or we won't have brakes, and who knows what else in this thing runs on air."

"Oh," Mr. Preston said and kept looking into the dark in the back of the RV. "Kind of creepy having a dead man in the back."

"Yeah," Eddie said, "it doesn't bug me much. I worked as a hospital orderly for awhile. We picked up dead bodies and took them to the morgue. After the first few, it doesn't matter anymore."

"You sure have had a variety of jobs," Mr. Preston commented.

"Yeah," Eddie was embarrassed. "I know. I guess I just haven't found my calling."

"I gather your brother has some issues," Mr. Preston said.

"Yes," Eddie told him. "My dad is a cop, a detective, actually. Travis doesn't always get along with him. Dad got angry that Travis couldn't keep a job. So Travis left home. He lived with some people that were kind of into drugs, and they got him in trouble. He's just angry all the time now. He can't seem to get his life straightened out."

"Does he want to straighten it out?" Mr. Preston asked.

"Good question," Eddie said. "I don't really know. He doesn't tell me much. He just likes to order me around and seems to get me stuck with his problems. He's the one that made me drive into this storm. I should have been at work, but Travis jumped in the truck and ordered me to go."

"Ordered you?" Mr. Preston asked. "You couldn't say no?"

"Do you have a mean older brother?" Eddie asked Mr. Preston.

"No, I don't. I'm an only child." Mr. Preston told him. "I always wanted an older brother."

"Well, when you have a mean older brother than pounds on you, teases you, blames his mishaps on you, threatens you, twists your arms, punches you when he walks by, makes you say 'uncle'...for your whole life, then you know you have to do what he orders you to do," Eddie said shaking his head.

"Can't you just walk away?" Mr. Preston asked.

"Look, Mr. Preston, sometimes he gets me into situations I didn't even know about," Eddie said.

"How could you not know about it?" Mr. Preston pressed.

"Ok, well, for instance. I realize you are a lawyer, but please hold this in the strictest confidence, or he'll kill me. The reason that lady in the Dominator said I looked familiar, is because she did see us before. A few hours ago at the diner. We stopped there to get something to eat, and those ladies were there. We'd just gotten our coffee when my brother got up, saying nothing to me, and he tried to hold up those ladies! Honestly, I did not know he was going to do that. He never said a word, just got up and shoved a spoon in his pocket as though it were a gun. The only thing that saved us was the diner lady. She put him in his place, and the ladies said they didn't want to take the time to press charges," Eddie confided.

Mr. Preston was quiet.

"You don't believe me," Eddie said, looking at Mr. Preston.

"I do believe you," said Mr. Preston, thinking back about how he rescued James from such a life, and now he was his trusted house manager. "Did the diner lady intend to file a report on you?"

"No," Eddie said with half a smile, "she put Travis in his place. I never saw anything like it. She made him sweep the parking lot, and mop the floor like a drill sergeant. She paid him though, saying she didn't expect anyone to work for free. She got us our dinner but docked his pay for it. Travis seemed to respect her for some reason. He didn't even argue."

Mr. Preston raised his eyebrows in amazement. "I think I met her when I stopped at the diner and got a bagel and coffee, but didn't take the time to realize how tough she could be. She deserves a handshake."

Eddie gunned the engine a bit. "I think we're ready to go."

The Dominator was still sitting there, waiting for the okay sign. Eddie tooted the blaring RV horn and flashed the headlights that he was ready to roll. The Dominator started to slowly head back around the drift, and Rita watched out her window looking at Eddie, still trying to figure out where she knew his face from.

Eddie carefully put the RV transmission into reverse to back it away from the wall of packed snow that it formed when it slammed into the drift. The RV had little trouble plowing the snow down under its huge tandem rear tires with the weight of the diesel engine over them. Eddie was only worried about accidentally slipping off the road down the embankment. On the outside lane, the embankment was steep and probably why the Minivan and the old Minibus rolled. Eddie could now feel how powerful the wind gusts were as it rocked the RV and caused it to sway a bit. It was impossible to tell if he'd driven to the shoulder, but Eddie held onto the wheel as it rolled farther back away from the drift.

"I think we're far enough," Eddie said as he stopped the RV. He let go of the wheel and shook his hands. "I'm tense," he said to Mr. Preston. Mr. Preston nodded. Eddie then shifted the RV into drive and slowly advanced the behemoth toward the south end of the drift. "It's just a school bus," Eddie said. "Just a school bus."

"Pardon me?" Mr. Preston said.

"This RV is about the same wheelbase as a school bus. That's one of the training classes we had to take. I know this belongs to that lady, and her husband is in here still, I feel responsible if anything happens."

"Don't worry. She won't sue you. I'll make sure," Mr. Preston said, then smiled at Eddie.

"Okay," Eddie said, "let's do it." And he goosed the accelerator, and the big vehicle began to move hissing out its air pressure and grumbling under the strain of the diesel engine moving the motor home on the deep snow. Slipping at first, but grinding the packed snow off the pavement, then grabbing hold, the RV moved forward.

Chapter 50

Articulating the Article

"Oh shit! Shit!" Barry nearly yelled. "I got something!" As he pulled himself out of a pile of magazines waving an old yellowed copy, "check this out, 1957 article, 'How to Build Your Own Short Wave Receiver.'"

Joe put his magazines down and stepped across the van to see what Barry had, "What does it say?"

Barry read from the article,

> " 'In times of hydrogen and atom bombs, air raids, and civil defense shelters or in your own fallout shelter, you might want to know what is going on in the world after communication is cut off. Here's how you can build a crystal radio receiver out of handy garage supplies. You'll have your own emergency short wave receiving radio.'

"Look at this Joe, it shows how to use crap to build a short wave. That'd be about a hundred times better than that CB radio they have." Barry was nearly ranting, he was so excited.

"Whoa, whoa, whoa," Joe said. "Calm down. This says it's a receiving unit, that's only half the battle. We'd need to send a message, this won't accomplish that."

"Yes, it does!" Barry went on, "Right here, at the end, it says, 'transmission unit coming in future issues.' It's got to be here in one of these issues. We can build a short wave system. Even if it's weak, it'd be good for a hundred miles, not one mile like the CB. My Grandfather always wanted a shortwave set. He talked about it all the time but never got one. He told me there were shortwave clubs all over that specifically tune in and look for calls of distress in a crisis or during disasters. If we can get any kind of a signal out, someone will hear it. One of these old farmers around here will have a set tuned in during this blizzard!"

Joe and Barry both heard a faint breathless, "Yessssss," coming from Early.

"See, he agrees, Joe. This is what we need to do. Here, you look through this year of these Popular Tinkering and see if you can find the follow-up issue with the transmission set. I'm going to see if we have enough supplies to pull this off," Barry remarked.

Joe sat on the pile and started sorting through 1957, page by page. They both heard the toot of the RV.

"Looks like they'll be coming around the mountain in a minute," Joe said as he glanced out the van window. It'll be good if we can all get in the RV. It'd be easier to build something if we had a flat surface and an outlet to use a soldering gun."

"Uh oh," Barry said and slumped his shoulders. "There's a problem."

"Yeah?" Joe said, still shuffling through magazines. "What's that?"

"It says we need a diode," Barry said. "I don't think there's a Radio Shack handy out here." And Barry flipped the magazine onto the front seat and stared out the window. "It was too good to be true."

Early started rocking his head a bit and said something.

"Huh?" Barry said, "Early, what is it?"

Joe stopped making noise with his magazines, and they both tried to listen to Early.

"Razorblaaade," he said breathlessly.

"Razorblade?" Joe asked.

"Yessss," Early said.

"Oh fine, you think you need a shave? Well, I'll just grab the extra one out of the glove compartment," Barry said with great sarcasm.

"Nooo," Early weakly rasped again, starting to act agitated, knowing he was not getting his message across, "make a diode from junk razorblaaaade." And his head drooped to the side, finally fainting away.

"Thanks for the help, Early!" Barry said, patting Early's arm but shrugging his shoulders at Joe.

Barry thought about what Early said for a moment, then the clarity beamed up from somewhere. "I think Early thinks we can make a diode. From junk. Okay, maybe we are still in business. Is anything else in those magazines about that? I see we can build a capacitor, we just need a couple toilet paper tubes, some foil, a paper towel core, or a piece of light cardboard...the RV might have that stuff. I will need a lot of copper wire, though. And the diode, how to build it, he said something about a razor blade. And tape, we'll need some of that damn tape you always have."

"Yep. I have some duct tape under my seat," Joe said.

"You always have duct tape, and now it'll come in really handy. We'll need a tin can," Barry said. "Hopefully, we can wrangle a piece of tin off one of the cars or something."

"What about the wire," Barry said. "If somebody had some jumper cables since they're about eight feet and single-stranded, we could strip them and get plenty of copper wire that way."

"Good plan," Joe said, "but nobody had them when we asked before."

"We didn't ask the lady in the Dominator, nor the RV lady, one of them might have a set, and if they do, we are in business," and Barry lit up with a big smile. "We're gonna get everybody outta here!"

"Don't get excited just yet, Barry. Wait until the RV gets back."

"I know," Barry said. "And first, we need to figure out how to create a diode. You keep looking for the transmission article, I'll study the schematic on this. We don't want any mistakes. I think we'll get one shot at this if we can get some wire."

Chapter 51

"Coming 'Round the Mountain"

"I see light comink around schnow mountain," Auggie suddenly said, looking up into his rearview.

"That should be the lady in the Dominator," Carol said as they all twisted around to see what would appear through the curtains of blowing snow.

Nick was still occasionally calling out on the CB, but he'd gotten tired of not getting any response other than static, and his enthusiasm was subsiding.

"Potty," Holly said, awakening from her sleep.

"You can wait a little," Carol said, comforting the toddler, not wanting to scare her.

"PottEEEE!" Holly said, a little more demanding.

"In a minute," Carol consoled her. "Watch for the big house coming! Daddy is coming too!" Carol tried to re-direct Holly's attention. Christie just made a face and rolled her eyes.

"I agree vit baby," Wilhelmine said. "Now vould be gudt time for pot to tinkle."

Slowly the big Dominator appeared through the snow shroud and pulled up behind Auggie's Lincoln. Jeff got out of the Dominator and quickly jumped into the Lincoln to share the news.

"That kid from the truck has the RV rolling. If they can make it between the snow dune there and the guard rail without tipping over, we'll be in good shape, I think. I know we'd all like to stretch our legs," Jeff said.

"Are we all going to fit in the RV?" Nick asked.

"It's pretty big, son," Jeff told him. "I think there'll be plenty of room. If nothing else, we can walk around for a minute, use the bathroom, wash our hands...." Jeff conveniently avoided mentioning Herman's body on the bed.

"I don't see any headlights yet," Nick said as he twisted around to look behind the car.

"I don't either," Jeff said, suddenly wondering if there was a problem. "They were moving when we left."

"If we go to the RV," Nick asked, "can I take the CB?"

"I don't think we'll need it there, son," Jeff explained. "The lady that owns it said there's a CB in it. Maybe she'll let you call from there."

"All right!" Nick said.

They all sat in anticipation, watching for the lights of the RV to come around the drift's southern end. But so far, they weren't seeing anything.

*   *   *

Incoming

Eddie had just about approached the edge of the drift driving the RV, when he looked into his assortment of rear-views, swallowed hard, and said, "Mr. Preston, someone is coming. It's an eighteen-wheeler, I can tell by the light pattern, and it's coming at a damn good clip."

"Then we need to get out of the way, Eddie," Mr. Preston instructed as though Eddie had suddenly become an idiot.

"No, no, Mr. Preston, that's not the point. It's not only about us getting out of his way. If that trailer is loaded and it's a big enough tractor, and if it's doing a decent speed and it hits this drift, it could plow through the whole mess and end up crashing through to everybody behind the drift under the overpass. My brother is over there, those girls, the reverend and everybody else. There's no way to tell them to move."

"Shit." was all Mr. Preston could say.

After just a moment of thinking, Mr. Preston said, "We have to figure out how to warn that trucker and slow him down."

"He'll never see the tail lights on this thing until he's fifty feet away," Eddie said in dismay. "I don't know if I can turn this thing around fast enough to face him so I could flash my brights in his direction."

"Do we have another choice?" Mr. Preston asked in his courtroom attorney voice. Eddie looked at Mr. Preston with a discouraged look.

"You realize," Eddie said as he shifted the RV into reverse and began to move it, "if I can't turn this thing all the way around and get his attention with the headlights to slow, he'll plow into the side of this RV with eighty thousand pounds. You know what that will result in."

Mr. Preston momentarily considered the situation and realized there was no other choice, they had to try. "Well, if he hits us broadside, it would probably keep him from plowing through to everyone else as I don't think he'll be able to push this entire RV through that drift." Mr. Preston quickly realized that he was committing to the paradox that to save the group, he might have to forfeit something really personal, then silently amazed himself at virtually volunteering to sacrifice himself for the total strangers on the other side of the drift. In one way, it felt good. In another, it was terrifying. "Let's turn this damn thing around, Eddie."

"Yes, sir," Eddie said in agreement with Mr. Preston's command to hopefully aim the headlights at the oncoming eighteen-wheeler, warning him, and hopefully stopping him from crashing through the drift and of course, not crashing through the RV either. Eddie was checking his mirrors to figure out how to execute a three-point turn on the interstate pavement to turn the great RV to face oncoming traffic without running the front end into the guardrail protecting the median nor running a rear wheel off the edge of the pavement, dragging the whole RV down the embankment into the ravine.

As he stepped on the accelerator in his flurry of excitement, the wheels slipped, and Eddie realized he had to calm down and remember all that he'd learned in his commercial truck driving classes. He took a big breath, and while he slowly blew it out, he slightly pressed the accelerator and slowly backed the RV to the shoulder, all the while Mr. Preston watched in the mirrors as the eighteen-wheeler lights kept coming.

"Steady, Eddie," Mr. Preston whispered, starting to feel a bit of panic setting in. He knew if this didn't go well, they'd both be dead along with the guy in the back.

Eddie backed it up as far as he thought he could without slipping off the shoulder down the embankment. Then shifted into forward and cranked the wheel hard to the left and pulled the RV forward until he felt the front bump easily into the guard rail. He needed all the space he could get on the two-lane interstate. Now he was totally broadside on the road, and there were just a couple courtesy lights on the sides of the RV facing the oncoming truck that the approaching trucker would never see in the swirling snow.

"Come on, kid," Mr. Preston whispered under his breath.

Once more Eddie shifted into reverse and angled the back of the RV toward the drift, slightly turning the front of the RV a bit more toward the oncoming traffic. Mr. Preston got out of the co-pilot seat to kneel on the sofa and look out the side window at the eighteen-wheeler bearing down on them.

"Come on, Eddie," he said quietly, hoping not to rattle Eddie's driving nerves.

"Working on it," Eddie said, slowly moving the RV backward, then turning the steering wheel hard again to bring about the RV to the next position as he shifted into drive. "Not gonna make it, not gonna make it," he muttered as he stopped the RV still cockeyed on the highway and reached for the headlight knob.

The RV was still pointing slightly toward the median instead of due East toward oncoming traffic, but Eddie prayed that just maybe there'd be enough of a headlight beam for the trucker to see if he was alert. So Eddie began to frantically flash his brights hoping the trucker would see it. Mr. Preston leaned over Eddie and saw the joystick switch on the side of the dash that said "spot" and flipped the switch, and to his joy, the two big spotlights on top of the RV lit up. He grabbed the little joystick and swung the spot-lights side to side, aiming as much as he could toward the oncoming truck. Even though the RV was mostly angled at the median, just maybe the trucker would be able to see all their flashing lights.

"Hang on, Eddie," Mr. Preston said as the truck lights grew bigger as it bore down on the RV. He gripped the back of the driver's seat and continued to furiously swing the spots back and forth, not able to look away but facing whatever fate was delivered.

*   *   *

Nick the Quick

Nick figured he'd lose his CB privileges when the RV got there, so he tried a few more times to hail help.

"Breaker, breaker," he said, not nearly as enthusiastic as he was in the beginning and sounding like one long run-on sentence. "Break one-nine, this is Nick the Quick, mayday, mayday, big pile up on I-70, westbound lanes. A 10-33. Seven or eight vehicles and an RV, mayday. Includes some injuries. Gigantic impassible snowdrift across all westbound lanes. Don't know our 20. Some point west of the Midnight Diner. Breaker, mayday, anyone got their ears on?"

Nick let up on the microphone key and looked back to the drift for the RV lights, but nothing. He repeated his message again and let up on the mike button, feeling like it was useless to keep chanting into it. He put the mike down and sat back in the seat, glancing out the window for a glimpse of the RV lights.

Suddenly, there was a crackle on the CB. "Yeah, good buddy, this is the Cockroach, I got your mayday signal. I'm west of the Midnight Diner. Slowing down, haven't seen the pile-up yet."

Auggie snapped around only as quickly as a man in his nineties could. "This is da cockroach I talk to!" he said with much excitement. "Tell cockroach ve are da butcher and vife!"

Nick picked up the mike fired up with excitement again, "Mr. Cockroach, this is Nick. I'm in a car with the Butcher and his wife. He says he knows you."

"Hey, little buddy, yes, I know the Butcher. Is he okay?" the call came back.

"Yes, sir," Nick answered. "There's a lot of us hiding behind a huge drift under an overpass. There is still a big RV in the lanes in front of the snowdrift."

"That's a 10-4, Nick. Thanks for the info," Chuck the Trucker answered back. "I'm slowing my rig, keeping an eye out. You did a good job, Nick."

By now, Nick was beaming as only a young boy could, feeling that he pretty much saved the day.

"So what," Christie said, once more plopping back on her seat with her arms folded.

"Mr. Cockroach," Nick said into the mike, "we have not been able to get help. We are sitting in cars, waiting for the storm to let up."

"Stay where you are," Chuck answered back. "I think I see some faint crazy lights up ahead. I'm going to slow down and try to figure out what the heck that is. Stand by."

"Roger that," Nick said and held the mike to his chest in glorious exhilaration of being in the center of the activity.

"Mom!" Nick said, "Did you hear that? The trucker was talking to me, and maybe I saved his life!"

"That's wonderful, son," Carol said. Jeff was looking back over the seat at his boy, smiling in pride.

*   *   *

The Driver's Meeting

"I'll be dammed! I think that damn truck is slowing," Mr. Preston said, looking out the side window with cautious amazement. "Maybe we will live to fight another day."

"I'll believe it when I see it, Mr. Preston," Eddie said. "He could lock up those brakes in ice because the temperature is so cold. He'll have no way to slow down other than taking his foot off the accelerator. In cold weather, sometimes the brakes freeze, and he'd have to get out with a hammer and bust them loose."

"Gee, Ed, you are always full of good news, aren't you?" Mr. Preston said.

Eddie saw that he now had a few extra seconds to put the RV into drive again and pull forward, so he was at least on the one inside lane of the interstate facing the oncoming traffic, then continued to flash the brights again while Mr. Preston was still fanning the spotlights from side to side.

Sure enough, they could both see that the big rig was slowing considerably and saw the rig flash his brights twice.

"Those two flashes, that's the all-okay-thank-you sign," Eddie said as he finally exhaled from holding his breath the past ten minutes, and was surprised that his eyes began to water a bit from both joy and stress.

As the big rig neared, they could hear the exhaust from his air brakes as he slowly rolled up alongside the RV next to Eddie's driver's window. Eddie opened his window to thank the trucker for not killing them.

"So, I couldn't help but notice you are facing the wrong direction, are you lost?" Chuck said in a teasing way. Eddie made a half-smile and Chuck continued, "I saw your warning, Thanks. I'd have never seen that drift, and I'd have plowed into it. Might have gotten through it, but I got a CB call from a kid warning me that there were people behind it, then saw your lights flashing around."

"It's okay, man. Thanks for not hitting us," Eddie said, noticing that his armpits were sweating even though it was cold in the RV. "We were moving the RV behind that big drift. We have almost two dozen survivors behind it and hoped this RV would be a refuge and shelter for everyone hiding under the overpass," Eddie told the trucker.

"Well," Chuck said, "that's good until another big rig comes along. If he's not paying attention, he'll blow right into that mega drift, and most likely, if he's loaded, he'll blow out the back and into you all."

"We didn't really have many choices," Mr. Preston leaned over Eddie to explain out the window, "there are already at least three cars buried in that drift. We moved everyone behind the drift out of the brunt of the wind where we've been for hours. We didn't want to freeze before we can get some help."

"Check," Chuck said. "Go ahead and turn this RV around again so you can maneuver it around that drift, looks like it'll be a tight fit. I'm going to back up and give you room."

"You can't stay here," Eddie told the trucker. "Bring your rig behind the drift. There's much less snow under the overpass. You could probably keep going, even if you don't stay."

"Naw...," Chuck was thinking that his rig was too big, too long, and way too heavy to try to pull it through that median. It could bog down or tip over. "I'm just going to situate it on the shoulder back there a couple hundred yards. I'll keep all my running lights on and set the hazard lights and radio out some warnings. Maybe I won't get clobbered by another truck, and it might keep them from plowing through that drift, or worse. I'm only guessing, but I have a feeling they've closed the interstate by now, and we're probably alone out here."

"Park your truck, leave your lights on as a warning and come with us," Mr. Preston said, "at least until the storm lets up."

Chuck thought for a minute, hating to leave his home on the road, but if he left his truck idling and lit up, it could serve as a warning to other drivers, and he might be able to help the travelers stuck under the overpass. And if his rig got sideswiped or clipped, at least he wouldn't be in it. "Ok. I'll go with you, but I still want to back up my truck so other truckers will get plenty of room to slow down. Follow me back."

Eddie agreed and followed the semi as it began backing up with every light on the truck and trailer lit, and all the hazard lights blinking. Chuck settled his truck back about a good half-mile from the drift, then pulled the rig as far onto the shoulder as he could. He set his rig, leaving the diesel and all the lights running. He grabbed his gear and climbed out of the truck into the wind and snow, his collar pulled up around his neck, and his hockey hat smashed onto his head. He tromped through the snow around his rig, setting a few extra flares off as warnings, then came around to the RV. Mr. Preston had opened the door, and Chuck hurried in, stomping the snow off his shoes and pants and dusting the snow off his coat.

"Damn," Chuck said, "that's just stupid cold!"

Mr. Preston helped him in, and they introduced themselves around and shook hands.

"Sit down," Eddie told them. "I gotta turn this thing around and head back to the drift before someone else comes along." And Eddie shifted it into reverse once again and worked the RV back and forth, actually making a decent five-point turn without the guardrails around. The RV was headed west again, and the plan was to get it behind the drift under the overpass. Eddie was slow but methodical, and as he completed the last point of the turn, Chuck complimented him.

"Nice and slow kid, that's the way it should be done. Some of these young guys I teach, they want to drive the big stuff like it's a Mustang."

"You teach truck driving?" Eddie asked.

"Naw. I only groom for my trucking company. The drivers come licensed, I just give them advanced training and plenty of horse-sense advice about driving for a living," Chuck said.

As they approached the drift again, Eddie saw that the space to drive around it was shrinking from snow being blown down in little avalanches from the top of the drift. Chuck sensed his hesitation.

"Just go slow," Chuck told him. "Feel the wheel. You want to make sure your steering tire doesn't get bogged down, or the back end will slide around in the opposite direction so you may have to fight it a little. Don't let the wheels win, you are in command."

Eddie listened to Chuck's advice, and squared his shoulders, and moved the RV slowly through the narrow pass between the guard rail, and the accumulating snow on the south end of the drift, hoping his tire didn't bog down. As he reached the drift, he could feel the right side of the RV rise as the tires took on the edge of the drift and Chuck was right, Eddie could feel the back end wanting to slide, but he took his time, inching the nearly forty feet of RV along.

Chuck sat on the sofa and watched Eddie drive the RV. As he looked around, he saw in the darkness back in the RV a shadow of a man laying on the bed. Chuck wasn't sure what was going on. Did this odd pair of men hijack this RV and knock the driver out? Chuck didn't really know what he should do. What if they were hijacking the RV with him inside? Would they clobber him and rob him too? Chuck suddenly felt some concern for his welfare.

*　　*　　*

Stunt Driving

Nick suddenly shouted, "I can see lights!" making everyone in the car jump. Jeff turned around, and Auggie looked in his rearview. Sure enough, they could see the faint shimmer of lights coming through the swirling snow around the drift. Auggie honked his horn to the others. Doris flashed her lights, and Delphia pushed on the horn of Ben's truck. They were all happy to see Eddie and Mr. Preston returning with the RV.

Chuck was still concerned about the body in the back room when Eddie answered back to the group blasting the RV diesel horn that reverberated under the overpass and shook a lot of the snow off the bridge, plummeting it down the back of the drift and making small avalanches in the loose snow that ended up right in front of Doris' Dominator. Chuck jumped up and stood between the seats, "Don't blast that thing under the overpass unless it's serious," he cautioned Eddie. Eddie understood.

Eddie was now trying to figure how to navigate the RV between the bridge abutments and the back edge of the drift. This would be tricky because of the length of the RV and having to make a turn between them. Chuck sensed his hesitation. "Slow," he told Eddie while standing between the front seats and watching the path they were going. "This is going to take awhile. You are going to have to do about six inches at a time, then crank the wheel, back up six, crank the wheel back, forward six, until you can get a straight line.

Eddie was making many small moves to move the RV around to get past the bridge abutments. Finally, Eddie stopped. "I don't think this is going to work," he said. "I think we are about two or three feet too long to get this thing through. It's like moving a sofa up a stairway that has a corner." Eddie put it in park and stood up, shaking his hands as though he could simply flip the stress off his fingertips. "How about you taking the wheel?" Eddie said to Chuck. "You're the professional." Eddie got out of the cockpit and sat on the sofa. Mr. Preston looked at Chuck for a positive response. Chuck looked at the dash, then out the window, he leaned over and moved the joystick to aim the spotlight at the drift and the bridge pillars and scanned it over then sat in the driver's seat.

"I can't tell if the guard rail goes up too far as it's buried in snow. If we hit it, we may have to go back and start over," Chuck explained.

"I hope not," Mr. Preston said.

"Well, I think, in my professional opinion, there's a better solution. I'm gonna want to go back to about where my truck is and open this thing up and see if we can get up to speed and hit that snow pile on the short end and try to plow through it."

"What?" Mr. Preston said in disbelief. "With us in here too?"

"Sure," Chuck said as he began shifting the RV back and forth to get it out of its current predicament. "There's seat belts."

"Oh, God," Mr. Preston sighed, "there's been enough drama tonight to last me a lifetime."

"Yeah. I know it sounds awful and might damage the front end some, but there's a big generator motor in the front, it won't crush the RV. And we simply don't have the room to maneuver this thing between the bridge pillars, abutments, guard rails, and the damn drift," he said as he started jamming the RV in and out of gears and rocking the RV back out of the grasp of the overpass pillars and assorted obstacles.

"The drift down on the south end looks to be about three or four feet high right now, maybe twenty to thirty feet back to the other side, and it's not too compacted yet. I think this old RV can handle it."

"Oh, Jeez," Mr. Preston said, "can't you drop me off or something?'

While Chuck manned the wheel and gearshift, he noticed the simple all-in-one CB mike on the dash and picked up the CB mike, "This is the Cockroach. Hey Nick, you still got your ears on?"

Eddie looked at Mr. Preston, both amazed that they had CB capability all along. Eddie shrugged his shoulders.

Nick's response was quick, and he was excited. "Yes, sir," he said into his mike, "got my ears on."

Chuck spoke back, "I have a job for you. Very important. Can you handle it?"

"Yes, sir!" Nick was even more excited because everyone in the Lincoln could hear Chuck's side of the conversation.

"I'm driving this RV now, and we can't make the turn between the bridge and the drift. So I'm going to back up down the interstate to flatten a path on the road and then come back, accelerating for about a mile, then plan to ram the south end of that drift and try to blow through the pile."

"Wow!" was all Nick could say, and everyone else in the car was dead silent.

"Nick, listen carefully," Chuck warned. "You have exactly ten minutes from now. What does your watch say?" Chuck was having a little extra fun with the kid on the other end of the CB.

"I don't have a watch, but wait, I'll get one," Jeff was already handing his watch over the seat to Nick.

"Got it," Nick responded. "I have twenty-seven after."

"Okay, Nick, I'm setting my watch to twenty-seven after. That means at thirty-seven after, on the dot, you must have this mission complete."

"Yes, sir," Nick confirmed, now sitting at attention on the edge of the back seat.

"Nick, you need to get all the people and vehicles to the north side of the highway as far as possible on the shoulder. When I come through on the south side, there will be a very big snow explosion of sorts, it'll blow snow from that drift everywhere. So you get people as far away and as protected from the snow as they can. Ten minutes. Got that?" Chuck said.

"Ten minutes," Nick repeated. "Thirty-seven after you'll blow the drift. Everyone as far away and to the north shoulder of the highway as possible," he confirmed back.

"Roger that. Ok, you have your assignment. This is The Cockroach. Over and out." And Chuck put the mike down smiling about making the kid's day.

"Always wished I had kids," Chuck said. "Always figure if you give them big responsibilities, they'll step up to the plate and do the right thing."

Mr. Preston nodded his head in agreement. "That's been my experience as well."

Eddie found himself disagreeing when thinking about his own brother, but he kept his mouth shut.

"I hope Nick gets the message to everyone that we're backing out of here, but we'll be back," Chuck commented.

Chuck spent a few minutes inching the RV out of its position and backing it back into the roadway around the south edge of the drift one last time. Chuck slowly moved the RV in reverse and kept backing down the interstate leaving the big tire tracks in the snow. And he kept going back, farther and farther. He passed by his own truck that resembled a traveling carnival with all his lights on, emergency blinkers, hazard lights, flares, and everything else, but he kept going. He drove far enough that he could barely see a glimmer of the lights from his rig through the blowing snow. He stopped the RV.

"Gentlemen," Chuck looked at them to say, "please put on your seatbelts and store your trays in the upright position. There will be some turbulence ahead." His little joke about being in an airplane was lost on Eddie, and Mr. Preston wasn't amused, he was too concerned for his own welfare.

Eddie found a seat belt stuffed down behind the cushion on the sofa, and Mr. Preston secured his in the co-pilot seat. Chuck got his on as well.

"Ready?" he asked. Eddie and Mr. Preston both said yes.

Chuck looked at his watch. "Forty-five seconds yet. We want to make sure everyone is away from the impact area. And just so you don't worry, this thing is going to hit a semi-solid surface, and it'll feel like we crashed into a brick wall, and some of the siding might come off depending on how frozen that drift is, I expect some of that. I'm hoping the cracked windshield will hold and not collapse in. I don't think the top edge of the drift will be high enough to come in heavy contact with the glass, but it's still a gamble. We will also do some fish-tailing on our way up there, but I think I can keep it in control."

"Well, whatever you do," Eddie said, "I'm sure it'll be better than anything I can do." Eddie snugged up his belt once more and grabbed a throw pillow and hugged it to his chest.

Chuck started revving the engine, checking the gauges, and trying his brakes to make sure nothing was stuck. He'd be needing those brakes. He knew he'd have to tease his brakes as soon as he broke through, and he'd try the jake brake to stop the RV only after he was free on the other side. His only concern was hoping there would be no damage to the generator or anything that would break a gas line or fuel line. He was hoping that none of the previous cars buried in the drift were in his way.

In the last few seconds, he asked Eddie and Mr. Preston, "Do you know if any vehicles are in that drift on the south end?"

Eddie made a face. "My dually is stuck about the middle, the back end might be just a teensy in the way. But that's the only thing on the left-ish side of that drift. That drift has grown over the past couple hours or so, and I can't tell you exactly where anything is."

"Ok," Chuck said. "I'll try to clip that drift as far as I can on the left edge. Won't be as much fun as plowing through five to eight feet of snow, though." And he winked at Eddie.

Chuck radioed to Nick once more, asking if he'd completed his mission, and Nick joyfully responded, "Executed as commanded!"

"Okay, Nick," Chuck radioed back once more. "Roger that. Get ready for impact. Incoming!" Then Chuck clicked the mike off and turned to Eddie and Mr. Preston, "Ok, it's time. Hang on. Say a prayer." And Chuck took a few seconds of prayer for himself, then shifted into drive, and the RV began to grumble again and started moving forward, at first creeping along, then picking up some speed. The grumbling smoothed into a roar as Chuck kept accelerating at an even pace. They were picking up quite a bit of speed. They all saw Chuck's rig lit up like a blinking Christmas tree on the side of the road as they nearly flew past it, the RV slipping on the snow now and then and rocking in the wind. Mr. Preston looked back at Eddie and crossed his fingers.

"Hang on. Impact in about 15 seconds," Chuck said. The RV was now moving at what seemed like the speed of light, and all Eddie could see was white streaks of snow flying by the windows.

"Five, four, three, two..." Chuck said.

But there was no "one," the RV collided with the determined snowdrift in one huge smashing jolt, jarring everything in the RV, including Mr. Preston's gritted pearly teeth. They saw nothing but a momentary field of snow plastered onto the windshield, and the RV came to what seemed like an abbreviated stop, throwing them all forward hard at the sudden interception of the drift, but amazingly, they were still moving and plowed through the rest of the snow until Chuck started to tease the brakes a bit to slow the RV. Eddie saw the back of the drift out the side window and realize they'd broken through. The front windshield was packed with snow.

"Hang on again," Chuck said as he hit the jake brake that jarred the whole RV so hard that most of the snow slid off the front of the windshield. Chuck's years of driving skill slowly brought the RV to a stop about a football field past the overpass. He could see the lights of one of the cars under the bridge as he put the RV into reverse and slowly backed up watching out for the vehicles parked under the overpass. He pulled the RV far enough under the overpass that it would provide some protection when the survivors were trudging to it.

He shifted into park, and it jarred the RV quite a bit, then in the momentary silence, they all heard the windshield crack and the accompanying gliss sound as the crack proceeded across the width of the dash before it slowly came to a stop. They held their breath for a moment and waited, but all was silent. Chuck exhaled heavily. "Whew!" he said, then took off his seatbelt and stretched. "So, how was that?" He good-naturedly asked Mr. Preston, who seemed frozen in his seat and Eddie, that was clearly thrilled that they found a stunt man to blow the pile of snow.

"Pretty damn cool!" Eddie was impressed.

"Well, anyway here we are, safe and sound," Chuck said as he doubled-checked the RV's parking brake. "I'm amazed that worked," he said, wiping a bit of sweat from his brow.

"What?" Mr. Preston was nearly aghast. "You mean you weren't SURE that was going to work?'

Chuck grinned and shrugged his shoulders.

Chapter 52

Moving Day

"I'm going out to check the front and see if there's generator damage or broken lines before we use this for a hotel," Chuck said. And as he got up to leave the cockpit, he looked back in the RV and saw a man lying on the floor crumpled up outside the bedroom door.

Mr. Preston saw the look of suspicion in Chuck's face when Chuck asked, "Is this going to be some kind of a problem?"

"Oh, sorry," Mr. Preston started to explain, "that is the guy that owns the RV. He hit the drift when he came in and was so upset at pushing cars into the drift that he dragged himself out to see if there were people still in the cars. The shock and stress of it all seemed to set off a heart attack or a stroke or something. His wife was a nurse, she dragged his body back in, and by the time she got him in, he'd already died. I told his wife we'd take care of him. Can you help me get him back up onto the bed?"

Chuck was satisfied with the explanation and helped Eddie and Mr. Preston pick Herman's lifeless body up and put him on the bed, but this time they fixed him up with his head on the pillow and tucked him in with a blanket as though he was sleeping. "We may have to tell those little kids that he's just napping or something," Mr. Preston said, once again amazed that he was concerned with what the kids might think.

Jeff was already coming into the RV. "How is everything?

That was awesome to see, you know, the headlights coming through that pile like angels coming through the clouds. Wow!" Jeff was clearly impressed.

"We did okay," Mr. Preston said. "This here is Chuck, he came up behind us in an eighteen-wheeler."

"Yes, I know," Jeff said, "my son was talking to him and radioing about the drift and the pile-up. The Cockroach, I presume."

"Tell your son he did a fine job," Chuck said as he shook Jeff's hand. "It all helped, or this could have turned out very badly for all of us."

"About the only mishap was when Chuck pulled the brake, the dead guy rolled off the bed," Mr. Preston said. "I told his wife, we'd do right by him, so we got him back into bed, and he's 'resting quietly' now. I think it'd be best if we didn't say anything to his wife about him taking a dive. She's been through enough."

Eddie tooted the RV horn as quietly as possible to indicate all was well, but the air horn was quite loud, and more snow fell from the overpass above them.

"Sorry," Eddie said sheepishly.

"You're okay," Chuck said to Eddie. "You could have a fine career in trucking if you wanted one. Come out and help me look at the condition of the front of the RV," Chuck said as he was buttoning up his coat and yanking on his hat again.

"Yes, sir!" Eddie said, pleased that Chuck asked him.

"I'm going back out to help the old couple out first. Let's get them in here and settled," Jeff said. "The old lady has been wanting a rest stop for the past hour. I hope she can make it from their car to here. They're slow, so it'll give you a little time to run your RV checks."

Jeff pushed the door open and tromped back out into the snow and wind to get Auggie and Mina.

Before Chuck went to check the exterior, he went to a control panel in the middle of the RV and pushed some buttons. "Looks like they have nearly a full fresh-water tank, but still, we should be careful about the water used for everything as we could be stuck here for a day or two." He opened a few cabinets and found a couple cooking pots handing them to Eddie. "When we go out to check the front, we'll find some real clean snow to fill these. We can warm it on the stove and use it for extra water for flushing, so we aren't wasting drinking water." Eddie took the pots and followed Chuck out the door.

*   *   *

The Gathering

Jeff opened the Lincoln door, "Okay, Mina and Auggie, get your coats on, you are going to the RV first."

"Already got coat," Auggie said.

"Leave your keys in the car and leave it running so your headlights keep shining out to the west in case anyone comes looking for stranded travelers," Jeff told him.

"Oh, I hate to leave her like dis," Auggie said.

Mina struggled to get out of the car before putting her fur coat back on. "Oh, oh, oh," she said, "artritis making joints stiff sitting so long." Jeff helped her with her coat as the wind was fighting Mina for it, and as soon as she got it on, Mina started to crawl back in the car. Jeff pulled her out by the hem of the coat.

"No, no, we are taking you to the RV there," Jeff knew she could barely see it.

"Vant to say mit Auggie," Mina said. Auggie was slowly shuffling around the back of the car, keeping one hand on it to remain steady, and she couldn't see him.

"He's coming to the RV," Jeff shouted over the wind.

"I vant to stay here," Mina was getting adamant.

"We'll be warm and safe in the RV," Jeff argued with her.

"Mrs. Buchbinder," Carol tried to explain, "you'll be more comfortable in the RV."

"No. I vant to stay vit my stuff," She wrangled around, trying to get Jeff to let go. "I got da crackers and cookies back dere." She was trying to reach over the seat to grab her bags.

By then, Auggie was coming around the trunk and, through his squinted eyes, saw his wife fighting with Jeff.

"Voman!" he shouted at her, "you go to RV!" He meant business.

"I vant to stay vit car, my stuff is here," she began to cry.

"Is okay, Mina. We can see dis car from RV. Nobody take our stuff. Vat numbskull vould be out in dis storm anyvay?" Auggie tried to appeal to her senses.

Wilhelmina broke loose from Jeff's grip and flung herself back into the front seat of the car, crying and cussing in German when Christie sat up and looked over the seat at her. "They have a nice potty in the RV with a door that closes, and it's warm."

Mina stopped and wiped a tear and looked at the young girl. "Dis true?" she asked her.

"Yes," Christie said and pointed to the RV, "you go first, Holly needs to go too, so hurry up."

For some reason, Mina saw the wisdom in the promise of the potty, and she struggled back out of the car, taking Jeff's hand as he helped the two old people plod through the snowy tire tracks as best they could to the RV.

Carol was smiling at Christie. "You are pretty wise for a teenager," she said.

Christie blew it off and sank back in her seat. "I just wanna get out of this obnoxious smelling car," she said and looked out at the barely visible lights of the RV in the swirling snow.

Jeff came back for Holly and Carol, then came for Nick and Christie.

Mr. Preston went out to tell the gals in the Dominator they could come to the RV, and take a number for the toilet but minimize flushing to every other person as a precautionary measure.

Then he trudged over to Ben's blue truck and told Travis, Matthew, and the girls to leave Brittany there and come to the RV, but Delphia refused to leave her.

"I'll stay with her for awhile yet. If she comes to and nobody is here, she'll be terrified," Delphia reasoned. "Has anyone heard anything from Ben yet?"

"Sorry, Delphia," Mr. Preston told her, "we haven't heard anything from him yet." Mr. Preston was getting too cold to have much of a discussion, so he let Delphia stay with Brittany.

"I'll stay too," Matthew said. "She shouldn't be sitting here alone."

Travis was already out the door and on his way to the RV to be with his brother, and Mr. Preston helped Tawnie out and over to the RV, then tromped over to the white van and knocked on the side. Joe jumped up to the window and rolled it down.

"RV is here, come on over. Bathroom privileges, too, if you need it," Mr. Preston told Joe.

"I don't think we should move Early," Joe told him. He's probably better off being still, besides, with all those people in the RV, I doubt there'd be room to lay him down. If we need the facilities, we'll come over, but so far, we just peed in the snow. Kind of cold, you know how it is when it's cold," Joe chuckled a bit.

"Well, if you change your minds, you know where we are," Mr. Preston said as he turned to head back to the RV.

"Tell him about the radio," Barry said as Joe rolled up the window.

"Not yet," Joe said. "I don't want to get their hopes up if this doesn't work. We've found how to receive a short wave signal, but we have to figure out how to hear it and how to transmit an SOS. We gotta find that article."

*   *   *

Introductions

Mr. Preston was returning to the RV just as the ladies from the Dominator were coming up to the door, helping Louise along, all gabbing and griping about the wind and cold, and complaining about the snow in their shoes. Mr. Preston took Jackie's arm to help her along.

"I'm so glad I grabbed my sneakers for driving," Doris shouted to Janet over the swirling snow. "I had sandals on. Can you imagine?"

"I know," Janet replied. "I was going to slip on a pair of flip-flops for the long ride and glad I didn't, my feet would be freezing."

"Oh my God!" Rita shouted loud enough that everyone stopped to see what happened, even Mr. Preston stopped and turned around. Rita had her hands over her ears, and her hair had blown forward over her face exposing the semi-bald spot on the back of her head. "My earrings are freezing in the cold and making my ear lobes freeze!!" she nearly screamed. Doris rolled her eyes at Janet, and the two resumed walking.

Jackie was getting fed up with the whole trip thus far, so she finally got a bit snippy with Rita. "I guess they'll get frostbite, and they'll have to cut them off," she said dryly and kept walking with Mr. Preston helping her along.

"What about helping me along?" Rita asked. Nobody answered and kept walking. Rita stood there by herself in the wind and snow, realizing that nobody cared, so she trudged along to the RV by herself.

Jeff opened the door, and Mr. Preston helped the women up the steps one at a time, himself last. He explained to the others as he shook the snow off his coat, "The reverend stayed behind with the smart girl in the blue truck. She didn't want to leave her friend that is still unconscious. Matthew didn't want to leave the girls alone," Mr. Preston explained. "The guys in the white van, one of them is injured, and they don't think it'd be safe to move him, so they are staying with him for awhile. So that's about it."

"There are injuries?" Louise asked.

"Yes." Mr. Preston said, then explained about the young girl that was apparently unconscious and the other guy that was in and out of it.

"I should go check on them," Louise said, thinking she was glad to have something to do other than think about Herman and the things she'll have to do from now on without him.

"I'll take her over there," Jeff volunteered. Louise took a small doctor's bag out of a closet and buttoned up her coat and put Herman's boots on, but before leaving, she fired up the generator and turned the heater on.

"This will help it warm up in here," she said. Then Jeff and Louise hurried out into the cold again. Twinkles stood at the door as she left, not understanding all this commotion. Tawnie went over to pet the little dog and talked sweet and small to her. Twinkles enjoyed that.

"My name starts with a 'T' too!" she cooed to the little dog.

It was barely a few minutes when the door opened again startling Tawnie and Twinkles, so Tawnie picked the dog up and sat back on the floor next to Christie and both shared petting duties. Chuck and Eddie were back from their inspection tour, both holding a pot of snow.

"Now, there's what we need," Rita snarked, "portable snow."

"It's to melt for water if we need it," Eddie said, facing the snow in his pot as he tried to avoid her recognizing him.

They put the pots in the kitchen area and stood there looking around for a place to sit. Eddie tried to get Travis to notice these were the same women from the diner that he attempted to rob at spoon-point, but Travis already knew.

"So, now what?" Doris asked as she returned from the bathroom. "Do we just sit here and wait?"

Everyone looked around, and it seemed no one had much of an answer.

"Well," Carol said, "we could say a prayer, then start fielding suggestions. Lots of heads here, someone must have an idea."

"The reverend is in the truck," Travis said, not quite interested in having another prayer. "Can we wait until he comes in to lead the prayer?"

There was some mumbling, but they decided to wait on Matthew.

"I'm sure I know you from someplace," Rita said, looking at Eddie again. Eddie shrugged his shoulders. The other girls were tired of Rita, so they didn't bother trying to figure out what she was talking about, but Travis heard it and made sure his face was always looking out a window away from those ladies.

"What about the CB?" Nick volunteered, remembering that he'd been told the RV has a CB.

"The CB is contained in the mike up there on the dash, young man." Chuck showed him how it worked.

"Who is going to call for help?" Rita asked while trying to re-mat her hair over the balding spot.

"I was using Mr. Auggie's CB in his car. No one was answering until the truck driver was near enough," Nick explained, only to have a few groans of disappointment come from the group.

"He's right," Chuck told them. "This heavy weather and the short distance a CB can call out to, it's almost useless, especially under a concrete bridge with all the wire and metal skeleton supports. If there was a base station that could hear us, he'd be strong enough to get us some help, but I haven't heard a base for the last 100 miles. If we had a short wave or ham radio, that'd be different."

"Auggie has nice radio in his car," Wilhelmina offered, "but I tink das radio is busted, only bad, bad music comes out. Notting like Glen Miller, or Dorsey boys or gudt music from war times."

"A car radio is only one way, ma'am," Chuck volunteered. "You can hear what is being sent out to you, but you cannot talk back to them."

"Oh ya? I talk back plenty," and Wilhelmina shook a fist causing Chuck to smile.

"Nick, why don't you work the CB and keep hailing for help like you were before," Chuck said and helped Nick climb up on the RV dash next to Twinkles' bed and made his space to continue radio hailing for help. Chuck continued, "I think the best thing to do is figure out where to park this thing while we wait for rescue. If snow plows come, they could run into us. If another big rig comes through, he might miss my warning lights or Nick on the CB, and plow through just like we did, but with about five times the weight of this RV."

"Do we all know each other?" Mr. Preston asked as he looked around and saw a few faces he wasn't familiar with. Auggie and Mina were sitting on the sofa, Carol next to them with Holly on her lap. The four gals from the Dominator were packed in the little dining booth intended for two. Mr. Preston was in one cockpit seat, and Travis had plunked into the driver's seat, looking out the windshield so the women couldn't see his face. Christie and Tawnie were sitting on the floor, and Eddie was leaning on the short counter space.

"I guess if someone needs a nap, we could send them back to the bedroom," Carol said, and immediately, Doris, Janet, and Mr. Preston started all at once making noise about not using the back bedroom and making such a deal out of it that Carol suspected something. Doris used her eyes to point at their kids and slowly shook her head no.

Just then, the door opened again, it was Jeff and Louise. Everyone was immediately curious about the welfare of the two injuries.

"The guy seems to have a simple concussion," she explained, "but because his face is bruised, he looks worse than it is. He'll be tired, but no fluids were coming from his ears or nose, nothing obvious. He's feeling sleepy, probably because of nausea and headache. He has some confusion but can communicate a bit. He knows his name and generally where he is. So I think he'll be okay after he sleeps for awhile and might end up dizzy and confused for a day or so, but he should still get some medical care. The young lady needs help as soon as possible. She might have bleeding in her head and/or a possible small skull fracture on the forehead. I don't think it'd require surgery, but you never know until you get a cat-scan or MRI. Both of them remaining cool and still is the best we can do for now. If one of them comes to, I can give them an aspirin or two for pain, but that's about all I can do for them. They've both passed that "golden hour" of getting optimum treatment after an injury, so all we can do is hope for medical help as soon as possible."

There was a bit of silence for a minute before Carol commented, "Yes, let's hope we get a rescue now."

Louise looked at the bedroom door again and felt the deep sadness of losing her life partner. She knew she had to keep busy and really didn't want all the kids to know about Herman. "I think I see a few people that would like some tea or coffee," and she set about to get a few pots of water and her coffee maker out of a cabinet. "It's small, but I have a lot of filters to make a couple of pots. I don't have a whole lot of food, but I do have a few things we can use up. Hopefully, you are right, and we'll be rescued soon."

There were more introductions, and lots of talking about coffee or tea, and Louise noticed a sad face on Holly. "I have some milk, would you like a little cup of milk?" Holly nodded her head, yes. Louise poured a little milk in a small juice cup and handed it to her. Holly gulped the milk and held the cup out for more.

"Holly, we have to share," Carol told her. "There's not much milk for everyone." And Holly made another sad face as she looked around the room at all the people packed together. "It's been a long day for the little one," Carol explained. "She napped a bit earlier, but this time of night she is usually fast asleep." The women all nodded that they understood. Jackie took her bracelet off and asked Holly if she'd like to wear it for a while, explaining that she'd need to have it back when the rescuers come. Holly smiled and took the bracelet, and it kept her occupied as she laid her head back onto Carol's chest.

There was some chatting between the RV refugees, and every few minutes, Nick would call on the CB with his mayday message needing help. They were all exchanging names, business cards, where they were from, and where they were headed. Christie saw Tawnie's phone and asked if she could get a signal, and Tawnie told her no, not since they passed the last diner. The two found that they both had offline games on their phones, but Christie's battery was nearly dead. Tawnie produced a charge cord from her purse that fit Christie's phone, so they plugged it into the outlet on the tiny counter to charge, and Tawnie shared her game with Christie.

Travis noticed that Eddie wasn't even looking at him. Travis stuck a leg out and nudged Eddie with his foot. "Hey man, I'm sorry," Travis said to Eddie. "Sorry I got you into this mess." And for once, Travis actually sounded sorry.

"It's okay," Eddie said, and he looked out the window as he felt his eye begin to water.

Louise was serving small cups of tea and coffee and pulled out a box of crackers and her tin of tea cookies. The guys were talking about where to put the RV to be in the least dangerous place, noting if they got hit now, there'd be a lot of human damage. Chuck mentioned that usually plows come three across on the interstates in what is called a conga-line, and they'd plow both lanes at the same time, and it'd be thrown off the shoulder down the embankment. If they came three across now, that would present a terrible problem. They discussed parking in the median, but they'd have to leave the protection of the overpass. They also asked if anyone knew the weather report, and no one did.

Everyone was settling in. Louise would glance back at the bedroom between sips of tea as though she expected

Herman to join them, but knew it couldn't happen. She concentrated instead on smiling at Holly and trying to make the toddler smile.

"What time is it anyway?" Rita said loud enough to startle everyone.

There was a lot of watch looking, but Mr. Preston was first.

"It's two-fifteen am." To which everyone groaned.

"I tink I vould like a nap soon," Auggie said. "Dis is much excitement for me, and now I am pooped."

"Ya," Mina agreed. "He is alvays pooped."

"We shouldt move big house here to safe place, then all take naps," Auggie said. "Ve may haff to dig snow or valk later, nap ist needed by oldt people."

"Yes, we could all use a nap," Jeff told him, "but first, we need to figure out the safest place for this RV. Then we can quiet down and take a nap for awhile."

"But DAD," Nick looked up from his little CB office on the dash, "if everyone is sleeping, we could miss a message!"

"Don't worry, Nick. We'll work something out," Jeff told him.

They all talked about it and decided to move the RV as far to the inside shoulder as possible. There just wasn't any totally safe place to park it at this time, but the shoulder next to the overpass abutments would be about the best for now. And the other vehicles should be on the outside shoulder lined up.

"You know," Jeff commented, "we might want to move the vehicles farther apart for better space to let exhaust fumes disperse. We don't want anyone getting carbon-monoxide poisoning."

Everyone agreed.

Mr. Preston got up once again and volunteered to go tell Matthew and the three guys what was going on, knowing he really wanted a breath of fresh air, even if it was extremely cold. Eddie volunteered to go along. "Just in case, Mr. Preston. You just don't know what might happen." Mr. Preston agreed, and the two buttoned up again, pushed the door open, and tromped down the RV steps into the blizzard once more.

Things were quieting down, and Doris got up from the edge of her seat and told Louise to sit. "You've had a really long day. You need to rest."

Louise nodded her head toward the bedroom, "Oh, when I'm tired, I can go lay down in the back. I don't mind," she said, knowing Doris would understand what she meant.

Doris shook her head, "You sit anyway. I've been sitting for five hours, I need to stand up for awhile." She convinced Louise to sit at the table so she could sip her tea. It was her RV, after all.

*   *   *

The Big Reveal

Travis was shooed out of the driver's cockpit seat, and Chuck took his place and began to check dials and mirrors out of habit. Travis had no place else to sit other than on the floor, where Rita got a good look at his face for the first time. It took her a minute, but it finally sunk in where she'd seen these two boys before.

"Oh, I remember now!" Rita loudly announced as she pointed a bony finger at Travis. You look like that guy at the diner that tried to steal my money!"

Doris and Janet snapped their heads around to look at him. "Hey, yeah," Doris said, "I think she's right. You tried to hold us up. Attempted armed robbery!" she announced. Everyone was now wide-eyed and looking at Travis.

Travis began to back-pedal. "It wasn't armed robbery. I only had a spoon in my pocket." He tried to excuse his actions. "And I didn't take anything anyway."

"You should have to sit outside to wait for rescue," Doris muttered. "Was your brother in on this?"

"No, ma'am," Travis lowered his tone. "He was trying to get me to stop."

"What is wrong with you? Did you think you were going to get away with that?" Doris asked.

Travis decided to try to explain and told them about going to the bar in East St. Louis and being attacked, and the gang members threatening to hurt his mother after they stole his wallet and identification. They wanted money and drugs in return to leave his mother alone and to get his license back. Travis explained to the gals that he didn't know what else to do. "It seemed like you ladies had cash to gamble with, it's not like it was rent or food money, and I figured you were all insured so rather than going to Colorado and buying a bag of pot and driving across state lines with it, it just seemed easier to hit up you ladies. Not that it'll do any good now, but I am sorry. I just panicked. Eddie was really pissed that I did that, and the lady at the diner gave me hell before she allowed us to leave. I am just scared. I can't admit to my little brother that I am scared." Travis hung his head and repeated that he was sorry. "Are you going to have me arrested now?"

Doris and her friends looked at each other for a few stressful moments. "No harm done," Jackie said quietly. Janet nodded in agreement.

"Well," Doris said to Travis, "my husband owns a contracting business. You are a big kid, you could use a little construction work. Maybe we won't say anything if you report to my husband right after the holidays and take on a job for a couple of months. It'll keep you out of trouble, and the other construction guys won't let anyone pick on you. Do you think you could manage that?"

"Sounds plenty fair to me," Chuck said, giving Travis one of those looks that means he better take the deal.

"I think so, but promise me you won't say anything to my brother," Travis said quietly while twiddling with the button on his shirt.

They all sat waiting for Mr. Preston and Eddie to return.

*   *   *

Reshuffle

Mr. Preston and Eddie got to Ben's truck and opened the driver's door scaring Delphia as she had been dozing and Matthew had been diligently watching over the girls as he said he would. Mr. Preston told Matthew what the latest plan was, moving the RV and other vehicles, so there would be less of a chance being whacked by a plow or another big rig coming through and putting a few more feet between the vehicles for air space. Then Mr. Preston and Eddie tromped over to the white van and explained to the guys about shuffling all the vehicles again.

Joe agreed and readied to move his van again as Mr. Preston and Eddie made their way back to the RV. "I wish they'd make up their damn minds about where to park. I have a few more magazines to hunt through. We have to be getting close," Joe said, referring to finding the transmitting radio article he needed. "We gotta get this going before we all freeze or are blown off the highway by some kind of truck."

Barry told Joe to calm down that getting aggravated wasn't going to help, and he needed his concentration so he would not miss the article or miss a magazine.

Joe piled his magazine stack in the passenger seat and started to move his van. By now, they had magazines everywhere in piles, some in boxes, some piled to sit on and more piled up like a desk to ease the sore necks they were getting scouring through hundreds of magazines. All the decades that Barry's grandfather meticulously kept those magazines, by date, month and year, each year bound with string, and now the magazines were strewn everywhere, and Barry was fretting to himself that maybe some of the magazines that he threw under the van's wheels to get out of the snow might have been the ones with the articles about building the shortwave transmitter, the shortwave antenna, or a speaker. He needed them all. He became acutely aware of what the phrase "thrown under the bus" meant.

* * *

More Shuffling

Mr. Preston and Eddie were going back to the RV when Eddie said, "Maybe it's wishful thinking, Mr. Preston, but I think the storm is letting up."

"I doubt it," Mr. Preston said. "It's just that we're changing the wind pattern under the overpass, so it just feels less. I bet if you go up on top the overpass, I bet there are forty to sixty mile an hour wind gusts."

"I'll take your word for it," Eddie said, clutching his pea coat up around his neck, but still suspecting the storm wasn't as bad as it was the last time they were knocking on vehicle doors.

"Okay," Mr. Preston told Chuck as they got back to the RV, "Everyone is ready to shuffle all the vehicles around."

"I'll move Mr. Buchbinder's Lincoln," Jeff said as he noticed Auggie snoozing on the sofa. Jeff bundled up one more time to move the Lincoln and asked Doris as he was buttoning up, "Doris, you want to move your Dominator, or do you want one of us to move it?"

"Keys are in it," Doris said. "I have no particular desire to go out again without a ski suit." Jeff thanked her as he left the RV.

"You know," Rita said rather loudly, "if they'd quit opening and shutting the damn door, it wouldn't be so cold on my legs."

"Shhh," Carol said, "it's getting late. Baby is sleeping now, and so are the old people." She pointed to the Buchbinders peacefully snoozing on each others' shoulders. Rita made a face like a brat and turned to stare out the window.

Jackie had put her head down on the little dinette table and seemed to be snoozing as well. Nick was quietly sending his useless messages out into the storm, and now Chuck was back in the driver's seat, getting ready to fire up the RV once again to nudge it to a safer position.

* * *

Nap Time

There was lots of vehicle shuffling before it all settled down. The final arrangement was everyone facing due West, the direction of traffic, with the guys in the white van backed up nearly into the drift, then Ben's truck, Doris' Dominator, and Auggie's Lincoln at the front with his headlights shining out to the west side's smaller drift.

As everyone returned to the RV, Louise was turning the heat up a bit. "Rita is right, we can warm up now if everyone is done coming and going," she said. "Anyone want more tea or coffee?" Christie and Tawnie held up their little cups for more tea as everyone else was settling in and trying to get comfortable. They were ALL stressed out and tired, now that it was nearly three in the morning.

Chuck had reclined in the driver's seat, and Travis was in the passenger seat. Eddie had taken a place on the floor, leaning up against the chair that Jeff was sitting in. Mr. Preston was about to take a seat on the floor when Eddie gave Travis a nod to vacate the seat for Mr. Preston. "Why can't some of us use the back room?" Travis said, and he was immediately hushed by three or four of them. "What?" He asked with his usual caustic attitude. Eddie got up and whispered something to Travis. "Oh, shit," he said as he looked at Louise, then mouthed "I'm sorry," to her.

"I think everyone should know something," Louise finally said quietly.

"Um, maybe not ma'am," Chuck said.

"No, I think everyone should know what's going on here," Louise said, and before anyone could say anything she calmly and quickly told the story of her husband going out to check the cars in the drift and had a medical emergency and passed on and he was now in the back bedroom until they could find some help. Carol leaned over and patted Louise on the arm and offered her condolences. Travis got up and gave his seat to Mr. Preston and sat on the floor with his brother, realizing that he was now part of this group of storm refugees, and his smart mouth wasn't going to bring any relief or help. It was quiet for a few minutes as everyone thought about their situation, Herman, and the blizzard that was still bearing down on them all. Nick broke the silence with a quiet call on the CB, then said, "Dad?"

"Son?" Jeff answered.

"Do you think I could see the dead guy?" Nick innocently asked.

"Shut up!" Christie whispered in a demanding tone.

"Nick!" His father reprimanded. "This is not a time for your morbid curiosity to be quenched, this is when we give people some compassion and peace.

"It's okay," Louise said to Jeff and Christie, "he's a boy and just curious."

"Well, then can we have kind of a funeral for him?" Nick asked. "Wouldn't that be compassion? We had a funeral for Hammy when he died."

"That was a hamster, you nerd," Christie whispered across the RV. "It's not the same thing."

"Calm down, kids," Carol whispered, "let's not wake everyone."

"Matthew is a minister," Tawnie softly mentioned, "maybe he'd say a prayer or some kind of a blessing."

"That's true," Eddie said. "He is a reverend. Maybe we should do something in case we get messed up by a plow."

"I think we should all just sit tight for awhile and let the RV warm up and all calm down for a bit. We don't need to send anyone else out there right now," Jeff said, and Mr. Preston nodded agreement as he rubbed his hands together and blew his breath over his fingers.

"If everyone doesn't mind," Louise said, "I can dim the lights, and we can all rest for a little bit."

"Yes, I think that's a good idea," Carol said as she looked around and saw two ladies at the table that were folded over on their arms and seemed to be napping, the two old people were still asleep, the truck driver looked like he could use a nap too, and Holly was sleeping again. "If everyone would just quiet down, so the rest of us can nap a bit, I think that would be sensible. Maybe the storm will let up, and we will be able to get some help."

"Can I keep using the CB, Mom?" Nick asked.

"Yes, just keep it very quiet and turn it down," Carol told him.

One by one, they all tried to sit back and relax. Carol scooted over on the sofa as best she could to give Doris a spot, but it wasn't working. Louise saw it and told her to take her place at the table and that she was going to spend a little quiet time with Herman, if no one minded. Most of the adults understood, but the younger ones considered it creepy. Louise noticed the kids' reactions. "It's fine," she told them in a peaceful whisper and a wink, "he always slept like the dead anyway." The kids weren't sure if she was kidding or not. She went to the back then came out with two small blankets to share and two throw pillows and handed them out. Janet covered Rita with one of the blankets but took a pillow for herself to park her head on the table. Travis and Eddie took the other blanket and shared it over their legs, flipping half to Tawnie and Christie. Louise propped up Wilhelmina's head on the other little pillow so her head wouldn't be all bent over. Wilhelmina adjusted herself a bit and never really woke.

It was quiet now. Other than a bit of the phone keypads clicking from the girls, a gentle snoring from someone and the generator humming away, it was peaceful, and only the howling wind outside was anything to worry about.

"Dad?" Nick whispered to his father.

"Hm? Shhh," Jeff answered.

"But, Dad, do you think this snow would cover this whole RV by morning?" Nick asked.

"I don't know, son," Jeff told him, "let's hope not. Now be quiet and do your job or take a nap." And Jeff adjusted himself on the chair and tried to rest.

One by one, in the dim RV light accompanied by the constant droning of the generator, it was almost soothing at this point. They all began to relax a bit, and eyes were closing. Except for Brittany and Christie. They were still playing a couple video games on their phones, sharing dog duty.

Chapter 53

Magazine Wracked

Meanwhile, the Geeks were not napping in their van.

"Hot Damn! And Hallelujah!" Barry suddenly shouted. "Here it is; *How to Make Your Own Radio Transmitter Out of Junk*, as he got up and stepped on the magazine mess to show Joe.

Joe used his penlight to study what Barry showed him. "Yes. I think that's it. This should work," Joe said. "And look, at the end of the article it says; next month's issue, *How To Make An Antenna*."

"Sheee-it!" Barry said as he plunked on top of the magazines in the passenger seat, feeling relieved. "We got it. I think the next month is on top of the pile I was looking at. Can we get all this stuff and make this work?" Barry seemed to have some doubts.

"I don't know, Barry," Joe said. "Wish Early hadn't whacked his face. He could probably do this with his eyes shut."

Barry fumbled with the magazine and turned on the map lights and aimed them both at the article.

"Oh no," Barry sounded like the life went out of him. "It says we need a transformer for this." Joe looked at Barry and watched Barry's shoulders slump.

"Well," Joe said, sounding beaten too, "we were heroes one minute, and back to being nerds the next."

"We can still build the receiving part as soon as I find the article on building the diode. At least we can maybe hear a weather report. At least it's something," Barry tried sounding positive.

"Oh hell, that old Lincoln's AM radio can probably find a radio station to listen to. What we needed was a transmitter to call Mayday. If nothing else, we could have alerted the state department of transportation that people are riding out the storm stranded on the interstate, and not to ram plows through here," Joe said.

"I know, I know," Barry's gloom hung in the air like thick cigarette smoke. He looked at the mess of magazines and knelt down on the piles and began to stack and try to re-organize them.

Joe suddenly turned off the engine of the van.

"What are you doing?" Barry asked with his arms loaded with magazines. "We'll freeze to death in an hour."

"I thought I heard something. Like a scratching noise," Joe said, cocking his head to listen carefully, "Stop moving for a minute."

"How can you hear anything? The wind is making enough racket whistling through the passenger window and rattling the van door," Barry commented.

"No, it's not wind, it's a scratching sound."

"This sounds like a movie, you know. Please don't yell squirrel," Barry said and went back to re-stacking his magazines.

"There it is again," Joe said, but Barry didn't hear anything and continued to try to get his magazines back into some kind of order. But a minute or two passed, and sure enough, the scratching sound happened again, and this time Barry did hear it. "You are right, Joe. It's coming from up front." Once again, Barry stepped on his magazine piles to get nearer to the front to listen again. And they both heard the scratching noise.

"It's Early!" Barry said. "Look. He's scratching the boxes with his fingers."

"That's probably not a good sign," Joe warned.

"No," Barry said, "I think he is trying to tell us something. Do you have a pen or pencil?"

"Uh," Joe said, looking on his messy dashboard and shuffling through the stuff to produce a black marker. "Here."

Barry uncapped the marker and put it in Early's hand. "Go ahead, Early, tell us what you need," he said, wincing at the mess of swelling in Early's face and forehead. There were some slow scratching sounds, and a few pen squeaks, the slow movements began to form what looked like letters or electronic notations.

"Oh, that looks like a Z," Joe said. "Is that for hertz or what? Ok, the second letter is an A, so ZA?" Joe said, scratching his head.

"Yeah," Barry said, "that's what it looks like, for sure. But he's doing more....a P? ZAP? That can't be right."

"What the hell does that mean?" Joe said. "I think he's probably having hallucinations."

Early dropped the pen, and Barry grabbed it and put it back in his hand. "We don't know what you mean, man," Barry said to Early. The pen began to move again like a slow planchette on a Ouija Board...so slowly at first, then sped up a bit and finally, the pen fell again, and Early's hand went limp.

"What did he spell out?" Joe asked, flicking on his penlight. "Looks like '*z-a-p-p-r-v-x-from*' with a little doodle at the end. What the hell?"

"Yes, I'd say that sums it up, but look, that last word is 'form' Joe, not 'from', and I don't think that's a doodle, that's a square with an oval in it," Barry said.

"That isn't some kind of game code, is it?" Joe asked.

"Nah, he knows we wouldn't know that. He must need something," Barry said.

Joe took the pen and re-wrote what he saw on a box lid. "R and V must mean he wants us to take him to the RV," Joe suggested.

"He didn't even know about the RV, did he? It must be something else," Barry said.

"I don't know....I've heard that people that are unconscious can still hear, so maybe he's heard us talking to the guys from over there."

"Well," Barry said, "that would make sense. So what is it about the RV? X and form? X, he wants us to cross out something. Or maybe it's a T that is written sloppy. T- form-X- form. ZAP with two P's or ZAPP?" I think he's dreaming of a video game."

Both guys sat and looked at the letters and tossed out suggestions, and nothing made sense.

"Well, I'll study it later. I want to get this radio thing going before Early has worse problems. I think the cold is helping him. If we took him to the RV where it's warmer, I think it would do more damage to the trauma in his face," Barry said. Then he looked at Early and told him in case he could hear the conversation, "You know, Early, the girls love scars on a man's face, you probably won't be able to beat them off with a stick after this."

Joe snickered at Barry's comment and started picking up magazines while Barry went back and sat on his pile and looked at the article with the transmitter plans.

"I don't see how we can do this," Barry said. "We need a transformer, and it's not like I have a spare one in my backpack or, orrrr....." Barry stopped and stood straight up. "Oh, hell yeah!" he shouted. "X and form....X, meaning TRANS, as in transform, transformer.....and zapper. He must mean the microwave, he always 'zaps' his microwave popcorn...I think he wants us to check the RV for a microwave, it'll have a transformer we can use! If we had the space in here, I'd do the dance!"

"So we need to head over to the RV," Joe said, looking out the side window at the RV that he could barely see through the raging snow. "What do we do with Early?"

"Let the engine run," Barry told him, "it'll keep it just warm enough that he won't get too warm. We'll pack him in sleeping bags. He'll be okay. He hasn't moved for hours, so I hope he'll stay put."

"You don't think he'll come to and try to get out of the van, do you?" Joe asked.

"I don't think so," Barry said, looking over at Early. "I gotta get his tool pouch and grab those magazines and let's get going. Those bruises on Early's head look like they are swelling more, I don't think we can afford to sit and waste time."

"I agree, but we still don't have the diode plans."

"You are right, we really gotta find that or this won't work at all." And they both buckled down to flying through the magazine table of contents around the year of the crystal radio set plans.

"I'm just not seeing it....I've gone twelve issues back, you've gone forward. It's not here," Joe said, sounding beaten again.

"I don't get it," Barry said. "They are really good about giving directions for everything." Barry flipped through the 1957 issue with the receiving radio directions and started to read the specifics when he suddenly shouted again. "Oh shit! It's been right here all along...in a sidebar next to the article! *How to Build a Diode Out of Junk.* Look at this list, a pencil, a razor blade, safety pin...it IS junk!" HA! Surely we can scrape together that stuff. Let's go!"

"Check," Joe said, as he reached under his seat and got his tool kit. "I don't think these will help much," he said, looking into his bag. "Mostly a couple of wrenches, pliers, screwdrivers, these are more mechanical tools. I'm sure Early has electronics tools."

Barry dug into Early's backpack. Sure enough, he yanked a small tool pouch out of Early's bag and held it up for Joe's approval.

"Score!" Joe said as Barry stuffed it under his shirt, then shoved the magazines in the pockets of his coat.

"Not cool, man," Joe said, pointing to the exposed magazines. "If those catch in the wind, they could blow away or get wet and ruin the print. Those are our lifesavers." Barry took them out and handed them to Joe, who put them under his own shirt, then zipped up his coat. Barry wrote a note on a box lid to Early that if he woke up to honk the horn and that they were over at the RV trying to build a radio. Then the two geeks were out the door and into the storm again.

Chapter 54

Scavenger Hunt

Joe pounded on the RV door. "Hey, it's us from the van, let us in!" he shouted over the snow that blew so hard it felt like it cut his eyes.

The door opened, and Joe and Barry quickly climbed in. Everyone was yawning and squinting their eyes and looking irked, even Twinkles was too sleepy to yap.

"Oh man, sorry if we woke you up," Barry apologized, "but we think we have a way to get rescued."

That wiped the irritated looks off everyone, and the looks turned into being cautiously curious.

"Look, we have an article in these old magazines about how to build a short wave radio out of junk. If we could borrow a few parts from this RV, we think we could build it," Barry said with an urgency that was out of his usual unemotional character.

"Tell us more," Jeff said, backed by a choir of mumbling and questions from everyone.

"Well, we need a few things first," Barry said. "Does this RV have a microwave?" As he looked around and saw the little microwave fitted into the cabinet over the stove.

Louise slid the door to the bedroom open enough to slip through after hearing the commotion.

"Ma'am?" Barry said to Louise. "Is this your RV?"

"Yes," she said with a curious look.

"I see there's a small built-in microwave there. We think we can build a short wave radio to call for help, but we need a little transformer. There should be one in the microwave, but we'd have to tear it apart, and the oven would never be useful again."

"That's okay," Louise said, "if it helps us get some help, that's fine. Besides, I can't use this RV without Herman."

"Herman?" Joe looked up and asked. "Which one of you is Herman?"

After a brief silence, Jeff explained what happened to Herman and where he was. Joe and Barry apologized to Louise for their abrupt push for parts and offered their condolences. Then they introduced themselves to her and to those they hadn't met yet. Joe recognized Tawnie from the diner and asked about her two friends. Tawnie explained how Brittany was still unconscious, and Delphia and the Reverend were staying with her.

"All the more reason we need to get help. I think we can do it with these directions to build a short wave radio," Joe said, slapping the magazines out on the table. "We'll need this table," Joe said, "if it's not a problem."

Doris and Janet looked at each other and slid out of the seats, then Jackie stretched and yawned and also scooted out, but Rita wasn't going to budge.

"You can sit right next to me..." Rita said to Joe, patting the seat next to her. She looked at Joe because he looked a bit older and healthier than the skinny pale Barry, "I don't take up much room with my tiny trim buns."

"Rita," Doris grumbled under her breath, "knock it off!"

"Oh, all right," Rita said, "but there's no more room in the RV to sit, and I'm not planning on sharing space with her husband," Rita pointed to Louise, "and I'm not taking up the whole seat here."

"It's okay ma'am," Joe said to Doris, winking at her as he was getting the gist of the situation, "she reminds me of my mother." That comment irked Rita so much that she sat back in her seat, folded her arms, and looked out the window into the storm.

Joe put Early's little tool bag on the table and rummaged in it, looking to see what he had, and Barry went over to examine the microwave.

"Phillips screwdriver?" Barry asked, and Joe pulled a multi-screwdriver tool out and handed it over. It didn't take long removing screws and some trim, then the two lowered the microwave, disconnected the power plug, and continued disassembling it with an audience of hopeful storm refugees.

"Finally," Barry said, while twirling out the last two screws, and handed the little transformer over to Joe as though it was a fragile newborn.

"Okay," Joe said, "we're halfway there. Now we need a few more items." And Joe mentioned the things they needed from the article. Some they got right away like cardboard core of a toilet paper roll that Louise took out of the trash, to the cardboard core of the paper towels after Louise and Doris unrolled all the sheets off of it. Jackie and Janet began to pull the sheets apart and stacked them up nicely. Louise produced some tin foil they needed.

"Now, we need a really large safety pin."

The women all began to scrounge in their purses, and Louise looked in a bathroom drawer. Two small ones were provided, but Joe said it needed to be bigger. A lot bigger.

Auggie made a face at Wilhelmina and jabbed her with his elbow. Wilhelmina made a face back, then sighed, "Ho-kay. I haff pin." And Wilhelmina slid a chubby hand into her fur coat and fumbled with the lining for a minute then produced a little silk purse that she'd kept pinned in her coat with a very large safety pin. She removed the pin and handed it to Joe. Everyone applauded Wilhelmina, and she blushed and wrapped herself tightly in her coat and pushed the silk purse down into a pocket.

"How about a pencil?" Joe asked. Everyone was able to produce an assortment of pens and markers, but no pencils. "Oh man, somebody has to have a pencil. It doesn't have to be big." Joe waited for a moment and added, "it doesn't even need an eraser, just a stub of a pencil??"

"Oh, wait," Mr. Preston said and stood to dig in his suit coat pockets. "Ahhh. Here," and Mr. Preston produced a golf scoring pencil.

"Ohhh, that's perfect," Joe said, thanking Mr. Preston and took the short pencil. "The Golden Sand Trap Country Club?" Joe read from the pencil and sniffed it like a fine cigar. "Mmmm, savory and salty with provocative new-mown fairway overtones," he teased, causing a few chuckles from the group.

"Yes," Mr. Preston said, seeming bummed. "It took me years to get invited to play there. I kept the pencil as a souvenir."

"I'm going to need to pretty much destroy it, is that okay?" Barry asked. Mr. Preston looked at the pencil for a few moments but nodded okay. He knew it was the least he could offer.

Travis looked up at Mr. Preston, who seemed to tower over him and his brother sitting on the floor. "Do you realize if you hadn't gotten invited to play there and didn't save the pencil that we'd all be screwed right now?" Travis then turned to ask Joe, "What are you going to do with that shrimpy pencil anyway? Write a note?" Eddie elbowed his brother in the ribs. Travis was just being Travis.

"No," Joe didn't mind explaining to everyone, "we need an electronic diode, but we obviously don't have one, so we can build one with a safety pin, a pencil, and a razor blade. Who has a double edge razor that will donate a blade to the project?" There was no answer.

"We really need this blade," Joe encouraged them all. They all looked at each other, hoping someone would come up with a blade. It seemed none of them used the big double edge blades, they only used disposable safety razors or electric shavers.

"Okay," Joe said, "this is a problem. Without the diode, this is a dead radio."

Louise clicked her fingers. "Wait!" she said and went into a cabinet back in the RV and rummaged in an old Sears toolbox. She came back to the group holding a small old yellowed box. "Razor blades," she said and handed the box to Joe. "Herman used to shave with them until he cut himself pretty bad, then bought an electric number. He used to pride himself on close shaves until that cut near his jugular that kept bleeding because he was on blood thinners. He saved the blades and used them for scraping bugs off the windshield."

Joe took out one of the blades that was folded in a stiff piece of paper. He unfolded it, and the blade was still shiny and new.

"Damn," Joe said when he saw the new blade. Everyone was puzzled, this is what he said he wanted, didn't he? "No, no," Joe realized he was scaring everyone, "this blade is new,

I needed a rusty old one. But I think I can fix this. Does this RV have a gas stove?" he asked Louise.

She pulled out a section of counter, revealing a small three-burner stove. "Yep...LP gas," Louise said. "Hope that isn't a problem."

Joe got a pair of pliers out of his tool bag and gripped the blade then explained to everyone that the blade had to be heated over the stove flame until it turned blue, or oxidized. He heated it until it glowed red, then yellow, then nearly white, but not blue. Everyone was watching and hoping whatever he was doing would work.

Joe then asked for a work surface that they could ruin with screws or pins. After a few suggestions of a baking pan, a cabinet door, and a cardboard box, Louise produced a small bulletin board and took off the business cards and phone numbers. "Awesome," Joe said.

"Now we need some paper clips, four double-A batteries, a couple screws, and some of those push-pins," Joe said, pointing to the pins Louise had just taken off the board. Janet had two paperclips at the bottom of her purse that got everyone checking, and two more were produced from Carol and Doris. No one had nails or screws.

"What about the screws you took out of the microwave?" Nick asked.

Joe and Barry looked at each other, wondering why they didn't think about that and went back to the microwave to take out a few of the brass screws. Nick sat back, glowing, knowing he came up with something else helpful. Louise remembered their map of America and the pushpins they used to mark the places they'd stayed and retrieved about a dozen more for the project.

"Well, now all we need is wire...a lot of wire," which was met with a collective groan from everyone.

"We could probably take Doris' Dominator around the front of the drift and cannibal some wires off the crashed cars. I'm sure we could pull one of the cars out of that heap somehow with that tank she's got," Jeff suggested. His suggestion was met with dismal silence. No one wanted to go out and drive around the drift again, much less try to hook up and tow a vehicle out of it.

"Vait!" Aggie nearly shouted. "I got oldt booster wire in trunk. Dat shouldt have plenty of vires!" He was quite happy to be able to contribute if it was needed. He still wanted to get to that christening if this all worked.

"Booster wire?" Joe asked. "What the heck is that?"

"That's an older name for jumper cables," Chuck volunteered.

"You mean we've had this wire available all this time, and nobody knew because of the different name?" Mr. Preston commented.

"More importantly," Joe asked, "will it work?"

"Not sure," Barry said but was still thinking. "If the wire isn't so old that the copper has oxidized, it might work. Those cables are probably stranded, so if we could get the sheath off, we'd have to untwist a lot of it and figure out how to put it together. Let's see what else is in Early's tool pouch," Barry said as he dug into the bag.

"Oh, wait," Joe said as he remembered something. "Doesn't the wire for the radio need to be coated? Stranded wire isn't coated."

"That's right," Barry said, "it has to be coated to wind around the toilet paper tube." Once again, everyone's hopes fell.

"Coated with what?" Doris asked. "Does it matter?"

"Well," Barry said, "I don't think it really matters, just so long as the copper doesn't touch copper when winding the coils."

"What about nail polish?" Doris suggested. "That's a coating." The other women nodded in agreement.

Barry and Joe both looked at each other in amazement, then once more, looked forlorn. "That might work, but we'll have to separate the strands of the cables, and we'll need a couple hundred feet if we can get that much," Barry said. "That'd require a lot of polish."

The women started digging in their purses, and Louise went back to the bathroom cabinets. They managed to dig up four mostly used-up bottles of nail polish, two were from Rita. "That won't be enough," Joe said, looking at the colorful little bottles.

"I bet Brittany has at least that many bottles herself," Tawnie volunteered, looking at the meager supply on the table, "she is always doing her nails and toes. But I don't want to go back out to the truck, I'm afraid I'll find Brittany dead or something."

"Would she have the polish with her in the truck, or would it be in her car that's stuck in the drift?" Eddie asked.

"I don't know if Delphia would have brought her purse and backpack when we were getting out of the car. I know she had a bunch of luggage in the trunk. I was so scared getting out I didn't pay attention and barely got my own purse."

Jeff stood and zipped up his coat again. "I'll go talk to the girl," and Jeff was headed out the door.

"Get wires out of trunk," Auggie reminded him. "Open driver's door and trunk button is on da door." Jeff thanked him and was gone.

"He shouldn't go alone in case there's some trouble," Mr. Preston said as he pulled up his collar and buttoned up his overcoat again, then offered his seat to Jackie. She graciously thanked him and sat in his co-pilot seat, and they both smiled at each other…a lot. Mr. Preston was then out the door, with a little flourish of fluttering snow as the door closed behind him. Doris and Janet noticed the brief flirtation between Mr. Preston and Jackie, but Rita didn't.

"Damn," Rita said. "I wish they'd stop flapping that door. It's really cold."

The geeks were busy assembling their supplies, and Barry nearly screamed when he saw that Early had a cold fusion soldering gun in his pouch. The batteries were dead, however, so Joe gave up the two batteries from his penlight. In the kit with the soldering gun were a few small coils of assorted solder. Bonus.

Barry made an announcement to the group holding up the cold fusion gun, "This my friends is a godsend, with this we can solder the ends of the wires together to make solid connections rather than relying on twisting the wire ends together and hoping it holds." None of them realized the importance of this tool.

* * *

Polish

"Hey, wait up!" Mr. Preston shouted to Jeff through the wind and snow. Jeff stopped with his back toward the wind as Mr. Preston tromped through the knee-deep snow. As he met up with Jeff, he commented, "We shouldn't go out alone in this." And the two trudged along through the blizzard to Ben's truck.

Jeff knocked on the window and saw Matthew jump at least a foot before he reached over and opened the door. Jeff and Mr. Preston climbed in and scooted over in the front seat. Delphia was still sitting watching over Brittney. Jeff turned to Delphia and asked her if she had any nail polish. Delphia looked at him, then at Matthew. Matthew raised his eyebrows, and then he and Delphia broke into a little bit of laughter.

"You need nail polish? Right now?" Delphia asked, sort of chuckling over it.

Jeff recognized just how silly this sounded out of the blue, and he and Mr. Preston got to smiling for a minute. Jeff explained that they needed it for coating wire. This did not escape Delphia at all.

"Oh, like magnetic wire. For a coil," Delphia commented as she began to dig on the floor to see what might be in the purses and bags. Jeff looked at Mr. Preston with a surprised look at what Delphia already figured out. Delphia managed to dig out two half-used bottles of mostly-dried-out nail polish from Brittney's backpack and purse and handed them to Jeff.

"Don't you women ever use up a whole bottle of polish before you start a new one?" Jeff asked nobody in particular.

"Do you know that nail polish dries faster when it's cold? It'll also spread better, so even though it's kinda thick and dried out, keep it cold, and maybe you can get a thinner coating if you need to stretch the polish. So leave it outside until you need it." And she sat back in the seat to make sure Brittney was comfortable again.

"Are you serious about that?" Mr. Preston asked her.

"Quite," she replied. Delphia was always handy with the facts.

"Well, thanks for the information, young lady," Jeff said. "Are you sure you two want to stay here? You can come to the RV at least for a bathroom break if you need it," Jeff told Matthew and Delphia.

"Maybe later," Delphia said.

"I took a leak a little while ago outside the truck," Matthew said, looking embarrassed. "I made Delphia promise not to peek." And he laughed a bit, making Delphia blush.

"So, you are making a coil for something?" Delphia asked as she stuffed the bags back on the floor of the truck.

"I guess," Jeff said. "The geeky guys in that white van, they think they can build a short wave radio out of some junk." And he shrugged his shoulders.

"Probably some sort of crystal set," Delphia said as she puffed up the sleeping bag around Brittany a bit.

"Huh?" Mr. Preston wondered. "Is that a real thing?"

"Oh yes," Delphia confirmed. "I don't know how it's done. It's really nearly lost knowledge in this day of technology and cellular towers. But as you can see, cell phones aren't always the answer."

Matthew sat there, impressed with Delphia's information. "Well, maybe this can work out then."

They exchanged information about using Mr. Buchbinder's booster wires and the microwave from the RV, leaving Delphia itching to see what was going on, but she wanted to stay with her friend Brittney. She asked if anyone had heard anything from Ben yet. She didn't like the answer but was still hopeful. It had only been a couple of hours since he left.

They all exchanged pleasantries, and Jeff and Mr. Preston left the truck and headed over to Auggie's Lincoln for the booster wires.

"That unconscious girl doesn't look so hot," Mr. Preston shouted to Jeff over the wind, once again thinking that Brittney was about the same age as his daughter. "I hope this radio thing works. I really want to get my life back."

"Me too," Jeff shouted back, hunching his collar up around his neck and heading for Auggie's Lincoln and the jumper cables.

*   *   *

Down to the Wire

Back in the RV, Joe and Barry were using the bulletin board as a base to assemble their makeshift radio. Using the pushpins, they began pinning things to the cork. The razorblade they incinerated on the stove had cooled off and left a blue glaze, giving them the oxidized coating they needed to create the diode. Eddie and Chuck were fascinated watching this live performance of inventing a communication device out of crap. Using Wilhelmina's safety pin and screwing its bottom loop to the cork with one of the microwave screws, they also screwed the razorblade blade down next to it. Then Joe used his diagonal cutters to break off an inch section of the pointy end of the golf pencil to use its graphite point. He stuck the point of the safety pin into the back end of the pencil's graphite section, creating one long component. Then bending the pin in such a way to touch the pencil's point to the oxidized razor blade and screwing it all in place, he made the whole contraption into a diode.

Other than the generator running and the cycling of the furnace, the only other sound in the RV was that of Barry and Joe's tools clinking. Everyone was mesmerized watching them like an operating room theater, and praying this would get them the rescue help they all needed.

As intense as everyone was watching the geeks work when Jeff and Mr. Preston returned to the RV and opened the door, everyone jumped.

Rita shouted, "Goddamit! Can't you knock?" And everyone chuckled a bit over her comment. Rita turned to look out the window and attempted to sneak a sip out of her flask, then quickly stashed it back in her purse, although everyone could see what she did in the reflection of the window.

"Here you go," Jeff said to Barry and Joe. "Here's some more polish," as he sat down the two bottles of partially used, nearly dried-up polish and explained what Delphia said about keeping it cold.

Mr. Preston had the jumper cables, and they looked as new as the day Auggie got them. "Where do you want them?" Mr. Preston asked.

"Here," Barry said, digging in the tool pouch. "There must be a utility knife in here." And he kept digging. "Does anyone have a sharp knife?" And every guy in the RV started digging into their pockets, and they produced an assortment of knives. Everyone got to laughing about all the pocket knives. Finally, Barry asked, "Can you guys cut the sheathing off the cables, then when it's off, begin to carefully separate the wires?"

Mr. Preston handed one of the cables to Jeff, and they stretched it, estimating it was about eight feet.

"So with the two cables, will we have enough wire after we cut the clamps off each end? That'll knock each cable down at least a foot," Mr. Preston figured out loud.

Barry got up and looked at the wire. He had small diagonal cutters and began to cut away at the sheathing and worked through the copper strands until he cut off one clamp, then looked at copper stranding at the end of the cable. "It's pretty thin wire and good to see that the copper hasn't gotten old and oxidized, it should be okay," he said. "And there should be plenty. But let's not try to waste any of it. When you get the sheath off, start unwinding it and let the girls use their nail polish to start coating it. We'll need a place to put the wire sections until it dries."

"Shower," Louise volunteered. "We can bend an end and hang it over the shower rod, I can plug in my blow dryer."

"Good," Barry said, nodding his head in approval.

The guys were busy cutting the coating off the cables and untwisting the copper strands. The women were working on coating the wires with the assortment of polish colors. It seemed like everyone was busy working on the project. Barry suddenly stopped. "Shit," he said, under his breath. But everyone heard it and looked at him. "I made a mistake." He looked at everyone, "I don't think we can build this. I need an oscillator chip," he said and hung his head.

"Can't you build one of those out of crap too?" Travis asked with a little sarcasm.

Barry thought for a minute. "Wait. Yes, maybe you have something there. I think we can build a rudimentary one," he said, and turned to Louise, "Ma'am, does this RV have metal ductwork?"

"I think so," she said. "I'm not very good about all this maintenance stuff. That was Herman's deal."

Joe stood on his seat and unscrewed the register from the ceiling, and sure enough, it was metal ductwork. "Ahh," he said, "bless these old machines! I bet the new ones have plastic. We might be needing a little piece of your ductwork, ma'am," he said to Louise. She nodded her head.

All they had were diagonal cutters, so Barry and Joe took turns working the diagonals to cut out a small piece of the galvanized tin ductwork. Eventually, they managed to hack out a two-inch by two-inch piece, big enough to make the chip.

"I'm going to have to heat this on your stove," Barry told Louise, and she nodded again. "I'm going to have to get it white-hot, and unfortunately, it's going to cause toxic fumes, can you run your exhaust fans?"

"There's one over the stove," Louise said. You have to take that cover off," she pointed to a shroud over the exhaust fan.

With the concerns about burning off the galvanized coating and all the nail polishes evaporating, Louise hit the exhaust fan and tried to crank open the roof hatch over the fan only to find the snow had piled up high enough that the outside hatch wouldn't open, or it was frozen.

"Not good," Chuck informed everyone. "All the fumes in here could cause a flash fire and incinerate all of us, and that's before you start to make the toxic fumes from burning the piece of tin." There were looks of concern all around. Chuck buttoned up his coat and pulled on his hockey hat. "I'm going to climb up there and get the snow off the hatches."

"I'll go with you," Mr. Preston said as he handed his end of a cable to Travis.

"No, man," Chuck told him, "you've been out there enough. Plus, you have to work on that cable wire. I'm just going around to the back of the RV, these old ones have ladders. I'm just going to climb up there and brush the snow off the vents. I shouldn't be out there for five minutes." Chuck seemed man enough to handle it, so Mr. Preston continued slicing pieces of sheathing off the cables as Chuck went out to do the chore.

*   *   *

Spit and Polish

The ladies were all painting wires when Barry explained, "Make sure you leave an inch or so on each end of those wires without polish, ladies." Barry said. "I'll need those bare ends to solder together into much longer wires."

The girls had formed two assembly lines with wire held between two of them and the other two painting to meet in the middle. The RV space was tight, so they figured out how to do it without moving around much or touching the wet polish.

As the polish dried Barry would twist the unpolished ends of two wires together, secure them with a dab of solder, then the girls would coat the connection. Barry showed Jeff and Mr. Preston how to carefully and neatly wrap the wire around the cardboard toilet paper core, explaining to count to twenty-five wrappings, then skip a space, then wrap ninety more on the little toilet paper tube. They would be using this to make a tuner. Barry began cutting seven-inch squares of aluminum foil to tape onto the paper towel tube to create a capacitor. He just needed a piece of stiff paper to cover with foil to be bent around the cardboard core to make an adjustable capacitor.

It wasn't long before Rita announced, "Doris and I have done two wires so far. How many will we need? There's not a lot of polish left." Barry looked up with a troubled look.

"Don't panic," Carol said, "Louise and I have done three. So now we have five so far."

Barry penciled the math. "Each wire from the jumper cable is about six feet, so that means we have thirty feet of good coated wire so far. Five and a half inches around the TP tube twenty-five times, so we'll need about eleven feet, then another wrapping of ninety turns, so that's about forty-five feet there. So with both wires, we'll need a total of sixty feet of coated wire. Can we get ten of those strands coated?"

"There's not going to be enough polish." Rita reiterated while looking at the side of the polish bottle she held up.

Once again, it was like air out of a tractor tire as the group's hopes sagged again.

Tawnie's small voice volunteered some information. "I saw Brittney putting lots of suitcases in her trunk. Maybe she has more makeup stuff in the trunk."

Everyone looked at Tawnie. She blushed so much it could be seen under her dark skin. "Well, Brittney is always fixing herself up. I was just wondering out loud," she said, almost apologetically.

"That means someone would have to go out and around the drift and dig her car out," Travis commented, looking at Eddie.

"Speaking of out," Mr. Preston said, looking at his watch, "what happened to the truck driver?"

"I guess we'd better go out and find out," Jeff said as he stood one more time to zip up his coat. Eddie got up and said he'd go along. He wanted to stretch his legs and grab some air that doesn't smell like nail polish. The two left the RV, slamming the door behind them.

*　　*　　*

Down the Hatch

"Do you think the snow is dying down any?" Eddie asked as they tromped through the snow to the back of the RV.

"I can't tell under the bridge here," Jeff said. "You can't tell with all the obstructions and barriers we have here."

"Do you think we could drive that Dominator around the drift where the RV came through and see if we could get that girl's luggage to see if she's got more polish?" Eddie asked.

"Might," Jeff said as they got to the rear of the RV.

"Well," Chuck said as the two guys rounded the rear of the RV, "this is embarrassing." Eddie and Jeff could see that Chuck's foot had slipped on the second rung of the icy RV ladder, and his foot had slipped between the ladder and the

RV, and he was trying to yank his foot out while hanging onto the ladder with both hands.

"Why didn't you pound on the RV or something?" Eddie asked him as Jeff tried to free his foot.

"Just thought I could get myself out," Chuck said, twisting his foot to try to get it out.

"That boot has to come off," Jeff said as he started to untie Chuck's big boot.

"Yeah, I figured," Chuck said. "my hands are freezing, and I can't let go of the ladder to undo the laces, or I'll fall back and break my neck."

Jeff made quick work of the laces and tugged a few times on the boot to free Chuck's foot. Chuck then easily slipped his ankle and foot out of the space. "Damn, that wind is cold when it sails through a sweaty sock!" Chuck commented.

"Did you get the snow off the vent cap?" Jeff asked him.

"No. Got my foot caught right off the bat," Chuck frowned.

"I can get up there," Eddie said, looking at the ladder.

"Not a great idea," Chuck replied. "If you stumble over the a/c, or step on a vent cap, you'll break it and let freezing air in the RV. Not to mention, you are kind of a small guy, and the wind will blow you off."

"I can do it," Eddie argued, and he didn't wait for an answer but started up the ladder.

Jeff helped Chuck get his boot back on, and Eddie was up and on the RV quickly. "We have to wait," Jeff said to Chuck.

"Yeah," Chuck agreed. "I know," as they both watched the edge of the RV. "How about you watch down that side, and I'll watch down this side in case the kid gets blown off."

Meanwhile, Eddie was on top of the RV crawling on his hands and knees, making sure he was hanging onto something after letting go of the ladder. There were two a/c units, a GPS dome, a small folded up television antenna, and a couple other antennas as Eddie crawled through the snow on his way over to the first vent lid and pushed the snow off.

"The kid must have gotten to one," Chuck shouted over to Jeff. "Just saw a pile of snow come down."

Eddie made his way to the other vent and pushed the snow off it as well, then tapped on it so the people inside knew they could open it. Slowly he saw the vent open, and the fan come on. Eddie smelled the nail polish and felt the warm air on his face from the exhaust fan and realized how cold he was getting, so he began his crawl back to the ladder.

You think that kid will be able to grab the ladder to get down?" Chuck yelled to Jeff.

"Hope so," Jeff said.

They both waited, looking up at the ladder.

Eddie wanted to turn around to crawl back face first, but he'd mashed the loose snow on the roof, and it made slippery bare places, and he was being pushed by the wind. Eddie realized now that his lightweight frame was nothing but tinsel to the blizzard wind. He began to slowly crawl backwards toward the ladder, laying as low as he could and hanging on to anything he could grab. The snow was still blowing so heavy that he couldn't see the ladder rungs yet. He was just guessing as he made his way back.

Chuck was getting a bit worried about what was taking Eddie so long up on the roof. He hadn't fallen off, or he or Jeff would have seen him. Chuck and Jeff exchanged a few worried looks but kept looking up.

Finally, they saw Eddie's feet breach the top of the RV, and both men crowded the bottom of the ladder. Jeff hauled himself up a few of the steps to help Eddie get his feet on the first rung or two. Then he was able to easily come down.

"Nice job, kid," Chuck said and slapped him on the back as they all made their way back to the RV. Jeff noticed Chuck was limping.

Both exhaust fans were running now, and when they opened the door, it only helped pull in more cold air, but at least it wasn't laden with nail polish fumes.

*   *   *

Running Out of Luck

The geeks at the table had already assembled the capacitor they would need by taping pieces of foil to the paper towel tube and taping another piece of foil to a section of a magazine cover that Barry had cut into a seven-inch by seven-inch square and bent the flat piece around the paper towel tube so it would slide over the foil-covered paper towel tube. By now, Nick had climbed down from his roost on the RV dash and was hanging over the back of Joe's seat watching the construction project.

Chuck apologized to the group for his clumsiness as Jeff explained what was taking him so long, but they were glad that he was okay and thankful to Eddie for going up and clearing the vent lids. Louise fixed up a plastic bag with some snow in it for Chuck to put on his ankle that was beginning to swell and she made Chuck sit with his foot up on the dash.

Everything was looking very promising and going smoothly until Barry announced that there wasn't going to be enough nail polish for the rest of the wire coatings. Nearly everyone groaned in dismay.

"We can take the Dominator and try to see if that girl has more polish in her trunk," Eddie said, chattering as he was still trying to warm up from his roof climb. Mr. Preston surprised himself by rubbing Eddie's arms to get him warmed up.

"Well," Joe said as he stood to tell everyone, "one other thing I forgot. The antenna. We have enough wire to get a decent signal, but it needs to be high enough to get out of this hole under the bridge. That bridge is about four feet over the RV. Even if we could toss something up there, the wire won't stay, it's too thin. The wind would blow it down."

Chuck patted the cold pack on his ankle and said, "He's right. We'd need a mast of some kind to wrap the wire around. I'm guessing we'd be needing at least ten or twelve feet to go up past the concrete railing on the overpass, high enough to grab a signal and another three feet or so to secure it to the RV. That ladder on the back of the RV is sturdy if we had a mast we could lash it to the ladder and move the RV so the top of the mast could be secured to the railing on the overpass."

Joe and Barry nodded in agreement and were bummed at not thinking this through.

"We've come a long way. We can't give this up now," Eddie said, still chattering.

"Can't we jerry-rig something to go up there? Broomsticks? Fishing poles?? Something??" Travis said.

"I don't think so," Joe said as he slumped in his seat, looking at his half-completed radio, "we'd need something sturdy enough that wouldn't blow apart when the wind gusts hit it. We simply don't have anything tall enough."

Other than a few coughs, there was a depressing silence in the RV.

"There's some stuff in the basement," Louise volunteered again.

"Basement?" Nearly everyone was asking.

"Yes, there is a lot of storage under the RV," Louise explained. "You'll need the keys from the ignition key to open the hatch doors." Once more, Jeff and Eddie buttoned up and left the RV with the basement keys.

Joe and Barry kept working on their radio and using the cold fusion gun to solder the wires together, making a long wire and used up the rest of the nail polish to coat the newly soldered connections.

Mr. Preston had been trying to do the wire wrapping around the toilet paper core, but he was clumsy with his fingers, and the wrapping wasn't going well.

"It needs to be touching all the way around," Barry said, after a brief inspection. "Maybe one of the ladies would have smaller fingers to wrap it better."

Mr. Preston looked around at the women. Rita wasn't doing much, but she irritated Mr. Preston something awful, and Wilhelmina was napping. The other women were coating the wires, and Louise was busy with the blow dryer drying the polish, only Jackie was left. Mr. Preston looked at her, sort of waiting for her to volunteer, but when Jackie saw his eyes looking at her, she blushed and looked away. Mr. Preston smiled as warmly as he could at her and stuck his toilet paper tube out in his hand in her direction. "Can you give me a hand?" Jackie blushed hard and felt her body heat up under her coat, but she nodded, and Mr. Preston leaned over to hand her his wire and toilet paper core that was now a rat's nest of wire and looked like a junked-up Slinky. Jackie took the toilet paper core from him, and as she touched his hand, she blushed more. She felt so shy around this attractive lawyer looking to her for some help.

"Um, so how does it need to be done?" she asked Mr. Preston.

He showed her how to wrap the wire, but he was fumbling it all over, so she held out her hand for him to hand it back to her, and she began to wrap the thin wire nearly perfect around the tube. Mr. Preston noticed her beautifully manicured nails and soft hands.

"I hope this doesn't ruin your hands," he said and noticed he actually felt concerned.

"I can always do my nails later," Jackie said without looking at him, "I'd really like to get rescued. So how many times do I do this?" She looked up, and it seemed Mr. Preston was just staring at her, and he realized she noticed it.

"I'm sorry," Mr. Preston said and switched his gaze to the TP core. "Twenty-five wraps. You are really doing a marvelous job with that wire," he complimented. Jackie stood from the co-pilot seat and indicated for Mr. Preston to sit again. He declined at first, but she wasn't taking no for an answer. He sat and unbuttoned his cashmere coat, and when he caught Jackie's glance, he patted his knee, indicating she could sit there again. Jackie backed up to lean on the counter instead when she saw his invitation to sit but was having trouble winding the wire while standing. Mr. Preston patted his knee once more and gave her a hopeful look. Doris noticed it and nodded to Jackie to go sit. Jackie took a deep breath and sat again on Mr. Preston's knees but never took her focus off working on the toilet paper tube. Barry handed them a very long wire and asked Jackie to coil up ninety more wraps on the other end of the TP core as they'd be needing that as well.

Barry did some calculations on the table and said,. "We're not going to have enough coated wire." And dropped his shoulders. Joe sighed and sat back in his seat, frustrated with all the rotten luck they kept having he was about ready to throw in the towel when Eddie and Jeff came back from rummaging in the basement of the RV.

"Nothing," Jeff said, "just some big tools, drain hoses, extension cords, a step-ladder, and some cleaning stuff. Nothing there we can use for an antenna mast."

And again, a big depressing sigh from the group.

*　　*　　*

Getting the Shaft

Mr. Preston had been surprising himself at how he had been helping out and amazed at his own benevolence at handing over his special golf pencil from The Golden Sand Trap Country Club, and he sat there thinking about his brand new set of unused custom golf clubs in his trunk. He knew each of the nearly two dozen clubs had a titanium shaft that was slightly flared from the club head up to the grip. If they could cut the heads off somehow and get the grips off, they would nest into each other about a foot and form a pretty damn sturdy pole. But did he want to give up the very expensive, custom-made gift he gave to himself that represented years of work, his successes, and achievements in his law practice? He hadn't even had a chance to play with them yet. They were pristine. Untouched.

He looked at sweet Jackie, working on the wire and looked around at everyone pitching in. He closed his eyes and thought for a moment before he took a deep breath and announced, "I have a set of golf clubs in my trunk. I believe if we can break the heads off, we can stack the shafts and make a decent antenna pole at least twenty feet if we need it." And he exhaled and hung his head.

There was dead silence for a few moments as the news sunk in, then slowly, there began a quiet round of golf-clapping that started with Eddie, then Jeff and Travis, and eventually it swelled into an appreciative golf applause from everyone as their hopes vaulted once more.

They began to devise a plan to retrieve Mr. Preston's clubs from his car in the drift, and while out there, see if they could get to Brittany's trunk to see if she packed more nail polish. Mr. Preston, Eddie, and Jeff were elected to drive Doris' Dominator back to the other side of the drift. Even though plenty of snow had fallen, they felt sure her Dominator Maximus would be able to get through the pass that the RV had made in the drift a few hours ago.

Jeff remembered the heavy-duty extension cords in the basement of the RV and suggested they could use those as tow-ropes to drag the cars out of the drift if they needed to. So as they headed for the Dominator, they visited the RV basement and got the extension cords and grabbed a broom to sweep the snow.

"This guy has nearly everything in that basement, you think he'd have a snow shovel," Jeff said as they took their tools to the Dominator.

The Dominator started right up, despite the cold and the time it had been sitting in the wind and sub-zero temperatures, not to mention the snow that had piled up around it.

"Ready?" Jeff asked the others.

"Yep," Mr. Preston said as the Dominator started to slowly roll once more.

"How long until we get heat?" Eddie asked, still chattering.

"You better be careful, kid," Mr. Preston said. "You aren't wearing decent winterwear, and you are kind of a slim kid, you don't want to end up with hypothermia. You just sit back there and try to stay warm."

Eddie sat back with his arms folded, "Smells like old ladies in here," he mumbled under his breath.

Back at the RV, Joe and Barry were finishing up making their oscillator out of the heated piece of duct metal and wiring up their radio. Another small piece of a pie pan that Louise donated was cut and folded and used as a radio tuning wand. Joe and Barry were wondering how they'd hook this entire contraption up to a speaker so they could hear responses.

"What about a cell phone?" Joe asked.

"Nahh, too digital," Barry said. "We really need older technology."

Joe wired together the double 'A' batteries, but they were weak, so he needed two more. Louise was able to get one from a remote and another from the garage door opener in the RV. If they needed more, they'd have to go back to the cars.

All they needed now was a good ground wire so it wouldn't short out the system and a decent antenna. They still needed more coated wire, so they all had to sit and wait on the results of what Jeff, Mr. Preston and Eddie could get from the cars in the drift, all the while Nick marveled at the contraption sitting on the table.

Louise stopped to look at her now scavenged RV that Herman loved so much. She knew if Herman was still with them, he'd be thrilled to be in the middle of the rescue himself, along with his brother barking commands from the other side. It seemed a good ending for both Herman and his RV.

Chapter 55

Goin' Back Around the Mountain

Doris' Dominator lumbered over the snow, and with the headlights and fog lights glaring out the grille, they could see where the RV had pushed through the smaller end of the drift.

"Does it look like it's letting up a bit?" Mr. Preston asked Jeff.

"Seems like it might be, just a little," Jeff replied. "Trouble is, if it's letting up, the plows will begin to roll, and we'll be in worse trouble. They'd never see us or know about us behind that drift. We need to get back there and get our vehicles out of the way."

"Ok, but let's see if we can get into that girl's trunk to see if we can get more polish and get into my trunk and get my golf clubs," Mr. Preston said.

"Sounds like a plan," Jeff said. "I saw that the Dominator has a real solid trailer hitch. I hope we can pull the girl's car out just enough to grab the keys for the trunk. Tawnie said she thought the keys were still in the ignition. We'll have to send Eddie in the window to get the keys if it's locked."

Slowly the Dominator inched its way around the drift as the men looked to see if they could see either Mr. Preston's Spectaculeer or the girl's little blue car.

"I can't see squat," Eddie said. "I can't see anything except the back corner of my truck covered in snow."

"Do you remember how far away the girl's car was?" Jeff asked.

"Maybe six feet. Not far at all," Eddie explained. "Mr. Preston's car will be just a few more feet over from there. The girl's car was jammed farther into the snow than Mr. Preston's."

"I have my fob with me, so if we can find my car and take the weight off the trunk lid, it should open right up. Nothing was smashed in the back end that would hinder the trunk opening mechanism, as far as I know." Mr. Preston told them as he dug his fob out of his pocket and held it up to the window clicking the button to flash his lights.

"I don't see anything," Jeff said. "Might be too much snow piled up."

Eddie added, "Maybe when the RV hit the drift, it pushed your car way in."

"Could be," Mr. Preston said. "Doesn't look like any other tracks have been here since we all went behind the drift."

"They close the interstates here in Kansas when we get these Siberian Express blizzards," Jeff said as he began to get the Dominator positioned to shine it's lights on the drift so they could find the cars. "They don't want anyone doing exactly as we have done, namely endanger all of us by parking on the road. Now let's see if we can find that girl's car."

Jeff threw the Dominator into park as the three got out, fighting the strong cold winds and blowing snow. Jeff had the broom and began jamming the broom handle into the snow to feel for one of the cars. It was only a half dozen jabs when he hit something hard.

"Found one," Jeff shouted to the others as he turned the broom around and began to sweep as much snow off the pile as he could manage. Eddie used his hands again and pulled snow away from the vehicle, and eventually, they found a bit of the back fender. "This yours?" he shouted to Mr. Preston.

"No, this is blue. Must be the girls' car," Mr. Preston said as he joined in trying to pull snow away from the car.

The three worked at pulling the snow away and trying to expose the back door on one side, and they finally were able to uncover a part of it. "We'll never unbury this whole door, so we can open it to get the key for the trunk," Mr. Preston said.

"The back window is half-way down. It sure blew a lot of snow into the car," Jeff said as he made a little headway, clearing the snow away from the window.

"How much extension cord do we have?" Eddie asked. "If we have enough, we can run it through both back windows and try to pull it out that way. We'll never be able to dig down enough to get the cord under the axle."

"Might be worth a try, Eddie," Jeff said.

"We will still need the key to open the trunk. Do you think we can bust out the rest of that window so maybe I can squeeze in to get the keys."

Jeff jammed his broom handle into the window several times, but he wasn't getting anywhere. The three were back to moving more snow by hand until they were able to open the rear door just enough for Eddie to squeeze through.

"We'd be digging for another hour if we had to open it wide enough to get my gut in there." Mr. Preston joked.

Eddie was able to squeeze in the back door and reached over the seat and felt around the steering wheel. Sure enough, the keys were in it. He grabbed the keys and handed them out to Jeff. Eddie squoze back out, smiling that his diminutive size was good for something.

"Eddie, you are shivering like crazy," Mr. Preston said. "Go get in the Tank and warm up."

"Check." Eddie wasn't about to argue and quickly jumped into the Dominator.

Jeff and Mr. Preston continued to scrape snow off the car to get to the trunk. "Let's get this thing opened. Hope there's nail polish," Jeff said.

"Yeah," Mr. Preston sort of joked. "Never thought I'd be standing in a blizzard looking for nail polish with another guy."

They finally cleared enough snow from the trunk to reveal a small trunk lid, but it was frozen down. They pounded their fists around the seal a few times, and eventually, it loosened, and they were able to pry it open. Inside was a lot of luggage.

Jeff started looking through the bags, but Mr. Preston told him to throw it all in the Dominator, saying they could look later.

"I'm freezing," Mr. Preston shouted to Jeff. "I need to warm up."

"Okay," Jeff yelled back. "Me too." As he threw the bags in the back seat of the Dominator, both men climbed in, shivering and covered in snow. Eddie was still cold as he sat at the wheel, goosing the accelerator, making the engine run harder because the heater air wasn't very warm.

"Eddie, are you okay?" Jeff asked. "Your lips look like they are slightly blue. You should have stayed at the RV until you got good and warm." Mr. Preston nodded in agreement.

"I'm here now," Eddie chattered. "So no point in ragging on about it." And he folded his arms to try to stay warm.

"Well, we did get the girls' luggage," Jeff commented. "Now, we have to find your car." He looked at Mr. Preston.

"I don't know how we're going to get my car out of that drift." Mr. Preston looked out the back window at his invisible car. "We won't be able to get the doors open. We can't put the cord around the window frames, as my car is a convertible, they don't have window frames. With all the snow packed around it, we can't get under it either. Eddie got me out cutting a hole in the convertible top."

It was quiet for some minutes while they were thinking.

"What about we use the Dominator's grille for a snowplow. If we run parallel across the front of the drift, we might be able to scrape away some of the snowpack," Eddie suggested.

"Well, I don't have any other ideas. Might as well give it a try," Jeff said.

"Yeah," Mr. Preston sighed, knowing his Spectaculeer was going to be beat-up worse. "Let's do it."

Eddie drove the Dominator and positioned it so it would take about six inches off the front edge of the drift. He shifted it down into low for extra torque and rolled the Dominator across the edge of the drift. Mr. Preston watched out the side window and saw that the Dominator indeed took a nice swipe off the drift.

"Let's do it again," Mr. Preston said.

Eddie turned the vehicle around and came back across, taking about a foot of snow off this time, and it all fell under the Dominator's tires. It was shaving off enough of the snow-pack to see they were making a little progress.

Eddie made a few more passes.

"I didn't think my car was shoved in there this far," Mr. Preston said.

"I think the RV might have pushed it in farther. That's probably why the old guy got out to try to see if anyone was inside the cars," Eddie commented.

Thankfully, the Dominator's heater was warming up as they were exchanging ideas on how to pull the Spectaculeer out of the drift.

"What about your wheels?" Eddie asked.

"Michelin," Mr. Preston said.

"No, no," Eddie said, "not your tires, your wheels, the rims. What kind of wheels do you have?"

"Uh," Mr. Preston wasn't much of a gear-head, "I don't know. I paid big bucks for some kind of special rally wheel."

"So, then they have spokes?" Eddie asked. Jeff got the gist of the idea before Mr. Preston even answered.

"I'll bet they have spokes!" Jeff brightened up. "We can run the cord through the wheel spokes. I think we'll only need to dig out one wheel."

Mr. Preston could only think that this idea will be one more thing of his that would be busted up in this disaster. "Okay," he sighed again.

The snow was so packed from its own weight that even the Dominator, with all its Maximus, had to work at pushing the snow, so Eddie was making the last possible pass across the drift edge when they all felt the clunk of bumping something more metallic than snow.

"I think we found it," Eddie said and backed the Dominator a couple of feet to shine the headlights at the source of the clunk. Mr. Preston pressed the buttons on his fob, but they didn't see anything or hear the horn.

"Shut the engine down, turn off the lights," Mr. Preston said.

Eddie shut it down and turned everything off. It was pitch black outside, not a streetlight, not a house light, nothing. And all they could hear was the storm blowing snow around.

Mr. Preston pushed the fob button again. And there, to the amazement of them all, one of his tail lights faintly lit up beneath a few layers of snow, and they could barely hear the honk of the horn.

"That's it!" Mr. Preston said. "That's her. Let's get her out."

Jeff and Mr. Preston buttoned up again and got out with the broom and jammed the broom handle into the snow about where they figured the trunk would be. They found there were just a couple inches of snow on the back bumper. Jeff began to try to sweep it off, but it was only packing down worse and creating an alcove of snow over the back of the car.

"This must be the damn earlier snow that was wet before the temperature bottomed out. It's frozen and packed down hard," Jeff said and started using the handle to wedge chunks of it off the bumper. Just as he was making headway, the broom handle snapped in two. "I can't believe it! Doesn't anything go right!!" Jeff yelled at the sky.

"It's okay," Mr. Preston told him, "now we have two tools." And Mr. Preston took one piece of the broom handle and began to dig at one side of the car to find a wheel.

"I think we'll have better luck just digging out the trunk," Jeff hollered over at Mr. Preston.

Mr. Preston stood and assessed the situation. "I don't know," Mr. Preston hollered back, "I'm concerned that if we keep digging this hole, that the top of the drift will collapse on us. I think we should try to pull the car out, at least until the trunk is out of the igloo."

Jeff looked at the bit of exposed bumper and had to admit that it would be safer to pull it out a bit. So the two used their broom handles to jam into the packed snow and pry the snow away from a back tire to expose at least one wheel.

Jeff knocked on the Dominator window and told Eddie the plan to pull the car out by a wheel.

"Check," Eddie said as he straightened up in the driver's seat as though he was on a mission. As he looked at the array of buttons and dials on the dash, he saw one lit up with a little yellow flame shape. He clicked it on. Nothing happened. But in a few more seconds, he could feel his seat warming up. "Seat warmers! Ahhhh," Eddie sighed and snuggled back into the warming seat.

With both men working as fast as they could with their broom handles, they managed to find the wheel and cleared the packed snow from around the wheel spokes.

"You think this will hold?" Mr. Preston asked Jeff as he looked at the wheel spokes.

"It's holding up the car, isn't it?" Jeff said, as he fished one end of an extension cord through the wheel and pulled it through. "But, I wonder if it'll hold trying to pull it out of the packed snow on the road."

Jeff and Mr. Preston knotted up the extension cords around the trailer hitch. Jeff threw a whistle to Eddie to get ready to pull, and then Jeff used his hand to signal Eddie to go forward slowly. Eddie began to move the Dominator as Jeff and Mr. Preston watched the extension cords tighten.

"Hope these cords aren't so old that the wires have deteriorated, or we could find our heads chopped off with a cord whiplash if they snap apart," Jeff commented to Mr. Preston, who immediately stepped back a few steps.

Jeff motioned to Eddie to keep going. Inch by inch. Mr. Preston and Jeff both stepped back a few more steps as they heard the cords groaning from the strain even over the wind and snow. The trailer hitch seemed to be holding fast. Then they noticed that the car budged just a bit, so Jeff motioned for Eddie to go a little more. The car moved a bit again. A half dozen more nudges and budges and the bumper and trunk were nearly a foot out of the drift. Jeff whistled again to Eddie to put it in park. Both Mr. Preston and Jeff were relieved that the extension cords didn't snap.

Mr. Preston used his trunk button on the fob, and they could hear the latch click, but the trunk didn't open. They pounded around the edge of the trunk lid to hopefully jar any ice loose. It still wouldn't open.

They thought they could use the broom handle pieces to wedge open the trunk, but the handles were too thick to put between the bumper and the trunk lid. Jeff dug out his pocket knife and began to whittle some of the broom handle down.

"Hope that works," Mr. Preston said.

"Me too," Jeff replied, "but it might just weaken the edge of the handle."

They wedged the newly whittled handle under the trunk lid edge and used the other as a fulcrum braced across the plastic bumper. Both men began to push on the handle piece as Mr. Preston pushed his fob button. They heard the trunk latch click and thought the lid moved slightly.

"More weight on it...." Jeff said. And they both put their weight into leaning on the broom handle, and Mr. Preston pushed his trunk button one more time. This time, the trunk yawned open, and through all the snow blowing around, they could see the beautiful golf bag sleeping peacefully up by the trunk's courtesy light. Mr. Preston took the bag of clubs out and held them like a long lost child and looked at Jeff.

"I know," Jeff said, understanding a little of how Mr. Preston was going to feel destroying his pristine set of very expensive clubs. "It's going to be tough."

"You have no idea," Mr. Preston said.

Both men hurried over to the Dominator, and they fitted Mr. Preston's clubs into the back seat. Mr. Preston chose to sit in the back with his clubs while Jeff and Eddie began the slow drive back around the drift to the RV.

Chapter 56

Fight-Clubs

"They are back!" Nick shouted when he saw the headlights coming around the mountain of snow. Nick watched in fascination as the Dominator climbed over the edge of the drift and parked along the shoulder near the RV.

It was taking the guys an unusual amount of time to get out of the Dominator, so Nick looked out the RV window. The interior lights were on in the Dominator, but it looked like the men were having a little three-way, hand-to-hand tussle, and appeared to be clobbering each other with big boxes or something.

"Gosh!" Nick said, "Are they having a rumble in there?"

Travis jumped up to look, and even Chuck leaned over to look out the window.

"People get fussy sometimes, son," Chuck told Nick. "Close quarters, missed meals, fears, cold, lots of things add up to short tempers," Chuck explained as he glanced out the window and saw what indeed looked like the three of them were having a little physical contact swinging at each other. Chuck lightly tapped the RV horn twice, its obnoxious blare dislodging plenty of snow from the overpass. But everything stopped in the Dominator. The lights on the Dominator returned the two headlight flashes indicating things were okay, then the squabble resumed.

"Not sure what's going on, but they seem to be working it out," Chuck said to Nick but didn't believe a word he said.

They watched the Dominator and saw Mr. Preston getting in and out of the opposite side of the vehicle, so was Jeff. The Dominator looked like it was having issues deciding on being in forward drive or reverse, going back and forth a foot or two each way. Then the guys got back in and scrapped with each other some more. This went on for some time, and it looked like Eddie was trying to drive off without them a number of times.

"What the hell!" Chuck finally said.

"Hope my Dad is okay," Nick said quietly as he watched the commotion.

"I'm going out there," Chuck said.

"You need to sit your butt down!" Doris told Chuck. "Let them work it out. Your ankle is swollen. You don't need to be walking out in the snow, putting your weight on it."

"She's right, you know," Janet said. "Just sit."

Louise also chimed in about him keeping his foot up.

Chuck wasn't going to argue with the tag team of, shall we say, assertive, women, so he dutifully sat and put his foot back up on the dash.

Some minutes later, Eddie threw open the RV door with three more bottles of nail polish in his hand. "We got it!!" He said with much joy as he set them on the table. Everyone was silent, waiting for his story of the fight.

"You okay, little brother?" Travis asked.

"Yeah," Eddie said a bit bewildered, "a little cold, but okay."

"So, you didn't get in the fight?" Travis asked.

"Fight? What fight?" Eddie asked as he looked around at everyone.

"We saw you all fighting in the Dominator. Looked like a real knock-down, drag-out," Travis explained. "You were slinging stuff at each other, slamming doors...".

"Fight...." Eddie mulled that over for just a minute before it dawned on him, "Oh, that. That was no fight," Eddie started to laugh. "We brought Mr. Preston's whole golf bag back and all the luggage from the girl's trunk. So at first, we were shuffling the bags back and forth to look through them for the nail polish. You didn't see fighting. You saw girl's luggage being shoved back and forth as we dug through it all. Did you ever have to dig through a teenage girl's luggage and try to figure out what all the stuff was and where she'd pack things? We saw stuff we'd never seen in our lives!" Eddie kept joking about it.

Eddie was seriously amused, thinking that everyone in the RV thought they were having a big brawl in the Dominator, and he struggled to stifle a laugh. Travis was nearly angry at feeling like a fool, but the smirk on the face of his little brother was a bit contagious, so Travis started to smile, then the ladies started to smile. Doris nudged Janet with her elbow as they felt a bit of a laugh coming on. Even Chuck began to struggle to chock back a laugh. As they looked around at each other, the smiling and chuckling gave way to soft laughter, they tried to stifle themselves as Holly and the Buchbinders were still dozing. It wasn't long before they all got to more giggling and trying to silence it by laughing into their sleeves and coats, laughing from both from the crazy idea of the fight in the Dominator and the stress and nerves of being stranded for hours.

As the giggles and laughter waned, the door flew open again, and everyone groaned at the cold air blowing in, but Jeff and Mr. Preston were carrying fourteen metal shafts from a set of golf clubs. Barry and Joe jumped up, grinning from ear to ear at the gold mine they were carrying.

"This is awesome!" Joe said. "This is going to do it!" As he took two of the shafts and inserted the smaller end of one into the larger end of the other, producing nearly four feet of very sturdy metal antenna. "How did you get the clubs off?" Joe asked them as he inserted another shaft and now had almost six feet.

Jeff and I held them under the wheels of the Dominator, and Eddie drove over them back and forth until we could break them off." Mr. Preston said with a sorrowful face as he looked lovingly at the bare titanium shafts.

Everyone felt heartsick for Mr. Preston, well, except for Rita.

"Don't worry, Mr. P," Rita said, "you can always get another set of clubs." Doris jabbed Rita with her elbow as she got up to help with the rest of the nail polish. "What?" Rita said, "It's true. He can get more clubs."

"I"d like to give you a club," Doris said with some contempt.

"So," Jeff interrupted, "how's the radio coming?"

"I think we are in good shape now," Barry said as he focused on soldering a few more wires together while Joe was pinning them down to the cork bulletin board. "The girls will have the rest of the wire coated, Jackie will get the wire wound nicely on the TP tube. So all we have left is making the antenna and ground wire. We'll need to get those extension cords back if you still have them. Those will be used for the ground wire and will have to have one end connected to this radio set, the other end will have to touch the ground, or the radio will just short out.

I think if we move the RV closer to the guard rail in the median, we can attach the extension cord to the guard rail, and it'll be plenty of ground contact through the guard rail posts so we won't have to dig through the snow to bury a wire. Then we need to make another wire for the antenna, and make it as long as possible, stack up those golf club shafts as high as we can make it, wrap the antenna wire around it and somehow hoist it up higher than the overpass. We may not be able to talk to someone in France, but we will be able to find a HAM operator nearby to get us some help. HAM operators usually get to their radios in emergency situations, and this storm would be exactly that."

"Wow, Barry, you haven't talked that much since you fried your fingers wiring your mom's circuit breaker box," Joe said with a laugh. Barry just looked at him then went back to soldering the wires.

"I'm going to go check on Early," Joe said, zipping up his coat. "I'll check on the kids in the truck too."

"Wear a hat," Chuck told him and tossed his nanook-of-the-north hockey hat at him.

"Oh...well, no, I don't think..." Joe said, but Chuck cut him off.

"I know it's not pretty, but it's warm, it'll keep the heat in your head and keep your ears from freezing off. You'll be walking into the wind. Just wear it." Chuck said. "We can't gamble with having a problem with the *engineers*," Chuck really emphasized the word engineers, "besides, when it's this cold out, you don't need to be making a fashion statement." Chuck smiled a mischievous grin.

Joe looked at the hat and sighed, then yanked it on his head. Nick started to laugh, and even Christie and Tawnie were giggling at how silly that big hat looked on Joe's smallish face. Chuck was encouraging, "You won't be sorry."

Joe flapped the door open and jumped down the steps, slamming the door behind him. "Someone should go with him," Jeff said.

"I'll go," Louise said as she jammed her feet in the boots again. "I should check up on both of the injured kids anyway.

It's been a couple of hours. I'll feel better if I can do something. Do you think Nick would want to go with us?"

"Nick," Jeff said, "do you want to go and get some air?"

"Yeah, Dad!" Nick was thrilled to feel important enough to be asked to accompany "the engineer" and the nurse. He zipped his coat, secured the hood, wrapped his scarf around his face, and Nick was out the door with Joe and Louise.

Mr. Preston had inserted five of the golf club shafts into each other. "This is about eight or nine feet. The rest of the shafts will give us at least twenty feet. But we can't get it out the door. We'll have to break them down into four smaller sections, short enough to get out the RV door, and then we'll assemble the whole length outside."

Mr. Preston, Eddie, Jeff, and Travis were jamming the sections together and tapping them on the floor, making sure they were jammed in tight. They had the four sections assembled plus the putter that still had the club end on it.

"Will this be enough?" Eddie asked.

Barry looked up from his contraption and looked at the sections of the intended antenna. "It'll have to be," he said.

"I left the putter head on," Mr. Preston said. "I figure we can use it for the topmost part of the antenna to attach wires to." Mr. Preston took one last grip on the putter and took a small putt in front of his feet as he said goodbye to his last club. It still had its little putter cover with the knitted "TAP" on it. Mr. Preston took the cover off and tucked it into his coat pocket. Jackie saw him do it and smiled at him.

Barry had assembled a long length of wire by soldering the rest of the wire strands together. He began winding the wire around the putter, loosely looping it many times explaining to the others that when they assemble the antenna outside, the putter goes on top, then slide the coil of wire down the shafts as they are assembled, sort of like dropping a slinky. Then they were to leave a tail on the end to connect to the radio wire he was going to trail out of the RV.

"Once you have all this all assembled, I'm going secure the whole thing to the RV ladder with some of the extension cord pieces," Barry explained. "Using the wire, it won't come loose in the blizzard like tape might. We have one shot at this."

Barry was so focused on his plan to make this work that he had no trouble running the whole radio show.

Chapter 57

Raising the Mast

"I think we're going to have to have someone go up on the overpass to lash the top of the antenna mast to the overpass railing to hold that steady. Once we find a signal, nothing should move, so we can keep the signal fine-tuned until we get our message out." Barry was intense as he explained the details. "While you guys are out getting the antenna up and the ground wire set, I have to cut the cord on the RV's CB radio microphone and attach it to my transmission side of the radio. Once that's all done, I think we can get a call out. Maybe twenty minutes to call time."

Barry became extra serious now. He didn't want mistakes this late in the game.

There was the feeling of excitement finally in the RV. Everyone was talking, and the girls had just about finished coating the wires with the nail polish and even had a bit of polish left to spare.

Joe suddenly swung the door open and helped Louise back into the RV, and he climbed in with Nick at his heels, stomping the snow off their shoes.

"How's everybody?" Jeff asked.

Joe shook his head. "Early doesn't look so good."

Louise agreed, "Yes, his face is very swollen where he hit, and it is starting to turn purple and black. The young lady doesn't respond to anything, and she's unconscious. I put some snow in a t-shirt to hold on the girl's forehead. They both need medical help. The reverend is fine and saying prayers. The other girl said she was going to come over soon and use the bathroom."

"You should see the stuff in the engineer's van, Dad!" Nick was excited about all the magazines in the geek's van. "Can we get a subscription to those magazines?"

Jeff told Nick when they got out of this, that he'd let Nick go to electronics camp next summer. Joe winked at Nick and smiled.

"I can make some more tea if anyone wants it," Louise offered then took orders around the RV. Everyone seemed to feel a bit more upbeat about this working and were counting on the geeks to know what they were doing. They'd begun using Chuck's "engineer" term instead of geeks as they began to regard the young men with new appreciation.

"Thanks for the hat, man," Joe said and tossed Chuck's hat back to him. "You are right...very warm."

"DONE!" Barry said so loud that everyone jumped. He apologized when he realized how much he startled everyone. "Now we're going to need that outside work. We will need a couple of you to jam the assembled shafts together and quickly wrap the rest of this wire around it, then twist the end of it to this lead wire that I'm going to drape outside the door. It will connect the antenna wire to the radio set. Then we'll need someone up on the overpass to grab the whole antenna when it's handed up and lash it to the rail up there while we get it lashed to the ladder down here. First, we need to move this RV, so the ladder is directly under the edge of the overpass and close enough to the median guard rail to reach it with the extension cords for grounding." Barry stopped to look at everyone waiting for volunteers.

"I can get up on the overpass," Chuck said. "I'm the only one with a down coat, my Eskimo hat, and decent Klondike boots."

"Nahhh," Doris scolded him again. "Your ankle is bummed up. You need to sit and rest it."

"Oh well, I'm going anyway," Chuck told her. "The cold will be good for my ankle, and I'm the highway man, I can get up around the bridge with my Klondike boots if I lace 'em up tight. So I'm the man. Well, right after I get this RV shuffled around so it's in place for the ground wire to reach the guard rail and the antenna mast to reach the edge of the bridge rail, Ma'am." Chuck saluted her in a teasing way and sat in the driver's seat and began adjusting mirrors.

"Ma'am," Joe said to Louise, "hold the tea until we move." And Louise stopped what she was doing and sat in Joe's spot at the little table.

Chuck turned the key to start up the RV, but it was slow to come to life, causing some concern among the group as they glanced around at each other with worried looks. Chuck saw Travis' wide-eyed look. Chuck turned the key again, and the RV rumbled a few times, and it died again.

"These old diesel engines need a little coaxing when it's this cold. It'll go, it just needs a good goose, then a few minutes to warm up so the air compressor works. It'll be a bit before we move." Chuck goosed it again, turned the key, and it grumbled a few more times sounding troubled, but sure enough, Chuck was right, it finally came to life. He nursed it until it smoothed out. "I'm ready to rumbleeeeee...!" Chuck announced, looking back at everyone in his mirrors, making a joke out of the announcement that the famous emcee shouts to the crowds. There were a lot of sighs of relief, and Chuck sat back, nudging the gas now and then.

"I thought the engine was running all this time," Nick commented to Chuck.

"No, son," Chuck explained to the curious lad, "the generator is what has been running. In front of this RV is a big generator that runs the things inside, like the hairdryer, coffee pot, lights, and stuff. The diesel engine is in the back, and it moves the RV. It's a mega-monster on the road." Chuck winked at Nick.

Joe put his coat on and zipped up. "I'm going to go out and signal you to get this thing into position," Joe said to Chuck.

"Check," Chuck said.

Joe was out the door and tromped to the front of the RV, then stood in the headlights and motioned to Chuck which way to move the behemoth.

The RV began to move while Joe gave directions to get it over on the shoulder by the guard rail and forward enough to line up the ladder with the overpass railing.

After some shuffling, it finally seemed to be in place. At last, this was one of the last big steps to getting them help.

Hopefully.

Joe came back in and asked if everyone was ready.

Chuck, Jeff, Mr. Preston, and Eddie got up and began buttoning and zipping coats, slipping gloves on, wrapping scarves. They had worked together, coming up with a plan to assemble the antenna sections and connect the ground wire as efficiently and quickly as possible. Each one had a section to put together and would hand over the wire after they got their section wrapped. After they assembled their sections, Jeff and Eddie would go to the Dominator and get the extension cords and plug them together for the ground, then cut off the plug end to wire it to the guard rail.

"I'll head up on the overpass," Chuck said. Even though he was gimping from twisting his ankle in the RV ladder, he felt he was the only one that would stay warm enough to accomplish the task and big enough to fight the wind. He put the RV in park.

They asked Barry for any last instructions. "No," he said, "we're ready. Let's do it." And the guys all piled out of the RV with their jobs to do. Barry stayed with his radio with Nick hanging over his shoulder. Barry was ready to call out as soon as they got everything connected, and he could send and receive. He wasn't sure how long this rinky-dink set up would last and wanted to make the calls as soon as he could.

"I don't get how that works without electricity," Nick said, staring at the pile of junk that Barry and Joe had assembled into a possible working radio.

"The copper wire wrapped in these coils is what provides the small amount of energy to make it work. If you take apart any motor, you'll see lots of copper winding," Barry explained to Nick, "but over here on the transmitting side, I have four double-A batteries to run the transformer that we got from the microwave.

The guys outside worked in the blowing snow and cold wind like a machine, jamming the sections together as they had practiced. Since Eddie had already been up on the RV roof, he climbed up the ladder again to hand the antenna up to Chuck. He had to wait until he saw Chuck up on the overpass before feeding the antenna up any farther. Jeff and Joe got the extension cords and plugged them together, adding a knot, and tossed Barry one of the plug ends. Barry cut off the socket and peeled back the wire sheathing exposing the bare copper wire that he twisted to the ground connection on his radio. Jeff and Joe draped the rest of the cord around the back of the RV and over to the guard rail, where Joe stripped the plug off, peeling back the sheathing and looked for a place to attach the bare wire to the guard rail. He was thrilled that one rivet was missing leaving a nice hole to wrap his wire through. "Gotta love those highway contractors," Joe said to the air.

Mr. Preston and Eddie were getting cold waiting for Chuck to show up over their heads. It was hard to keep looking up with snow blowing in their eyes.

Joe and Jeff were done grounding the radio and met up with Mr. Preston at the back of the RV.

"Chuck show up yet?" Jeff asked.

"Not yet," Mr. Preston said, "I expect him any second."

But still no Chuck.

"Do you suppose his ankle gave out?" Jeff asked, not really wanting to know the answer. Then Jeff looked at Joe and said, "Maybe this will work without lashing it up there."

"I am concerned," Joe said, "he's got a bum ankle and is only on this mission because of me and Barry, so I'll go after him."

Just then, they heard a wolf whistle, and there was Chuck, hanging over the railing above them on the overpass. "Get that damn thing up here. It's cold!" He shouted down to them as the wind blew the ear flaps on his hat around like a happy puppy.

They passed up the antenna to Eddie, who handed it off up to Chuck. It was sturdy enough not to fold in the wind. Chuck was able to grab it after a few misses from the wind swaying it around, then lashed it tightly to the overpass railing with the extra extension cord pieces. There was a glove-muted applause of the mission accomplished when Chuck was done. When Joe got the base of the antenna secured to the ladder, Joe banged on the side of the RV, a signal to Barry to make his calls.

"Let's go get warm!" Eddie shouted as they high-fived each other with much back-patting and talking about the radio and being rescued.

They all piled in the RV again, and everyone was hovering around Barry and watching him slowly sliding the bent piece of pie pan over the copper coils. "This is the tuner," was all he was saying. He was able to hack open a small weather radio Louise had and attach wires from his radio to the tiny speaker on the weather radio and the other side to the wires from the scavenged CB microphone. The old weather radio had a volume knob, that was a plus.

"Shhhhh," Barry hushed everyone. "This isn't going to be loud or strong if we get a signal. How high over the overpass is the top of the putter?" he asked.

"Looked like we got it about five feet higher than the railing. Chuck will know," Jeff said. "By the way, where is Chuck?"

"Didn't he come back with you?" Doris asked.

"No," Eddie said, looking out the window. "He was up on the overpass hooking up the antenna. He's the only one with boots, down coat, and that crazy hat, but I don't see him." Eddie looked at the group.

"Shouldn't he be back by now?" Mr. Preston looked at Jeff.

"I would think so," Jeff said, cupping his palms around his eyes and pressed them up close to the window to see better. "I don't see him coming either."

"We gotta go get him," Mr. Preston said. "We can't leave it to chance that he's okay. He was gimping when he took off for the overpass. If he's limping or hurt that ankle, we can get him down at least to the Lincoln. I don't think we can carry a big guy like that through the snow."

"I'll go too," Joe said.

"Nahh, you stay here. Eddie stays here too. We'll need someone to drive this thing if Chuck is hurt."

Once more, Jeff and Mr. Preston zipped up and buttoned down everything they had and prepared to take a serious walk to find Chuck.

"You know, I could have used a pair of boots," Mr. Preston said as he wrapped himself up to head out again.

"I hear ya," Jeff said as he bundled up preparing to go out again too.

"You shoult take mine fur," Wilhelmina said through sleepy eyes. "It is varm for you."

Jeff thought about it, but he had a decent winter coat with a hood and gloves and borrowed his son's scarf, Mr. Preston thanked her for her thoughtfulness and declined her offer. The two men were out the door once again.

"I could have been heading to Vegas," Mr. Preston said. "I keep visualizing the warm desert air on the golf course. Maybe it keeps me going."

"You still going to try to get there?" Jeff asked him as they tromped across the snow.

"I don't know. It would have been a lot of business contacts, but right now, I could care less about business. I never realized just how unimportant all those contacts are. They don't give a crap what happens to people, and I had become part of that culture. I'm not such a jaded lawyer that I can't see how we all came together in this storm to hopefully make this radio work to get help. It's like a community project. I've learned that sometimes a community of a bunch of odd people, each with their own abilities, can make great things happen. If I'd have been alone. I'd be dead. Little skinny Eddie pulled me out of my car using a big filet knife he had handy. Look at all we've done to help each other." Mr. Preston philosophized.

They stopped at Ben's truck and explained what they were doing and how the radio was coming along to Matthew and

Delphia. Matthew decided to join the guys to find Chuck since he felt like he hadn't done much but babysit, and Delphia could clearly manage taking care of Brittany.

After they all left the truck, Delphia told Brittany, "I hope our parents don't kill us when they get the phone call."

Chapter 58

Touching Base

Barry was slowly sliding the v-shaped stick from the pie pan over the carefully coil-wrapped toilet paper tube, listening for anything, and adjusting the cardboard and foil capacitor tubes hoping to hear something. There was nothing, not even distant static.

"I don't get it," Barry said, running his hands through his hair, obviously frustrated at this point. "This should work." Barry ran through all his connections again, and it all seemed good. He double-checked his speaker connections and hushed everyone in the RV, then slid his tuning stick again.

"Nothing!" he fumed. "Not a diddley-damn thing!" Everyone was silent as Barry aired his frustrations.

Mr. Buchbinder slowly pushed himself off the couch and stood. Stretching his legs and arms a bit, then shuffled over to get a closer look at the radio, adjusting his glasses down on his nose. Barry looked at him.

"Dis ist your mayday set? Ja?" Auggie asked him.

"Yes," Barry said.

"Vell, it is pretty vith all de colors on de vires. Maybe too many colors. Reminds me of radio set I saw at POW camp after V-E Day. Soldiers at das camp were so happy to see us come. Those sets were not so colorful, budt they didt haff *shiny copper strip across top*," Auggie said, as he stood there studying the array of wires and paper tubes, emphasizing the part about the copper strip. "Hope you can get it to vork." Auggie patted Barry on the shoulder then shuffled off toward the bathroom.

Barry thought about what Auggie had said for a few minutes as he looked at his fabricated device that sat there useless. Auggie came out of the bathroom and shuffled back to his seat. He winkled at Barry on his way by.

For a moment, Barry considered that Auggie knew something he didn't, and how could the old man know something or even remember something from seventy-some years ago. Why didn't he say something? Barry looked again at his radio, recalling what Auggie said. "The POW's sets were not colorful, but shiny copper strip…"

"Holy shit!" Barry said and turned to Auggie, "You are right….it has to be shiny! Any of you ladies have a nail file?"

The ladies started digging in their purses. "I have emery boards in the back," Louise said.

"Nah, I'd rather have a file that won't leave grit if I can get it," he said, looking hopefully at the women digging in their purses.

Rita pulled out a long metal file out of her very small purse. "Did I hear someone ask for a file? This one could get you out of jail free," she teased as she waved it in the air like a snake. "Diamond file, best there is. It makes my nails look like a goddess."

"Can I borrow it for a minute?" Barry asked as he watched her waving it around like a magic wand.

"Of course," Rita said, "anything for the greater good." And she tipped the edge of it to Barry that was both happy to get it and demoralized he had to take a personal item from her and touch it with his bare hands without disinfecting solution.

"Thank you," he dutifully told her. "I just need it for a minute." Barry began to barely file off a thin strip of the nail polish on the top edge of the coil that Jackie so carefully wrapped for him. "Auggie is right. It has to be shiny copper without the polish coating to make the electrical contact with the tuner. I forgot."

Wilhelmina made a surprised face and patted Auggie's hands. "You have good memory still."

"Ja. Maybe," Auggie said, "it was a day I can always remember."

Barry was very carefully working on the coil as he explained, "I have to be able to touch the copper coil with my tuner stick, so I have to carefully file off a little thin strip of the nail polish but not too much, the coil wires still can't touch each other." He did his work carefully and blew the dust off every second or two. When he was satisfied with his work, he handed Rita back her file. She took it and tapped it on the table to dislodge any additional polish dust, then touched up a few of her own nails with it before returning it to her purse.

"Okay," Barry said as he re-assembled the tuner-stick. "Let's try it again." And he began to slowly slide the tuning stick across the bare copper coil again, ever so slowly. He was beginning to sweat when he was two-thirds across the coil that he hadn't heard a peep. Then, at about three-quarters of the way across the coil, he heard a brief bit of static. He pulled the tuner back and forth over the spot to hone in on it and adjusted the capacitor paper towel tube a few times.

"I got it!" he said as he put his ear nearly on top of the speaker and listened to the glorious sound of static fading in and out.

"Mayday," Barry said into the microphone. "Mayday."

But that's all he heard, nothing but faint static. He pushed the tuning stick some more, very very slowly, bit by bit across the coil. Everyone in the RV was holding their breath, hoping for a reply.

Barry kept going. "Mayday. Foxhole radio call. Mayday. Blizzard victims stranded on I-70. Mayday. Need medical help. Mayday."

Still nothing.

"I need to run the wires. This should work better," Barry said, quite intent on rechecking all of his work. He started following each wire and checked the soldering, he went out the door and followed the wire to the antenna then followed the ground wire to the guard rail. Finally, he came back to the RV, quite cold and frustrated.

"This should work," he said as he slumped in his seat, looking at the contraption he'd built.

"Can we see if we can pick it up here in the RV? The RV is old enough, it must have AM radio," Joe commented, looking at the dash of the RV.

"Yeah, we can try that," Barry said.

After turning on the RV radio and a few minutes of tuning the coils and adjusting the capacitor, they finally got some of their own static on the AM radio. Barry picked up the mike and pushed the button "Mayday?" And they all heard it faintly through some static on the AM radio, and everyone was oohing and ahhing.

"Ok, we'll try it again," Barry said, making a tiny adjustment in the foil-wrapped cardboard capacitor tubes. "Maybe I can get the capacitance better." Barry seemed hopeful once more.

Barry tuned with the pie pan stick, slowly up the coil range, occasionally stopping to make a mayday call. At least he could hear occasional static.

"Mayday," he called over and over, and he was becoming disappointed and knew he was disappointing everyone. He readjusted the capacitor tubes and adjusted the pencil point diode a few times and tried again going slowly up the coil calling his mayday message over and over and even turned the little radio volume knob up as high as it would go.

Then, just about when he was going to give it up, he thought he heard a distant weak voice. Barry waved at everyone and shushed them.

Barry lightly tapped the tuner, and the voice became a bit clearer. A calm, pleasant voice that said, "Come back, mayday. This is station KZXQ-7797, Center, Kansas. State your location. Come back, mayday, state your location." They all heard the angel-like voice from the little speaker.

Barry carefully spoke into the mike, not daring to touch anything on the table for fear of knocking it out of adjustment.

"We are not HAM, repeat, not HAM. This is Mayday. Foxhole radio. Kansas blizzard trapped 24 people in a half dozen car collision on I-70, westbound lane. Unknown location other than maybe an hour west of the Midnight Diner. Two injuries, one casualty, children, senior citizens. Giant snowdrift across the interstate, a few vehicles buried in it, the survivors are behind the drift, under the overpass. Built fox hole radio, no cell coverage, no phone, no GPS. Mayday. Need help."

"Copy," the distant weak voice came back. "Nice job on foxhole radio. Will notify Kansas Highway Patrol. The storm should weaken in another couple hours or so, hang in there. Very bad through Western Kansas. Highway closed from Salina to Goodland and might be awhile before we get you help. Lots of drifts and blowing snow. Will pass along your position, somewhere west of the Midnight Diner. Repeat: Will notify Kansas Highway Patrol of twenty-four people stranded under an overpass on I-70 west of Midnight Diner, Medical Help requested. Over.

"Roger that," Barry said. "Thank you, Sir. This is Foxhole Radio, over and out"

"This is KZXQ-7797, Center, Kansas, over and out," the voice said.

Barry sighed a huge sigh and sat back in his seat, staring at his miracle on the table. For a few seconds, there was dead silence. Then a quiet round of golf clapping started and increased as voices of appreciation and relief began flowing. Barry sat there jostled by back pats, and the women ruffing his hair, and a little tear trickled down his cheek. He hoped no one would notice, but Jackie handed him a tissue. Everyone was chatting and even a bit of laughing.

"Tea?" Louise announced again, and she began preparing tea for just about everyone.

"I'll give you a hand with the tea," Janet offered.

Rita sneaked another sip out of her flask and noticed Jackie looking at her. "They're small sips," Rita commented without looking at Jackie.

Barry stood as if to say something and cleared his throat. Everyone stopped and gave him the floor. "I need to thank you all for your help. You all donated parts to make this radio possible, especially Mr. Preston sacrificing his golf clubs and his very special pencil. And we can't forget Louise letting us destroy her RV, the young ladies handing over their nail polish, and Auggie's jumper cables, or booster-wires, or whatever you want to call them. Then using Doris' Dominator back and forth, and even Wilhelmina donating her extraordinary safety pin that helped make the diode. And you guys, going in and out, up and down, and all over, freezing your butts off. And finally Auggie's 70-some-year-old memory about what a foxhole radio looked like. So much from so many to produce this radio. If just one of you didn't crash into the pile, we might not have been able to create this communication device.

It reminds me of the stories of young men in WWII that my grandfather told me. Those young men were ten years younger than me and sat in foxholes and prison camps and together developed the strategy to communicate during the war, and today, we are standing on their shoulders to get ourselves rescued. I'd like a moment of silence for the men and women in uniform that gave their lives for our American freedom so we can take vacations across our great land, even if it ends with a Siberian Express. We'll never forget this pile-up, and even though we aren't out of the woods yet, I think we will be rescued soon. We'll tell this story for the rest of our lives."

Everyone sat in silence, glancing at the makeshift radio and looking around at each other acutely aware of being storm refugees sharing both the RV space and a desire to be rescued. The long quiet minute passed. "Thank you," Barry said and sat back down to marvel over his radio.

"And thank you, Barry," Joe said, "for sacrificing your grandfather's magazine collection, so we weren't stuck in front of the drift all this time, as Chuck might have come flying in and crashed right through us all, and thanks for building that radio."

More thank you's and back pats for Barry went around in the RV that night. Barry felt a little self-conscious yet proud of himself but remembered that Early, even though he was bashed up, still made his own contribution. So he took the time to explain to the group about Early managing to tell them through his daze about making a radio set.

"Truly amazing," Doris said. "I think we should all get together next year. Maybe at that Midnight Diner and have a reunion." Travis made a face. He wasn't particularly interested in going back to the diner.

Carol suddenly said, "It's Christmas Eve, isn't it? After midnight this became the early morning of Christmas Eve."

"I think so," Janet said as she handed Carol some tea.

"Well, then, today is my birthday, and in view of everything, I think I got the greatest gift of all…. new friends and a rescue."

A few Happy Birthday comments were made, and a suggestion to sing Happy Birthday, but Carol decided it wasn't appropriate to celebrate her day, not under these circumstances and on this Christmas Eve.

"I'd rather we sing 'Silent Night' considering all that has happened to us," Carol said.

"That was Herman's favorite Christmas song," Louise said as she delivered tea around. "I know he'd enjoy hearing it."

There were a few nods, and they slowly began to sing, "Silent Night...Holy Night..." Even the Buchbinders quietly joined in and were singing in German, "Stille Nacht...."

Just about when they got to the second line of the song, the door flew open again. Jeff and Mr. Preston were back, but they weren't happy.

"Where's the truck driver?" Doris asked. "Did he wreck his ankle?"

Mr. Preston shook his head. Jeff took off his scarf and slammed it onto the chair and kicked it.

"What happened?" Carol asked with great concern.

Mr. Preston was clearly distressed and spoke to the group, "Looked like Chuck was coming back down the incline by the overpass. Either the wind or his bum ankle made him miss his step, and he fell over the guard rail near the top of the overpass. He was laying on the pavement when we got there. It looks like he fell the whole way down the incline, probably twelve to fourteen feet maybe broke his neck or back on the pavement or the guard rail or something,"

Jackie stood and looked at the pain in his eyes and helped him back to his seat.

Louise stood and grabbed her stethoscope to go and check him. Mr. Preston put his hand on hers and looked in her eyes and slowly shook his head, "No pulse, Louise. We checked."

"We tried to get him going again, but nothing," Jeff added. "There was no point in us trying to get him back to the RV. We got him back to Auggie's Lincoln. We'll wait for rescue if we ever get it."

Carol and Jackie sniffed back some tears. "He was such a wonderful, thoughtful man," Doris said, handing Jackie a tissue. "I told him he shouldn't go, but he demanded taking up the challenge.

Nick started to cry. "I liked him," he said through his tears.

"We all did, Son," Jeff told Nick. There were a few minutes of quiet and sniffles.

"This is tragic," Carol said. "If it wasn't for him climbing up on the overpass to secure the antenna, we may have never gotten that weak signal."

"You got a signal?" Jeff asked through his despair and looked around.

"Yes, Barry made contact with a HAM radio operator. He's notifying the highway patrol. He said the storm should break in about another couple hours or so," Carol told him. "We should be rescued shortly after the storm dies down."

"Aw jeez. Well, that's just great," Jeff said with some aggravation. "Chuck could have made it if we didn't let him climb around on the overpass. We didn't take the time to find out much about him. He sacrificed himself for all of us. It was odd, too, when we found him, he looked at peace, his eyes were open looking up. Reverend Matthew gave him last rites and closed his eyes."

"I would like to think that he was able to go be with his wife for Christmas," Jackie said quietly. "He told me when you guys were out in the Dominator that he drove on the big holidays because he didn't like to be alone during them since his wife died a couple years ago. Maybe he's gone to be with her for Christmas." Jackie began to sniffle, and then tears began to flow. Mr. Preston once again motioned for her to sit with him. Jackie took a couple more tissues and sat with him and broke down sobbing while Mr. Preston wrapped his arms around her and patted her back. Mr. Preston looked at Jackie sobbing into her tissues and noticed how sensitive she was and how classy the long line of her neck was with the single strand of pearls until his thoughts were interrupted when Tawnie spoke.

"Is Reverend Matthew back at the truck with Delphia?" Tawnie asked.

"Yes, he said he wanted to be quiet for a bit, so went back to the truck," Jeff explained.

"Someone should go tell him that help is on the way," Christie said, looking at her new friend Tawnie.

"I'll go," Joe said. "I want to stop by my van and check on Early and tell him help is on the way as well. He needs to know that we built the radio. He knew we could build it even though his head was smashed up. He even knew we could get parts from the RV. Maybe it'll help him to heal if he knows his idea worked."

"Bless his heart," Jackie said quietly though a few sniffles. "I hope your friend is going to be okay." Mr. Preston patted her back.

"Can I go with him, Dad?" Nick asked his Dad.

"It's okay with me if it's okay with Joe," Jeff said.

Joe nodded, and Nick was overjoyed at being able to buddy up with the engineer to deliver information. They bundled up again and left the RV.

*　　*　　*

Mixed Emotions

"How do you know so much stuff?" Nick asked Joe as they trudged through the snow and wind.

"I don't know that much," Joe told him. "It's Barry and this other guy that know all the electronic and computer stuff. They spend a lot of time reading and experimenting. It's fun to goof off at school, but if you use your time to learn things, you never know when something might come in handy to know."

They got to Joe's van, slid the door open, and climbed in. Joe put his hand on Early's shoulder. He was still breathing, which was a relief. "Early? It's me, Joe," he said. "Barry built the radio, and it worked. Help is on the way, so hang on. We'll get you to a hospital soon." And he patted Early's shoulder. Early didn't seem to hear or acknowledge the message. Joe repeated it while Nick climbed over the boxes and magazines to get a closer look at the injured guy.

"Look, he moved his finger!" Nick exclaimed.

"Are you sure?" Joe asked. "How can you tell in the dark?"

"I'm sure I saw it!" Nick said. "Tell him again or ask him to move his hand."

Joe repeated it and asked Early to move his hand. They both saw it this time, just a tiny twitch of his mouse finger. "Hang in there, man. We'll get you out of here real soon. You are going to have one hell of a story to tell." And Joe patted his shoulder again and re-tucked his sleeping bags around him.

They left the van and headed over to Ben's truck and knocked on the window, making Delphia jump as she had been napping. Matthew opened the door, and Nick and Joe slid in.

"We made contact," Joe told them. "They said the blizzard would die down some in about another hour or so. They are contacting the Kansas Highway Patrol."

"Praise God," Matthew said and folded his hands to his chest. Joe explained how the radio was built and all the contributions and problems of making a shortwave radio out of junk to Delphia's delight, and then he asked Matthew if he'd come over to say a few prayers.

Matthew started to button up his coat when Delphia said, "Wait. Has anyone heard from Ben?"

They shook their heads no and felt lousy that he hadn't come back. "I hope he's made contact with someone by now," Matthew told her. "Have faith."

Delphia was disappointed but was hoping Ben would come back soon. By now, nature was calling, and Delphia needed to use the restroom and said she would go back to the RV with them. "Brittany's been out for hours, I doubt a few minutes will matter." They waited for her to button up, then they piled out into the snow. Matthew took Delphia's hand and led her through the snow behind Joe and Nick.

As they climbed in the RV, a few more introductions went around, and Delphia politely asked Louise where the bathroom was. Barry showed Matthew the radio, and they all talked about Chuck's heroic efforts to lash the antenna to the overpass rail.

"You know, a trucker saved my life earlier tonight," Matthew explained, fighting tears. "I was freezing half to death in my Minibus, and a trucker simply invited me to warm up in his truck. He shared his dinner with me and told me how he and many of the truckers are road warriors helping people along the way. He gave me these ugly socks and this ball cap to help keep me warm. He was such a wonderful, giving man." Matthew hung his head. "It's like a trucker to tackle the hard jobs. Our trucker wasn't only road warrior, he was a road angel."

Jackie was so overwhelmed that she went over to give Matthew a hug. She held him for a minute until he composed himself. Jackie looked over to Mr. Preston, and they locked eyes for a quick moment. Jackie blushed again and glanced away.

"Would you like to say a prayer for all of this?" Jackie asked Matthew. "Or would you rather wait a bit."

"Now would be good, while we are all here," Matthew said, then wiped his nose on a tissue. Mr. Preston helped Jackie sit in his seat while he stood next to her and patted her shoulder. Jackie looked up and smiled at him. It made Mr. Preston blush this time.

Chapter 59

According to Matthew

Matthew glanced around at the storm refugees and their hopeful, yet tired and weary faces.

"I see all kinds of people here that were on their way to a holiday or some event not dreaming of the consequences of colliding with this storm of God's making, or Mother Nature, or whatever your faith holds for you. But I don't believe in accidents. I believe God finds purpose in the destiny of each soul he puts here and of both the good and the unpleasant circumstances each soul comes to endure. Humans seem to learn more from the difficult lessons, and so perhaps this storm was thrown into our paths to teach us lessons that we need to learn before we move on or leave this life.

I've seen a few of us that have made some positive changes, something deep inside us stepped up to the plate when needed. We worked together without conflict for the common good. Like so many refugees and survivors of the world, we found ways to overcome the problems with some teamwork. The armies, countries, and governments of the world could learn a valuable lesson from this."

There was much nodding and agreement with Matthew's comments. Matthew continued.

"I hope we all realize the coincidence of us running into each other, so to speak, at the drift. This is not luck. I believe this whole experience was divinely inspired to teach us all something. That we'd all be here at the same time with the abilities we have that are getting us rescued, is truly fate. I believe God rewarded Chuck for his work. As Jackie mentioned, he missed his beloved wife, especially around the holidays, so I think God gave him that gift today so he could spend Christmas with his treasured wife. Herman, what I've heard of him, driving for hours and the mystery of his brother's spirit pushing him to keep going so he'd be right here when we needed him and his RV. Then he left us to be with his brother that he'd missed so much. The young man in the van pummeled in the face, yet his spirit let him get a valuable message out. Barry's grandfather that saved magazines, and Barry's abilities with electronics, and Joe driving them in his van. Auggie's CB radio to hail Chuck, and having jumper cables and the ladies with the Dominator. A pair of brothers each helping the other learn some lessons about themselves. And, of course, Mr. Preston's new golf clubs. Even the crazy girl wanting to see a boy that put her here with lots of nail polish. Oh, and Mrs. Buchbinder's safety pin."

Rita interrupted, "And Mr. Preston's little pencil." She tried to look like she didn't say anything. Jeff had to stifle a smile to that comment.

Matthew continued, "had any of us not been pushed by a divine spirit to be here, we may not have rescuers on the way. Even though some of us may not be into faith and believing, I believe He blessed us all by putting us here at this time so we could learn that we are more than just ourselves. We each have a sacred spirit, and like radiant threads, it connects all of our souls in a divine woven tapestry giving us an inner need to help each other in a way we can't explain. This is the blessing that God, or whatever your higher power might be, has given us. So I would like to pray for a moment." And Matthew bowed his head, others followed.

"Most Holy Spirit, Hallowed light of our human souls that watches over us as we journey to our destiny on this holy night of Christmas Eve. Bless us all, those of us that are faithful and those that aren't there yet. Watch over the rescuers as they make their way to us, and bless their ability to relieve us from the grasp of cold and snow and the harsh memories that might haunt us. Heal the broken spirits, calm the worries and fears, watch over the injured, and shine your light in each of us so we can feel how valuable we are in this life and to each other. And dear Lord, have us hold this day in our hearts so we can remember how deeply we have been moved to help total strangers, to sacrifice for the common good, and let that compassion reside in our souls from this day forward. Amen."

"Amen," Mr. Preston heard himself say, and Jackie patted his arm.

There were more 'Amens' from most of the others and a few tearful eyes at the message Matthew gave them.

"Thank you, Reverend," Doris said. "That was lovely."

"Yes," Jackie followed. "Beautiful." She felt Mr. Preston lightly squeeze her shoulder that made her eyes close with a smile.

Chapter 60

HAM Helper

Rescue At Last

Everyone was talking about everything that had happened so far, and being distraught over Chuck and Herman. Yet they were marveling over all the fortuitous events leading up to now.

Rita was busy trying to help herself to another sip from her flask when she bumped the table hard with her elbow jarring the radio set when she heard a weak voice. "Sh, sh, shhh," Rita whispered to everyone, "this radio get-up is talking again."

Barry manned the radio and everyone hushed. "This is KZXQ-7797, Center, Kansas, HAM operator looking for the foxhole mayday. Come back, mayday," the radio said.

Barry picked up the mike and spoke, confirming the connection. "Go ahead, KZXQ-7797. This is mayday."

"Just heard from Kansas Highway Patrol that a young man on skis showed up at Agnes' Midnight Truck Stop Diner awhile ago. He indicated he is involved with your group. They are going to send help and medical, and the young man is going to lead them there right away."

"Roger that, Center. Thank you, KZXQ-7797. Mayday, out." Barry sat the mike down and looked at the group.

Delphia smiled, thinking Ben will come back for his cow pitcher.

Well," Rita tried to stand as best she could in the corner of the booth, "I think this deserves a toast!" And she took out her little flask of booze, held it up and shouted, "To Everyone!" and she took a good gulp. "Anyone else?" Nick stuck up his hand, but Jeff grabbed it by his wrist and yanked it down. No one else offered to take a sip. Rita gave a snide look to everyone and took another sip. "Suit yourselves," she muttered, "it's more for me."

Doris and Louise were still fixing tea and handing out little foam cups. "I hope it's not too long before they come for us," Louise quietly told Doris. "I'm getting a little anxious about how we are going to get out of here, and I'm running out of foam cups."

Carol overheard the conversation and suggested that even though the storm will let up in a little while, that it may be some time before someone comes to get them. "They have to get the plows, and they only do about fifty miles an hour, so it'll be awhile for them to plow their way here."

Auggie overheard that too. "Dat means we might not get back on dis road tonight. Ve vill miss dis Christening." He looked beaten and looked to his Wilhelmina for comfort.

"Not so bad," Wilhelmina said as she patted his old wrinkled hand, "vould have been vorse had ve toldt dem kids ve vere comingk! They vouldt be so vorried by now. It vould ruin Christening of Augustus Heinrich Buchbinder V. So Reverend is right. It is blessing."

"I can sing the Lord's Prayer," Tawnie offered to Louise. "I know all the words."

"That'd be lovely," Louise told her. "I would like that."

"Me too," Janet and Doris chimed in.

"Yes, that'd be nice," Carol added.

Rita rolled her eyes and continued to stare out the window.

Tawnie stood, and handed Twinkles over to Delphia, then leaned against the counter, and everyone quieted down. She cleared her throat a few times and started so softly, and quietly, they could barely hear her over the heater running. "Our faaaa-ther, whooo art in heavennnn, hallowed beeee thy name...." As she went through the song, she got braver and felt the prayer's power so strongly that by the time she got to the end, Tawney was belting it out in beautiful, clear, teenage soprano voice, "for thine is the Kingdom, and the Power, and the GLORY...."FOREVER! Ahhhhhhhhhhaaaah"...and ended it as peacefully as she began "....mennnnn."

Many wiped tears from their eyes from the sweet song that touched their hearts and left them with the peace that only such a song can have on a memorable Christmas Eve morning. Some tears were from thinking about the events leading up to this point. So many ups and downs. So much agony, so much worry, yet so much joy.

There was light applause, and once again, Tawnie blushed.

"Thank you, Tawnie," Louise said as she patted her shoulder. "That was beautiful. I bet Herman could hear it. I know he and his brother like to hang around this old RV, and I hope it brought him some joy and peace."

"Thank you, ma'am." Tawnie sat back down next to Christie and Delphia, and they all shared hugs. Even Christie had tears in her eyes. Carol was surprised to see her daughter that emotional.

"This has been a hell of a day," Doris said. "No offense, Reverend."

"I'll say," Mr. Preston said. "I started out with major plans to land some big deals and new clients at a golf tournament day after tomorrow in Vegas. That is obviously off the table now.

But now I think I'd rather spend some time with my daughter. Those big business deals will never care about me or my life." He sighed a big sigh. Jackie patted his hand that was still on her shoulder.

"I understand," Jackie said. "We were going to Vegas too, to gamble for the holidays. It seemed important until this happened."

"Well, now we'll have a better story to tell when we get home," Janet added.

"What?" Doris asked, "You want to go home? The tank only has a few scratches. We can wait a day or so, then continue on. Our reservations are paid up for the week."

"Oh, I don't know, Doris," Janet said. "Seems like maybe we ought to go home."

"Go home to what?" Doris asked. "My kids are spending the holiday with hubby's family. Jackie's niece is out of town with her family. Nobody expected us to be home for the holidays, so they all made other plans. Rita will still want to go to Vegas too. So what will you go home to?"

"You're damn right I want to keep going," Rita chimed in.

Auggie piped up, "If you can drive in a day or two, I can drive too. I want to see my great-great-grandson, August Heinrich Buchbinder, the fifth!"

"What about Matthew, Jeff and his family, Mr. Preston, the girls, even Eddie and Travis there, their cars are wrecked. They won't be continuing on," Janet said.

"Well, I'd like to continue on, but I can't drive this RV," Louise said. "I'll have to go back home and have a funeral for Herm. It'll be a long cold winter in Minnesota. Maybe I can stay with one of our kids for awhile, at least through the holidays until we get insurance and things squared away.

Herman always had things in order just in case." Doris and Janet comforted Louise.

"My truck should run," Eddie said, "it just needs to be dug out of the snow. I don't think anything is wrong with it other than a couple of dents. I think Travis and I would just like to go back home.

"My folks are less than an hour from here, I think," Jeff said. "If I can get to a phone, I can call my mother. She can come get us, or my sister can come for us. We need to be there soon as my dad isn't doing very well."

"What about these young ladies?" Doris asked. "The one in the truck is going to need a hospital. They won't chopper out the other two. And what about the young man that owns that truck?"

"His name is Ben," Delphia told them. "He'll be back for his truck."

"I hope he's okay," Doris said. "And Louise, what about you?"

"I suppose when the police come, they'll want to make sure there hasn't been any funny business and they'll take Herman to a funeral home around here. They can make travel flight arrangements to get him back to Minnesota, and I suppose I'll accompany him, and figure out what to do with Twinkles on a plane." Suddenly Louise looked very sad, as though she'd been holding up until she knew help was on the way, and then broke down sobbing and apologizing for it. Doris hugged her, and Carol got up and hugged her too while she sobbed her heart out.

"You let it out," Doris told her. "You have saved all of us, or we'd have frozen to death by now or worse." And Louise cried while still trying to make more tea.

"If they get a medivac chopper in here that takes that girl to the hospital, I can drive the other two girls back to St Louis," Eddie volunteered.

"My van runs," Joe offered. "I suppose if they take Early to the hospital, we can follow there until we know how he is. Then we can take him home."

"I can call the church," Matthew said, "I'm sure someone can come get me. Or maybe just stand my bus back up on its wheels." And he let out a little joking laugh.

"Mr. Preston, there's plenty of room in my Dominator, if we continue to Vegas, you can ride along and still make your golf outing," Doris invited.

Jackie quickly looked up to Mr. Preston. Mr. Preston was making the kind of face that looks like no, but he glanced down at Jackie, and his expression changed, "I might just take you up on that, Doris," he said and smiled at Jackie and squeezed her shoulder once more. "I can still make it back to take my daughter to the New Year's dance."

"Hey, hey," Rita said as she watched Mr. Preston taking an interest in Jackie and vice versa, "no hanky-panky in the back seat you two. She's old enough to be your mother."

Mr. Preston nullified Rita's comment with a raised eyebrow, and his lawyer voice aimed directly at her, "Well, Rita, I like experienced women."

Jackie blushed so much she started to sweat, and her French twist felt like it tightened up.

"Oh, well, I have more experience than she does," Rita snipped, flipping her stringy hair back.

"Could be," Mr. Preston continued, "but I think the packaging suits me better." And he winked at Jackie.

Doris and Janet were jabbing each other with their elbows as they saw a budding romance with the lawyer and their long-widowed friend. "I should have gotten a manicure before we left," Janet said to Doris as they watched Mr. Preston and Jackie, "it seems like that was the starting point for them." Both chuckled as they sipped their tea.

"I think the snow is stopping," Nick said as he looked out the front window. "I wonder who will be here first, the plows, or the cops."

"You nincompoop," Christie snipped at her little brother. "They said the Highway Patrol will come."

"That's the same as 'cops,' you ninny," Nick snapped back.

"Mom!" Christie looked at her mother.

"Kids!" Carol shouted, then quickly calmed herself so she wouldn't wake Holly, "It's Christmas Eve! After all that's happened, can't you be nice for five minutes? We've been given an awesome gift today, let's appreciate it for awhile." And Carol puffed out a breath of air.

Nick and Christie nodded to each other. For a moment there was silence, then way off in the distance over the blustery wind, they heard what sounded like a chopper.

"Is that a chopper? Jeff said. "I thought it'd be hours before we got help. I didn't think they came out in blizzard conditions."

"I didn't either," Joe said as he peered out a window to see if he could see anything other than flying snow. "Maybe it's letting up where they take off."

"Does anything else make a noise that sounds like that? Like maybe a conga-line of plows?" Eddie asked. Everyone froze and looked at Eddie. "Don't look at me, I don't know, I'm just asking!"

Suddenly everyone was alert and concerned and asking each other questions that no one had a clear answer for. It wasn't long though before the sound became louder, and it was more apparent that the noise was most likely an incoming helicopter. A big one.

"Pretty sure that's a big chopper," Mr. Preston pointed out, attempting to ease the anxiety he felt in Jackie. "We're going to be okay. It's a rescue ship."

Within the next few minutes, yes, they could all hear the blades of the chopper in the air.

"Will they be able to find us?" Nick asked his father. "They won't be able to see us under the overpass."

Delphia leaned over to Nick, "Don't worry. Ben, the guy on the skis, he is going to show them the way. He's smart. He knows how to deal with snow too. You can bet he'll lead them right to our overpass.

"But how can they land in all this snow?" Nick asked.

Mr. Preston jumped in to answer, "I suspect they'll hover, son. One of my clients owns his own helicopter and pilots it himself. He flies to Canada to fish and lands in snow-covered areas. He hovers for a while, and the air-wash blows the loose snow away, and he can land his chopper on the ice pack. The other alternative is to drop in medical personnel to help with the injured and drop supplies until they can safely evacuate us. Either way, they'll notify the authorities so we'll get whatever help we need as soon as the weather eases up and we won't be plowed off the road. Rescue is a few minutes away."

There was a general sigh of relief from almost everyone as they listened to the distant sound of the chopper getting closer, and there was a feeling of peace for a change.

Ever so quietly, Tawnie started to hum Jingle Bells, Christie and Delphia heard it, and they began to hum it too as the three girls smiled at each other. Jackie now felt confident that the chopper was coming, and she got up and hugged Mr. Preston to Mr. Preston's surprise and enjoyment. Then Nick heard the song, and he started humming along. Auggie knew this song too, and he started singing the words, "yingle beltz, yingle beltz"...and one by one they joined in and were all singing and getting louder, even Holly woke and joined in,

"Dashing through the snow, in a one-horse open sleigh,
Oe'r the fields we go, laughing all the way,

Bells on bobtails ring, making spirits bright,
What fun it is to laugh and sing a sleighing song tonight,

Oh, Jingle Bells, Jingle Bells, Jingle all the way,
Oh what fun it is to ride in a one-horse open sleigh, HEY!

Jingle Bells, Jingle Bells……..."

They sang until the chopper drowned them out as it began its landing preparations, with Ben waving out the chopper door and Eddie sitting in the RV's driver's seat, waving the spot-lights into the air.

THE END

Alternative Ending: When they heard the chopper, they all ran over to the one side of the RV to look out the windows when their weight and the wind tipped the RV over and killed them all. The end.

This Disclaimer In Tiny Print Is To Be Read Really Fast and Quiet
Like the Disclaimers of Drug Ads on TV

Characters in this book or digital version do not represent anyone living or dead or anywhere in between, including the dog. The characters and their names are made up and only figments of my imagination and nothing else. These are fake characters. I developed the storyline out of my own head and not copied from anyone. I've never read a blizzard pile-up story in my life, so there's no way this would have been plagiarized. I also tried very hard not to step on anyone's copyright or trademarks, but I did use a couple so the readers can visualize what's happening in my story, such as a line from the song White Christmas and mentioning Bing Crosby's name, a Lincoln Town Car (best ride ever!), Minibus, Spectaculeer (which doesn't really exist), Pinnacle golf balls (awesome!), Dominator-Maximus (that doesn't exist either), and Ouija, all of which makes me crazy because technically putting it in my story would be free advertising and they should owe me like they do with product placement in movies. But apparently the written word doesn't work the same, so I get nothing.

The world is nuts.

Love my readers!

www.ingramcontent.com/pod-product-compliance
Lightning Source LLC
Chambersburg PA
CBHW021212260626
47172CB00002B/388